TALK RADIO

Suddenly, there was the sound of a door banging in the background. Then the clatter of something falling over. A muffled voice said, "Get out of here, you can't come in here, we're recording!" Then another shout and a blurt of thick static as if somebody had knocked the microphone.

At first, Martin thought this must be part of the plot. But the shouting and struggling were so indistinct that he realized quickly there must be an intruder in the radio studio, a *real* intruder, and that the actors and technicians were trying to subdue him. There was another jumble of sound and then an extraordinarily long-drawn-out scream, rising higher and higher, increasingly hysterical.

Then the most terrible thing Martin had ever heard in his life. He turned away from the open door to stare at the radio with his eyes wide and his scalp prickling with horror.

"Oh God! Oh God! John! John! Oh God help me! He's cut me open! Oh God! My stomach's falling out!"

A noise like somebody dropping a sodden bath towel. Then more shouts and more thumps. A nasal, panicky voice shouting, "Ambulance! Get an ambulance!" Then a sharp blip—and the program was cut off.

from *The Heart of Helen Day,* by Graham Masterton

Contents

Introduction

In his introduction to Raymond Van Over's MONSTERS YOU NEVER HEARD OF (Tempo Books, The Berkley Publishing Group, N.Y., 1983), Colin Wilson observed that the author had tried to "open creaking doors into other dimensions of life that show us other realities, as they terrify us."

And so, the versatile British writer-thinker concluded, Van Over's book was far more than "nasty." It is, said the creator of THE OUTSIDER, MYSTERIES and BEYOND THE OCCULT, "the myths and fairy tales of fear that symbolize the deepest problems of human existence." As if anticipating the authors of the present book, Wilson noted we never fully outrun "the horrors" of our childhood frights; "we have merely learned to look the other way."

Although your present writers created fiction, not analyzed our "five-year old self" (in psychological parlance), many have enabled MASQUES, by this combined third and fourth volume, as though creating credible myths and fairy tales for adult readers. Some such authors, I believe, include John Maclay (twice herein), Diane Taylor, Gary A. Braunbeck, Mort Castle, (again, twice here), Stanley Wiater, the poets Boston, Frazier, Ray Bradbury and Denise Dumars, Dan Simmons (in two appearances in this book), Kristine Rusch, John Keefauver, Ed Gorman, Kathryn Ptacek, F. Paul Wilson and the late Steve Allen. As editor, I am pleased with all the contributions but those wordsmiths elevated the horror/supernatural genre to new, different heights. Simultaneously, because of or despite connections to some painful realities, they are rediscovering the element of our race's eldest concerns.

We must throw open those ancient, creaking doors to see *us*—even those we pray are little like us at all—in order to experience the "wonder and excitement," as Wilson put it, of what we have come to recognize from time to time is the reality of our individual and collective existences. So I say as I have said before in introducing these collections . . . let the masque begin!

J. N. Williamson
Indianapolis, Indiana
April 2002

Drifter

Ed Gorman
for Michael Seidman

The Denver rig driver dumped me fast when he caught
me trying to stuff a pint of his whiskey down the front of my
pants. I'd figured that with the dark and the rain and the way
even this big mother was getting blown around on the two-
lane blacktop, he'd be too busy to notice. He flipped me his
middle finger as he pulled away.

So I landed around seven o'clock that night in some town
named Newkirk ten miles south of the Nebraska border,
with half a pack of Luckies, two Trojans, and maybe three
dollars in change to my name. I had a pocketknife, one of
those babies that will do the job but that the law can't bust
you for in most states, and a backpack filled with my one
change of clothes, which was exactly like the ones I was
wearing except they were more or less clean.

Newkirk had a single main street three blocks long. In the
October night only two lights glowed, one for a DX station,
one for Chet's café. No doubt about which one I needed
first.

The kid at the DX station was trying real hard to grow a
mustache—you could almost *hear* him trying to will that
sucker into existence—and he had already grown an attitude.

"You ain't got no car," he said when I asked him for the restroom key.

"So?"

"You're some stranger and you ain't got no car."

"I need to pee real bad, friend. I figure you'd like me to do it in your rest room rather than your street."

The kid had spooked blue eyes. "Strangers never been good for Newkirk. Just last year—"

I interrupted him. "Friend, if I was a bad sort, I would've already hauled out my piece and stuck this little joint up. Ain't that about right?"

He relaxed, but not much. Over his grease-stained coveralls he wore a brand-new high school letter jacket. He probably had a girlfriend with a nice creamy body and they got to spend a lot of time in front of the TV, out of the wind and cold, watching horror flicks and having the kind of sex only teenagers can have. At thirty-one, I felt old and envious. I also felt filthy. It had been four or five days now. I said something I rarely do. "Please, friend. Please."

I put my hand out and he filled it with one of those keys that are attached to two-pound anchors so you won't steal them.

"Thanks, friend."

He didn't say anything, just sort of nodded.

October had stripped the trees and put a coat of frosty silver over everything. The cold only made the dimly lit rest room smell all the worse. It was more in need of a cleaning than I was. The mirror had been shattered by somebody's fist and I saw myself in a dozen fragmented pieces. There was a brown lump floating in the john. I didn't need to ask what that was. I flushed the john. Or tried to. It didn't work.

Laid over everything was this sickly sweet smell from this black-and-white air-freshener deal hanging off the edge of a condom machine. The air freshener was in the shape of a cute little skunk.

I got to work. On the road this way—the last real job I'd had was back in Cincinnati just before the '82 recession, when I'd been working construction—you learn how to sponge-bath yourself fast. You take a rough paper towel and you soak it with cold water (they never have hot or even warm water) and then you soap it till it's nice and silky almost like a real washcloth and then you do your face first and then you do under your arms and then you do down in your crotch and then you do down in your behind and then you take the BIC and you careful-like shave your face. I say careful-like because the road leaves you looking rough enough. You don't need any help with cuts on your face.

I finished off by combing my dark hair and brushing dust from my denim jacket and dousing a little Old Spice on the collar of my black turtleneck. There'd been a time when I'd done all right with the ladies and, looking at myself fragmented in the shattered mirror there, I thought about those days as the wind screamed outside and the light in the small, filthy rest room wavered. I used to always think, You're a long way from home, sonny boy. But lately I've realized I was always kidding myself. I wasn't a long way from home—I'd never *had* a home. Never.

I was two steps out of the rest room when I saw the guy. I should have known what the kid would do. Small town, distrustful of strangers, me walking in out of the night.

He wore a kind of baggy dark suit and a gray business hat like they always wear in '40s movies. He had white hair and a nose that looked almost proud of how many times it had been broken. The only thing different about him from any other cop in any other town was his eyes. You rarely saw cops with eyes sad as his.

He came right up to me and said, "I'm afraid I'm going to have to ask you for some identification."

I shrugged. "Sure." I pulled out my wallet and showed him my driver's license.

"Richard Anderson. Six feet. One hundred fifty-two pounds. Blue eyes. Black hair. Place of residence, Miami." As he read each of these off in the light on the drive, he'd look up at me to verify that what the license claimed was true. "You're a long way from Miami."

As if to prove what he'd said, a dirty truck filled with bawling cattle on the way to the slaughterhouse went rumbling by.

"Miami was a long time ago," I said.

"You doing anything special here?"

"Thought I might get something to eat."

"And then?"

"Then push on, I guess."

"That'd be a good idea." He handed me back my wallet. "I'm Jennings, the Chief of Police."

I wanted to laugh. The Chief? How big a force could he command in a place like Newkirk? People's fondness for titles always gripes me. It makes them feel like somebody. Me, I know I'm nobody and I've learned to face it.

He made a big production out of looking at his watch. "You see Chet's over there?"

Chet's was the diner. From here you could see a counter and a row of seats with only one guy in a Pioneer Seed Corn hat sipping coffee and forking off big chunks of what looked to be apple pie. Other than that the place was empty.

"Yep," I said.

"Good. You go over there and you tell Mindy that you're a friend of mine and that I told her to give you the special tonight—that's Swiss steak and peas and mashed potatoes and apple pie—and let me tell you, Mindy's apple pie is a pisser—and then I want you to have her put it on my tab."

"Hey," I said, "that's damn nice of you."

He stared at me with those sad eyes of his—so sad they made me a little nervous—and then he said, "Then I want you on the road. You can pick up the highway about a quarter mile east of here and you can get a ride in no time. You understand me?"

"Yes, sir."

He was just about to say something else when a pack of kids, dressed up variously as Freddie in *Nightmare on Elm*

Street, Darth Vader, Spock, and several others I didn't quite recognize, pushed past us.

"Hi, Chief Jennings!" several of them called. And then, "Trick or treat!"

They encircled him.

From his trouser pocket he took a fistful of change and then, standing right there on the DX drive with gasoline fumes strong on the bitter night wind, he gave each of them a quarter.

He also gave them a small lecture. "Now you be sure to all stay together, you hear me? And I want you in by"—he glanced at his watch—"seven-thirty." He nodded to the one who looked like Freddie. "Walter, I'm making you responsible, you understand?"

"Yessir."

"Seven-thirty."

"Yessir."

Then they were off again, caught up in themselves and the chill night.

I saw how he watched the kids. He looked sadder than ever.

"You don't want to be a stranger in this town tonight, son," he said softly. He sounded almost as if he was going to cry. Then he corrected himself by clearing his throat and said, "You go have Mindy fix you up."

"Yessir," I said, watching him wave to the kid in the DX and then walk back to his squad car.

"Yessir," I whispered again.

I sounded like one of those kids he'd given a quarter to.

The food was just as good as he'd said it'd be: big chunks of Swiss steak floating in tomatoes and so tender you could cut it with a fork, whipped potatoes with big yellow pats of butter, and some juicy green peas; all capped off with a wide wedge of apple pie and a cup of fresh coffee. It was one of those moments when you didn't want to leave, when you wanted to freeze the world in just one place, when you regretted things you'd been and done, and never wanted to be or do those things again.

The place smelled pleasantly of frying grease and cigarette smoke as I sat there finishing up my after-dinner coffee and talking some with Mindy, a short woman with unnaturally red hair and a grease-spattered pink uniform and horn-rimmed glasses that kept slipping down her nose.

She was saying, "You sure can't beat the Chief now, can you?" She wanted me to be grateful and a part of me resented that, but another part of me understood, so I said, "You sure can't. You sure can't."

I was about to say more when the door opened up and two farmers leading a bunch of kids got up in Halloween costumes came in. They all took over the place instantly, some of the kids to the johns, others sitting along the counter or at the tables.

I'd been planning on shooting the breeze with Mindy before taking off. I knew she figured me for scum, just another drifter, but it was just one of those times when I needed some conversation and I didn't much care about what or who it was with.

In lieu of talk, with her making a big fuss over all the cute little kids, I pointed to the coffeepot, and she nodded and even gave me a little smile, and then I had me some more java and another Lucky and took to staring out the front window.

Which was when I saw the little red VW bug all shiny sitting just outside, with the young blond girl—I figured her for eighteen or so—sitting there and staring inside Chet's. She seemed to be staring at me, even though I knew better. She was just as shiny as her car and there was no way she'd be looking at me.

Then she sort of grinned and took off. But her image stayed on the night air—her blondeness and her quick girl grin—long after she was gone.

I finished my coffee and Lucky and got up to go. Mindy

was so busy with the kids that all I could do was kind of wave and mouth a big thank-you. She nodded back to me.

One bite of the cold night and I was right back to being me again. My heels crunched through ice as I moved down the street, hefting my backpack, heading for the highway.

I walked from one streetlight to another, and in between it was as dark as nights ever get, and for a minute or two I felt like a kid, sort of scared of how vast and black the night was. I touched the pocketknife in my jeans.

I had just reached the highway when I heard a familiar straining engine noise. I'd just come up a steep grade and the motor was laboring to climb the same grade. Tiny VW engines always make that particular sound.

She whipped across the center line and pulled in right in front of me, cutting me off.

She rolled down the window and said, rock 'n' roll blaring on the radio inside, "You look just about as lonely as I am."

"You don't look like the kind of girl who has to be lonely if she doesn't want to be." Up close she was even better-looking. The only slightly disturbing thing was that she looked familiar somehow.

"The men around here are strictly dull."

I smiled. "I guess we've all got our crosses to bear."

She said, "What's your cross?"

There was something serious in her question, and again, for a reason I couldn't explain, I felt disturbed. I shrugged and said, "I ain't got it half as bad as some people I know. It just gets a little wearying sometimes."

"You going to get in?"

"Can I ask you a dumb question?"

She laughed. "People ask me dumb questions all the time. Why should you be any different?"

"You legal?"

"Huh?"

"You legal? Age, I mean."

"You asking if I'm jailbait?"

"Yeah."

She laughed again. She had a real nice laugh even above the loudly idling engine. "Honey, you do wonders for a woman's ego. I'm twenty-four years old."

"Oh."

"So get in."

"Where we going?"

"How's my place sound?"

"Right now that sounds about as nice as any place in the world."

She lived in a trailer court out on the highway, in one of those long silver jobs that was now almost white with frost in the cold moonlight.

The last stragglers of Halloween ran up and down the dirt roads between the trailers. Hers was set off from the rest by a good city block, over by a grove of elms forming a windbreak.

I know it's not supposed to happen this way but it did. We went inside her trailer and she didn't even turn a light on. We just stood there in the moonlight coming through the window and she put her arms around me and kissed me with a mouth that was warm and tender and frantic, and it had been so long for me that I nearly went crazy.

It didn't take long before she was undoing my shirt and leading me back to the bedroom.

We were spreading out, getting ready, when I said, "You smoke cigars?"

"You're so romantic," she said, reaching behind her with slender graceful arms and undoing her bra.

"I mean it smells like cigars in here," I said.

"My dad's. He comes over sometimes."

"Oh."

"Why? Who'd you think they'd belong to?"

"I wasn't sure. I mean, this . . ." I paused.

"This what?"

"Well, this sort of makes me nervous."

"Why? I thought you'd be having a good time. *I* am."

"So am I. Just . . ."

"Just what?"

"Well. Why would you just sort of—"

"—pick you up?"

"Yeah. Pick me up."

"Because today my divorce from Larry is final and I need to do something to make it real and I don't happen to want to do it with anybody from Newkirk. If it's any of your goddamn business, I mean."

"I didn't mean to make you mad."

"Well, you did."

"I'm sorry."

She was naked from the waist up. She sat there in the moonlight, letting me look at her, and believe me, I did look at her.

"You don't like guys or anything, do you?"

"No. I just kind of wanted to know where you were coming from," I said.

"Well, I guess you know now, don't you?"

"I sure do," I said. "I sure do."

The funny thing was, the first part of it was as sweet as doing it with your girlfriend back in high school, you know, when you really love somebody and do it as much to convey your feelings as to get rid of your needs. Her hair there in the darkness smelled wonderful and so did her perfume, and her flesh was soft and beautiful and there were nooks and crannies in her body that almost made me cry, they were so wonderful, and we went very slow then and her breath was pure as a baby's and her fingers on the back of my neck were gentle as any woman's had ever been, making me feel wanted and important and somebody.

And then, just as we were rolling over to the other side of the bed, she said, "Now I'm going to ask you to help me."

Something in the way she said it made me real nervous. "Help you?"

In the shadow I saw her nod.

I tried to make a joke of it. "And just what if I don't help you?"

She didn't move or speak. I saw the lift of her breasts as she sighed. "Then I'll kill you," she said. "And you'll be dead, just the way I am."

He came home, just as she said he would, ten minutes later. Now I knew who the cigar smoke belonged to.

She had the tape recorder set up for me and she had me set up in the chair next to the recorder. She also had a .38 Smith and Wesson, a policeman's gun, to put in my hand.

I sat there in the darkness listening to the gravel crunch as his heavy car pulled up to the trailer. The car door squeaked open and a big engine trembled into silence and then his shoes snapped through ice and then he put a key in the door and then he came on inside and turned on the light and then he said, "Jesus Christ! Just who the hell are you?"

He was a big guy, six-five maybe, and fleshy. His face was mottled from drinking. He smelled of cold and he smelled of booze. He wore a cheap rumpled sport jacket and cheap rumpled pants.

"I want you to sit down over there," I said.

"You a thief, or what?"

"I want you to sit down over there and tell me about the night you and your friend Frank Campion raped and killed the girl two years ago tonight, on Halloween."

"What the hell are you talking about?"

"You know what I'm talking about."

"I never raped no girl."

I pointed the gun at him. *"She* put me up to this."

"You're crazy, mister. You some kind of dope addict, or what?'

"She put me up to this. The girl you killed. Meaning,

she's controlling my hand. Anytime she wants she can force me to pull this trigger."

"You really are crazy."

I shot him in the leg.

He looked totally surprised. I guess because of the way I'd been talking—crazy and all with her controlling me—he'd started to feel as if he were in control of the situation, that he might have some kind of chance of getting the gun from me.

But she was in my mind now, and she eased my finger back on the trigger.

"I want you to tell me about that night, everything you did," I said.

He was crawling backward and shouting for help. He kept looking at his leg as if he hoped it might belong to somebody else. "I didn't rape no girl," he said.

I shot him in the arm, the right arm.

This time he vomited. I'm not sure why. Maybe fear.

But it worked. He started talking.

"We was drunk, Frank and me," he said, and then he said it all and it was pretty simple, really right up to and including how they'd buried her at the bottom of a grain elevator, where nobody would ever find her.

I turned off the tape recorder and let it run back and then I tested it and his voice was good and loud and clear. She had what she wanted.

He was crying, the big guy was. He was bleeding a lot and getting weaker and crying.

He said, "I can't even shout no more. You call an ambulance, okay? Okay?"

I got up and went to the phone and picked up the receiver. I started dialing, but then she turned me around abruptly.

As I realized what was going to happen, I jerked the gun to the left so that it misfired into the wall.

She came out of the bedroom and he saw her, and he started screaming louder than anybody I'd ever heard.

She tore the gun from my hand and walked over and stood above him. She fired four straight shots into his face.

When she was finished, she threw the gun to me and I caught it from reflex.

Down her cheek ran two tears like drops of mercury.

Then she was gone, the trailer door flapping in the wind, with her disappearing over the edge of the hill along the line of moonlit horizon.

I stood staring down at the corpse on the floor, the gun grasped in my fingers, as the first neighbor peered into the cabin and said to the second neighbor, *"Look.* This man shot John!"

The Chief made sure that nobody else rode back with us to the jail.

I'd told him everything that had happened, the girl and all. I knew better than to expect he'd believe me.

The funny thing was, as he listened, his sad eyes got sadder. He said, "I figured she'd be back tonight."

"You knew about her then?"

He looked over at me. "She was my daughter. I knew those two men raped and killed her but I could never prove it and I could never find where they'd buried her. Last year she used another drifter the same way—that's why I warned you to get out of town. He killed Campion, except Campion didn't confess before he died. So I figured she'd use another drifter like you to get the second man." He sighed. "And she did."

"Where's this other drifter now?" I said.

He shook his white head. "Death row. Tried and convicted of first-degree murder."

For the first time I saw what had happened to me. What had really happened to me.

"But if you tell them the real story, they'll believe you, won't they?" I said, sounding like a little kid, all pleading and desperate.

The Chief's car shot through the chill darkness. I could still see her in bed. Feel her . . .

"Son," he said, "that's why I warned you about being a drifter in Newkirk on Halloween night."

He shook out a cigarette from his pack and offered it to me.

"Son," he said. "I like you, so I'm going to do you a favor. I'm giving you a half-hour head start before I come looking for you."

"But . . ."

He looked at me with those sad eyes and I knew then why she'd looked so familiar from the start. She'd had the same sad eyes.

"Son," he said, "they're not going to believe you any more than they believed that other drifter." He paused. "You know what it's like on death row—just waiting?"

Twenty minutes later I was on the highway headed north. Three trucks rushed by, nearly knocking me over with their speed. A couple of carloads of kids came by, too. They just saw me as somebody to have some farm-boy fun with—calling me names and flipping me the bird and challenging me to a fight.

Then they were gone and there were just the unending prairie darkness and the winter stars overhead, and the lonely crunch of my feet on the hard ground.

I kept thinking of her, of how good and loving she'd felt in my arms, even though all the time I held her she'd been . . . dead.

I don't know how long I walked or how many cars and trucks roared by. After a while I faced frontward and just started walking, forgetting all about thumbing.

Then I started thinking about my own life. The years being raised by my uncle in a one-room apartment in the city. And the wife who'd dumped me for a grinning young Marine. And the years of drifting after that . . .

I heard it from a long way off. It came up over the sound of the wild abandoned dogs roaming the night, of the distant train smashing through the darkness of the distant prairie, of the crunching sound of my feet . . .

I recognized it immediately, that sound.

A slightly laboring VW engine.

At first I was scared and started running along the shoulder of the road, my backpack slamming against my shoulders. But the faster I ran, the closer she drew . . .

When she got alongside me, I decided there was no use fighting it anymore. Chest heaving, warm now from sweat, I turned and looked at her there inside the red VW.

She leaned over and rolled down the window. "Would you like a ride?"

"Just leave me alone, all right? Just leave me alone."

"If I didn't like you, I wouldn't have come back. When we were making love, I realized how lonely you are . . . being a drifter and all, and I thought I could help you." She smiled and held her hand out to me. "I thought I could take you with me."

I didn't want to hear any more. Throwing my backpack down so I could run better, I set off, trotting back down the road, away from her as fast as I could get.

For a long time I could hear the VW sitting there, engine idling, but finally I heard her grind the gears and set off over the hill, leaving me alone.

The blackness again; the sound of my own heart racing; the texture and smell of my own sweat.

I stopped. She was gone. I no longer needed to run.

And then I saw the headlights headed toward me and heard the engine with the idle set too high, the laboring VW engine.

As I watched her come closer, an exhaustion set in. All I could think of was the time I'd had mono. For three weeks I hadn't even been able to walk down the hall to the bathroom . . .

She pulled up. This time she opened the door for me.

"I'll drive around till you get used to the idea," she said.

"So you won't be so scared, I mean." Blond hair hiding part of her face, she said, very gently, "It's really what you want, you know. No more bitterness . . . no more pleading . . . no more pleading."

The door opened wider.

"We can drive these highways all night and look at how beautiful the forest is on the hills, and by then—"

"—by then I won't be scared."

"By then," she said, "you won't be scared."

"My backpack—"

She smiled again. So soft. "You don't have to worry about things like that anymore. I'm going to take you with me."

She put out her hand once more, her warm, tender hand, and I took it and let her draw me inside her car, the red VW that set off now into the unceasing black prairie night.

And it was just like she'd promised. I didn't worry about anything.

Not anything at all.

Reflections

Ray Russell

This timeworn city of ours is a place of many shops. I have often reflected that they are like voluptuous sirens, luring us with the enticing wares that beckon from behind the shining panes of their windows. A person could stand—as I stood last night—outside Alecu's pastry shop, and simultaneously see the mouth-watering cakes and tortes as well as one's own face, licking one's lips at that delectable display. At certain hours, when the light is right, the windows of those shops are as good as any looking glass. Frequently, with their aid, I have straightened my hat or smoothed my mustache before going on to keep a rendezvous with my beloved.

Last night, I waited for her in front of the pastry shop. It was closed—dark inside, each windowpane a perfect black mirror. I could see myself, lit by the combined rays of the street-corner lamp and the full moon: the respected physician, elegant host, pillar of society. All those qualities and attributes seemed to be reflected there. I fancied I could see them clearly.

But would I see *her?*

I feared that I would not. I feared that my most morbid suspicions would be confirmed. I shivered, and not only with the cold. Soon I would know the truth. I had set a trap for her and had asked her to meet me in front of the shop at midnight.

Somewhere, in the chill darkness, a distant bell tolled that hour, and at the same time I heard the delicate click of her approaching heels. I turned away from that sound, to face the shop window. The click of her heels drew nearer.

And then I saw her beautiful reflection in the glass. I was filled with a welcome warm flood of relief.

"Good evening, Ioan," she said in that sable voice.

I turned to her. "My dear . . ." I began to say, but my voice faltered.

"Is something wrong?" she asked. "You seem ill at ease."

"I am an ingrate and a fool," I replied. "I misjudged you. Can you forgive me? I actually had come to think that you were—"

"A vampire?" she said, as her lips stretched wide in a ghastly smile, revealing hideous fangs.

I recoiled, in disbelief as well as horror. "No!" I cried. "Impossible!" I gestured wildly toward the window. "Your reflection . . ."

"Ah yes," she said, admiring her lovely image in the window.

"A vampire cannot be reflected," I pointed out. "Everybody knows that."

"You are a famous scholar of the healing arts, Ioan, but I am afraid you have not studied the lore of my kind closely enough."

"I have," I insisted.

"If indeed you had," she replied in a mocking tone, "you would have known that our forms, even as yours, can be reflected in many things—in water, in windows, in gleaming china . . ." She began to move closer to me. "But not in silver, or in mirrors backed by a coating of it."

"The killing power of silver bullets is known to me," I murmured, "but . . ."

"Silver," she crooned, slowly moving ever closer, "was the coinage paid to Judas for the betrayal of your Lord. And the old legend has it that, to compensate the spirit of that metal for the base use to which it had been put, it was forever granted the power to repel evil. Hence, when a creature of my sort stands before a silvered mirror, the glass refuses the reflection. But a shop window, with no silver behind it . . ."

"I understand," I said.

"You understand too late, my poor Ioan."

Baring her fangs again, she moved quickly toward me. From under my cloak I drew the syringe. It was filled with glittering fluid.

She laughed. "Poison? That will avail you nothing."

"Not poison," I said sadly. "Medicine. We prescribe it in cases of epilepsy."

"I do not suffer from that complaint," she said, and laughed again.

"No, my dear. Your affliction is far more terrible. And this will cure you."

She lunged at me like a panther. I sank the needle deep into her smooth white throat and pressed down the plunger. *"Argenti oxidum,"* I whispered, as she fell dead at my feet. "Oxide of silver. Farewell, my love. And may you rest in peace at last."

The shop window reflected my anguished face and my tears.

The Happy Family

Melissa Mia Hall and
Douglas F. Winter

Skin so pale and body pencil-thin. Hard. Cool to the touch. Put your head against that unmoving breast and hold tight; everything's going to be all right.

She stares blindly at the track lighting of the department store. Her arms are crossed protectively in front of her, as if she's embarrassed by something he said. There's a slight arch to her back, and she's too tall, her legs long and bare. She is modeling lingerie, or a swimsuit that could pass for lingerie. A bicycle leans against the Plasticine rock behind her. Two steps to her left, another mannequin, not as fetching or desirable, scans the distant menswear section, as if she's lost a boyfriend to the racks of disconsolate ties.

Walter stares at her and thinks about the movie where a mannequin turns into a girl. A real-live girl.

That is not what he wants. He just wants her.

There is something special, something right, about this mannequin. She is so much like the others, the ones he has collected. They wait for him at home, perfectly coiffed, perfectly clothed, perfectly arranged down in the den.

Rachel doesn't particularly like them. Neither do Laurie or Rob, his children. Laurie seems afraid of them. He can never understand why. She always liked playing with her Barbies.

Walter pats his pocket to make sure that he brought his checkbook. He'll have her. Somehow he will have her. All you have to do is name the right price to the right person.

But there's no rush. She's not going anywhere.

He smiles crookedly, amused with himself. No one at work thinks he has a sense of humor. His secretary walks on eggshells around him. She's afraid of him. But the name partners of most blue-chip Dallas law firms tend to be frightening, don't they?

There aren't many shoppers this early on a Saturday. Give it an hour and that'll change. He savors the silence, marred only by the throb of rock videos warming up in the junior department. At least that's what they used to call it. Now it's something like "Connections" or "Upbeat." Laurie once liked to hang out in those places, but now she seems to prefer the same expensive boutiques as her mother.

Walter has always loved department stores. He liked them when he was a kid and Sears was top of the line and Penney's just for window-shopping. He never thought he'd marry a woman who would consider Saks Fifth Avenue slumming.

Her arms are crossed so tightly.

Walter turns to watch a grim-faced clerk march past, his arms filled with pantsuits. Then he looks back toward her.

Her wig is styled in a short, punkish bob, laced with spiky curls that dance on her forehead with comic intensity. He'll take the wig off. Let her go bald.

Her eyes are blue. A beautiful blue, wide and watery bright. Her nose slices the air. Imperial. Her cheeks are hollowed as if she were sucking air, preparing to say how lost she is, how defenseless. Her skimpy pink underwear would make anyone feel defenseless. Who could ride a bicycle like that? She's not even wearing decent shoes, just flimsy white sandals, half-on, half-off.

She's so scared.

He'll buy her. He has to save her.

He wonders what to name her. Amy? Leigh? She doesn't have a name. She doesn't have anything, really. She is penniless. Her friend, over there by the bicycle, could care less. She's alone—except for me, he thinks with a curious satisfaction. And she's not going anywhere unless I take her with me. And I will. I will buy her; but not now. Later.

She's not going anywhere.

He walks away from her and wanders over to the menswear department, with its shirts and slacks and jackets, wallets and belts and ties. He never buys ties. His secretary buys ties. The receptionist buys ties and the receptionist's secretary buys ties and the secretary's receptionist buys ties. Even his wife buys ties. But he does not. His partners—and even, on occasion, his associates— say that he fancies himself as the Don Johnson of north Dallas. It's true that, in the summertime, he does not wear socks at home or on the golf course. Or on the *Fairweather,* his boat—or, as Rachel calls it, his yacht. But he doesn't look like Don Johnson. He shaves everyday. And he doesn't feel like Don Johnson. Women don't hang on his every word and he's never been in *People* and he's never been on TV (well, maybe once), and he's never cut a record. Not a record record, but he has cut some record-making deals.

He looks in a mirror, holding a red necktie against his chest. It's silky and shiny and absolutely uncouth. He tells the bored clerk he'll take it and tucks the package under his arm. The paper crackles reassuringly. He doesn't like the plastic bags that most stores are giving out these days. Nonrecyclable. He thinks of all that plastic still lying around, long after he's dead and gone. It bothers him.

He gazes into the distance and sees the two mannequins in their "Sportif" ensembles. The bicycle gleams. She could ride away in a minute, if she wanted. If she could. But it wouldn't be long before they were together again.

These things are inevitable.

He suddenly wants to walk away. Especially from her.

She's so vulnerable, so needy. Rachel was like that once. He'd believed her. It was only later that he discovered it had all been an act; but by then he had also discovered that it didn't matter. Or he chose to believe that it didn't matter. He's still uncertain; perhaps she simply changed. But Rachel is a good woman. Patient. Understanding. Demure.

He does like Florida. On occasion. The right occasion.

And he likes the song that Don Johnson sings. He has heard it on the radio, on MTV. Something about a heartbeat. Looking for a heartbeat.

The multilevel mall opens before him, vast, impersonal, glittering, and real. So real. Rob's favorite word is "real." Everything's "real"—like real radical, real stuff, real right, you know? *Real.*

Walter's hair is going silver at the temples. Terry Bragg accused him of coloring his hair, because it was just too distinguished-looking to be real. Really real. He charges down the mall, taking huge strides, burning calories, being aerobic, healthy, stirring the blood.

People are pouring into the mall now. It's like an awakening beehive. They all look so wonderful. The men purposeful and fatherly. The women smelling of perfume and money. The children circling and laughing, circling and laughing. He finds himself smiling again.

He pictures Rachel and Laurie somewhere in the crowd. They're pretty, Rachel and Laurie: Rachel's fair hair with its faint reddish streaks, Laurie's redder hair catching and holding sunlight until her head looks as if it were on fire. They both have green eyes and a dusting of freckles across their perfectly matched noses. Both are petite and slender, their breasts like half-opened buds. Short and flashing-quick on their feet, their hands sporting the fingernail polish of the week, Laurie's showing signs of teeth marks.

He stops in a bookstore and heads for the magazine section. Tchaikovsky is playing over the sound system. This bookstore sells music, videos, calendars, postcards. He glances through the array of foreign publications that marks the stand as an upscale, trendy sort of place. A lovely girl holds a *Madame Figaro* closer to her face. She's obviously pretending to read it. She squints at the French and then notices that he's watching her. She blushes and puts the magazine back.

"Hello," Walter says. He has no intention of carrying this further, but she looks so innocent and sweet. Like the mannequin.

"Hi," she says and blushes again. She's about average height, with brown hair and hazel eyes—or are they brown, too? Her clothes look old but clean. Her sandals are worn. She's not as young as he thought at first. There's gray in her hair. Maybe she's over thirty.

"Ever been there?" he blurts out, gesturing toward the magazine.

She glances at him, uncertain. "To Madame Figaro's?"

"No. To France."

She tugs at her shoulder bag. One of the straps is splitting. She shrugs.

He has lost count of how many times he has been there. To France. But never to Madame Figaro's. He visualizes a comfortably fat woman wearing a lace shawl and holding a wooden spoon, red with tomato sauce, in her hand. A good name for a restaurant or a fortune-teller. But for a fashion magazine?

"I've been to France lots of times."

"Great," she says coolly, as if she were unimpressed; but her eyes seem wider. Perhaps she is envious. Perhaps not.

"You read French?" he asks her as she picks up the *Madame Figaro* again and heads for the cashier. She glances over her shoulder at him and says, "A little," and then pays for the magazine. She's ignoring him. She doesn't want to talk to him. It makes him angry. She's a nothing. She's just a woman he doesn't know. It doesn't matter.

Why would a woman who doesn't read French buy a French magazine? But she said she could read it. A little. She was probably lying. Probably she has fifty dollars in her checking account, if she has one at all. Maybe she doesn't even have a car. Maybe she rides the bus. Is there a bus stop near here? He thinks of the mammoth parking garage and of all the cars on the expressway girdling the mall.

He finds himself following her. She looks so old-fashioned, wearing her faded black pants and her faded black shirt. The amber necklace was probably plastic. Or was it carnelian? She couldn't afford carnelian. Glass?

She's almost five stores ahead, but she's walking slowly. He catches up to her in no time. She turns and enters a chocolate shop. There are small tables and chairs out front, so that patrons may watch passersby as they eat. She comes out and sits down, clutching a small bag of truffles. A plastic bag. She eats a truffle and, when the waitress arrives, orders a cappuccino. She glances up and sees him. She looks trapped. Captured. He sits down across from her.

"Do you mind?"

"I guess not," she says, but he can see that she's scared. He finds this oddly thrilling. The waitress comes back and hands him a menu. He orders chocolate ice cream with almonds.

"My name is Walter."

He waits for her to tell him her name. She just stares at him.

"So?"

He wishes that he could think of something witty to say. He feels very young and very foolish. He hasn't felt this way in years.

"So. I'm a lawyer."

"Okay."

"What do you do?"

"Whatever I have to do to get by," she says. The waitress brings their orders. She stirs and sips her cappuccino without looking up.

"I find you fascinating," he says.

She says nothing. She won't look at him. Her body, he realizes, is like white enamel. Porcelain. The only place with color is her cheeks. They bloom like pink roses.

"You don't get out in the sun much, do you?" he says.

"I burn easily," she whispers.

"What's your name?"

"Look, pal, I really don't know you and I don't think—"

"I don't mean any harm. I'm not a mad rapist or anything."

Now she almost gulps her cappuccino.

"I just want to know you."

Is this love at first sight? Her hands come to rest on the sack with the French magazine. Her hands are beautiful. She doesn't wear any rings at all. Rachel wears a ring on almost every finger. She especially likes diamonds. This girl has probably never owned a diamond. He wants to give her diamonds, rubies, emeralds. But she probably wouldn't wear them. He sighs.

"I think I'd better leave," she says, half-rising. He stops her with an over-eager hand. She freezes; the fear turns into shock.

"Don't go."

She sits back down. Their eyes lock. She's not afraid at all. Walter glances around, checking reality. The sun slides through the glass ceiling. Shoppers whip past, and the plants seem to rustle in their clay pots. The noise escalates. A child screams and laughs with another child. A mother tells them to stop running. He glances back at the young-old woman and she's not there. The sack with the magazine is still on the table. She forgot it like she forgot him. He leaves the waitress an overlarge tip and takes the magazine.

His enthusiasm for his Saturday at the mall has waned. He heads for the exit closest to the parking garage where his Mercedes is parked. He does not even have the heart to go bargain for his mannequin, with her crossed arms and big blue eyes. The girl from the bookstore had big eyes, too; lost eyes. Now he feels lost. He knows he's being childish. Rachel will get a good laugh out of this.

For all her faults, Rachel usually understands. It all comes from being thirty-nine. He's going to turn forty next year. It's only natural to have days like this. But he has so much to live for. He's done so well. His father's proud of him. He's proud of himself. He has a good life, a happy family.

And that mannequin's not going anywhere.

He finds the exit. In a minute, he stands in the parking garage, looking for his car. He does this a lot. He's always forgetting where he parked his car. One time, he spent two hours searching for his car at the Beverly Center in Los Angeles. To this day, it has made flying to the West Coast a pain in the ass. He's always afraid it will happen again. Consequently, he never goes to shopping malls in California anymore. It's a matter of principle.

He is sweating profusely. Rob loves to say that, too: "sweating profusely." His face cracks into another lopsided smile. He walks past a Porsche, and sees her staring at him. The girl from the bookstore. It's her Porsche. He can't speak. She stares at him, crosses her arms defensively. As if he's going to attack her. As if he's going to grab her and hold her against his chest. Though he does want to do that. But she's gone and slammed the door of her Porsche and it's squealing past him. He catches one last glimpse of her startled face, her mouth open, a crack of red in her porcelain skin. He breathes in the exhaust and coughs. His Mercedes is right there, right next to the space where her car was parked.

Poor little rich girl.

He feels worse than cheated. He feels dumb.

Sighing, he sinks into his car and leaves.

Walter likes driving. He's got a sports car in the shop. A black Ferrari. He drives and drives and drives. He drives fast. See Walter go. See Walter go fast. See Walter get a ticket for speeding. It's no big deal.

Late afternoon in Dallas. It's been a hot summer. It's cooler right now, but not by much. He cranks up the air conditioner. He feels hungry—the ice cream went untouched—but he doesn't want to head for home. Not yet. His family is probably not there anyway. He can't remember, but he thinks they're gone. Somewhere.

Saturdays are always busy. Laurie had a dentist's appointment. A dance lesson. A friend's birthday party. Rob had a baseball game. A Scout meeting. A sleepover. Rachel had a date with the girls—or maybe, with the boys. He thinks she has lots of affairs of the heart.

That's what she calls them: "Affairs of the heart."

Has Walter had affairs? He doesn't think so. He has held a mannequin in his arms, but he's never screwed one. He wouldn't do that. That would be perverse.

Walter may be many things, but he's not perverse.

Not really.

It's almost twilight. The sun is watered down and mellow. Mellow-yellow, orange and red. He clicks a cassette into the tape player. The Moody Blues sing of nights in white satin. He's dated and old. Never reaching an end. Floundering.

The expressway is almost empty. Soon it will be overcome with exhaust and taillights. He's driving home the way he's always driven home from the Galleria. The light shines in his eyes. He might have a wreck. Just in time, the sun winks and is gone.

He's approaching an overpass. His favorite overpass, a sleek angle of white concrete and sunbaked steel. He sees something dangling in the shadows overhead. It looks like a body, hanging at the end of a rope. But it can't be a body. He puts on the brakes, and the Mercedes slides. He brings the car to a stop on the shoulder and gets out, gaping back at the body, twisting and turning above the highway. An eighteen-wheeler wheezes by. It doesn't stop. Another car passes. Doesn't anyone care? He's got to save that poor girl. But he knows that it's probably too late.

Why do people kill themselves? *Selves*. He sees a multiple image of himself trying on a suit. Did she plan this, or was it spontaneous? Panting and sweating—sweating profusely—Walter manages to scale the earthen bank. He boosts himself onto the pavement of the overpass. It would have been easier to move the car, but maybe she's still breathing. Maybe she's alive.

He carries a pocketknife in his jacket. His father always told him to be prepared. But he can't haul her up by the rope; he's not that strong. And if he cuts the rope, she may die from the fall. He pulls tentatively on the rope and discovers that she is not very heavy. She is not very heavy at all. He pulls the rope, hand over hand, and soon holds her in his arms. She does not breathe. Her heart is silent. He cradles her against his chest, uncertain whether to laugh or cry.

It is a joke of some sort, isn't it?

He hears a siren, and from the corner of his eye, he sees a police car's knowing lights. They're coming to get him.

He looks at her again and still can't believe what he sees. He knows this lady. But she's so far from home. It's Christine. The shaggy blond wig he had glued on her himself; he had glued it well. And dressed her in the silk Kamali blouse and sleek faded jeans. One of her spike heels is missing. He kisses her cheek and the policemen approach him carefully. There's a crowd gathering. The policemen may arrest him. They must not do that.

He is a lawyer. He can talk himself out of anything. He starts talking. The policemen listen. They listen as they finger the long rope, the thick noose. They listen as they go down to the patrol car. They listen as they escort him to the Mercedes. They marvel at the nut case—or perhaps it was a high school prankster—who planted the mannequin at an unusually busy section of the Interstate.

The policemen shake his hand. Walter says good-bye. He watches as they carry Christine to the patrol car. He checks an impulse to wave. He'll miss her. Did he do this? Did he hang Christine from the overpass? When could he have done that?

It is almost night. The cars zip by, one after another. Their headlights are bright, probing, like flashbulbs. If he didn't hang her, perhaps Rachel did. But how would Rachel know when he would pass? How did she know that he would be the one to stop? And why didn't anyone else stop to see if it was a real body? Real body. Real. His brain feels fuzzy.

Doesn't anyone care?

Rachel would not have done this to him. He's a good husband. A good father.

A Porsche drives past. The girl from the bookstore. He starts to follow her, but the car is white, and he knows that her car wasn't white. But it wasn't black. He thinks it was silver. Gray. He's not sure. Two Porsches in one day.

He sits behind the wheel of the Mercedes and cries. No one understands. No one cares. No one but Rachel.

Ahead, the highway curls into darkness. In the rearview mirror, he watches the shadows lengthen. And sees someone hanging from the overpass, twisting at the end of a rope. A trick of the fading light. He turns the ignition key, tries a new tape in the cassette player. But he doesn't listen.

He has decided to drive straight home. He follows the highway to the third exit. Turns right at the end of the ramp. Passes two traffic lights, then takes a left, another left, a right, another left. He's there.

All the lights are on. The station wagon, a Volvo, sits in the driveway. Maybe everyone's home. Maybe dinner is ready. Maybe a chilled Martini is waiting on the table. Maybe they'll play gin rummy.

Walter trembles as he slides the key in and out of the lock and walks into the living room. He clutches the sacks with the magazine and the red tie. Rachel prefers Italian fashion magazines, but she'll be glad he thought of her. They'll laugh about the tie. It's a joke, he'll explain. They'll laugh. He should have bought something for the kids. Of course, Laurie's not a kid anymore. She has a boyfriend named Chad.

They're not in the living room. He tries the kitchen, the

dining room. He can't find them. The bedrooms. They're not there. He hears music coming from the den. With enormous relief, he heads in that direction. Down the stairs. They're safe. They've been waiting for him. All the lights are on. They're sitting on the couch, staring at the TV.

"Welcome home, Daddy," he says for them. He kisses Laurie on the cheek, scuffs Rob at the back of the neck. Then he sits next to Rachel, touches her beautiful hair, her eyes, her lips.

He loves her.

"We love you."

He pulls her to his chest. Her breasts are cool and hard. He listens between them for the sound of a trapped heart.

Maybe, someday and always.

He listens.

Dew Drop Inn

D. W Taylor

Ten hours on the road and Rick couldn't remember it ever being day, the night thickening around the highway like grave dust and all he could think was move, move, move, eating up the road with speed. Jonesboro 46, take it; 35 more to Johnson City, maintain the strain. Yeah, this was how the truckers did it—lost in the rhythm of the road, on the move and in the groove. Sixty-five mph, seventy; the BMW was a silver bullet. Didn't matter. The cops were good ol' boys too. Besides, everyone was in a hurry. It was Christmas.

"I wanna hear Madonna. See if you can find Madonna." The irritation went through Rick like a jolt of current, settling right in the amalgams of his teeth. Chrissy had developed one hell of a whine this year. She and her little buddies in the second grade must practice it at recess, trying out different versions at home and comparing notes the next day—honing their art until they had developed the perfect whine, guaranteed to rattle fillings. Make a man do anything. He had seen the little devils giggling together triumphant, out on the Academy's playground. The *expensive* Academy's playground. And this was what he got for his money?

"Jesus, honey, do something to shut her up, will ya?"

Rick glanced over at his wife. Mary Beth was just sitting there sliding the needle across the radio's dial, slowly, expectantly, deliberately, with all the patience of a god-damn saint.

"You always get to listen to what you want to. I *never* do." Absolutely perfect. Her child's vowels drawn out just so and blended with a touch of the nasal. A pitiful little singsong on the edge of tears.

"Mother of God, hurry up. She's driving me crazy." Still nothing but crackle and arruphs from the radio; voices from outer space. They were somewhere in the tip of Tennessee, that sawblade state on the road atlas with a blue stripe called Interstate 40 wriggling like a vein across its middle. Nowhere, man. In between Bristol and Knoxville it was just you and the hayseeds and the stars, good buddy.

All Mary Beth could get was some soul station with Ray Charles singing Christmas carols: "Shepherds quake—Oh, *say* now, can't you hear them quakin'—at the sight."

Rick knew it was coming.

"That's not Ma-don-na."

"Mary Beth, do something with your child. *Now.*"

She bent over into the backseat, her rear end kissing the windshield, and began talking in her Mommy Voice to the pouting face with its little conceited mouth all screwed up. "Daddy's trying to drive, honey, so we . . ."

God, whatever happened to the good old days? Just the two of them cruising down south to visit Mary Beth's parents for Christmas. Then maybe to Florida for a few days. They used to go anywhere they wanted, buy anything, anytime. Then the nightly DoveBars got traded in for an Aprica stroller. And ever since *it* was born, all Rick could remember was dirty diapers, sleepless nights, its constant presence, feeling manacled to it—*its* slave at home, at the law office earning money for *it,* watching Mary Beth do everything for *it.*

He even knew the precise instant everything changed: Mary Beth up on the delivery-room slab, legs in those stirrups, gown pushed up to her waist. She was grabbing at his arm, her face washed in sweat, eyes pleading. Then her mouth made that ugly, grotesque oval of pain while everybody stared between her legs as the plastic-gloved hand reached into her.

Something clicked, snapped, broke; whatever. But his Mary Beth, the slim, sexy, long-blond-hair-on-her-shoulders Mary Beth, the girl he used to wait for at the college dorm while she floated down the stairs like an angel, the girl who took his breath away when she walked into class that day— she was gone. Just like that. She wasn't his anymore. The *it* took her away, destroyed her. And now sometimes, only *sometimes,* mind you, he wished they would both just go away. Just leave him alone. Silently, carelessly, at the low brilliant stars littering the sky with promises, he intoned: "Star light, star bright . . . I wish I may, I wish I might . . ."

"She can't help it, Rick. Ten hours. Why don't we stop for dinner? It's almost six."

"Terrific. Why didn't you say something before we got past Bristol? We're in the middle of nowhere out here."

In the backseat Chrissy was singing to herself: "Like a vir-gin." What did an eight-year-old know about virgins? He hadn't even noticed that Annette Funicello had breasts under that Mickey Mouse emblem until he was ten, much less speculated on her sexual status vis-à-vis Frankie Avalon. What was the hold this "Madonna" had on kids? His daughter looked like a miniature bag lady with those droopy socks and fingerless gloves.

"Must have been subconscious," Mary Beth said. "I'll die if I have to eat at another Pizza Hut."

"What's wrong with franchises? At least you always know what you're getting." Rick realized his mistake too late.

"It's not the food, it's the people." Mary Beth launched into her "They're-so-gross" speech—one of her specialties—describing how the fat women lined up, haunch to haunch, at the all-you-can-eat bar. How the men piled their

plates like pharaohs building pyramids, one of every top-
ping, stuffing it all into their faces as if they were scared of
ever being hungry again. She added a seasonal twist: "They
make me *sick,* especially at Christmas."

He had her this time. "Okay, then, at what *new* place
would you like to watch the local yokels stuff their faces?"

But she had learned to ignore loaded questions during the
cross-exam. "Look, we *have* to stop someplace. You
promised to call your mom before they shut off the switchboard at seven. You know how she worries."

Obvious but effective. Rick imagined his mother in her
room at the Bronxville nursing home, sitting hunched over
in the wheelchair, staring at the phone, arthritic hands curled
in her lap like twisted roots. A shy stab of guilt made all the
lies troop forward on cue, defenders of the conscience: It
was the right place for her. My God, the woman had
rheumatoid arthritis so bad she could barely get in and out
of the wheelchair or feed herself. And with him and Mary
Beth both at the office all day, they'd just have to hire someone anyway. She was better off there with others like her.

Then he remembered the conversation by the Christmas
tree the year before, his mother gripping his arm with her
cold, gnarled hand, the same way Mary Beth had in the delivery room, making him look at her, making him promise
never to put her in one of those homes. "Son, I'd go crazy.
Son, *please . . .*"

"Rick, look. The Dew Drop Inn. What do you think?"
Mary Beth moved to the edge of her seat. Chrissy popped
up out of the back, instantaneously. "I wanna stop. Can we
stop? *Ple-ease?* " Right in his ear. There went the amalgams
again.

They had driven this route at least five or six times and
he couldn't remember ever seeing a "Dew Drop Inn." But
there it was, halfway up a dark hillside, red neon "Dew" and
"Drop" and "Inn" flashing in tedious sequence. Obviously,
Tennessee's terminal case of corniness had struck again.
"Only because my ass is pleading its case for mercy," Rick

said. "But don't blame me if the real name of this place turns out to be the 'Do Drop Dead' after we eat." Chrissy cheered when he took the exit.

No cars in the gravel parking lot, yet lights were on inside. Strange; usually every pit stop along I-40 was doing good business this time of year, jammed by station wagons with presents stuffed in the back, presents flowing out the windows and up onto the roof—the bounty of America runnething over.

"We must've missed the ptomaine warning on the radio. Everyone's left already." Rick was really getting into this. "Oh, look, it's built of logs, just like in the old days. Isn't that clever? Chrissy, I think this could be a valuable educational experience for you."

"Park it, Dad." The brat. He'd pay her back later. She was all business now, getting her bag-girl costume ready to impress any potential rival second graders. It would be so easy to show up these hick kids. They probably thought Madonna had something to do with Christmas.

Interior decor was definitely "Early Davy Crockett": oak barrels and fake log counters. There were racks of toy outhouses for sale with tiny doors that opened onto the best in scatological humor; shell ashtrays with a map of Tennessee painted in the middle; a bounty of corncob pipes and Rebel T-shirts. Expensive, classy stuff that you just could not *get* at Neiman Marcus anymore.

But Rick couldn't understand how, with no cars out front, there could be people dotting nearly every booth and table in the restaurant section. And they all looked like travelers, too—definitely not local yokels. There was a skinny brunette in one of those trim business suits that made any woman look like a schoolmarm, a salesman type in polyester, a dapper gray-haired gentleman, even a trucker leaning on meaty forearms over his coffee. No kids. Sorry, Chrissy. Just adults sitting quietly alone, one to a table, staring into space, speaking to no one. Not even to the dwarf waitress who waddled from table to table.

Rick smiled privately. The waitress looked just like Mother Teresa—an ancient angular face with great folds of skin, a wide trunk that seemed to stretch almost to the floor, definitely to her kneecaps. Her shoulders swayed up and down with each step. One stumpy leg was shorter than the other—Rick had it figured out by the time she did her little duck walk over to their booth.

"Evening, folks. What y'all gonna have tonight?" Her voice was low and full of gravel, making you want to clear your own throat. All three stared down at her, mesmerized. Her chin was exactly level with the table, which hid the rest of her, leaving just a decapitated head talking on top of the table. John the Baptist come back to life to scold Salome. Silence as she handed out the menus, her little hands brown and fragile as dead leaves.

"I'll be right back. Y'all take your time now and don't be in no hurry." She was saying the usual corny things, but the edge to her dry country-biscuit voice was somehow condescending—maybe even menacing. "That's a real cute outfit, honey," the turning talking head said to Chrissy, who started to smile but caught the dwarf's small sneer and stared quickly down at her children's menu.

All right! Rick thought appreciatively. Took the starch right out of those mesh stockings! He was beginning to take a shine, as they say, to this little table-waiting curmudgeon. Maybe he could learn a few things. One part churlishness and two parts sarcasm; he'd have to try her recipe.

"I hate her, she's ugly!" Chrissy blurted out after the dwarf had gone. She was almost beside herself, hurt and angry, the pout threatening to mutate any second into a full-fledged, scrunchy-faced bawl.

"Now, Chrissy, sometimes people don't mean . . ." Mary Beth went into her mother act about understanding others, how *some* people just *look* different, the need for tolerance, and blah blah. Did she really think it would do this kid any good?

Time for the payback. "Here's a quarter, honey," Rick

said. "See if you can find any good songs on the jukebox."
That should take her at least ten minutes of searching in vain
for the one name he knew would definitely not, in this hick
joint, be found alphabetically between *L*oretta Lynn and *M*el
Tillis. Rick watched her wriggle her little butt across the
floor. Too bad, Chrissy. No one else even looked up. They
just stared at their plates or at the darkness pressed like a
hand against the windows, their faces expressionless, as if
in a trance, mouths chewing slowly.

"Can you believe that damn little witch? Saying something like that to a child?" A curse word! Saint Mary Beth
must really be hot. "What was on her name tag—'Ida'? I'd
a-like to trip her next time she goes by!" Not bad, not bad.

"What's really weird is the customers," Rick said. "Look
around. Everyone's alone, no one's talking, no one's even
leaving. And where are their cars? The lot was empty when
we drove up." He leaned forward for emphasis. "This is *definitely not* the Pizza Hut."

Ida appeared suddenly at the corner of the table. These
damn little midgets could really sneak up on you! The look
on her face made Rick feel like a prisoner plotting an escape
or something. Maybe she had heard Mary Beth. She looked
directly at Rick, though, as if he were the only one at the
table, and rasped, "Y'all know what you want yet?" Ah, that
southern charm had returned.

Mary Beth said sharply, "Yes, we're having coffee—*to
go*. Chocolate milk for my daughter. And please hurry." She
slapped he menu down on the table as if she were playing a
trump card an stared out the window. That was telling her!

"Uh . . . one more thing, if you don't mind." Rick just had
to know. "Did I park in the right place? I mean, there are
all these people in here but no cars out there. For future
reference, you understand." He smiled. Funny how quickly
you adapted. It seemed normal talking to a decapitated head
with its chin on the table.

"Overnighters. Cars in the permanent lot. Cain't be too
careful, 'specially at Christmas." She started to waddle off,

her broad ugly shoulders dipping up and down, tilted slightly to starboard. Then she turned. "You folks welcome to stay, if you've a mind to."

"Gosh, right kindly of you," Rick said, hoping he wasn't being too obvious; but this one was for Chrissy and Mary Beth. "But we'd better be moseyin' on down the road a spell." The dwarf's old face lit up in a repulsive grin. She loved it! This was the kind of thing she fed on. You could never get to a person like that. The more you gave, the more they wanted.

Chrissy waited until Ida had disappeared before slinking back into the booth. Now she was really depressed. No Madonna in this place, only midget witches. While Mary Beth and Chrissy went to the rest room, Rick slipped a tip under his coffee saucer before leaving. Mary Beth would have said the second curse word of her life if she had found out—but, he told himself, you had to maintain your class around hicks. Besides, the old crone was a bit scary.

It was a relief to be back inside the BMW, the silver bullet of I-40, strapped in and ready for ignition.

Nothing.

He tried again. Still only that helpless sinking feeling in the pit of his stomach and a voice at the back of his head saying, "No, no, no!" as the engine growled over and over, lifeless, recalcitrant, inexplicable.

"Goddamn *son* of a *bitch*." Rick slapped his palm against the leather-covered steering wheel, took a deep breath, and tried again, telling himself this wasn't happening even while the engine kept grinding. "Come on, come on, come *on*." Mary Beth and Chrissy, perfectly still—watching, listening, depending.

The grinding slowed as the battery weakened. And Rick finally gave in, slamming his fist against the padded dashboard above the digital AM/FM stereo cassette combination, throwing himself back into the anatomically contoured bucket seat and announcing to the dead cold silent night all around them, "This lousy piece of *shit!*"

Mary Beth waited until it was safe. "Rick," she said softly, ever so cautiously, "I think we might be out of gas. Look at the gauge." It couldn't be. He always filled up when it got just below half-tank. They'd had plenty of gas, pulling in here; he'd checked. But the little red stick was lying flat on its back under the big "E," asleep or dead. Same thing. He flipped the ignition switch off, and back on. Still no sign of life.

Dew Drop Inn. And they sure as hell had.

Rick shifted restlessly in one of the rickety beds; Mary Beth and Chrissy were curled up together in the other. He had been sleeping alone since *it* was born, but tonight, sleep wouldn't come because those damn faces were there, racing back and forth in front of his eyes like a film in continuous forward and reverse. When he'd walked back in—defeated know-it-all city slicker—every blank face from every table and booth had turned toward the door, given a collective suck of air, and stared in wide-eyed greater knowing, straight at Rick. Then there was the little hag's face from behind the register where she perched on her stool, her mouth twisted into the same wicked grin as before, victorious, eager for its pleasure.

Nope, fillin' stations done closed around here. Yup, might as well stay here till the mornin' and things open up. We'll take care of ya then.

God, what did these people have against vowels and inflectional endings anyhow? Like a mouthful of marbles! Why did everyone stare . . . Damn zombies . . . Ugly bitch . . . Early start . . . Tomorrow . . .

Blades of light from the closed venetian blind fell like prison bars across the room, casting a faint gray light against the walls, along the hardwood floor, and beneath the furniture where it was trapped in the tiny ghost balls of dust and hair that hid there, glowing dimly.

Rick pressed his fingers hard into his eyes and released, blinking as the bare room took shape around him—tan dresser and nightstand, wrought-iron beds, an old chifforobe that towered beside him like a guard. No ashtrays, no phone. Not even a Gideon's Bible in this hellhole.

And no Chrissy or Mary Beth.

Damn, it must be late! But they knew better than to awaken him. They were probably eating breakfast. Now he'd have to hurry around like a . . . what did Beth's mother always say, a chicken with its head cut off? How *utterly* charming. No, that was a cow. He absolutely had to get this farm talk straight.

Rick lifted one of the slats on the blind but caught only a glimpse of orange and white below before having to shut his eyes and turn quickly from the bright sun. Squinting, he edged the slat up and saw an ambulance backed up to the entrance, its rear doors flung open like two welcoming hands and the attendants lifting a stretcher into the back. The familiar, predictable lumps of a body pressed up against the heavy sheet that lay over it, head to toe. *Jesus, must be dead,* Rick thought.

Then he saw them next to the BMW: Mary Beth and Chrissy, shepherded by some tall, thin guy in coat and tie. He was carrying the goddamn suitcases. He said something to Mary Beth. She shook her head and stared at the ground. Chrissy looked up, toward the window.

Rick jerked down on the cord, sending the blind flying up, flooding the room with light. He grabbed both handles of the window and pulled up. Stuck, of course. Again—this time with everything he had. *Damn* motel windows. By now the thin man was loading the *suitcases* into the trunk while Mary Beth and Chrissy stood by the car. What the hell were they *doing?*

Rick cupped his fingers and rapped his wedding ring

against the glass as hard as he dared. But they just stood there, oblivious, casually glancing up at his face in the window, then down again. He shouted, "Mary Beth! Chrissy!" Nothing. They were watching the ambulance, waiting for something.

"They can't hear you, Ricky." The gravelly voice was a low, patient growl rubbing against his back. He knew what he was going to see even before he spun around—the stump of a body covered in the white gown of Mother Teresa, twisted shoulders that loathed pity. "They can't hear you. Can't see you either." Ida's mouth curled into a vile sneer, not for Chrissy this time, all for him now.

"What the hell. . . ?"

"You know what they say, Ricky: 'Careful what you wish for—you might just get it.'" The hillbilly accent was gone. These vowels were round and cruel. And ancient.

"You bitch! Are you crazy? Let me *out* of here." He tried to move toward her but suddenly his chest was gripped by a hammering pain that spread like wildfire to his arms and throat, his whole body gnawed by an agony that lived and breathed. He opened his mouth to scream but could make only a small dry sound like a trapped animal begging to be released.

"How does it feel, Ricky? Does it hurt? Does it make you want to cry out to someone you love? Why don't they *come* to you?"

The pain released him as quickly as it had begun, leaving him bent over, eyes closed. He breathed in slow, deep, measured relief. "A heart attack is a terrible thing," she said in mock pity. "You were so young, so alone in your pain. You reached out but there was no one to take your hand."

Rick straightened, carefully, slowly, considered the hag's hungry face and smile. He turned away to the window and leaned heavily on the sill, weak from the pain but with something cruel holding him up, not allowing him to fall. He saw the attendants buttoning up the ambulance. Chrissy and Mary Beth were getting into the BMW.

"Please. Let me go." He was whispering now, pleading. "They're going to leave without me."

"Out of my hands, Ricky. I'm just the care nurse at this facility." Then irritation raised the growl a half octave. "What's the complaint, anyhow? Isn't this what you wished for? All alone, nobody to intrude on your little world?"

Now the mocking and sneering were back. "Don't bother even looking out the window, Ricky baby. There's nothing out there for you. You gave it up a long time ago." She was in heaven and used the word "baby" like a knife. "This is the world you wanted, what you and others like you have created, and it's my job to see that you enjoy it."

Still watching the two people that he loved now more than his life, two humans whom he wanted to hold and caress, to feel their soft hair against his face, the comfort of their arms, wanting all that at once and knowing it was lost forever, squandered, ground into dust beneath a boot heel, he said quietly, like a shamed little boy, "My name's not Ricky. Nobody calls me that."

The growl from the tiny body was now everywhere in the room, more real than the dwindling life he watched distantly through the window. "It's whatever I say it is—from now on." And those last words became three hideous things, set free, scuttling around the room, flying against the ceiling, finally lurking in the corner like enemies. *From now on.*

What he felt then was far worse than the burning and searing of before. He never knew pain could be so deep, the loneliness like drifting in a cold, faithless universe of night that swept across his heart as he watched his wife and precious daughter drive off into a wash of sunlight on Christmas Day.

He turned slowly from the window and knew that he would always turn in just this way, again and again, a motion as ancient as the planets and stars he had carelessly prayed to. And standing against the door, dressed in white, crooked shoulders and crooked smile, the face of eternity stared back at him.

Refractions

Thomas Millstead

Sheila dabbed a few tears from the corner of her eye. The new contact lenses bothered her, but she thought they'd be comfortable enough to leave in for the rest of the evening.

She felt a trifle self-conscious. None of the members of the Aura of Light had ever seen her without glasses before. At first she'd felt conspicuous, almost naked. Then she'd noticed herself in Millicent's mirror and liked what she saw.

Of course, she knew it was all psychological. She was neither more nor less attractive because of the absence of those heavy framed bifocals. No sleeker. No younger. But the contacts had definitely given her an emotional lift.

"My dear, I never realized what lovely eyes you have!" Millicent—exuberant as ever—hugged her and introduced her to tonight's speaker, a Dr. Negruni.

"Lovely eyes, indeed." He stared intently at her, then bowed to kiss her hand.

She felt suddenly on the verge of giddiness. How long since she'd received a compliment? Of any kind? From anyone?

How long since Russell had last praised anything about her?

So very long. He'd seen her wearing the new lenses for the first time this afternoon, before he left for his overnight sales meeting. He'd puckered his thin, derisive lips and whistled mockingly.

"Whoa! Look at *this* hot number, would you!"

"Well, I'm not trying to look like a . . . a . . ."

"Hot number? I know. Believe me, I know."

Hurt, she'd turned away. "No. Not like one of those . . ."

"One of those what?"

"At your sales meetings. Those . . . women in the hotels that you pay to . . ."

"That I pay to what? Say it! It's a simple Anglo-Saxon word!"

"To . . . consort with."

"Consort with?" He laughed harshly, puffy jowls quivering. He slammed shut the lid of the suitcase. "God, is it any wonder you and I have *not* . . . 'consorted' for lo, these many years?"

Abruptly, his voice faded to a gruff whisper, more baffled than bitter.

"My God, the wonder is why I've put up with this . . . this *farce*. For so damn long! Why?"

And why have I? she asked herself as Millicent led the members of the circle into the evening's meditation period. Sheila concentrated on the question. All those hostile years. His infidelities. The occasional beatings. *Why?*

No answer emerged. It was time for their speaker.

Dr. Negruni had traveled widely and studied Eastern mysticism in India, Nepal, even Tibet. His voice was accented and soothing, rising and falling in gentle tones like the mesmerizing murmur of a mountain stream. He spoke eloquently of karma, of kundalini, of chakras.

What magnetism he exerts, Sheila thought. She could not imagine how old he was. But his age must be great, for many of his journeys dated to the early decades of the century. Yet he was vibrant, his face hardly lined. A small sparrow of a man, his skin was velvety olive and his eyes lustrous and penetrating.

Afterward, she clasped his hand and thanked him warmly.

But she did not stay for the punch and croissants. Her lenses were increasingly irritating her and she did not want Dr. Negruni to see her squinting and grimacing.

On the sidewalk, as she sought a cab, she felt her forearm softly squeezed.

"Always it is such a pleasure to meet those who aspire to learn the secrets of the ancients," Dr. Negruni purred. "In all modesty, I have mastered more than a few. You know, it is the fusion of the Siva and the Shakti—the male and female principles—that generates prana. Which is the very energy of life. You are quite beautiful, if you permit me. In Western culture, mature beauty is not justly prized. Ah, here is a taxi!"

Idiocy! So stupid! At *your* age! Shameful!

Accusations raced relentlessly through her mind. But she smiled lazily in the darkness, her body glowing with a fulfillment she'd not known in—how long?

Never before, really, she admitted. Never, certainly, with Russell.

The sleep of satisfied exhaustion crept over her. But she fought to remain awake, to cherish every moment. To marvel again at the exquisite pleasures Dr. Negruni had awakened in her.

Drowsily, she reached out to slide her fingers once more over the silky, diminutive body beside her.

His arm was cold. She touched his chest. Icy, frigid. There was no heartbeat.

Panicked, Sheila bolted upright. She shook him, pounding his breastbone, desperately blowing breath into his sagging mouth.

It was too late.

She was stunned but she knew she must get out. This was ghastly, but there was no helping Dr. Negruni. She must not be found here!

She struggled to her feet, groping in the dark, unfamiliar room. Where were her glasses?

Then she remembered: contacts. She'd taken them out before she and Dr. Negruni . . .

Sheila scooped up her clothes, scuffled to the bathroom. She flipped on the light and saw the lenses, hazily, on a tissue on the counter over the sink.

Now she was sniffling, sobbing. *Be calm,* she commanded. She dressed hastily, then wetted the contacts and, with trembling hands, inserted them.

She glanced in the mirror, briskly brushing her hair into place. It would not do to look disheveled when she slipped out of the hotel this time of night. She must *not* be remembered. Nor could she report this.

How would she explain it? Alone with a naked dead man in his hotel room? Her reputation! Her daughter Cindy in college! And Russell?

Would he merely smirk? Or come at her again with his hamlike fists?

One last tug at her blouse. But her arm froze in midair.

Behind her—she saw it distinctly in the mirror—stood a man. Only a few feet away.

It couldn't be! her mind shrieked.

At first, the irrational thought: Dr. Negruni!

But no. This man was tall, heavy, pasty-faced. Wearing a long, caped, Victorian greatcoat buttoned to the throat and carrying a small satchel. A black slouch hat was pulled low over his forehead, shielding his eyes.

He smiled at her.

She thought she couldn't move, yet instinct spun her around, to confront him.

She was alone.

Sheila fled.

She sank onto the chair in front of her own vanity. Her face was sickly pale as she studied it. "Shock, of course," she remarked aloud. Some hallucination. But predictably, after the trauma of tonight.

Once more her contacts were bothersome—gritty and grating. With her index finger, she stretched the skin of one eyelid, attempting to pop out the lens just as she'd learned. It remained nestled against her cornea.

Again she tried, with no success. Finally she was digging, gouging, and *still* the lens wouldn't budge.

She scowled, bent forward to the mirror. Strange: Her eyes looked brown. Yet—when she wasn't wearing glasses—the bright lights over her vanity had always brought out the vividness of her sky-blue irises.

She blinked. Brown? Yes. Deep, deep brown.

It came to her like an electric jolt.

These lenses must have been laid out beside hers at the hotel. Brown-tinted lenses. Dr. Negruni's.

Frantic, she pried, poked, squeezed. And could not eject them. In her agitation she did not—for a few moments—perceive the large man reflected in her mirror.

He was still in his greatcoat, still clutching the satchel. A commanding presence; solid. He placed one hand on the back of her chair.

From under the wide brim of his hat, his eyes were barely visible. They locked on hers. They were a phlegmilke yellow, glittering, feral as a leopard's.

As in a trance, she half-turned her head to look behind her. No one was there.

"Of course," she said matter-of-factly.

And buried her face in her hands, hearing high, keening whimpers she knew were her own.

Millicent, Sheila thought in the morning. She *must* see Millicent.

Millicent would be consoling. Millicent with her serenity and compassion. Not that Sheila would relate last night's circumstances. Not that she would compromise herself . . . or Negruni's good name.

But Millicent was uncanny about arcane matters. So wise

and experienced. It had meant so much to Sheila—in the torment of her marriage to Russell—to be part of Millicent's circle.

She found it difficult to separate what had happened from what she must have imagined. Certainly she hadn't fantasized the death of that dear little man. Still, she wore his lenses, unable to remove them—and, it being Sunday, she could not seek help from her optometrist. But the other horror: that *creature* in the mirror . . .

Sheila nodded to the doorman at Millicent's apartment building, as she always did. He tipped his cap, as he always did. "How are you today, ma'am?" He was beefy, with the broiled-lobster flush of a heavy drinker.

A young woman in tight jeans sauntered past them, out of the building. The doorman winked at Sheila. "Just moved in," he said. He licked his lips. "Some hot number—ain't she?"

Rage exploded within her, a scorching flash fire of fury.

A "hot number?" *Russell's* stupid words! Exactly the kind of filthy remark Russell would make! She had never before been engulfed by such a frenzy of anger. This damned *degenerate!* Sheila fumbled wildly in her purse; what could she use?

The manicure scissors—yes!

In Sheila's mind's eyes, she already saw the slice in this cretin's throat. How *jolly* that was—how *very jolly!*

She opened and closed the scissors convulsively, biting her lip to stifle her eagerness.

Wait! Someone—behind the doorman. Odd; she hadn't seen him before, the bearded man in coarse seaman's garb.

Never mind! Do them both!

Sheila's hand faltered. Suddenly she was shivering, drenched with fright. She flung herself through the door, into the lobby.

Merciful God, she prayed, *what was I thinking of?*

The elevator was ornate, paneled on three sides with mirrors bordered in gold leaf. Sheila held tightly to the burnished brass beside her, sucked in her breath.

The caped man was there with her. All around. He loomed above her in each of her three reflected images. He was so close that she might have smelled his breath.

She reached out her arms and swung them to and fro, touching nothing. Confirming—something.

"Who are you?" she asked softly, staring at one of the images.

His lips moved. Sensual lips, drolly amused.

She felt sound vibrations somewhere behind the back of her skull—as if from his voice. She tensed, listening. No; not his voice. Nor a whisper. More the shadow of a whisper.

Should've gone for the windpipe. Never a squawk out of 'im. Then into the carotid—and rip! Remember those bloody trollops? Oh, jolly!

With his left hand, the figure in the mirror brandished the satchel, laughing.

She squeezed her eyes shut and pressed her hands against her ears.

"Do have some tea, dear." Millicent smiled sweetly. "You seem distraught."

"Well, Dr. Negruni . . ."

"Yes, a terrible shock. I got the call this morning. Such a gifted man. So animated—just last night. But the transition was peaceful, I'm told."

"You'd known him long?"

"Eons, casually. He was away for years at a time. He'd made a fortune from his technological innovations, he was a genius in the field of optics. He could . . . well afford to pursue his passion for the occult." She tapped Sheila's knee. "Of course, you are upset. We all are. Yet it's merely a passage from one dimension to another."

Sheila sipped her tea, desperately searching for the right words. She must be discreet, but she had to have an answer. Somehow, Millicent would understand. She must!

"It's just that . . ." she began, but let her voice trail off.

She nodded toward the corner of the room. She could not confide in the presence of a stranger. It was so unlike Millicent not to observe the social proprieties. Weakly, Sheila smiled at the woman, who gazed back at her.

"I don't believe we have met . . ."

"Who's that, my dear?"

"Your friend. In the beautiful sari."

"My *dear.*" Millicent clapped her hands and chortled heavily. "How sensitive of you! Why, you surprise me."

"I don't understand."

"Dr. Negruni saw her, too! Last night—before our meeting. I haven't, unfortunately. But he had this rare ability—and now you. Remarkable!"

"Ability?"

Millicent's face radiated delight. "To see who we once were. In our last *incarnation,* don't you know?"

"Please . . . ?"

"I was a high-caste Indian woman, a teacher, in the early nineteen hundreds, Dr. Negruni said. The form . . . the identity . . . in which we last materialized—it clings to us, follows us, influences us. We carry with us the ghosts of those we were. He was often able to perceive those apparitions of our past. Something to do with his discoveries in optics."

The cup slipped from Sheila's hand, shattered on the floor.

Dr. Negruni's *lenses.*

Merciful God, that's *me* then . . . who I was, *what* I was. That abomination! That . . . *thing.*

Millicent talked on but Sheila couldn't hear for her throbbing pulse. It was like the crashing of heavy surf; then the waves formed words that were remote, blurred, insistent.

Remember? The nights? Whitechapel? The fog? The empty streets? Remember what they called us? The police, the yellow press?

It emerged, then—the recollection. As though a trapdoor had creaked open deep within Sheila. A dim memory, only fragments, sensations. But real.

As true as any other memory—of last week, last year, childhood even.

The bony faces of the prostitutes, petrified with terror . . . the dank midnight air. Echoes of boots on cobblestones mere yards away. The scalpel pulled from the surgeon's satchel . . . The uncontrollable orgasmic roar with the first thrust! . . . The *thrill!*

"My dear, what is it?"

Remember? They called us "Jack."

Gagging, Sheila stumbled from the apartment.

That evening she sat quietly before her vanity, wearing only a slip. Her mind was empty, drained. She looked steadily into the eyes of the other image in the mirror. She held a steak knife in her lap.

He was also silent; motionless. He hovered, erect, over her, returning her gaze with a kind of detached insolence.

Hours ticked by while they shared their wordless communion. A key rattled in the front door and Russell entered.

He dropped his suitcase loudly. By the stamp of his feet she knew he was very drunk.

When Sheila swung around to face him, her single thought was mild disgust. Now he'd had the effrontery to bring into *her* home one of those scummy tarts he patronized on his sales trips!

The girl looked cheap—Sheila was sure anyone Russell favored would be—her cheeks heavily, ludicrously rouged. And dowdy, with boxy buttoned shoes that were more like boots. Archaic, too, with a shapeless dress that fell to her instep, hair twisted into a crude bun.

She lingered in the doorway, partially hidden behind him, ill at ease, shifting nervously from one foot to the other. Russell ignored her, stepped toward Sheila.

"How's Miss Priss?" he demanded. His narrowed eyes roved over her, his voice dropped to a slurred, sarcastic whisper. "Damn if you don't look half appealing for a change. To a guy that hasn't gotten any—since last night, anyway!"

Sheila stared past him. Her heart began a trip-hammer beat. She'd *seen* women who looked and dressed like that. But in photos, faded, stilted photos of a time long gone.

That girl was *Russell,* she realized. Russell of the past—of a *century ago!*

Instantly, the roaring filled Sheila's ears, cascaded over her. She glanced in the mirror. Yes, *he* remembered this girl. He trembled, excited; one hand dipped into the black satchel.

Remember her? Liz Stride. Recall what we did to her? Recall that throat, ripped open and bubbling . . . ?

Sheila got slowly to her feet.

"Time we . . . consorted . . . again," Russell sneered, reaching for her. He whipped the back of his hand across her face almost casually, his knuckles bruising Sheila's jaw.

She brought the steak knife up for him to see. It was as if swarms of angry hornets buzzed within her veins then. A lust sprang to life; a clamoring. An awful appetite to be fed, so *long* dormant. Sheila's hand itched to lunge with the blade—to feel it slide in, penetrate flesh.

Now! Just as before . . .

Russell gaped, disbelieving. He threw up his arms to ward off the thrust.

Sheila struck, then crouched, waiting to strike again.

"Damn you!" Russell spat out, weaving from side to side, frightened and enraged. She had cut his shoulder and it was bleeding freely. Russell clutched his wound, reeled backward. "You bitch—this is what you *always* wanted!"

"Yes!" she shouted, exulting. And remembered the question she had asked herself so often—the one they had each asked, so often: *Why have I put up with this, year after year? Why?*

Now . . . she knew. Why they were irrevocably bound. Eternally linked.

He bumped the chair, fell. He sprawled against the vanity, brushing aside jars, bottles, brushes. She stood over him and read in Russell's face the cowering, gibbering horror she recalled so exquisitely well.

The horror in the waxen faces of all those women. Those pathetic, anguished women. As they stared up at the sight of the poised, glinting scalpel.

Now! Stab! Revel!

She shot a sidelong look into the mirror. The caped man wasn't there. No, he was *in* her now—squirming in spasms of rapture.

She saw him reflected in her own eyes—glaring and merciless. And in her own face, hot with delicious anticipation.

It was a face so hateful that she staggered backward at the sight of it. So repellent that she clapped a hand to her mouth, her entrails twisting repulsively.

No, she thought, screaming it inside.

She was *Sheila*—not *him.* Never again, dear God—dear God, let me be free of him. Let the damned debt be paid, forever!

Sheila hurled the knife to the floor.

Russell gave a sobbing sigh.

And *he* pounced on the knife, crying aloud with triumph. Then he raised it, studied the blood-flecked blade.

Through Dr. Negruni's lenses, Sheila saw the gawky, dowdy woman—that rouged harlot—drift forward until her body melted into Russell's.

Did *he* know? she wondered almost indifferently. Did he recall that life, long ago . . . how it had ended? Did he understand why vengeance was his at last?

Yes, she thought. His eyes were slits of searing, red-rimmed, wholly irrational hatred. But in their depths there lurked some wisp of . . . remembrance.

It seemed to startle Russell, to bewilder him. He paused.

You know why you must do this, she thought. *You know.*

She nodded, granting permission.

He plunged the knife home.

The Spelling Bee

Adobe James

Gabe and I were playing chess in the garden when Peter, who serves as in-house security, put in an appearance. "Company," he said, looking troubled.

We glanced in the direction of his gaze and saw the dust cloud of the twice-weekly Greyhound bus creeping down out of the hills like a silver beetle.

The game was put on hold. I went into the shop to wait.

At the far end of Oasis's only street, which intersects the sunbleached asphalt highway, the bus stopped and disgorged a tall, rather debonair, older man. He stood, motionless, until the bus headed back out into the desert. Then he began walking toward us. With the sun low in the late-afternoon sky, he cast a shadow thirty feet long that glided smoothly in front of him like a black mamba coming after prey.

Even though it had been a long time since we had last seen each other, when the bell tinkled and Trancredi walked into the shop, I knew instantly why he was there.

He made small talk while sizing me up. "You haven't changed a bit," he said. "Not one day older."

I refrained from commenting that the same could not be said for him; the poor devil looked as if he had gone through hell . . . a couple of times! Instead, I replied, "Is that so surprising? After all, Trancredi, look around you. Oasis is peaceful. No stress. No competition."

He merely smiled.

I waited. In a small town like Oasis, waiting was the one thing I did best. Next to spelling.

"You were number one," he said. He meant it. Because it was the truth, I accepted it without comment, even though his use of the past tense "were" was duly noted.

His eyes never left me; if he was searching for weaknesses or uncertainty, there would be no overt signs of it. Finally he asked, "You are prepared for a new challenge?"

"Do I have any choice?"

He snorted, then laughed. "Well, yes. Of course! The Committee simply names a new champion. You know the rules."

I knew the rules. Still, though, I hesitated. It had been years since I had last been in a real competition. I still kept my hand in with dilettantes, but without recent challenges from the professionals, I wasn't all that sure of my immediate readiness.

"How long," I asked, "do I have to prepare?"

He shrugged. "A week."

"A fortnight," I countered.

Trancredi smiled. "Ten days."

I paused again. Stalling, really. Ten days was enough time. You either remembered the words, the phonetics, the nuances, prefixes, suffixes, and origins—or you didn't. Finally I nodded my acceptance.

"Who is the challenger?"

"A girl. Fresh out of high school." His eyes became hooded. "She can spell anything." A slight smile, then his gaze met mine. "A natural. Like you. But better. And much younger, of course."

Now it was my turn to smile. "The last time you bet against my spelling, Trancredi, it cost you dearly."

"I plan to win it all back with the girl. All of it . . . with interest! I've waited a long time. She will depose you."

"It's possible." Like tennis players, politicians, movie

stars, and gunslingers, we worry about novices; they are always a threat . . . always disturbing the status quo, dethroning acknowledged champions. To paraphrase something once said about history: "Competition is nothing more than the sound of newcomers' wooden clogs clumping up the front steps while silken slippers whisper down the back."

"So be it," I said.

"I shall notify The Committee that you have agreed to defend your title. Some of them"—he grinned nastily—"were sure you would resign."

"What? And not give you an opportunity to regain your very substantial losses?"

Trancredi closed his eyes slowly, then smiled, and laughed. He was still barking out his amusement when the bell tinkled to denote his departure.

You should know that the next ten days were not easy. I closed the shop; it was a necessity because so many new words had been added to our language during the last few years that I had to spend twenty-four hours a day reading and doing research.

Most competitive exhibitions have their legions of fanatics whose only standard of speech is hyperbole. Spelling is no different. A flighty female reporter, one of my supporters, from a magazine devoted to spelling, began her article with the statement, "The eyes of the universe will be focused on Oasis next week . . ." A bit of an exaggeration, but tame compared with the publicity from Trancredi's group.

When the evening of the contest arrived, I was ready. I drove to the announced site in my convertible, top down, enjoying the balmy desert air as the sun sank beneath the ridge of hills and one by one the familiar stars started popping out.

A large circus tent had been erected for the event, and a white banner bearing the words SPELLING CHAMPIONSHIP flapped listlessly in the torchlight.

Inside, The Committee—all twelve of them—was already in the Jury Box.

A hush fell on the crowd as I walked down the dirt aisle and made my way up onto the fifty-five gallon oil drums and wooden planks which constituted a makeshift stage. There were two speaker stands about ten feet apart. A young, dark-eyed, dark-haired, slender girl—not much more than a child—dressed all in white, was stationed at one of the stands. I took my place behind the other and stared out at the audience. There must have been close to five hundred spectators here for the event, not including the thirty-five gamblers en route to Las Vegas this morning when their bus had lost its brakes coming down the grade and sideswiped a bridge before coming to a halt just outside the city limits. Mostly, the gamblers were unhappy about being stuck here but, in their parlance, this was the only game in town. Most of them, willing to bet on anything, had already wagered on the spelling contest. On the girl. To win!

I gazed around. Identified those who were my supporters . . . recognized others who would give anything to see my defeat . . . saw a large number of undecideds who, traditionally, chose sides fairly early in a competition. My glance came back to Trancredi with his entourage in the front rows. He appeared relaxed, perfectly composed, untouchable. And yet, there was a wariness about him. A lot was at stake. He almost looked as if he were having some second thoughts. Good! He could still withdraw the challenge and slink away like a jackal in the night. But he wouldn't. Pride. His one weakness . . .

I turned my attention finally to my challenger. The girl stared back at me, appraisingly, not yielding. A pretty little thing, she wore a loose-fitting peasant blouse, and the soft shimmering cloth clung to her unconfined breasts. Her nipples were erect from the material against her bare skin, from the excitement! Under her muslin-thin skirt, the almost imperceptible shadow of her pelt of Eve was a perfect triangle as the cloth sought out the body's natural conformation. It was all too obvious she wore nothing beneath her garments. Trancredi had made his second mistake; the girl's physical attractions would never distract me, although most of the gamblers loved what they thought they saw.

The spelling contest began. The first word KHEPERA was for the challenger. She went through it effortlessly, and drew some polite applause from the audience—except for the gamblers, of course, all of whom now were looking as if they wanted to be elsewhere.

"ANGRA MAINYU" the voice of the unseen moderator called out my word to me.

I pronounced it, then spelled. Applause, a bit louder than that given to the girl.

"AHRIMAN." The challenger's second word came out of the darkness. She paused for dramatic effect, inhaled so her breasts were uplifted in promise again, all this intended to distract me, then spelled. Another top mark for her from The Committee. Trancredi led the applause.

In quick succession then came SHAITAN, ARALU, BELILI, MICTLANTECUTLI, ABADDON, APOLLYON. The girl seemed at ease, growing in confidence as she spelled each of hers. With each success she won more supporters from the undecideds. Understandable, in a way. She had a flair; there was something sensual about the way she mouthed each word, then proceeded to spell.

By the end of the first period, the temperature inside the tent had risen considerably because of the close-packed bodies. And it was then, during prolonged applause for the girl, that I noticed two things: one, the gamblers were creating an intolerable disturbance, something would have to be done about them; and, two, the challenger made her first mistake—not in spelling, but in using a feminine little gesture to push back a stray curl from her perspiration-streaked forehead. Vanity? Or simply not concentrating on the task at hand? Either could be fatal!

Trancredi noticed her movement and he stood to motion angrily at her. Uncertain of his meaning, she frowned and bent forward to peer at him. Quite unexpectedly, I had been granted an opportunity. It was not the kind of opening that I care for particularly, but nonetheless I went for an early kill as the darkness regurgitated my next word, MALEBOLGE.

You should know that in a major spelling contest like tonight's, it is a relatively easy thing to create a spell which will bring about a simple manifestation of Angra Mainyu, Apollyon, Belili, Khepera, Mictlantecutli, Shaitan, or any of the other 2,603 forms of Satan, but it demands real power and concentration to spell forth the whole subregion of Malebolge—better known as the eighth circle of hell.

"Malebolge," I intoned, using powers older than time itself. *"Tempera scelerisque . . ."* and felt the nether regions slowly bending to my will. *"Asmodeus semper . . ."*

And Malebolge began taking shape. We were above it, looking down into the inferno as the earth peeled back and the sulfurous flames roared skyward.

The gamblers were screaming in fright.

"Scelerisque . . ." I cried, pointing at them, and their screams became shrieks, then squeals, as they turned into swine and began fighting each other in terror, snapping brittle-boned legs and losing ears and eyes to razor-sharp hooves in their frenzied scramble to get away from the crevice crumbling beneath them.

Trancredi, suddenly frightened and aware he was losing, attempted to change into his real form, but I was already far ahead of him and, slowly, his head became a giant beetle while his torso thickened to a white repulsiveness, which in turn became an elongated maggot that began feeding on itself amid his cries of agony.

Flames were everywhere now. Sure of my victory, I let my followers go, and they rose on great white wings to rip through the top of the burning tent.

The girl, unafraid and still composed, was attempting to assert her powers. Trancredi had been correct; she was surprisingly strong and cunning for one so young, but I had caught her off-guard with my spelling, and, in truth, she was no match because I knew her weakness now.

Vanity!

There is no greater weakness . . . except, perhaps, pride . . .

I spun toward her and held up a large silver mirror. The reflection that shone back at her showed a toothless old crone—besotted with dripping, leprous sores that had eaten away the right eye. Her hair had fallen out, her clothes were gone. Her once proudly uplifted breasts were now only slabs of gray lifeless flesh that hung below her navel. She screamed and kept on shrieking as her belly distended in a pregnancy of putrefaction before exploding, and a million white grub worms flew out into the audience, each growing instantly into incredible size, exuding the stench of sulphur and death as they clung to and began feeding on new hosts.

The moans and screaming from Trancredi's followers were deafening, even above the sound of thunder and flames from below and the insane squealing of pigs trampling blindly back and forth in terror over the bodies of other gamblers.

"Malebolge," I chanted, and the seas of the world heated up, boiled, and then licked inward with scalding tongues three hundred feet high and a hundred miles long. The earth shuddered in its orbit, then moved backward, and the malevolent red eye of the sun appeared once again above the western horizon while ten thousand volcanoes orgasmed and became Roman candles of death.

At almost full power now, I had built up enough energy to destroy all of current creation if I wanted to. I turned toward The Committee. It would be so easy to nullify them—to send them all to a frightful place from which release could be made only by someone far stronger than I . . . if such a being still existed somewhere.

But I am a caring person.

I acquitted them, then turned back to the old hag who screamed and writhed in unendurable agony on the oil drums which were red-hot and about to melt. Green saliva gushed in a malodorous fountain from her mouth and nostrils, and her fingernails clawed great bloody furrows in her boil-infested flesh. The Malebolge spell was good for 20 years of her time and compounded so that each and every tick of the clock would be as 100 years. The same time frame, of course, would apply once again to Trancredi, whose torment now was too terrible for even me to witness. The poor devil. He would never learn.

I made to depart.

And the unseen moderator announced, in reverence, "You remain the champion."

I made a slight bow to The Committee; the courtesy was acknowledged and, I sensed, with considerable relief.

Leaving the screams, the piteous entreaties, the stench, the flames, the squealing behind, I went out into the cool night air where the sky was black with my hovering followers.

I motioned to end the spelling, and the ground on all four sides of the tent reared up like gigantic hooded cobras . . . and then struck! The land trembled as the tent and all within were devoured.

The planet earth was now back in its normal orbit. Time, which had fled, returned. A three-quarter-old moon was just rising in the east. A meteor flashed across the firmament in approval.

It was such a nice night that I decided to join my followers, and fly home . . .

Better Than One

Paul Dale Anderson

Stubbornly, Bob pushes to regain control. He wills his hand forward, but again the hand halts in midair and his fingers twitch uncontrollably, like earthworms skewered on the barbed ends of fish hooks.

"Give up," the voice insists. "Give up give up give up."

Frustrated, frightened, Bob searches for an opening. Like a cornered rat, he perceives that his adversary would rather play than pounce. He talks to buy time.

"You'll have to kill me," he says. "You killed Laura. You'll have to kill me, too."

"You know that's impossible, Bob. Your wife wasn't the slightest bit necessary, but you are. What would *I* do without *you?*"

"Rot in hell," Bob suggests.

"I can punish you without killing. Perhaps you'd like a sample . . ."

Intense pain rips through his lower body, sending Bob to his knees in tears. *This isn't real,* he tells himself. *None of this is real.*

His intestines feel as if they're being pulled from his stomach, an inch at a time. A red-hot nail enters his urethra, penetrating all the way into his bladder before he screams. The pain continues even after he loses consciousness.

Stop! his mind cries. *Oh, please! Stop!*

"Have you learned your lesson?" the voice asks.

Yes! I'll do anything you want! Anything!

"Good," the voice says.

The pain goes away and Bob sleeps like a baby.

"Did you enjoy my little demonstration?" the voice asks when Bob returns to consciousness.

"How . . . ?"

"How? Divert endorphins from your pain center, secrete acetylcholine, pressure the pituitary, and *voilá!*"

"It seemed so real."

"Oh, it was. Not the injuries, you understand. But the pain. The pain was real, exactly the same as if your guts had been ripped out or your penis penetrated. You felt the same pain you would have felt had those things actually happened."

"Where did you learn to do that?"

"From books and magazines, of course. Things you've read over the years and don't remember. But *I* remember. I remember everything."

"I never read about acetyl-whatever-you-call-it."

"You skimmed a newspaper article eight and a half years ago that mentioned the importance of acetylcholine as a neurotransmitter—the synaptical junction for nerve impulses. Though you paid little attention at the time and can't even pronounce the word, you obviously know what it means. Don't you?"

"Vaguely."

"That information, all information—everything you've read or been exposed to—is stored in billions of chemical receptors in a part of the brain you don't normally use. The part of your brain I now occupy."

"What *are* you? You're not me. You can't be me. Am I going crazy?"

"I'm you, but not *you*. I'm a cancer, a growth, a cellular

mutation of your neocortex. I'm the next step in human evolution."

"I am going crazy."

"No. I won't let you."

"You can control my sanity?"

"Yes. And everything you say and do, too. I can control every aspect of your body and brain except . . ."

"Except what?"

"Forget it."

"Tell me!"

"I said forget it."

"I want to know!"

"I'll punish you again if you don't forget it. Do you want to be punished?"

"No." Bob shudders uncontrollably. The memory is too fresh, too real. He has already had enough pain to last a lifetime, and he can't stand the thought of more.

"You made me kill Laura," Bob says. "You took control of my body and made me murder my own wife. I hate you for that."

"I know. I, too, have fond memories of Laura. It was a difficult decision but absolutely necessary. She was about to phone a doctor and have you committed to a mental hospital. I couldn't permit that."

"Why not?"

"Because they'd discover a cancerous growth on your brain and want to *remove* it. They'd lobotomize you to get at me. In their ignorance they'd destroy us both."

"You didn't have to kill her. Couldn't you have talked to her explained things?"

"Did you think she'd believe? You didn't believe, either, until I made you kill her. But you believe me now, don't you?"

"Yes," Bob says. "I have no choice. Do I?"

"None whatsoever."

I'd rather die than be your slave, Bob thinks. *I'll bide my time, wait for an opportunity, kill myself.*

"Impossible," the voice says. "I know your thoughts even before you do. I'm a part of your brain. I can intercept nerve impulses before your muscles can react. You'll do nothing without my permission. You must obey or be punished."

Fear and trembling take control of Bob's body at the mere mention of punishment. He feels trapped between the proverbial rock and hard place, unable to choose between two evils. To obey this monstrosity is unthinkable. To disobey and be punished is impossible.

"Pick up Laura's body," orders the voice. "Show me you can be trusted, and I'll let you dispose of your wife on your own. Put her in the bathtub, cut her into tiny pieces, and cover her flesh with Draino until it dissolves. Do this and I won't punish you. Fail me, and I'll . . ."

This time when Bob reaches for his wife, his hand isn't stopped. His fingers touch her face, her hair. A rush of emotion overwhelms him and tears flood his eyes.

He remembers his fingers worming around her neck against his volition, squeezing the life and breath from her body as her screams slowly died in her throat. He'd tried to scream himself, but no sound emerged from his mouth, no tears stained his cheeks.

Now, at least, he can cry.

He picks her up in his arms and carries her to the bathroom. There he undresses her, peeling away her clothes as if she were still alive and he were planning an act of passion on the tiled floor.

He almost expects her to respond as he opens her legs and slides a pair of lace panties down her thighs, over her knees. But her flesh is cold to his touch, the panties soiled.

He thinks he's going to throw up. He crawls to the toilet bowl and holds his head over the sweet-smelling, blue-tinted water until his nausea passes. His guts wrench but nothing comes out.

He sits on the floor in front of the toilet and stares at his wife's naked body, unable to complete his task despite the promise of painful punishment. Inevitably, he knows, the punishment will come. But for now, he cannot bring himself to touch his wife again.

"You do it," he challenges the cancer. "Clean up your own mess. I won't help you anymore."

He waits for the pain to hit but it doesn't come. Any minute now, he reasons, the cancer will again take control of his limbs, like a puppeteer manipulating a mannequin, forcing him to cut Laura's body into bits of bloody flesh the way a butcher slices steaks and roasts from a side of beef. But, inexplicably, that doesn't happen, either.

"Do you hear me?" he shouts. "I won't *help* you anymore! You can't make me!"

The cancer doesn't answer. Hope buds anew. Bob struggles to his feet and takes a tenuous step toward the door; then another step, expecting to be stopped in his tracks before he can leave the bathroom.

Then he is out of the bathroom, into the bedroom. He sees the telephone on the nightstand, and his hand reaches out to touch it . . . and does!

He lifts the handset, places the receiver to his ear, dials 911, and counts the rings. "Ni-yun wun wun e-mergency," announces a woman's voice on the fourth ring.

Frantically, Bob searches for the right words. *I killed my wife* comes immediately to mind and is quickly discarded. *I'm possessed by a cancer* requires too much explanation. *What can I say?*

"Try 'Help me,'" a familiar voice says to his mind.

Panic.

Help me! Bob tries to scream, but his tongue and jaw don't want to cooperate. *Help me!*

"This is ni-yun wun wun po-lice e-mergency. Your call is being recorded. Is anyone there?"

Yes!

Help me!

Please!

"This isn't funny. If this is a prank . . ."

Help me!

"It's illegal to dial nine-one-one and tie up this line unless it is a bona fide emergency. Is anyone there? Hello?"

Help . . .

CLICK!

Buzzzzzz . . .

"Too bad," the voice says. "You had your chance. You blew it."

This time the pain feels like a thousand splinters pricking his skin, sliding under his toenails, his fingernails, his eyeballs. Every hair on his body is painfully plucked out.

"Stop!" orders another voice.

"Stay out of this."

"You'll destroy him completely. Destroy his *soul.* I can't let you do that."

Two? There are two . . . ?

"Tumors? Yes. One is malignant and the other benign. Look in the mirror. You can see us both."

Bob glances at his reflection. "No!" he screams when he catches sight of his face.

Protruding from each temple, an inch above each eye, are miniature replicas of his own visage.

The one on the right—"The one that controls the left side of the brain," the new voice explains—smiles back at Bob like a happy-face cartoon drawing. The one on the left looks dark and devious, cruel.

The face in the middle, contorted in terror, isn't familiar at all.

Ever, Ever, After

Graham Masterton

The road was greasy; the light was poor; and the truck's braking lights were caked in dirt. Robbie saw it pull up ahead of him only ten feet too late, but those ten feet were enough to send a scaffolding pole smashing through the windshield of his Porsche and straight into his chest.

The medical examiner told me that he never would have known what hit him. "I'm truly sorry, Mr. Deacon; but he never would have known what hit him." Instant death; painless.

Painless, that is, to Robbie. But not to Jill; and not to me; and not to anybody who had known him. Jill was his wife of thirteen weeks; and I was his brother of thirty-one years; and his humor and vivacity had won him more friends than you could count.

For a whole month afterward I kept his photograph on my desk. Broad-faced, five years younger than me, much more like Dad than I was; laughing at some long-forgotten joke. Then one morning in early October I came into the office and put the photograph away in my middle desk drawer. It was then that I knew it was over; that he was really gone for ever.

That same afternoon, as if she had been affected by the

same feeling of finality, Jill called me. "David? Can I meet you after work? I feel like talking."

She was waiting for me in the lobby, at the Avenue of the Americas entrance. Already the sidewalks were crowded with home-going workers, and there wasn't a chance of finding a cab. The air was frosty, and sharp with the smell of bagels and chestnuts.

She looked pale and tired, but just as beautiful as ever. She had a Polish mother and a Swedish father, and she had inherited the chiseled face of one and the snow-white blondness of the other. She was tall, almost five feet nine, although her dark mink coat concealed most of her figure, just as the dark mink hat concealed most of her face.

She kissed me. She smelled of Joy, and cold October streets.

"I'm so glad you could come. I think I'm beginning to go mad."

"Well, I know the feeling," I told her. "Every day, when I wake up, I have to remind myself that he's dead; and that I'm never going to see him again, ever."

We went into the Brew Burger across the street for a drink. Jill ordered tomato juice; I ordered Four Roses, straight up. We sat by the window while torrents of people passed us by.

"That's my trouble," Jill told me, picking at her freshly lacquered fingernails. "I'm sad; I keep crying; but I can't really believe that he's dead."

I sipped my whiskey. "Do you know what he and I used to play when we were younger? We used to pretend that we were wizards, and that we were both going to live forever. We even made up a spell."

Jill stared at me; her wide gray-green eyes were glistening with tears. "He was always full of dreams. Perhaps he went the best way, without even knowing what was going to happen."

"*Immortooty,, immortaty—ever, ever, after!*" I recited.

"That was the spell. We always used to recite it when we were scared."

"I loved him, you know," Jill whispered.

I finished my whiskey. "Haven't you talked about it with anybody else?"

She shook her head. "You know my family. They practically disowned me when I started dating Robbie, because he was still married to Sara. It was no use my telling them that he and Sara were already on the rocks; and that he despised her; and that they would have been divorced anyway, even if I hadn't shown up on the scene. Oh, no, it was all my fault. I broke up a healthy marriage. I was the scarlet woman."

"If it's any consolation," I told her, "I don't think you're scarlet at all. I never saw Robbie so happy as when he was with you."

I walked her back to her apartment on Central Park South. Thunder echoed from the skyscrapers all along Sixth Avenue; flags flapped; and it was beginning to rain. In spite of the swanky address, the flat that Jill and Robbie had shared together was very small, and sublet from a corporate lawyer called Willey, who was away in Minnesota for most of the time; something to do with aluminum tubing.

"Won't you come up?" she asked me in the brightly lit entrance lobby, which was graced with a smart black doorman in a mushroom-colored uniform and a tall vase of orange gladioli.

"I don't think so," I told her. "I have a heap of work to finish up at home."

There were mirrors all around us. There were fifty Jills, curving off into infinity, fifty doormen, and fifty *me's*. A thousand spears of gladioli.

"You're sure?" she persisted.

I shook my head. "What for? Coffee? Whiskey? More breast-beating? There was nothing we could have done to save him, Jill. You took care of him like a baby. I just loved him like a brother. There was no way that either of us could have saved him."

"But to die that way. So quickly; and for no reason."

I grasped her hand. "I don't believe everything has to have a reason."

The doorman was holding the elevator for her. She lifted her face to me, and I realized that she expected me to kiss her. So I kissed her; and her cheek was soft and cold from walking in the wind; and somehow something happened between us that made both of us stand for a moment looking at each other, eyes searching, not speaking.

"I'll call you," I told her. "Maybe dinner?"

"I'd like that."

That was how our affair began. Talking, to begin with; and spending weekends together with a bottle of California chardonnay; listening to Mendelssohn's violin concertos, while Christmas approached, our first Christmas without Robbie.

I bought Jill a silver Alfred Durante cuff watch and a leather-bound book of poems by John Keats. I left a silk marker in the page which said,

> *Love! Thou art leading me from wintry cold,*
> *Lady! Thou leadest me to summer clime.*

She cooked wild duck for me on Christmas Day, and Robbie's photograph watched us, smiling from the chiffonier while we drank each other's health in Krug champagne.

I took her to bed. The white wintry light arranged itself across the sheets like a paper dress-pattern. She was very slim, narrow-hipped, and her skin was as smooth as cream. She didn't speak; her hair covered her face like a golden mask. I kissed her lips, and her neck. Her oyster-colored silk panties had tucked themselves into a tight crease between her legs.

Afterward we lay back in the gathering twilight and listened to the soft crackle of bubbles in our champagne, and the sirens of Christmas echoing across Central Park.

"Are you going to ask me to marry you?" said Jill.

I nodded.

"It's not against the law or anything, is it? For a widow to marry her late husband's brother."

"Of course not. In Deuteronomy, widows are *ordered* to marry their late husband's brothers."

"You don't think Robbie would have minded?"

"No," I said, and turned over to pick up my glass, and there he was, still smiling at me. *Immortooty, immortaty, ever, ever, after.*

Robbie, in Paradise, may have approved, but our families certainly didn't. We were married in Providence, Rhode Island, on a sharp windy day the following March, with nobody in attendance but a justice of the peace and two witnesses whom we had rounded up from the local bookstore, and a gray-haired old lady who played the "Wedding March" and "Scenes from Childhood."

Jill wore a cream tailored suit and a wide-brimmed hat with ribbons around it and looked stunning. The old lady played and smiled and the spring sunshine reflected from her spectacles like polished pennies on the eyes of an ivory-faced corpse.

On our wedding night I woke up in the early hours of the morning and Jill was quietly crying. I didn't let her know that I was awake. She was entitled to her grief, and I couldn't be jealous of Robbie, now that he had been dead for over six months.

But I lay and watched her, knowing that by marrying me she had at last acknowledged that Robbie was gone. She wept for almost twenty minutes, and then leaned across and kissed my shoulder, and fell asleep, with her hair tangled across my arm.

* * *

Our marriage was cheerful and well organized. Jill left her apartment on Central Park South and moved into my big airy loft on Seventeenth Street. We had plenty of money; Jill worked as a creative director for Palmer Ziegler Palmer, the advertising agency, and in those days I was an accountant for Henry Sparrow, the publishers. Every weekend we compared Filofaxes and fitted in as much leisure time together as we could; even if it was only a lunchtime sandwich at Stars on Lexington Avenue, or a cup of coffee at Bloomingdale's.

Jill was pretty and smart and full of sparkle and I loved her more every day. I suppose you could have criticized us for being stereotypes of the Perrier water generation, but most of the time we didn't take ourselves too seriously. In July I traded in my old BMW for a Jaguar XJS convertible in British racing green, and we drove up to Connecticut almost every weekend, a hundred and ten miles an hour on the turnpike, with Beethoven on the stereo at top volume.

Mega-pretentious, *n'est-ce pas?*—but it was just about the best fun I ever had in my whole life.

On the last day of July, as we were sitting on the old colonial veranda of the Allen's Corners hotel where we used to stay whenever we weekended in Connecticut, Jill leaned back in her basketwork chair and said dreamily, "Some days ought to last forever."

I clinked the ice in my vodka and tonic. "This one should."

It was dreamily warm, with just the lightest touch of breeze. It was hard to imagine we were less than two hours' driving from downtown Manhattan. I closed my eyes and listened to the birds warbling and the bees humming and the sounds of a peaceful Connecticut summer.

"Did I tell you I had a call from Willey on Friday?" Jill remarked.

I opened one eye. "Mr. Willey, your old landlord? What did he want?"

"He says I left some books round at the apartment, that's all. I'll go collect them tomorrow. He said he hasn't relet the apartment yet, because he can't find another tenant as beautiful as me."

I laughed. "Is that bullshit or is that bullshit?"

"It's neither," she said. "It's pure flattery."

"I'm jealous," I told her.

She kissed me. "You can't possibly be jealous of Willey. He's about seventy years old, and he looks just like a koala bear with eyeglasses."

She looked at me seriously. "Besides," she added, "I don't love anybody else but you; and I never will."

It thundered the following day and the streets of New York were humid and dark and strewn with broken umbrellas. I didn't see Jill that lunchtime because I had to meet my lawyer Morton Jankowski (very droll, Morton, with a good line in Lithuanian jokes); but I had promised to cook her my famous *pesce spada al salmoriglio* for dinner.

I walked home with a newspaper over my head. There was no chance of catching a cab midtown at five o'clock on a wet Monday afternoon. I bought the swordfish and a bottle of Orvieto at the Italian market on the corner, and then walked back along Seventeenth Street, humming Verdi to myself. Told you I was mega-pretentious.

Jill usually left the office a half hour earlier than I did, so I expected to find her already back at the loft; but to my surprise she wasn't there. I switched on the lights in the sparse, tasteful sitting room, then went through to the bedroom to change into something dry.

By six-thirty she still wasn't back. It was almost dark outside and the thunder banged and echoed relentlessly. I called her office but everybody had left for the day. I sat in the kitchen in my striped cook's apron, watching the news and drinking the wine There wasn't any point in starting dinner until Jill came home.

By seven I was growing worried. Even if she hadn't managed to catch a cab, she could have walked home by now. And she has never come home late without phoning me first. I called her friend Amy, in SoHo. Amy wasn't there but her loopy boyfriend said she was over at her mother's place, and Jill certainly wasn't with her.

At last, at a quarter after eight, I heard the key turn in the door and Jill came in. The shoulders of her coat were dark with rain, and she looked white-faced and very tired.

"Where the hell have you been?" I demanded. "I've been worried bananas."

"I'm sorry," she said in a muffled voice, and hung up her coat.

"What happened? Did you have to work late?"

She frowned at me. Her blond fringe was pasted wetly to he forehead. "I've said I'm sorry. What is this, the third degree?"

"I was concerned about you, that's all."

She stalked through to the bedroom, with me following close behind her. "I managed to survive in New York before I met you, she said. "I'm not a child anymore, you know."

"I didn't say you were. I said I was concerned, that's all."

She was unbuttoning her blouse. "Will you just get the hell out and let me change!"

"I want to know where you've been!" I demanded.

Without hesitation, she slammed the bedroom door in my face; and when I tried to catch the handle, she turned the key.

"Jill!" I shouted. "Jill! What the *hell* is going on?"

She didn't answer. I stood outside the bedroom door for a while, wondering what had upset her so much; then I went back to the kitchen and reluctantly started to cook dinner.

"Don't do any for me," she called out, as I started to chop up the onions.

"Did you eat already?" I asked her, with the knife poised in my hand.

"I said, don't do any for me—that's all!"

"But you have to eat!"

She wrenched open the bedroom door. Her hair was combed back and she was wrapped in her terry-cloth bathrobe. "What are you, my mother or something?" she snapped at me. Then she slammed the door shut again.

I stabbed the knife into the butcher block and untied my apron. I was angry, now. "Listen!" I shouted. "I bought the wine, and the swordfish, and *everything!* And you come home two hours late and all you can do is yell at me!"

She opened the bedroom door again. "I went round to Willey's apartment, that's all. Now, are you satisfied?"

"So you went to Willey's place? And what were you supposed to be doing at Willey's place? Collecting your books, if my memory serves me. So where are they, these precious books? Did you leave them in the cab?"

Jill stared at me and there was an expression in her eyes that I had never seen before. Pale, cold, yet almost *shocked,* as if she had been involved in an accident and her mind was still numb.

"Jill . . ." I said, more softly this time, and took two or three steps toward her.

"No," she whispered. "Not now. I want to be alone for just a while."

I waited until eleven o'clock, occasionally tapping at the bedroom door, but she refused to answer. I just didn't know what the hell to do. Yesterday had been idyllic; today had turned into some kind of knotty, nasty conundrum. I put on my raincoat and shouted through the bedroom door that I was going down to the Bells of Hell for a drink. Still she didn't answer.

* * *

My friend Norman said that women weren't humans at all, but a race of aliens who had been landed on earth to keep humans company.

"Imagine it," he said, lighting a cigarette and blowing out smoke. "If you had never seen a woman before tonight, and you walked out of here and a woman was standing there . . . wearing a dress, with blond hair, and red lipstick, and high-heel shoes . . . and you had never seen a woman before—then, *then*, my friend, you would understand that you had just had a close encounter of the worst kind!"

I finished my vodka, dropped a twenty on the counter. "Keep the cha-a-ange, my man," I told the barkeep, with a magnanimous W. C. Fieldsian wave of my hand.

"Sir, there is no change. That'll be three dollars and seventy-five cents more."

"That's inflation for you," Norman remarked, with a phlegmy cough. "Even oblivion is pricing itself out of the market."

I left the bar and walked back up to Seventeenth Street. It was unexpectedly cool for the first of August. My footsteps echoed like the footsteps of some lonely hero in a 1960s spy movie. I wasn't sober but I wasn't drunk, either. I wasn't very much looking forward to returning home.

When I let myself in, the loft was in darkness. Jill had unlocked the bedroom door but when I eased it open, and looked inside, she was asleep. She had her back to me, and the quilt drawn up to her shoulders, but even in the darkness I could see that she was wearing her pajamas. Pajamas meant we're not talking; stay away.

I went into the kitchen and poured myself the dregs from a chilled bottle of Chablis, switched the television on low. It was a 1940s black-and-white movie called *They Stole Hitler's Brain*. I didn't want to sit there watching it, and at the same time I didn't want to go to bed either.

At a little after two, however, the bedroom door opened and Jill was standing there, pale and puffy-eyed.

"Are you coming to bed?" she asked, in a clogged-up whisper. "You have work tomorrow."

I looked at her for a long time with my lips puckered tight. Then I said, "Sure," and stood up, and switched off the television.

In the morning, Jill brought me coffee and left my Swiss muesli out for me and kissed me on the cheek before she left for the agency, but there were no explanations for what had happened the previous evening. The only words she spoke were "Good morning" and "Good-bye."

I called, "Jill?" but the only response I got was the loft door closing behind her.

I went to the office late and I brooded about it all morning. Around eleven-thirty I telephoned Jill's secretary and asked if Jill were free for lunch.

"No, Mr. Deacon, I'm sorry. She had a last-minute appointment."

"Do you happen to know where?"

"Hold on, I'll check her diary. Yes . . . here it is. One o'-clock. No name, I'm afraid. No address, either. It just says 'Apt.'"

"All right, Louise, thank you."

I put down the phone and sat for a long time with my hand across my mouth, thinking. My assistant, Fred Ruggiero, came into my office and stared at me.

"What's the matter? You look like you're sick."

"No, I was thinking. What does the word 'apt' mean to you?"

Fred scratched the back of his neck. "I guess it means like 'appropriate,' you know. Or 'fitting.' Or 'suitable.' You doing a crossword?"

"No. I don't know. *Sheila!*"

One of our younger secretaries was bouncing along the corridor in beaded dreadlocks and a shocking-pink blouse. "Yes, Mr. Deacon?"

I wrote 'apt' on my notepad and showed it to her. "Does that mean anything to you?"

She grinned. "Is this a trick? If you'd been looking for someplace to rent as long as I have, you'd know what that meant."

"What do you mean?"

"*Apt.* Don't you read the classifieds? Apt equals apartment."

Apartment. And whenever Jill mentioned "apartment," she meant one apartment in particular. Willey's apartment.

Fred and Sheila stared at me. Fred ventured, "Are you okay? You look kind of glassy, if you don't mind my saying so."

I coughed and nodded. "I guess I do feel a little logy."

"Hope you haven't caught a dose of the Szechuan flu," Sheila remarked. "My cousin had it, said it was like being hit by a truck."

She realized suddenly what she had said. Everybody in the office knew how Robbie had died. "Oh, I'm sorry," she said. "That was truly dumb." But I was too busy thinking about Jill round at Willey's apartment to care.

It was still raining, a steady drenching drizzle; but I went out all the same. All right, I told myself, I'm suspicious. I have no justification; I have no evidence; and most of all I have no moral right. Jill made a solemn promise when she married me: to have and to hold, from this day forth.

A promise was a promise and it wasn't up to me to police her comings and goings in order to make sure that she kept it.

Yet there I was, standing on the corner of Central Park South and the Avenue of the Americas, in a sodden tweed hat and a dripping Burberry, waiting for Jill to emerge from her apartment building so that *I* could prove that she was cheating on me.

I waited over half an hour. Then, quite suddenly, Jill appeared in the company of a tall dark-haired man in a blue raincoat. Jill immediately hailed a passing taxi and climbed into it, but the man began to walk at a brisk pace toward Columbus Circle, turning his collar up as he did so.

I hesitated for a moment, and then I went after him.

He turned south on Seventh Avenue, still walking fast. The sidewalks were crowded and I had a hard time keeping up with him. He crossed Fifty-seventh Street just as the lights changed, and I found myself dodging buses and taxis and trying not to lose sight of him. At last, a few yards short of Broadway, I caught up with him. I snatched at his sleeve, said, "Hey, fellow. Pardon me."

He turned to stare at me. He was olive-skinned, almost Italian-looking. Quite handsome if you had a taste for Latins.

He said nothing, but turned away again. He must have thought I was excusing myself for having accidentally caught at his raincoat. I grabbed him again, and said, *"Hey!* Pardon me! I want to *talk* to you!"

He stopped. "What is this?" he demanded. "Are you hustling me, or what?"

"Jill Deacon," I replied, my voice shaking a little.

"What?" He frowned.

"You know what I'm talking about," I replied. "I'm her husband."

"So? Congratulations."

"You were with her just now."

The man smiled in exasperation. "I said hello to her in the lobby, if that's what you mean."

"You know her?"

"Well, sure. I live along the hall. I've known her ever since she moved in. We say good morning and good evening in the lobby, and that's it."

He was telling the truth. I knew damn well he was telling the truth. Nobody stands there smiling at you at a busy intersection in the pouring rain and tells you lies.

"I'm sorry," I told him. "I guess it was a case of mistaken identity."

"Take some advice, fellow," the man replied. "Lighten up a bit, you know?"

I went back to the office feeling small and neurotic and jerkish; like a humorless Woody Allen. I sat at my desk staring at a heap of unpaid accounts and Fred and Sheila left me very well alone. At four o'clock I gave up and left, took a cab down to the Bells of Hell for a drink.

"You look like shit," Norman told me.

I nodded in agreement. "Alien trouble," I replied.

Maybe my suspicions about the Latin-looking man had been unfounded but Jill remained irritable and remote, and there was no doubt that something had come adrift in our marriage, although I couldn't quite work out what.

We didn't make love all week. When I tried to put my arm around her in bed, she sighed testily and squirmed away. And whenever I tried to talk to her about it, she went blank or scratchy or both.

She came home well after ten o'clock on Friday evening without any explanation about why she was late. When I asked her if everything was all right, she said she was tired, and to leave her alone. She showered and went straight to bed; and when I looked in at the bedroom door only twenty minutes later, she was fast asleep.

I went to the bathroom and wearily stripped off my shirt. In the laundry basket lay Jill's discarded panties. I hesitated for a moment, then I picked them out and held them up. They were still soaked with another man's semen.

I suppose I could have been angry. I could have dragged her out of bed and slapped her around and shouted at her. But what was the use? I went into the sitting room and poured myself a large glass of Chablis and sat disconsolately watching Jackie Gleason with the volume turned down. "The Honeymooners," blurred with tears.

Maybe the simple truth was that she had married me because I was Robbie's brother; because she had hoped in some distracted and irrational way that I would somehow become the husband she had lost. I knew she had been nuts about him, I mean truly nuts. Maybe she hadn't really gotten over the shock. Robbie would live forever; at least as far as Jill was concerned.

Maybe she was punishing me now for not being him. Or maybe she was punishing *him* for dying.

Whatever the reason, she was cheating on me, without making any serious effort to hide it. She might just as well have invited her lover into our bed with us.

There was no question about it: Our marriage was over, even before it had started. I sat in front of the television with the tears streaming down my cheeks and I felt like curling myself up into a ball, going to sleep and never waking up.

You can't cry forever, though; and after about an hour of utter misery I wiped my eyes on my sleeve and finished my glass of wine and thought: right, okay. I'm not giving Jill up without a fight. I'm going to find out who this bum is who she's been sleeping with, and I'm going to confront him, face to face. She can choose between him and me, but she's going to have to do it right out in front of us—no sneaking, no hiding, no hypocrisy.

I went to the bedroom and opened the door and Jill was lying asleep with her mouth slightly parted. She was still beautiful. I still loved her. And the pain of still loving her twisted inside me like a corkscrew.

I hope you live forever, I thought to myself. *I hope you live to know how much you've hurt me.* Immortooty, immortaty. Ever, ever, after.

On the dressing table her key ring lay sprawled. I looked at it for a long moment, then quietly picked it up.

Next day it was windy and bright. I sat in the coffee shop opposite Jill's agency building, drinking too much coffee and trying to chew a bagel that tasted of nothing but cream cheese and bitterness. At a few minutes after twelve, I saw

Jill march smartly out of the front of the building, and lift her arm to call a cab. Immediately I ducked out of the coffee shop and called another taxi.

"Follow that cab," I told the driver. He was a thin Puerto Rican with beads around his neck and a black straggly mustache.

"Wheesh cab?" he wanted to know.

"That Checker, follow that Checker."

"You thin' this some kinda movie or somethin'? I ain't follnin' nuttin'."

I pushed a crumpled-up fifty into his hand. "Just follow that Checker, okay?"

"Whatever you say, man. Your fewnral."

As it turned out, I paid fifty dollars plus the fare to follow Jill back to Willey's apartment on Central Park South, where I should have known she was going anyway. The Puerto Rican saw Jill climb out of the cab ahead of us. Those long, black-stockinged legs, that smart black-and-white suit. "Hey man, she's worth fifty, that one. She's worth a hund'ud!"

Jill walked without hesitation into the apartment building. I allowed her five clear minutes, pacing up and down on the sidewalk, watched with unwavering curiosity beside an old man selling balloons. Then I went into the building after her, through the lobby to the elevators.

"You're looking for somebody, sir?" the black doorman wanted to know.

"My wife, Mrs. Deacon. She arrived here just a few minutes ago."

"Oh, sure." The doorman nodded. "You go on up."

I went upward in the small gold-mirrored elevator with my heart beating against my rib cage like a fist. I could see my reflection, and the strange thing was that I looked quite normal. Pale-faced, tired, but quite rational. I certainly didn't look like a husband trying to surprise his wife in flagrante with another man. But then, who does? People die with the strangest expressions on their faces. Smiles, scowls, looks of total surprise.

I reached the third floor, stepped out. The corridor was overheated and silent and smelled of lavender polish. I hesitated for a moment, holding the doors of the elevator open. Then I let them go, and they closed with a whine, and the elevator carried on upward.

What the hell am I going to say, if I actually find her with somebody? I thought to myself. *Supposing they turn around and laugh at me, what can I possibly do then?*

Reason told me that I should walk away—that if I was sure Jill was cheating on me, I should call a lawyer and arrange a divorce. But it wasn't as simple as that. My ego was large enough to want to see what dazzling hero could possibly have attracted Jill away from me after such a short marriage. Such a passionate marriage, too. If I was lacking in any way, I wanted to know why.

I reached the door with the name-card that read "Willey." I pressed my ear against the door and listened; and after a moment or two I was sure that I could hear voices. Jill's, high-pitched, pleading. And a deeper voice; a man's voice. The voice of her lover, no less.

I took out the extra key that they had made for me at American Key & Lock the previous evening. I licked my lips, took a deep breath, and then I slid it into the door. I turned it, and the door opened.

You can still go back. You don't have to face this if you don't want to. But I knew that it was too late and that my curiosity was overwhelming.

I quietly closed the door behind me and stood in the hallway, listening. On the wall beside me were framed Deccan paintings of the eighteenth century, showing women having intercourse with stallions. Highly appropriate, I thought. And sickening, too. Maybe Jill *was* having an affair with Willey, after all. He seemed to have a pretty libidinous turn of mind.

I heard murmurings from the bedroom. The door was

slightly ajar, and I could see sunlight and pale blue carpet. The sheets rustled. Jill said, "You're marvelous; you're magic; if only I'd known."

God, I thought, *I shouldn't have come. This is almost more than I can stand. And what am I going to look like if they discover me? A creeping cuckold; a jealous husband who couldn't satisfy his wife.*

"Promise me," said Jill. "Promise me you'll never leave me."

The man said something indistinct.

"All *right,*" Jill replied, with tart satisfaction. "In that case I'll get the champagne out of the icebox, and we'll—"

I hadn't realized, listening to her talking, that she had climbed out of bed and crossed the bedroom floor. She opened the door, naked, flushed in the face, and caught me standing in the hall.

"Oh my God!" she exclaimed. The color emptied out of her face like ink spilled from a bottle.

Without a word, I pushed past her, and threw open the bedroom door.

"All right, you bastard!" I roared, in a voice so hoarse that it was almost insane. "Get up, get dressed, and get the fuck *out!*"

The man on the bed turned, and stared at me; and then I froze.

He was very pale. He was almost gray. His eyes had a stony faraway look that was more like a statue's than a man's. He was naked, his gray penis still glistened from sex. His chest was bound tightly with wide white bandages.

"Robbie," I whispered.

He drew the sheet right up to his neck but he didn't take his eyes away from me once.

"Robbie?" I repeated.

"That's right." He nodded. "I was hoping you wouldn't find out."

When he spoke, his words came out in a labored whisper.

Massive chest injuries, that's what the doctors had told me. *He didn't feel a thing.*

I managed one mechanical step forward. Robbie continued to stare at me. He was dead; and yet here he was, staring at me. I had never been so frightened of anything in my entire life.

"What happened?" I asked. "They told us you were killed instantly. That's what the doctors said. 'Don't worry, he didn't feel a thing. He was killed instantly.'"

Robbie managed a tight, reflective smile. "It's the words, George. They work!"

"Words?" I demanded. "What words?"

"Don't you remember? *Immortooty, immortaty, ever, ever, after.* I saw the truck coming toward me and I shouted them out. The next thing I knew, it was dark and I was buried alive."

He raised his hand, and turned it this way and that, frowning at it, as if it didn't really belong to him. "I don't know, maybe 'alive' is the wrong word. Immortal, sure. I'm immortal. I'm going to live forever—whatever that means."

"You got out of your casket?" I asked him in disbelief. "It was solid Cuban mahogany."

"The one you paid for might have been solid Cuban mahogany. The one I kicked my way out of was pine, tacked together with two-inch nails." He gave me a grim smile. "You should sue your mortician. Or then again, maybe you shouldn't."

"Jesus." I was trembling. I couldn't believe it was he. But it really was. My own brother, gray-faced and dead, but still alive.

"Jill!" I shouted. *"Jill!"*

Jill came back into the room, wrapped in a red robe.

"Why didn't you tell me?" I asked in a whisper, although I couldn't stop myself from staring at Robbie. He remained where he was, wrapped in his sheet, his eyes fixed on me with an expression that was as cold as glass. God Almighty, he *looked* dead, he *looked* like a corpse. How could Jill have . . . ?

"I love him," Jill told me, her voice small and quiet.

"You love him?" I quaked. "Jill, he's dead!"

"I love him," she repeated.

"I love him, too, for Christ's sake!" I screamed at her. "I love him *too!* But he's dead, Jill! He's *dead!"*

I snatched hold of her wrist but she yanked herself angrily away from me. "He's not dead!" she shrieked. "He's not! He makes love to me! How can he be dead?"

"How the hell should I know? Because of a rhyme, because of a wish? Because of who knows what! But the doctors said he was dead and they buried him, and he's *dead*, Jill!"

Robbie slowly drew back the sheet from the bed and eased himself up. His skin was almost translucent, like dirty wax. From the bandages around his chest, I heard a whining inhalation and exhalation. The scaffolding pole had penetrated his lungs; he hadn't stood a chance.

"I dug my way out of the soil with my bare hands," he told me; and there was a kind of terrible pride in his voice. "I rose out of the earth at three o'clock in the morning, filthy with clay. Then I walked all the way to the city. *Walked!* Do you know how difficult that is, how far that is? And then the next day I called Jill from a public telephone in Brooklyn; and she came to rescue me."

"I remember the day," I told him.

He came up close. He exuded a strange, elusive smell; not of decomposition, but of some preservative chemical. It suddenly occurred to me that embalming fluid must be running through his veins instead of blood. He was my brother; I had loved him when he was alive. But I knew with complete certainty, now, that he was dead; and I loved him no longer.

Jill whispered, "You won't tell, will you? You won't *tell* anybody?"

For a very long moment I couldn't think what to do. Jill and Robbie watched me without saying a word, as if I were a hostile outsider who had deliberately set out to interfere and to destroy their lives.

But at last I grinned, nodded, and said to Robbie, "You're back, then! You're really back. It's a miracle!"

He smiled lopsidedly, as if his mouth were anesthetized. "I knew you'd understand. Jill said you never would; but I said bull. You always did, didn't you? You son-of-a-gun."

He rested his hand on my shoulder, his dead gray hand; and I felt the bile rise up in my throat. But I had already decided what I was going to do, and if I had betrayed any sign of disgust, I would have ruined it.

"Come on through to the kitchen," I told him. "I could use a beer after this. Maybe a glass of wine?"

"There's some champagne in the icebox," said Jill. "I was just going to get it."

"Well, let's open it together," I suggested. "Let's celebrate! It isn't every day that your brother comes back from the dead."

Jill dragged the sheet from the bed and wrapped it around Robbie like a toga. Then they followed me into the small green-tiled kitchen. I opened the icebox, took out the bottle of champagne, and offered it to Robbie.

"Here," I told him. "You were always better at opening up bottles of wine than I was."

He took it but looked at me seriously. "I don't know. I'm not sure I've got the strength anymore. I'm alive, you know, but it's kind of *different.*"

"You can make love," I retorted, dangerously close to losing my temper. "You should be able to open a bottle of champagne."

His breath whined in and out of his bandages. I watched him closely. There was doubt on his face; as if he suspected that I was somehow setting him up, but he couldn't work out how.

"Come on, sweetheart," Jill coaxed him.

I turned around, opened one of the kitchen drawers.

String, skewers, nutmeg grater. "Yes, come on, Robbie. You always were a genius at parties."

I opened the next drawer. Tea towels. Jill frowned and said, "What are you looking for?"

Robbie began to unwind the wire muzzle around the champagne cork. "My fingers feel kind of *numb,* you know? It's hard to describe."

I opened the third drawer, trying to do it nonchalantly. *Knives.*

Jill knew instantaneously what I was going to do. Maybe it was genuine intuition. Maybe it was nothing more than heightened fear. But I turned around so casually that she didn't see the nine-inch Sabatier carving knife in my hand; she was looking at my eyes; and it had penetrated Robbie's bandages right up to the hilt before she understood that I meant to kill him. I meant to *kill* him. He was my brother.

The champagne bottle smashed on the floor in an explosion of glass and foam. Jill screamed but Robbie said nothing at all. He turned to me, and grasped my shoulder, and there was something in his eyes that was half panic and half relief. I pulled the knife downward and it cut through his flesh as if it were an overripe avocado: soft, slippery, no resistance.

"Oh, God," he breathed. His gray intestines came pouring out from underneath his toga and onto the broken glass. "Oh, God, get it over with."

"No!" screamed Jill, but I stared at her furiously and shouted, "You want him to live forever? He's my brother! You want him to live *forever?"*

She hesitated for a second, then pushed her way out of the kitchen and I heard her retching in the toilet. Robbie was on his knees, his arms by his sides, making no attempt to pick up his heavy kilt of guts.

"Come on," he whispered. "Get it *over* with."

I was shaking so much that I could hardly hold the knife. He tilted his head back, passive and quiet, his eyes still open, and like a man in a slowly moving nightmare I cut his throat from one side to the other; so deeply that the knife blade wedged between his vertebrae.

There was no blood. He collapsed backward onto the floor, shuddering slightly. Then the unnatural life that had illuminated his eyes faded away, and it was clear that he was truly dead.

Jill appeared in the doorway. Her face was completely white, as if she had covered herself in rice powder. "What have you done?" she whispered.

I stood. "I don't know. I'm not sure. We'll have to bury him."

"No," she said, shaking her head. "He's still alive . . . we could bring him back again."

"Jill . . ." I began, moving toward her; but she screamed, "Don't touch me! You've killed him! Don't touch me!"

I tried to snatch at her wrist, but she pulled herself away and ran for the door.

"Jill! Jill, *listen!*"

She was out in the corridor before I could stop her, and running toward the elevator. The elevator doors opened and the Italian-looking man stepped out, looking surprised. Jill pushed her way into the elevator, hammered wildly at the buttons.

"No!" she screamed. *"No!"*

I went after her but the Italian-looking man deliberately blocked my way.

"That's my wife!" I yelled at him. "Get out of my goddamned way!"

"Come on, friend, give her some breathing space," the man said and pushed me in the chest with the flat of his hand. Desperately, I saw the elevator doors close and Jill disappear.

"For God's sake," I snarled at the man. "You don't know what you've done!"

I shoved my way past him and hurtled down the stairs, three at a tune, until I reached the lobby. The doorman said, "Hey, man, what's going on?" and caught at my arm.

He delayed me for only a second, but it was a second too long. The swinging doors were just closing and Jill was already halfway across the sidewalk, running into Central Park South.

"Jill!" I shouted after her. She couldn't possibly have heard. She didn't even hear the cab that hit her as she crossed the road and sent her hurtling over its roof, her arms spread wide as if she were trying to fly. I pushed open the swinging doors and I heard her fall. I heard screams and traffic and the screeching of brakes.

Then I didn't hear anything, either.

It was a strange and grisly task, removing Robbie's body from Willey's apartment. But there was no blood, no evidence of murder, and nobody would report him missing. I buried him deep in the woods beyond White Plains, in a place where we used to play when we were boys. The wind blew leaves across his grave.

We buried Jill a week later, in Providence, on a warm sunny day when the whole world seemed to be coming to life. Her mother wouldn't stop sobbing. Her father wouldn't speak to me. The police report had exonerated me from any possible blame, but grief knows no logic.

I took two weeks away from work after the funeral and went to stay at a friend's house in the Hamptons, and got drunk most of the time. I was still in shock; and I didn't know how long it was going to take me to get over it.

Down on the seashore, with the gulls circling all around me, I suppose I found some kind of unsteady peace of mind.

I returned to the city on a dark, threatening Thursday afternoon. I felt exhausted and hung over, and I planned to spend the weekend quietly relaxing before returning to work on Monday. Maybe I would go to the zoo. Jill had always liked going to the zoo, more to look at the people than at the animals.

I unlocked the door of my apartment, tossed my bag into the hallway. Then I went through to the kitchen and took a bottle of cold Chablis out of the icebox. *Hair of the dog,* I thought to myself. I switched on the television just in time to see the end credits of "As The World Turns." I poured myself some wine; and then, whistling, went through to the bedroom.

I said, "Oh Christ," and dropped my full glass of wine on my foot.

She was lying on top of the comforter naked, not smiling, but her thighs were provocatively apart. Her skin had a grayish-blue sheen as if it would be greasy to touch, but it wasn't decayed. Her hair was brushed and her lips were painted red and there was purple eye shadow over her eyes.

"Jill?" I breathed. I felt for one implosive instant that I was going mad.

"I used the spare key from the crack in the skirting," she said. Her voice was hoarse, as if her lungs were full of fluid and crushed bone. I had seen her hurtling over the taxi, I had seen her fall. I had seen her *die.*

"You said the words," I told her dully. "You said the words." She shook her head. But it was then I remembered watching her asleep, and reciting that childish rhyme. *Immortooty, immortaty, ever, ever, after.*

She raised her arms, stiffly. The fingers of her left hand were tightly curled, as if they had been broken.

"Make love to me," she whispered. "Please, make love to me."

I turned around and walked straight to the kitchen. I pulled open one drawer after another, but there wasn't a single knife anywhere. She must have hidden them all, or thrown them away. I turned back again, and Jill was standing in the bedroom doorway. This time she was smiling.

"Make *love* to me," she repeated.

Prometheus' Declaration of Love for the Vulture

Alan Rodgers

In the ten thousand years
        that I lay chained
        on this mountain
        in the Caucasus,
when you would wake me each day
        with your beak upon my belly,
            tear my gut,
            and feast upon my liver,
I came to love you, bird.

It seems to me
        that you have always
        understood our love
        better than I could—
for I every moment loathed you,
        despised you,
        plotted against you
            (but came to *know* your touch,
            to tell your mood
                by the feel of your spittle
                in my veins . . .

and even to be jealous,
    though I could not
    then confess it,
    of the carrion
       I would sometimes smell
       on your breath)
—for I saw sunlight catch
    on a tear
    falling from your eye
the day Heracles freed me.
It haunted me,
and does so still.

O Eater of My Liver:
come away with me,
    the love
       who has returned to you;
follow me
    out into the corridors
    of light and pain and love
that are the world.

And live with me.

Long Lips

R. Patrick Gates

Fog slips in from the sea like blood sliding from a wound. It drips over the seawall, stains the cobblestone streets. It chills the air like the icy breath of Death. With it slinks a shadow; thin, quick, ethereal. It dances like fine rain in the night. It slithers and laughs, filling the night with a hideous tinkling, like razor-edged slivers of glass ripping into dead flesh . . .

She paused, listened, and shivered. She closed her coat against the fog and hurried toward the friendly lights of the tavern. A black cat skittered through the fog, howling like a human baby in pain. Chills ran over her spine like ice down the back of her blouse. She gasped, exhaled loudly. Dead laughter floated on the fog but she mistook it for the echo of her own frightened breathing. She didn't see the shadow dancing close behind her.

The music from the tavern was distant, fading in the mist. It sounded like a dirge played in the depths of a mausoleum. The woman shivered, fumbled out a cigarette. A man stepped out of the fog.

"Good evening," he said in a deep but vaporous voice. She relaxed. Just another john. She lit the cigarette and ran her tongue seductively over her lips.

"Hello, sugar," she said in a sweet southern drawl. "What can I do you for?"

The man smiled, showing luminescent teeth.

"You shy, honey? That's okay. You can tell me. What you want Mama to do?" She peered into his face, but the swirling mist shrouded it. She could see only his eyes. They were deep purple and seemed to glow.

She shook off the sudden chill that rippled her skin, took his hand. "I can't help, sugar, if you won't talk to me."

He pointed to a nearby alley.

"Now we gettin' somewheres! Come on, don't be scared."

In the alley, her open blouse revealed large brown breasts frosted with mist. His tongue glided over them, licking them dry. She giggled at the sandpaper feeling. He pushed her to her knees. She unzipped his pants. He sighed.

"*Oh* my God!" she said in amazement. "I'm sorry, sugar, but I can't. I—" Her voice was cut off suddenly. She gave a muffled cry, then gagged. The fog carried away the sound of her death and the thin, mean laughter rejoicing in it.

"What have we got?" The captain barked the question as he stepped out of the cruiser. His voice was hoarse from too many cigarettes and too many years in the damp, seaside town. He was a short man, stocky and wide. With a little more height on him he would have made a fine football player. His face was windburned and weathered, making him look more like a lobster fisherman than a cop. His hair was getting gray. He never combed it, leaving it to wave wildly in the wind.

"There's . . . ah, been a homicide, of sorts," said a tall lieutenant named Hedstrom, trying to hold back a lecherous grin.

"No shit, Dick Tracy? I thought we had a mad jaywalker on the loose."

An unsuppressible giggle bubbled from Hedstrom.

"What's the MO?" the captain asked, scowling and heading into the alley. Hedstrom giggled again and his face turned bright red. The captain pushed past him. The dead hooker, covered by a worn woolen blanket, lay against a trash can. The captain knelt, lifted the blanket from her body, and almost jumped back in horror. He'd seen murdered corpses before but never anything like this. He covered his shock—he was too much of a pro to let it show—yet he felt it, inside. It assaulted his innermost being.

She was half-naked, but he barely saw that. His eyes were drawn to her face. Her eyes were open. They stared at him and the horror of death lingered in them. She might have been a pretty girl once, but the ravages of her profession and the violence of her death now made her ugly. Long strands of milky fluid hung from both nostrils. Her jaw had been broken and hung on her upper chest. Her face and neck were blotched with bloody bruises.

The captain stared out the window. His feet rested on the top of the old desk and a cigarette hung from his mouth. Opposite him sat Lieutenant Hedstrom, the medical examiner, and the DA.

"This isn't for real," muttered the captain. The DA coughed and the captain pulled his eyes away from the window. "Is there any way the guy could be faking this?"

Hedstrom giggled.

"I mean," the captain continued after an angry glance at the lieutenant, "is there some way he can make it *appear* that he has—" The captain fumbled for the right word.

"Fellatioed his victim to death?" offered Hedstrom. "Maybe oralicide, or headicide? How about blown away?"

"Knock it off!" barked the captain. He turned to the medical examiner. "Is there any way to *fake* this—make it *appear* he killed her this way?"

The medical examiner sighed. "Not in this case. Abrasions at the back of the throat, coupled with sperm and skin cells found in the victim's mouth and on her teeth, prove conclusively that the murder took place the way I described."

The captain took a deep breath. "So it looks like we've got a killer with an unusual modus operandi."

"He shouldn't be too hard to find," Hedstrom commented. "All we've got to do is look for a guy with a third leg."

The captain glared at him.

"Actually," the medical examiner interrupted, "that's not far from the truth. By measuring the bruises in the victim's throat, I'd say the killer has a twenty-inch penis—with a circumference of seven inches."

"Holy Christmas," mumbled the DA. "You know, if we catch this bastard, there's no way we can *try* him! It'd be a side show. If we catch him, he'll have to be put away quietly. Heaven help us if the papers get wind of this!"

"Putting him on trial is the least of my worries," the captain answered. "But I do want to keep this out of the papers. We'll put out a standard release saying the guy is a strangler; nothing more." He pointed at Hedstrom. "Circulate a description of the murderer's, ah, anatomy to the hookers in the red-light district, but do it discreetly. You'd also better check the doctors and hospitals within a fifty-mile radius. It seems to me there should be a record somewhere if this guy is such a freak."

Hedstrom nodded.

"And double the night patrol downtown. We're going to crack down on the johns until we find this guy. Anyone soliciting sex is to be picked up and examined."

Hedstrom started to laugh, then smothered it quickly under the captain's harsh stare.

The sign read: BLACK LEATHER CAFÉ. When the door opened, the stench of stale smoke poured out of it like steam from a caldron and mingled with the sea fog. A shadow, hidden by the mist, slid under the sign and lingered near the entrance. The door opened and two young men holding hands came out. They paused in the open doorway to kiss, passionately. The shadow slid past them, inside.

The smoke was thick. The smell of sweat and urine was strong. The flickering jukebox played low, perverted jazz. Conversation was low and rumbling, stopped when the door shut. Bloodshot eyes under visored leather caps looked up. Mustaches bristled, chains rattled, leather squeaked as the men in the bar strained to get a look at the newcomer. Lips were licked, eyes winked, heads nodded, but the stranger in the long black cape stared through them. Moving as if he rode a cushioned wave of air, he traversed the floor and went into the bathroom. A collective chill ran through the patrons of the bar, was shrugged off. The conversations resumed.

In a corner, a thin young man in tight pants and a fishnet jersey eyed the stranger as he floated past. Their eyes met momentarily and the young man nodded. A trembling smile quivered on his lips. He knew what the glance meant. He had exchanged the same glance with men hundreds of times at the café. This time, though, there was something different. A thrill like nothing he'd ever felt coursed through his loins like an electrical current.

He ran his tongue over dry lips and followed the stranger in the bathroom.

The captain stood in the doorway of the men's room, fought back the sickness rising in him. "All right, you know what to do," he said to the officers outside the door. "Question everyone who was in here tonight. Move it! Stop gawking like a bunch of idiots."

The officers moved off to carry out his orders and Hedstrom stepped forward. "What do we call this, Chief?" he asked. A sarcastic smile twitched at the corners of his mouth. "A *homo*cide?"

* * *

"There's someone to see you, Captain."

The door opened and a woman in black entered the office. She was in her fifties, with gray hair and stern, rock-hard features. The first impression the captain had was that she looked like Indira Gandhi. The second impression was that she was a weirdo. She remained near the door, eyes staring straight ahead, lips moving silently as if she were reciting the rosary.

"Can I help you, ma'am?" the captain asked, making a mental note to chew out whoever had let her in his office.

"*I know what he is,*" she said.

A chill ran over the captain's brow.

"And I know how to stop him," she added. She continue speaking and the captain listened with amusement, fascination and, finally, dread.

The DA and Hedstrom were back in the captain's office. The former smoked a cigarette nervously while Hedstrom stared at the ceiling.

"Before I say anything, I want to get one thing straight," the captain said to Hedstrom. "This is no joking matter. We have a serious situation on our hands that has reached a point where I'm ready to take drastic measures. If you feel the need to joke—*don't!*"

Hedstrom coughed into his hand and nodded sheepishly.

"What I'm about to suggest is unorthodox but at this point I'll try anything. If we let this go on any longer, it's going to attract national attention. The local media has been cooperative, but that can only last so long. Sooner or later, this story is going to break big. That's why I want you *both* to listen to me seriously."

The DA and Hedstrom nodded.

"As you may know already, I had a visitor yesterday who

was a little strange. Strange or not, she made sense about how to nab this guy."

"What did she say?" Hedstrom asked.

"She claimed to be psychic and most of what she said was crap, delusions about the killer being a demon; she called him an *incubus,* which I gathered is some kind of sexual vampire. But that isn't important. While she was babbling she gave me an idea of how we can get him. We need someone he *can't kill.*"

The DA looked mystified and leaned forward. "I don't understand."

"She said this guy feeds on death created through sex. I think that's true, though not in a literal sense. If we can get someone, a hooker—even a gay—who can handle his size, we might frustrate him to the point where we can nab him. We bait this guy with someone he can't kill in his usual manner and, with surveillance, we'll grab him. Or at least have an eyewitness description."

"You really think it will work?" the DA asked. "I think he's too smart. He's been baiting *us* all along."

"Yeah," Hedstrom interrupted, "this guy's been a real *master baiter.*"

The captain ignored Hedstrom.

"Yes, I think it'll work." He turned to Hedstrom. "And *you,* Mr. Comedy, are going to find the right bait!"

Hedstrom's face turned crimson. For the first time in days, the captain smiled.

The phone rang in the middle of the night. The captain started from sleep, cursing loudly. Without turning on the light, he fumbled on his nightstand for the receiver.

"Chief? It's me, Hedstrom. I think I've got something."

The captain threw back the covers, got out of bed. Next to him, his wife groaned and rolled over. "What is it?" he asked quietly.

"I called a friend of mine in San Francisco. We went to

collage together; now he's a pornographic film producer. One of his stars is willing to help us. You ever hear of the movie *Deep Throat?*"

"Yeah."

"I've got someone who makes Linda Lovelace look like a lollipop sucker. I've got Long Lips," Hedstrom said proudly.

"What the hell is *that?*"

"*Lorna Lipps,* of course—Linda Lovelace's *suck*cessor! She'll do if for ten grand plus expenses. Pretty expensive blow job, but considering the risks, she won't do it for less."

The captain nodded his head in the dark. "Okay. Get her on a plane out here and keep her *quiet.*"

The captain was surprised by how tall and blond she was. He wondered briefly if she was a natural blonde. She towered four inches over him, and he was five-nine. She was a pretty woman, not scuzzy-looking like most porno queens. There was a little age showing in the wrinkles around her eyes and in the tiny lines at the corners of her mouth, but those small flaws were easy to overlook when gazing into her large, crystal-blue eyes. They held and mesmerized. Her mouth was full, sensual under a thin, noble nose. Her chin melted gracefully into a neck that was long and aristocratic. Her shoulders were broad, supporting breasts that were huge, firm mounds pushing out the seams of her tank top.

The captain caressed her with his eyes and found it hard to look away. She smiled at him and cocked her hips. Her hot pants looked as if they'd been painted on. They rode up her thighs, creased around her crotch and firm buttocks. The captain licked suddenly dry lips.

"I'm pleased to meet you, Miss Lipps."

"I can see that." She smiled down at him.

"Did Lieutenant Hedstrom give you the plan?" he asked nervously and crossed his legs.

"He gave it to me, all right," she said.

The captain mumbled, "I should have known."

"Don't worry," she said, placing a leather travel bag on the desk. "He also told me what I'm supposed to do." She opened the bag to pull out a pair of black satin pants and a red see-through peasant blouse. She laid them carefully on the desk.

"First things first. You have some money for me?"

The captain fumbled an envelope out of his pocket and handed it across the desk to her. She took it, tucked it inside the bag.

"While I get changed into my working clothes, why don't you give me the details of this operation?" She slid the tank top over her head. Her breasts bulged and lifted before flopping free of the stretchy material. They made a soft smacking sound as they settled back against her body—full, luscious things with small, ripe-red, perpetually hard nipples.

The captain couldn't take his eyes off her. She smiled at him and ran her hands over her breasts. She unbuckled her belt and slid the tight shorts seductively down her thighs. With a sharp intake of breath, the captain noticed she was wearing no underwear. He smiled.

She was indeed a natural blonde.

Hedstrom clicked the radio off and watched Lorna Lipps standing on the corner in her tight black pants and flimsy blouse. He smiled, glanced at the captain in the seat next to him. He was holding his head as if it hurt.

"She'll give you a real *headache* if you let her, Chief," he chuckled.

The captain frowned, but not at Hedstrom. The thought of banging Lorna Lipps had certainly crossed his mind. He knew he'd had his chance when she stripped in his office. But unlike Hedstrom, the captain had a conflict; namely, marriage. Even though his wife showed all of her forty-five years, he didn't think he could ever cheat on her.

Not that he hadn't been tempted.

"Where'd she go?" Hedstrom asked suddenly. The captain glanced up. The corner was empty. Lorna was gone.

The captain sipped coffee, looked at the clock. It was 3 A.M., and Lorna Lipps had been missing for five hours. A dragnet had failed to pick up any trace of her. The captain was afraid he was going to have to chalk her up as another victim. The problem was, she wasn't just another victim; she was a celebrity of sorts. He was responsible for her.

The telephone rang, startling him. He snapped up the receiver.

"Hello?"

The voice was distant and weak. His heart skipped a beat. It was Lorna Lipps.

The small, dingy hotel room was at the end of a long, dark corridor. The captain hurried toward the room, his footsteps echoing like ghostly shots. The building smelled of sweat and garbage; it reeked of perversion, and of death itself.

He called Lorna's name, heard a muffled explosion. Panting, he reached for the doorknob, afraid of what he would find. The knob felt as if it was coated with Vaseline. He opened the door. Gasped.

The room was filled with thick, pungent smoke. Waving his arms, the captain made his way inside. The air began to clear. Lorna lay on the bed, naked, covered head to toe in gooey black slime.

She was alive.

"Where is he?" the captain asked, his gun ready.

"There," she said, pointing at the wall. "And there," she added, pointing to the ceiling and floor. The smoke was escaping into the hallway and the room was clear enough now for the captain to see.

From the ceiling hung a hand, suspended by a string of

gelatinous slime. The walls were covered with bits and pieces of goo-covered flesh: an eyeball over the door; part of a foot in the corner; an ear plastered against the grimy window. On the floor, he saw the twenty-inch piece of flesh that had been the murder weapon.

"What the hell happened?"

Lorna Lipps shrugged and smiled weakly. "Some guys just go to pieces when they can't get off."

Sinners

Ralph Rainwater, Jr.

I'd always admired the way David wedded intellect with action. But this latest terrorism went too far. Riding our bikes through the quiet back roads of the Georgian countryside, once again I gathered my courage and told him so.

"Listen," he replied, "you're like a broken record. You keep repeating the same old doubts, yet you never convince me they're justified."

"That's not fair," I argued. "You know that. Even when I'm right, you *always* win our arguments!"

"Then you should learn to debate better. In any case, if you don't like what we—and I emphasize that 'we'—are going to do, why are you pedaling alongside me now?"

"Because you're my older brother," I said simply. Given our rough family history, I knew this answer would soften him.

In the dark separating us, I saw him nod and I sensed the smile on David's face. "Okay, then, because you're my *younger* brother, I'll try to explain one more time." He paused for a moment to collect his thoughts.

In the silence, the only sounds we heard in the still, humid night were those of our bikes rolling over the crumbling country road and of millions of crickets singing their mating songs. With no moon overhead, the weak headlights on our handlebars illuminated only a few feet of ground at a time, barely giving us enough opportunity to swerve around the abundant potholes and occasional crushed animals.

The canvas bag, containing a plastic human skeleton David had ordered from a novelty horror catalogue, hung around his neck, resting on his back. Also inside the bag were several accessories: a claw-toothed hammer, some nails, and three pre-cut lengths of rope (in case pounding in nails proved too loud or difficult).

Finally, he spoke again. "We're agreed that this whole area is stuck in the past by willful ignorance, right?"

"Right."

"And the biggest holdback keeping these rural people from joining the twentieth century is their primitive brand of religion?"

"Okay," I said.

"So it follows, then, that anything done to discredit religion is good. Think of what our little book did."

By "our" book, he meant the parody of the New Testament he'd written, "The Breeder's Digest Condensed New Testament," in which all the human characters had been replaced by dogs. I had merely provided a few ideas and helped distribute it by leaving copies in strategic points around town—at night, of course. The parody, printed on our home computer, created a stir that lasted for weeks. The local paper had been filled with letters from ardent churchgoers and civic leaders, expressing outrage and shock.

I'd had doubts at first about belittling a holy book. But we bathed in private glory over the vehement reactions our parody's anonymous authors had caused. The faithful had revealed their insecurity, just as David predicted they would.

"Yeah, you were right *that* time. But isn't this going to extremes?" I asked.

"Yes, it is. But no more extreme than these fanatics are. It's 'an eye for an eye,' Mark."

"We're talking about nailing a *skeleton* to their cross. They'll go nuts!"

"Maybe not. Consider what their fanaticism is based on. That they've *seen* God. He lives amongst them, *inside* their church." He paused, waiting for comment. When I offered none, David continued, "Think—who could believe such a fiction? Only the most ignorant, the poorest types. And that's precisely who belong to this country church. You've seen them around town. You know what the congregation is like. That freak this morning is a perfect example."

I didn't want to think about him. There'd been too much weirdness to that skinny, ill-dressed man's manner as he exhorted everyone in the town square to join "The Church of an Angry God." There'd been an unnatural gleam in his eye, a too-frenzied spinning of his arms. He kept shouting, "Praise God! He has come! Come to step on those who have stepped on us! Vengeance is His!"

"Well then, if they're not going to get violent, what *do* you think will happen?" I demanded.

"Imagine all these zealots coming to worship tomorrow." My brother sounded excited now. "These are people who save welfare checks to buy Cadillacs. That car is a sacred symbol of the 'good life' to them. It's a *religious* token! And then, with their perpetually pre-scientific minds, they enter the church and stare at their cross! Instead of *imagining* Jesus . . . this *thing* will be up there. A skeleton! Signifying how dead their religion really is.

"Can't you hear them now?" David went on. "'Oh Lordy, Lordy—someone's come in here and done the Devil's work!' Don't you *see*? If we pull this off, the congregation will think that God would never have *allowed* such a transgression!"

"So He was never there at all." I nodded, understanding.

"Exactly," David replied. "Don't you think this little joke is worth it to end such fanaticism?"

No; I didn't. David's escapades had always been contrary to my nature. His intellect was somehow too sharp, his condemnation of others' blindnesses too unforgiving. I didn't have the courage of his convictions.

Yet here again I was acquiescing to his plans, a faithful though doubting sidekick. Why? Because David was the only person in our atavistic town I could conceivably admire. Because we were *both* sharp, and all I saw around us were blunt, dull surfaces. Because where my brother went, I had to follow.

It was as simple as that.

By now our pedaling had taken us to an impoverished backwater area nearly fifteen miles from town. Scattered here and there were ramshackle, decaying homes occupied primarily by unemployed or, at best, seasonally employed, poor families.

By the light of day the homes were embarrassments; eyesores. Front porches sagged, roofs had holes, broken windows had newspaper covering them. In the yard around each of these shacks lay assorted garbage and the wrecks of old Cadillacs. Anybody driving through this part of the country during sunset usually spotted the massive families economically clutched by sitting together on rusted chairs or splintering steps. The adults would be smoking, the children chatting.

Having until recently given up on prosperity in *this* life, these people clung to the promise of reward in the next with a peasant's simple faith in reward and retribution from a personal God. Not for them was God some abstract Deity Who, if He existed at all, did so as a mass of disincorporated energy. To them, God was an angry old white man with a long beard Who'd never forgiven people for killing His son. They awaited the sound of His massive feet stomping across the land—an all-powerful giant Who'd set things right.

For the past month their message had been this: The wait was *over.*

And sitting in the midst of this poverty, the nucleus around which every one of these families revolved, was the church. We saw its square, whitewashed outline beckoning to us from out of the darkness when we approached.

We hid our bikes in some kudzu growth a few yards from the front entrance. The entire area was deserted, but I couldn't shake off the feeling that somebody was watching us. I mentioned this to David. He shrugged it off.

We'd been prepared to break a window and climb in, if need be, but the front door's knob turned easily. We slipped quietly into the empty church, David carrying our sack of goodies. At first, there seemed nothing unusual. There were the expected polished pews, the imitation stained-glass windows, the podium sitting on a dais in front.

We were, however, surprised to see a life-size representation of the crucified Christ on the large oak cross behind the podium. Fundamentalist churches tend not to believe in such graphic depictions. They smack of "graven images."

It was when we neared the cross that another oddity struck home with me: Unlike most such figures, where Jesus' head is down and his eyes closed, this one's head remained erect, his eyes open. Even more disconcerting was the unmistakable sneer his lips were set in.

"How fitting," David said.

"Fitting? It's downright *scary!*" I said.

"Well, at least we know for sure what his church is about," he replied and walked steadily forward. He stopped when he realized I had not followed. "This statue is likely to be heavy. I'll need your help in taking it down."

I couldn't pull my gaze from Jesus' eyes. Whoever had painted them had given the sculpting an almost sentient quality. "I've really got the creeps from this," I admitted. "It truly looks like he's watching us."

David frowned. "Sometimes, Mark, you show yourself to be yet a child. Hurry now. It does us no good to waste time chatting. The *real* danger is that of late-night worshipers dropping by."

The idea of fanatics catching us in the act of desecrating their church scared me enough to rush to David's side and hold the bag open for him. While he busied himself trying to yank out a large nail pounded through the left hand, I stared at the front door, nervously expecting it to fly open any second with a contingent of pitchfork-carrying parishioners intending to skewer us.

"This might take a bit longer than I'd planned," David said ruminatively. "The nails are pounded flush with the plaster, so I'll have to dig into the statue itself to get a grip on the nail head." I managed a nod. A minute later, when David spoke again, there was something foreign in his voice: uncertainty. "Mark . . . look at this."

I looked. Where David had chipped away the plaster, it was not a chalky-white, but blood-red.

"These people go to some lengths for realism, huh?" He smiled, composure outwardly restored. "Want to bet it bleeds when I pull this nail out?"

I shook my head. "David, don't do it!"

"I was only joking," David said. Grabbing the thick nail with the hammer's claws, he pulled. The nail moved perhaps a half inch. He tugged again. This time it slid out nearly all the way.

And a thin stream of blood followed. It trickled steadily from the wound, onto the dais floor. "Oh, shit," David said.

I didn't say anything because my feet were flying up the carpeted aisle, taking me outside toward the bikes. If David was stupid enough to continue this stunt, I thought, he'd have to do it alone.

He wasn't stupid, however. He was never that. His feet pounded close behind me.

I tried to turn the doorknob, to leave in one smooth motion. But it was locked now, and momentum caused me to smack hard into the heavy wood and bounce off. By the time I'd regained my feet, David was already rattling the door. Frantically. Still, it refused to open.

The tinkle of metal striking the floor caused both of us to spin around. What I saw literally made me pee my pants.

The statue's head twisted back and forth, as if stretching its neck muscles. Its mouth changed from a sneer into a chilling, mean smile. Its arms and legs flexed plaster muscles, causing the nails binding them to pop out.

I heard myself screaming incoherently. Even though he surely was as frightened as I, David kept his wits enough to speak. "Get *away* from us! I'll knock your goddamn *head* off!" he yelled, still clutching the hammer in his white-knuckled hand.

Hesitantly, as if not entirely confident of its balance, the statue took one single step forward. When it began to speak, however, its voice seemed to come from the church itself, not the plaster-filled mouth. It was an appropriately deep voice, filled with authority—and menace.

"By the depth of their hatred did they create me. By their need for revenge against the fortunate, the well-constituted, did my suffering children cause me to be. I was created in their image; their faith sustains me."

While he spoke, he moved steadily forward, arms outstretched in a welcoming embrace. When the figure was some ten feet distant, David threw the hammer at it with all his youthful strength. It struck, bounced off, taking a chunk of dark, red plaster with it. The statue paid no heed.

"I am yet but a weak god. My children are few, and simple of intellect. I need an anger fed by knowledge." The head veered toward my brother. "I need . . . *you*," it said, and stared directly at David.

My brother scooped me up with a brave vigor born of hysteria and charged toward the nearest window. Numb of mind, I did nothing to resist. An instant later, amid shards of broken glass, I landed on the grass outside. Somehow, I escaped with only a few cuts—

But I was alone.

I leapt to my feet, ran to the window, and then discovered why David had not followed.

The god had him. My brother was locked in his embrace. Before my eyes, I saw the impossible: David, struggling in horror—but then his body began to take on an ethereal quality. Then, quit slowly, gradually—inexorably—it started to merge with this god's . . .

Until they were one.

Since David's back was to me, thankfully, I did not have to see the incalculable terror that must have been reflected in his young face.

Then they were gone.

Shock and adrenaline gave me the energy to pedal madly back home. An hour and a half later, I returned to the church with my disbelieving and disgruntled mother, her newest boyfriend, Max, and a very dubious, irascible policeman in tow.

We found nothing to corroborate my story. The statue was back in place, head down and eyes closed. The window had been repaired; even the shards of glass on the ground were gone, as were David's bike and the bag he'd carried inside the church.

They all thought David had run off, and that I'd used his disappearance to concoct this wild story, trying to explain away the trouble I'd obviously been in.

What none of them noticed, and I did not point out, however, was this: Embedded in the statue's face, David's own features could still be discerned, indelibly frozen in a grimace of awful terror.

Sunday Breakfast

Jeannette M. Hopper

Having been bedridden for nearly ten months with an impressive list of real and imagined ailments, Carlotta Pierce was quite a surprise to her daughter-in-law, Maureen, who found Carlotta sitting at the kitchen table, bathed in golden Sunday-morning sunshine. Permed white hair glinted violet against the blue-green backdrop of Monterey Bay visible through the patio doors. Carlotta ignored Maureen's entrance and continued her concentrated chewing.

"Mom, what's that you're eating?" asked Maureen, steadying herself with one hand on the kitchen counter. The shock of finding the woman suddenly mobile was compounded by the sight of her breakfasting on raw meat—three-dollars-and-eighty-nine-cents-a-pound raw meat, from the looks of it. Maureen had bought it the day before for their Sunday barbecue.

Carlotta appeared not to have heard the question. She went about the systematic task of ripping chunks of muscle and gristle from the T-bone, mashing it between toothless gums, swallowing through a throat grown accustomed to Cream of Wheat and pureed vegetables.

Maureen scratched at her scalp, pitching a drapery of auburn curls over her cheek. This she tossed back, making a mental note to allow time for a shampoo before church.

She glanced at the clock and calculated the time needed to cook breakfast, take her shower, get Tricia up, bathed, and dressed, feed Carlotta—or would that be necessary after her meal of steak tartare? Looking over her shoulder at the woman by the wide glass doors, Maureen asked, "Will you be wanting any cereal when you're done, Mother?" Carlotta grunted, shook her head. "Okay. Then you just go on with your breakfast. I don't suppose Andrew will mind. He doesn't care about anything else you do."

From the back, Carlotta looked like any octogenarian having a go at a tough steak: shoulders hunched, head bobbing with the effort, ears sliding up and down the sides of her oversized scalp. Her jaws emitted dull clicks as the thin muscle bulged and hollowed. Maureen couldn't tell whether the old lady was enjoying the meat, or simply satisfied to have gotten her way once more.

Maureen put coffee on to drip, then stood at the sink and gazed out over the sloping backyard, down on the glittering Pacific water. This should be Paradise, she thought, but I'm stuck caring for a senile invalid who takes, takes, takes, and never gives a damned thing back but shit, piss, and vomit. Not that that's anything new for Carlotta Pierce . . . She looks like she's ready to croak, but with my luck, she'll live forever. Maureen let a deep, weary sigh escape, and the silence was broken by Andrew's arrival in the dining room.

"God," he moaned, "didn't sleep worth shit last night. Damned kids down on the beach till all hours, drinkin' and carryin' on. Goddamn access laws and the—Mom, what in holy hell are you *eating?*" He'd stopped in mid-gripe, crouched halfway to the chair, butt poised a foot from the cushion. Black hair lay glued to his head, but his eyes were a startled electric blue. When he received no answer from either woman, he repeated his question without profanities.

"An early lunch, I think," Maureen said.

Andrew Pierce stared at his wife. "You just gonna let her—eat that?"

"She's up, isn't she? She's eating the first solid food she's had in months. Besides, we can't go calling Dr. Patterson just because Mom's suddenly taken it into her head to eat raw steak." Maureen brought two cups of steaming coffee to the dining room table and set one in front of her husband. She kept the other in her hands while she stood behind the chair opposite him. "He'd just tell us what he's told us the other times: 'Keep an eye on her and make sure she doesn't hurt herself.' You know she only does these things for attention."

"Well, she *got* it, all right." Andrew smeared his hair back from his forehead, blew into his coffee. After taking a cautious sip and grimacing at the heat, he asked, "Is Tricia fed and ready for services?"

"You kidding? I'm letting her sleep in. She was cranky last night, and I don't want her missing another day of Sunday school."

Andrew replaced his cup on the table and blinked. "But I just went in to check on her, and she's not in her room."

"She's probably in the bathroom. You know six-year-olds—"

"No, I checked both bathrooms. I thought she'd be in here with you."

"Oh, God," murmured Maureen, splashing the tablecloth as she nearly dropped her cup. She padded down the long hallway, peeking in doors and calling her daughter's name. Andrew followed close behind.

"I told you," he said to her robed back, "I looked in the bathrooms, in Mom's room, and—"

"Oh, damn, damn, *damn,*" chanted Maureen as she opened closets and turned back draperies. "Tricia Eileen Pierce, if you're hiding from me, so help me I'll blister your little behind, but good!" No reply came, and after a moment, Maureen hurried into her own bedroom.

She threw on jeans and a sweatshirt, poked her feet into loafers. Forgetting about her mother-in-law in the kitchen, she trotted down the front steps, crushing shade-happy snails beneath her heels, and ran to the front gate. "Tricia!"

she yelled. Her voice was all but lost in the thunder of rolling surf. *"Tricia!"* Pulling tendrils of copper hair from her mouth, she shouted orders to Andrew, who peered inside his tarp-covered sailboat in the driveway. "Go down to the beach. See if there are any signs of her down there. I'll walk up the road and check the dunes!"

They met back at the front gate, both without success, and Maureen leaned against the rock wall. "What if she's drowned? I *told* you we should have taken her for swimming lessons, but *no-o,* your mother wouldn't hear of it. And Tricia, naive child that she is, takes your mother's word as law!"

Andrew shuffled in the sandy gravel, gazed off across the dunes. "Don't make this all *my* fault. I don't like having to look after Mother, but she'd raise hell if I tried to put her in a home." His feet stopped moving and he shoved his hands up into his pockets.

"Your mother," sneered Maureen, "would probably eat her roommate."

He turned to her, his brows knotted, mouth set in a hard line. "That doesn't happen anymore, and you know it. Mother never actually *ate* anyone." He snorted bitterly. "Hell, do you think I'd have let her move in with us if there was any danger whatsoever that she had inherited the curse?"

"What about your sister? Sammy bit her nipple off when he was two months old!"

Andrew swallowed, looked away. "That could happen to anyone."

"But when it happens in *your* family . . ."

"Sammy never did anything again."

"He's only two. Give him time."

Andrew pushed away from the wall and started for the house. "This is getting us nowhere. I'm going to call the Adamses and the Hendersons. Maybe Tricia walked down to see Judy or Dwayne."

Maureen trudged off in the opposite direction, toward the

field across the road. Tricia could have fallen into the tall grass, or become lost in the thick stand of trees on the other side. Maureen refused to think of the possibility that her child had been . . . kidnapped.

Twenty minutes later, after searching the field and coppice and finding only a mangled cat, she returned to the house. As she approached the door, she heard Andrew screaming angrily inside.

She found him standing in the middle of the kitchen, staring in disbelief at Carlotta. The old woman had finished her steak; she was now working hard on a pile of raw liver.

"First Tricia disappears and now this," yelled Andrew. "What the hell is going *on* around here?"

Maureen, hands held before her, approached her mother-in-law slowly. "Now, Mother," she said as if to a child, her teeth clenched until they ached, "we don't eat that until it's cooked. Why don't you give it to me, and I'll cook it for you?" Her smile was strained. She knew that if she didn't get the slimy organ from the old woman, she'd come apart inside and stuff it down that scrawny throat. "Please, Mom . . . just give it to me."

Carlotta hugged the wobbling flap of meat to her chest, cuddling it. Streams of liquid like tobacco spit squirted between her bony fingers. She shook her head vehemently, her wet brown eyes locked on Maureen's. Her mouth worked like some senile monkey's to gum the glob inside. Then, while Andrew and Maureen looked on in disgust, she tore off another strip and swallowed it without chewing.

"I can't take this," whined Andrew. "A man can handle only so much, even from his own mother!"

Maureen glared at his back as she stumbled down the hall toward the den. She felt her face grow hot; the itch of anger crawled across her shoulders, building to a scream. After all, the old woman was *his* mother, not hers.

She lurched forward and yanked the liver from Carlotta's grasp. Enraged, the old woman clawed at Maureen's arms, drawing blood with unified fingernails. Fresh red streaks mixed with the slimy brown juices of the liver, and for a moment the organ was strained between the two women, pulled taut like a wad of taffy.

Then it broke.

Carlotta smashed backward into the patio doors, bowing the safety glass. Tiny spider-cracks appeared at the corners near the aluminum casing, but the old woman bounced back, colliding with Maureen where she landed, seated on the edge of the dining room carpet. Both halves of the liver had flown through the kitchen to land on the counter; one lay in the sink near the disposal, and the other had slid into the crevice between the microwave oven and the refrigerator.

Maureen shoved Carlotta off and struggled to her feet. "You stinking cow," she growled. She backed away from the old woman's still-clawing hands, into the dining area.

The revelation struck Maureen full-force, driving her into the edge of the table. "No!" she cried, waving her arms to ward off the advancing horror. *"Not*—no . . . you couldn't have—you *wouldn't* have!" She dodged Carlotta and ran to the refrigerator, where she touched the red mass wedged between it and the oven. "Tricia . . ." she groaned, "oh, my poor baby . . ."

Maureen wiped her face on her sleeve and turned to face her mother-in-law. "What have you done with the rest of her?" Maureen demanded. Her voice was icy, measured, almost calm. "You couldn't have eaten her bones, could you? No, I don't think so." Maureen's hand fell upon the bread knife.

The old woman's rheumy eyes followed Maureen's hand as the fingers curled around the rosewood handle. Her mouth curved and stretched with moist smacks.

Blade in hand, Maureen advanced on the frail figure before her. "Your own granddaughter," she wailed. "And on *Sunday!"*

The long knife sliced through Carlotta's face and breast as easily as it had sliced through the air. Dark-red droplets rained on Maureen's hair, blending with it, and drizzled down her arms to run off her elbows. Carlotta's gnarled, blue-veined hands rose stiffly to her cheeks to spread blood into her cottony hair and blinded eyes. The blade descended once more and cut through the fingers of her right hand before plunging up to the handle behind her collar bone, where Maureen left it.

The younger woman stepped back, dazed, and whispered, "Die."

The sound of the front door opening—of light footsteps across the foyer—spun Maureen around. She gaped, both in relief and horror, at her daughter standing just inside the dining room. "Baby!" Maureen cried.

The old woman sank to her knees, remained there. Her eyes stayed wide open, obscured by thick red film. She stared at the Congoleum while her fingertips explored the knife handle.

Maureen ran to Tricia and threw her arms around the little girl. She drew her to her bosom tightly, rocking on her heels until she stood and brought the child up with her. She carried her to the kitchen counter, all the while ignoring the glazed expression on her mother-in-law's face. "What happened, love?" she begged, wiping at the streaks of blood on the girl's face. "Who did this to you? Where have you *been?*"

Andrew appeared in the doorway, hung there a moment, then rushed to his mother.

"I was sure she'd eaten Tricia," said Maureen, still dabbing at the crimson blotches on her daughter's face and arms. "I did what any mother would do in the same situation!"

Andrew eased his mother onto her side and reached for the telephone. "Should I call the police? I mean—what would we *tell* them?"

"I don't care." Maureen slid Tricia upright and studied her. "I don't see any wounds, baby. Can you tell Mommie what happened?" Her own hands shaking, she lifted Tricia's and turned them over, inspecting each finger. She peered into the child's dark-blue eyes and was startled by their sharpness. "Sweetie, what *happened?*"

Still holding the phone, his breathing quick and shallow, Andrew said, "Maybe she had a nosebleed?"

Maureen backed away from her daughter. The girl scrambled off the high counter and dropped to her feet, stared at her grandmother with hard eyes, then glanced up at her parents. Neither adult moved when she took several tentative steps toward the fallen woman to stand in the growing pool of blood; neither made an effort to stop her when she bent, tore off the old woman's nose, and stuffed it into her mouth.

Andrew hung the receiver on its hook and joined Maureen. "She *was* Tricia's favorite grandmother."

"Yes," agreed Maureen, watching her daughter chew. "And it's not as if the old bitch didn't *owe* us . . ."

Third Rail

Wayne Allen Sallee

Clohessy watched Raine's blue Civic head back toward the Kennedy on-ramp; then he turned, zippering his jacket as he took the down escalator steps two at a time to the concourse leading to the El train. The Kennedy overpass was deserted and he stood for several minutes staring out at the eight lanes of weekend traffic—four on each side of the Jefferson Park/Congress/Douglas rapid transit line.

Then he noticed the girl.

Before looking back at her a second time, Clohessy—time-scheduled commuter that he was—glanced north, saw that the train was nowhere near arriving at the terminal. He had been chilled crossing the parking lot, yet the girl below him was wearing only a pair of jeans and a white sweater that clung tight to her waist. A loose gilded belt completed the image. Clichéd as it was, she looked as if her body had been poured into her clothing. The sweater was pushed up around her elbows. Maybe he'd offer her his gloves after he'd handled business.

Clohessy walked briskly down the glass-and-stainless-steel corridor to those stairs leading to the El platform. It was after 10 P.M.; the ticket agent's booth was closed. He'd have to pay on the train and took a second to make certain he had small bills. The conductor wouldn't be able to break a twenty.

Clohessy never carried a comb, so he ran a hand through his thin blond hair (not that it would matter in the sharp late-September wind), pushed through the gate and took the down escalator. Halfway to the platform, he caught a flash of the girl's sweater, a creamy slice of arm. As cold as it was, and my, how the hair on her arms *danced*.

Clohessy had been disappointed to leave Raine's place so early, but he'd had a two-hour trek on public transportation to the Southwest Side ahead of him; he enjoyed Raine and Peg's company and likely wouldn't see them again until Lilah Chaney's party in Virginia next February. Yet seeing the girl on the platform made him momentarily forget the last few hours.

As Clohessy's shoes clacked onto the concrete, she turned to look at him. He met her gaze and she glanced quickly away. She did not seem concerned about whether the train was coming; she didn't seem impatient in her movements, and, after the first five minutes Clohessy had watched her from the corner of his eye, she hadn't once leaned out, over the tracks (as most people—himself included—usually did).

He looked at the digital clock on the Northern Trust Bank across the Kennedy: 53° at 11:09. If he was ever going to strike up a conversation with the girl, he'd have to do it now; the train would be there by quarter after.

Walking the ten or so steps to where she was standing, Clohessy jammed his fists into his pockets, realizing just as he neared her that he was wearing his spring jacket and that he'd sound pretty damn stupid offering her his gloves when he'd left them on his coatrack back in his apartment! Embarrassed, he swung away.

The platform rumbled; he turned to stare north. It was only a plane leaving from O'Hare, a mile away. Clohessy whistled tunelessly, rubbernecked. The sign above him read BOARD HERE FOR TRAINS TO LOOP & WEST SIDE. The dull white neon lines flickered. The clock at the bank now said: 52° at 11:11. A huge tanker truck obscured the red neon Mona Koni restaurant sign as it made wide turn into the parking lot of Dominick's.

Sighing, Clohessy began watching for signs of life in one of the lighted upper floors of an office building to the far side of I-90's left lanes. When he turned again, the girl was gone. Clohessy glanced up at the escalators. From where he stood, he saw the bottom fifteen steps of the two stairwells, with the escalator in the middle, before they disappeared out of sight behind the overhead ads for Camel Filters and Salem Lights. He was still surprised by how well kept and graffiti-free the El station was.

Clohessy saw a blurred flash of color.

The girl was riding the rails on the *up* escalator. He smiled, amazed. Slipping back into sight from above, she'd slide down nearly to the bottom before stopping, then glide back up. Clohessy watched her straddle the moving stairwell a half dozen times, saw her ride up in a kind of swimming sidestroke. She was gorgeous. Her sweater had hiked up over her hip, exposing more flesh. Her hair fell across her face.

She turned to stare at Clohessy, winked. He touched his collar, glanced away at the bank clock again, too flustered even to notice the time. He looked back; again she was gone from sight.

Clohessy heard whistling and catcalls from above. *Male* voices. The voices came nearer, accompanied by the sound of sneakers on the concrete stairs. Clohessy calculated four separate voices, fretted for the girl. All four men wore slicked-back hair, he saw when they reached bottom; all wore lime-green fall windbreakers. Each carried a bag of some kind. They walked closer. Behind them, the girl slid back down the rail. She stared at the men, but with boredom.

Once they had reached the glare of the sodium lamps, Clohessy realized why the girl wasn't afraid of them, and, for what seemed like the twelfth time that night, he felt extremely stupid. They weren't gang members. The jackets advertised Szostak's Tavern.

The four guys were a Polish bowling team.

Within minutes, the southbound train pulled in. The bowlers got on, heading toward Milwaukee Avenue; Clohessy was certain. He glanced at the time. 11:18. Still plenty of time to catch the Archer bus downtown. He'd wait around to see what the girl was going to do. She seemed in no hurry to leave. Maybe she was waiting for Clohessy to make his move.

The southbound train was now far in the distance. The girl hadn't come back down the escalator since the train was in the station. Clohessy, inching closer to the stairwell and her, heard a shuffling sound from the concourse above. Probably her boyfriend showing—

He saw something white, lying flat on one of the escalator steps lowering to the platform. White with splashes of red.

Descending.

Red nails on a girl's hand.

Red veins at the wrist.

Descending. Catching on the edge of the platform grille and flipping up. Her hand, severed at the wrist, hideous in the green glow seeping up from the escalator's bowels. Creating a ghastly cast of shadows from her dead veins and finger joints.

Then her corpse followed, riding the rail down, lines of blood sprayed across the chrome. Her eyes, forever open, still had the bored look she had given the bowlers.

Then, also riding the rail down, toward Clohessy, the man with the knife.

Coochie-Coo

Mark McNease

Eddy's eyes burned when he opened them, each brown iris floating in a pool of red. He jerked his head forward, as if the receding nightmare had shaken him by the shoulders or drilled like a fist into his spine with its vicious images. His muscles, constantly alert and prepared, contracted sharply and he bolted upright in his seat. Sweat adhered his clothes to him; sweat unrelieved in the hot, stagnant air of the bus.

He listened with the nerves of a rabbit to the sounds around him—nothing now but the hum of the engine.

Time had passed. He guessed it had been a long while, judging from the empty seats. Only one other passenger remained, a woman sitting directly in front of him with a baby peering over her shoulder.

A curious baby with wet blue eyes.

A fat, hairless baby sucking its thumb. Staring at him.

Everyone else was gone.

Eddy's sleep had been fitful at best, plagued by a dream he'd floated in and out of for hours. It was more like a memory than a nightmare: stabbed in the Portland depot, cornered in the men's room by a thief like himself who thought nothing of putting a blade in him over ill-chosen words. A skinny black man with yellow teeth whose knife hand he remembered too clearly for dreams; a thumb and three fingers twisting into his belly.

Plunging in.

Digging.

He clenched his shirttail, pulling it up to expose his abdomen. *God I don't wanna die don't let me die.* Without looking down he ran his palm over the skin, expecting to feel dried blood with the sweat. *Not on a bus please not on a bus.* Nothing. It had been a dream after all.

He exhaled loudly, following it with a laugh that cut through the stillness. He slapped his thigh. "Goddamn, Eddy boy," he said half-aloud to reassure himself, "you got the luck. You sure do got the luck!"

He carefully rubbed his eyes, trying to soothe the sting that bit with every blink of his lids. The smell of his hands made him grimace. It was the odor of long days and nights on the road, the pungent aroma of sweat and the dirt of traveling that builds from a film to a tangible layer of filth. He sniffed, familiar with the places it came from—doorknobs and benches and cigarette butts plucked greedily from the sidewalk. His grimace changed to the smile of a child who has found his way home.

Eddy leaned back and wiped his hands on the knees of his jeans. He immersed himself in that feeling of *home.* This was it: riding down a deserted highway with a dozen destinations to choose from. He wouldn't let them kick him out this time, or lock him up with common drunks. He wouldn't let them give him rules and regulations, or wag their righteous fingers at the kid gone bad, saying, "Why can't you be like your *brother?* He made something of himself in the exciting and challenging world of data processing. *He* gets to meet interesting people every day. But you, Eddy Brisk? You're a schmuck. A zero."

He flinched at the memories. They were useless to him, like love or duty to the family he'd detached himself from five years before. A family content with being slaves to boredom while he, Steady Eddy Brisk, insisted on freedom. Unconditional freedom.

Certain law-enforcement agencies argued that he wouldn't keep it for long. They said stealing wasn't freedom, but crime. *Well,* Eddy thought, grinning with the teeth he had left, *they ain't caught me yet. I got the luck. I sure do got the luck.* Secure in the knowledge of his good fortune, he leaned forward to spit on the floor. When he lifted his head he realized that the baby was staring at him, its fingers dug into the gray cotton of its mother's blouse. Eddy winked and made a face, sticking his tongue out while crossing his eyes.

The baby was not amused.

Eddy nodded. "Name's Brisk," he said. "Rhymes with risk." He laughed, certain the mother would turn around to glare down her nose at him. When she didn't respond, Eddy assumed she was asleep. *Dumb bitch is out of it,* he thought with a smirk. *Just as well. One less mom to snatch her brat away from me.*

He curled his index finger, hooking it several times like a worm sticking up from an apple. "Coochie-coo," he said, his voice more a grate than a whisper.

The baby just kept staring, its cool blue eyes too large for its face; round blue eyes that were oddly developed for a child so small.

Eyes that didn't blink, gazing intently with what Eddy suddenly took for contempt.

He drew back in his seat, not wanting to play anymore. "You're weird," he said. "Can't be more than two years old and you're fucking weird." He ran a grimy hand across his forehead, wondering why sweat had beaded there. He passed it off with a phlegm-stained chuckle and turned his attention to the landscape outside.

Dust covered the window. Most of it was external, but not all of it. By wiping the glass with his sleeve, Eddy was able to see into the darkness. He peered out, expecting to catch a glimpse of the hills they were surely descending as the bus wound down through northern California. Relieved that they must be hundreds of miles from the redneck bastion called Oregon, he grinned as he gazed inches from the windowpane.

His smile dropped quickly, his mouth opening in a gape. *Desert.* He wiped frantically at the glass. *Desert. Long endless cold desert.*

He sat back, perspiring heavily, cursing himself for drinking so much. *Damn,* he thought. *I got on the wrong bus! Jesus. How long was I asleep?* He closed his eyes and slowed his breathing, trying to calm himself. Thinking. He decided he must be headed for Vegas. Of course. Where else would his drunken mind have thought to take him? He was always grand when he drank. Always had his plans.

He slumped into the seat cushion. He opened and closed his eyes several times, squinting tightly, attempting to dispel the tension building just inside his skull. He didn't want to go to Vegas. He'd had trouble there. *No problem.* Somebody might remember him. *You got the luck.* Maybe it would be all right. Maybe he was on a roll. His fear began to subside.

And the baby stared.

It dawned on Eddy that the child had been watching him all this time. *Obnoxious little shit.* He looked away, surveying the seats across the aisle. *Where is everybody?* Apparently no one was much interested in Vegas. *Awful damn dark in here.*

He brought his head back around only to discover that the baby was still staring. He glared back, his annoyance mixed with apprehension. "It's not polite to stare," he said.

The baby paid him no mind. It had taken its thumb out of its mouth and used its hands to climb up on the woman's shoulder. A little bit farther.

A little bit closer.

Studying the man whose sweat blended with fear to spice the air.

Staring.

Two small, pudgy hands alternately digging into and releasing the shoulder it perched against.

Staring.

Its androgynous yellow jumpsuit failing to be cheerful.

Staring.

Eddy squirmed in his seat. He laughed nervously, thinking how foolish it was to be disturbed by a baby. Still, it had the strangest eyes he'd ever seen. As if they knew everything—where he'd been and where he was going. All that he'd done in his thirty-two years, and all he'd never accomplished. He found himself caught in its unblinking gaze, slipping away, his eyelids growing heavy.

He snapped out of it with a quick, jerking motion. He thought of other things—anything but the bus and the baby. *Headed for Vegas.* He covered his face with his hands, smelling the filth on them. *Portland to Vegas.* He turned to the window, confused by the stretching desert. *Stabbed in Portland. Left for dead. Son of a bitch took my money. Bleeding.* He grabbed his stomach, pressing his fingers into the flesh, feeling for a gash. *No gash. No money either.* He patted his pockets. *Going to Vegas no money.*

Eddie threw himself against the cushion behind him. His breathing had accelerated; he could hear it escaping in short, fierce puffs through his nose. As panic heightened his senses, he saw the woman's purse nestled between the seats. A common purse, it was, beige cotton with one dark letter in a pattern like a designer item, or a cheap imitation. A clearance-sale purse that no doubt held lipstick, Kleenex, sunglasses, and money. *Got to have some money.* Not much, but some. *Got to have some money.*

He debated with himself for the next five minutes. If he reach up slowly, cautiously, he could slip the pocketbook out of the purse without a sound. But he could get caught. The woman could wake up, start screaming, have him arrested at the next bus station.

After weighing the consequences, he quietly leaned forward.

And *it* watched him.

He slid his arm between the seats, taking what seemed an eternity to get to the other side.

And it wouldn't take its eyes off him.

With just the slightest pressure, he pushed his forearm through. Years of skill paid off when he grasped the latch. Muffling the noise with his palm, Eddy snapped the purse open.

And *it* grabbed his arm, digging its fat little fingers into his flesh.

Eddy gasped, looking up, found himself pierced by those ice-blue eyes.

"Coochie-coo," it hissed. A shrill laugh escaped its mouth. A squeal of delight.

Eddy tried to pull his arm back. It was stuck between the seats, partly from his twisting away from the baby's grasp but mostly from fear.

Out of the corner of his eye he saw the woman's torso move. He glanced up, knowing she would glare at him, accuse and loathe him. He dreaded what he would see in her face.

What he saw was nothing. No eyes. No nose. No mouth. Just the front of a skull covered tightly with skin. Turning away with his heart racing, Eddy saw where the woman ended and the baby began—up near her right shoulder—growing and wriggling and laughing. Sprouting like a tumor. Being her eyes. Her mouth. Her terrible shriek of pleasure as *it* dug into his arm, pulling it up to cut its teeth on him.

A wetness began to spread near Eddy's waist. It could have been urine. He knew it was blood.

The Wulgaru

Bill Ryan

Michael Aloysius Curry was nineteen when Caitlin O'Shea fanned his desperate love into an act of revenge. Revenge for his brother, Dion. Mick's and Caitlin's plastique had left one paratrooper legless in the Falls Road, another's brains running down his back. The legless one rose somehow, a spray of petrol smoldering on his flak vest. Caitlin ran as the para bore Mick through the broken bow window of Fihelly's florists, where Cup Final wreath crisped.

The para knew the Brothers Curry from the papers. Dion's suicide in Belfast's Maze Prison had given the press a martyr and they'd plastered young Mick's confirmation picture everywhere. Eamon Curry's eldest had looked angelic with his arm around the lovely Caitlin.

But an unchristian eye might have noted the kerosone burns Dion had suffered in lighting the neighbors' tomcat.

The soldiers had wanted names, read Mick's terror as defiance. Even as the bayonet burned his knuckles, though, he was no Judas. One finger fell among the charred Cup flowers.

Then, cheek to cheek, he betrayed every IRA lad he had met through Dion. The girl? No, he'd never grass on Caitlin, never! The para began to cry for the woman in Kingussie who would soon be his widow and lopped off another of young Curry's fingers as he died. Mick wriggled out of the glass and embers, and ran . . .

Ten years had left him graying, ruddy, and soft; only the brittle green eyes remained of the boy Mick. Sucking brandy, he decided this vigil for wild boars on a pile of rocks in outback Australia had been a mistake. His ghosts were no more bound to Belfast than he.

"You won't see the pigs at this rate, sport." Jo Pitman retrieved the bottle, took a slow swig of amber. Under her Stetson the brassy sunset glowed in her eyes.

"Yeah." The two fingers of Mick's right hand checked his rifle for the tenth time. The dum-dums hadn't walked away.

"They're coming down," Jo said.

He heard faint squeals and snorts. He looked down from his rocky perch. The waterhole burned. The pigs were black shadows against it. He brought the rifle to his shoulder, jerked the trigger. His slug bounced off a boar's skull, knocked it to its knees. It struggled up, squealing. Mick put a round through its chest. *Reload . . . slow.* Pigs, they were running. But two more dropped before the rest were gone.

"Thought they'd be bigger."

The sun was fat and red when they reached the first carcass.

"Like that movie, *Razorback?*" Jo showed Mick a crooked smile. "You want a buffalo, sport!"

She slid a hunting knife from her boot, then hacked a tusk three inches long from the pig's jaw. "In Spain, you get the bull's ears and tail. Reckon this'll look better round your neck."

Mick laughed, then noticed the fine silver links hanging from the boar's mouth. A bracelet was bent around the peg-like teeth. Jo's knife levered them apart and he worked it free. Earth removed the blood and pus.

Jo snatched the dangling diabetic ID bracelet and raced back to her antique Jeep. Mick weaved after her.

"Where are we going?" he asked.

"Nev Yagunjil's the only diabetic round here. An aboriginal, not far off."

Still muzzy, he managed to puke overboard as they bounced over ruts. Like a dream, the Jeep growled across a dry lake, and the red-and-gray waste took wing. The parrots were the colors of the clay, invisible until startled into flight. The eye of a raucous hurricane, Mick clutched the Jeep's roll bar and his head.

In no time, Jo's apricot singlet and shorts were soaked. Her sandy hair swung in damp rattails. His own shirt was a sweat rag and his skin glowed pink where he wasn't caked in dust.

Jo braked at a steep ridge and dug out a first-aid kit. Mick followed over red earth and boulders peeled like onions by sun an frost. Shards cut the soles of his Nikes.

The granite fell to a sapphire pool ringed by pale mulga trees, which sheltered a monstrosity of corrugated iron and slabs of bark. Tarpaulins made the shanty resemble a shipwreck.

"Nev?" Jo slid down the loose rock without waiting for a reply that never came.

Most of Nev Yagunjil was on the far side of the shanty. The pigs had scattered him like terriers with a rag. The aboriginal's face and scalp hung from a spiny bush, a child's discarded mask watching blowflies troop on his bones and goanna lizards squabble for any morsel left by the pigs.

Jo turned green but choked it down. The awful find had no effect on Mick: this wasn't a corpse, it was a jigsaw. He held Jo until the spasms eased. Finally she stuck that pugnacious cleft in her chin up at him and said, "Thanks."

The peeled skull turned to face them. Jo screamed. It nodded sadly at Mick's approach. The left temple was staved in; a red goanna unraveled from inside the cranium and fled on its hind legs. The skull spun and stopped with the jagged hole up.

"Could pigs have done that, Jo?"

She shook her head.

"Looks like someone took a shillelagh to him."

"Or a rock." Jo turned it with a twig.

A wedge of flint was embedded in bone near the hole. Mick steered her toward the shanty before she bit through her lip.

Under the tarp awnings, a toadlike paw had drawn an aboriginal hunter into the hollow stump of a baobab. Yagunjil had carved him skinless, after the black style. Each knot of muscle, each filigreed vein, stood out. So did the terror in those naked features. Mick resisted the temptation to cover that nightmare with Yagunjil's own face.

"Pretty horrific," he said.

"His Dreamtime Legends series," Jo grunted. "Nev even had the wood and stone trucked in from the original tribal lands."

The workshop was dark. As their vision adapted, they saw a carpet of bloodstained sketches. Flies ran down the crusty streaks on walls.

Another of the artist's flayed men stood by a hurricane lamp burning with the tiniest blue spark. The wood smelled old; rotten. Flies delved the incisions for blood and swarmed on its horrible right hand. The limbs and the fingers were articulated with knotted human hair.

Mick winced. "What's that great ugly thing?" he asked.

"The wulgaru legend." She shuddered, pulled herself erect. "A *kurdaitcha* man supposedly freed an evil spirit from a tree by carving it into human shape. Then it ran amok; real Frankenstein stuff. I don't recall all the details. This was to be Nev's last piece. He was months finding the right Gidgee log."

Mick squinted. "Are those eyes opal?"

"Quartz." She shuffled paper. "These drawings . . ."

"What about them?"

"Nev was fanatical about 'feeling the spirit in the wood,' then paring away 'all else.' He never before planned a work, Mick."

"So he put *this* spook on paper, eh?" Mick turned the

sketch. There was a thumbmark in the charcoal rendering of a rough log. He could almost see hateful eyes and hair like smoke. Caitlin O'Shea, he thought, seen through tears.

Jo was gone. The chop of a shovel led Mick to her. She was digging a grave. He offered to spell her.

"Lousy holiday for you, Irish."

"It's different."

They collected the bones in a rusty oil drum and rolled it into the grave. The sun died behind the mulga as they tamped dark soil on Yagunjil's impromptu bier.

"Have we just illicitly disposed of a body?" he asked, suddenly anxious.

"Sport, the nearest cop is six hundred klicks east. I radio him from town, he gets Homicide to fly up from Brisbane. Three days. This way, there's something for them to poke at."

"Oh." Mick wiped his forehead. His wrist left a stripe of sunburned skin in the ocher dust. Jo drew circles on his cheeks.

"Let's lose the warpaint, chief."

After a stiff progress to the pool, their tension scraped away with the dust. Jo stepped out of her shorts. Scanties white against her tan, she jackknifed into the pool. She spat and slicked her hair back. "Well?"

No great swimmer, Mick was worried by the depth. Despite her whistle he felt ridiculous in his boxer shorts. An explosive belly-flop proved the water both deep and cold. He swallowed a howl and kicked for the surface.

"Unique style, Irish," said Jo.

Mick's dog paddle barely kept him up. "That's how we do it in the Auld Sod."

He floated, watched the first stars appear. The cool quiet recalled a boy mounting rotten steps in a Belfast boarding-house. Whitewashed glass turned the light to sour cream and cobwebs. He'd perched breathless on the widow's walk as the world rolled away to the mountains of Mourne. His dreaming place, refuge from Dion's malice. He'd trusted it to Caitlin and she'd made it a deadly cache.

He remembered fierce love and the hate that fed it. Mick had joined the Na Fianna Eirann after the Orangemen smashed his father's kneecaps, but even that shining hate hadn't nourished itself as Caitlin's did. If Mick hadn't loved his brother, he'd done his duty.

Love, hate and duty! No wonder he was enchanted by this uncomplicated Australian lass.

Jo splashed him. She laughed and swallowed water. Coughs lured him in for another volley. They caught each other's wrists and traded fierce grins.

"Ten dollars says I can duck you," she said.

"You're on." Mick knew he had the weight advantage, but Jo was solid and fitter than he'd ever been. He kissed her to break her grip. Even though it was necessarily hard and clumsy and he held it too long, Jo didn't back off.

"Cards on the table, Mick."

"Not quartz, eh?"

"Color, mate. Worth a packet."

"So why are we talking about it?"

Jo refilled the lamp and threw light on Nev's wulgaru and its stone eyes. She chewed a knuckle in thought. "Jeez, I'll be yanking Nev's gold teeth next."

"Didn't have any."

She made a face. "Real funny. I hate myself for doing this."

A shrug. "Then go."

"And hate myself for passing it up?" Jo's exasperated smile made him laugh. "So make yourself useful, sport!"

He chose a knife and chipped away the dark resin holding the opals. As he pried one loose, his hand slipped. A flint tooth drew blood. "You bastard!" he yelped.

Getting a solid grip on the jaw, he yanked the opal out.

But his triumphal laugh was punctuated by the clasp of stone—and pain. Confused, he jerked back his hand—

And his right *thumb* was gone. Mick stared at where it belonged in agony, disbelief. His knees turned to water then, making him sag, sparing him Yagunjil's fate. Incredibly, a graven arm skinned his cheek. *(A* kurdaitcha *man freed an evil spirit from a tree.* . .) Striking the worktable with all his weight, Mick inadvertently tipped the lamp onto the littered floor.

From there, astonished, he watched the unbearably ugly wulgaru creak and writhe. Behind the fire. Flies rose from it in a lazy swarm. Mick's hand was a red rubber glove, so Jo, glancing back up at the horror, knotted something white around his wrist.

"It got my *thumb.*" He said it wonderingly, feebly. The world was eating his *hand,* bits at a time.

"Keep pissing claret like that and it'll get the rest of you kosher." Her panties stanched the blood but not before covering her, making her an abstract in red below the navel. "We've got to—"

Suddenly, wagging limbs writhing with human hair, the wulgaru splintered a bark wall and fled the fire. The shanty groaned alarmingly; that sound and the icon's terrible, carved face penetrated the shock that had held Mick paralyzed. He grabbed Jo's wrist and they dodged under flapping sheets of flame that had been the canvas roof. Scarcely escaping, they saw that the wulgaru had lurched between them and the ridge. Now it was herding them back toward the water and into it with a loud splash. Holding onto Jo, Mick dashed quickly to the deepest point, pursued by the monster.

Its ghastly head cocked its remaining eye at them and then sank . . .

"We're safe!" Mick exclaimed. "The bastard can't swim!" Treading water, he sucked his thumb joint, fought weakness.

"C'mon, we can't lose too much—"

Abruptly, silt boiled up around them.

Jo stared at Mick. "It's . . . *walking*. Along *the bottom!*"

Then the water promptly closed over her with a hiss.

With their fingers twined, Mick was dragged under also. He tried to see. Silver bubbled from her nose but her cheeks were full. Jo had had time for one quick breath. He wriggled down beneath her arm, into the milk, saw the living legend.

The wulgaru had hooked her calf muscles! Mick tried hard, couldn't budge so much as one claw. The wulgaru grinned at him. Content to hold her, it flaunted Mick's helplessness. In desperation, he gnawed at wood and sinew alike but was ignored.

Raw lungs decided it. Mick had no choices. He kicked away after seeing Jo's lips as a blue circle, her eyes already mercifully shut.

Nikes on, hand bundled in his shirt, Mick ran up the ridge. Granite scattered beneath his feet and his knees became thoroughly barked before a final spill dropped him near their Jeep, and the rifles. He had never been so frightened, quite.

Above him, the wooden horror crested the ridge. Even from there it reeked, it stank. But Mick was waiting. He blew splinters out of its chest, cast around for something with more clout, then fumbled with the key in the ignition.

The Jeep croaked to life. Momentarily, the wulgaru seemed bewildered by the contraption thundering at it. Mick whooped, elbowed a steady bleat from the horn. Claws exploded the windscreen and tore the headrest off the driver's seat. Mick ducked and brained himself on the wheel as wood smashed under the back wheels.

Mick braked as the wulgaru got up, designs crushed and scored, the wicked jaw ripped off. It swung the severed left arm like a scythe . . .

* * *

That last Belfast summer, a shoelace had saved his life. He'd balanced against a lampost with blistered green paint and wished for more fingers or fewer jars of Guinness under his belt. Five minutes spent on the Gordian knot (ties were still insoluble) gave black fatigues with Heckler-Koch automatics time to cordon off his street. One scanned the crowd for a face in a Polaroid.

From Malone's tobacconists, Mick could see the gabled bulk of his boardinghouse. Caitlin would have rung Malone's if she'd escaped. Was she hiding under the widow's walk? With the plastique?

It was quiet such a long time, Mick almost believed she'd surrendered . . . then the roof of the brownstone vomited into the street.

And such shameful peace swept over him! Mick had always imagined Caitlin O'Shea's driving hatred as a separate entity, even a demon; how else could he love her? Her death opened cellars of his mind that loved Caitlin not at all. Love a black fire that devoured Dion and would have destroyed him? His heart rebelled against that cold vision and he'd run so far this time.

And the hate had found him, after all.

The brandy bottle tapped his heels. He screwed it open and watched the monster advance through the glass. He never took that swig.

The Jeep had bled oil and petrol over the wooden man . . .
Inspired, Mick bit a linen strip from his shirt and soaked it well. He wadded the rag down the neck and lit it from the Jeep dash. When he could smell the rot, Mick gunned the engine and threw the bottle. The wulgaru was cloaked in blazing mist. Sinews of hair spat and melted as it smacked the flames in mute parody of a burning man.

Stones rattled the Jeep's belly. The grade was too steep, the left wheels chewed into thin air. Mick jumped—his shirt was tangled in the roll bar.

The steel banshee crushed him.

Consciousness hurt.

The moon wept a rainbow tear that stung his eye and lip. Gasoline. The "moon" was the skewed lid of the gas tank. The Jeep had capsized, pinned him.

A giant eye hanging by its nerves, one headlight threw its beam down the broken slope. The wulgaru hobbled through the light, blackened chest alive with fiery worms.

Only a flood of adrenaline kept Mick out of shock.

"You look like I feel, Woody," he muttered.

Rotten wood crackled in answer.

Another drop of gasoline burned Mick's eye and was ignored. That cold purpose Caitlin must have felt on the widow's walk filled him. His free arm was nerveless meat; the cap of the gas tank was slick, jarred off its thread. He lacked the strength to turn it. He didn't need to. As his hair sizzled in the wulgaru's fist, Mick kept a death grip on that cap.

He didn't feel the gasoline sluice over them.

The Luckiest Man in the World

Rex Miller

"Zulu six, Zulu six." He could imagine the PRC crackling, the bored tone of somebody's RTO going, "Dragon says he's got movement about fifty meters to his Sierra Whisky, do you read me? Over." And the spit of intercom garble. Guy in the C & C bird keying a handset, saying whatever he says. Fucking lifer somewhere up there generations removed from the bad bush. Yeah, I copy you, Lumpy Charlie, Lima Charlie, Lumpy Chicken. Whatever he says. Bird coming down. Charlie moving at the edge of the woods. Thua Thien Province. Northern Whore Corps. The beast killing for peace, back then. Dirty-Dozened out of the slammer by military puppeteers. Set in place by the spooks. Very real, however.

"Chaingang" his nickname. The fattest killer in the Nam. Thriving on blast-furnace heat like some fucking plant. He was the beast. He had killed more than any other living being. Over four hundred humans, he thought. A waddling death machine. "Gangbang" they would call him out of earshot. "Hippo." He had heard them. Other names he ignored. These arrogant children who knew nothing about death.

He flashed on the woods, so similar to these, and to a pleasant memory from long ago. He was about two miles from the house.

"There goes Bobby Ray," the woman called to her husband, who was bringing logs in, and watched a truck throw gravel.

"Nnn," he grunted in the manner of someone who had been married a long time.

"He's another one don't have anything to do but run the road all day."

The husband said nothing, loading kindling.

"Drive up and down, up and down, drive a daggone pickup like he was a millionaire." She had a shrewish, sharp voice that grated on a man, he thought. He put a large log down in the hot stove.

"Now you gonna' run to town to pick up that daggone tractor thing an' you coulda' got it yesterday when you was in there at Harold's, but *nooooooo*." She was a pain in the ass. "*You* couldn't be bothered." She was working herself up the way she always liked to do, he thought. He knew the old bitch like a damn book. "You waste a fortune on gas for that truck and—"

He spoke for the first time in hours. "Go get the boy."

"Then you expect us to get by with the crop money bad as it was last year and—" She just went on like he hadn't said anything. He looked over at her with those hard, flat eyes. She shut her mouth for a second, then said, "I don't know where he's at. He'll be back in a minute. Anyway, you don't seem to realize . . ." And she was droning on about how he always thought he could write it off on the tax and that. Christ on a *crutch*, if he hadn't heard that a thousand blamed times, he hadn't heard it once!

Wasn't that the way of a woman? Worry you to damn death about some little piddling thing all the time! He sat down at the kitchen table and pulled out his beat-up wallet, opened it. She had the food money. He had the gin check and the check ol' Lathrop had given him, what—three weeks back?—and he better cash that dude if it was any good anyhow. He'd dump the woman and the boy and he'd go cash the checks and make the deposit and there'd be enough left over to get some suds. He could taste the first one right now. Sharp bite of the shot and then that nice cool taste of the foam off the head of the beer.

She was running that mouth all the time, man couldn't even count his money. Going on about Bobby Ray Crawford but he knew it was her way of goading him. He'd get her in the truck and that would do it. She always shut up when they went someplace. He was getting warm in the kitchen with the hot fire going, but *damn* he couldn't stand to listen to that shrill hen anymore, and he got up and pulled his coat off the peg and stomped back outside to find the boy.

The boy had just come out of the woods on the south of the house. Thick woods maybe ten meters from the edge of the fields in back of the house, and he and the dog had been kicking around in there looking for squirrel sign and what not. Shit, the boy thought to himself, fuckin' Aders done killed off all the fuckin' squirrel. Otis and Bucky Aders had hunted all this ground to damn death for ten years. You didn't hardly see no sign at all no more. Once in a while where they cut but shit, they was plumb hunted out.

The dog was what the beast had heard as he entered the woods from the south side; just a faint, yapping bark that had penetrated one of his kill fantasies as he walked down the pathway that obviously led to a treeline. (Hearing the faint noise on another level of awareness and tucking it away in his data storage system for later retrieval.)

Life for the beast had been largely lived that way, in fantasy, daydreaming half the time, living out the fantasies the other time. Imagined flights to lift him first from his hellish childhood of torture and degradation, and mind games to alleviate the pain of suffering. Then, later, the thoughts to vaporize that claustrophobic ennui of long institutionalization.

So it was not in the least unusual for the hulking beast to be fantasizing as he cautiously made his way through the woods.

For a time he had daydreamed about killing—the preoccupation that was his ever-present companion, the thing he liked the best, the destruction of the human beings—and the terrain had triggered pleasant memories. As he carefully negotiated the swampy area around a large pond, he imagined the vegetation-choked floor and green, canopied ceiling of a South Vietnamese jungle, and the shadows of tall trees and wait-a-minute vines, and the triggering of a daydream alerted him to the presence of possible danger.

There were always parallels to be found. This, for example, was rice country. Here in this flatland in between the old river levees you could easily imagine a field crisscrossed by paddy dykes. Where he would have been watching for traps, falls, mines, and the footprints of the little people, here he watched for hunters.

The beast loved to come upon armed hunters in the woods and he had been fantasizing about a dad and his son; shotguns he would later take; a dog. How easily he would do the man, then stun the boy and use him before he did him, too. The thought of the boy filled him with red-hot excitement that immediately tingled in his groin and plastered a wide, grotesque smile across his doughy countenance. His smile of joy was a fearsome thing.

How easy and enjoyable it would be to do the daddy first. Take the boy's shotgun away. *Lad,* he thought. Take the *lad's* shotgun, then bind and gag and hurt him. How easy and necessary it would become to cause the pain that would bring his relief. He had the killer's gifts—the survival talents—but he'd learned that it was in those times of biological need, when the scarlet tide washed through him, that he had to be particularly cautious. Sometimes when he did the bad things he became careless.

He was not an ignorant man and in some ways he was extremely intelligent. According to one of the men in the prison where the beast had been confined, a Dr. Norman, he was a sort-of genius. "A physical precognate," Dr. Norman had told him, "who transcended the normalcy of the human ones." He was grossly abnormal. He did not find this an unpleasant thought.

The beast saw himself as Death, as a living embodiment of it, and he had availed himself of all the death literature during long periods of incarceration, devouring anything from clinicians to Horacio Quiroga. And none of it touched him. Death was outside of these others. He thought perhaps Dr. Norman was right, in his rather bizarre theorizing. But it was of no consequence to him either way.

The beast knew nothing of presentient powers. It was simply a matter of experience; preparation; trusting the vibes and gut instincts; listening to the inner rumblings; staying in harmony with one's environment; riding with the tide; keeping the sensors out there.

He could not fantasize because of inner rumblings that had intruded upon his pleasureful thoughts, but these were the demands for food. His appetites were all insatiable, and he was very hungry, had been for the entire morning.

Instinctively, he knew the small animals could be had. Their tiny heartbeats were nearby and he homed in on such vibrations with deadly and unerring accuracy, but this was not the time for game. He wanted real food and lots of it. He salivated at the thought of the cheese and the meat of the enchiladas he'd eaten the evening before. He was *HUNGRY.* It had been the last food he'd had in thirteen, maybe thirteen and a half hours, and his massive stomach growled in protest.

The beast was six feet seven inches tall, heavy with hard, rubbery fat across his chest, belly, and buttocks. Four hundred pounds of hatred and insanity. His human name was Daniel Edward Flowers Bunkowski-Zandt, although the Zandt part wasn't even on the official dossiers or the sophisticated computer printouts. They also had his age wrong by a year, but the fact that he had weighed fourteen pounds at birth was quite correct. His powerful fingers could penetrate a chest cavity. He had once become so enraged that he had squashed a *flashlight battery*—so strong was his grip.

It would be incorrect to say that the beast hated humans. In fact, he enjoyed them. Enjoyed hunting them just as sportsmen enjoy killing game; much the same. He differed only in that he liked to torture his game first, before he killed it. Cat-and-mouse games with his play pretties. Sex sometimes. But then when the heat and the bright-red waves were at their highest ebb, he would take their hearts. He would devour the hearts of his enemy—the human beings—and that was what he loved.

The beast whose human name was Danny-Boy wished that it were summer or at least that the pecan trees to the west had something for him. There would be nothing on the ground, either, he knew. *No sweet pecan nutmeats for Danny*. But that was all right. He'd be out of the woods, literally and figuratively. And with that he stepped daintily over a rotten log in his big 15-EEEEE bata-boos, and he *was* out of the woods, in plain view of houses and traffic. With surprising quickness the huge beast dropped back into the cover of the trees.

"Them fuckin' river rats done hunted *out* ever'thing awready. Pah-paw," the kid whined as he patted the hound absentmindedly. "Fuckin' Punk," he said without malice.

"Them fuckin' river rats enjoy life ten times more'n *you* ever will," his father told him. Let him chew on *that* a bit. "Let's go," he said, and got into the Ford pickup.

Bunkowski saw the woman leave the house from where he stood, frozen immobile behind a massive oak. Watching the faraway tableau from his vantage point. He saw the boy climb over the side and get into the bed of the truck, for some reason. The woman came out, did something and went back inside momentarily, came back out and got into the truck. The gate was lowered and the hound jumped into the truck; the beast saw it pull out slowly, go out of sight, then reappear to the east of the tar-papered home.

The beast looked up and the sky corroborated his inner clock, which ticked with a frightening machinelike precision at all times. He saw that it was after 9:30 A.M. (It *was* 9:32, at that second. He had not looked at a clock or watch for over thirteen hours.) In a second's camera-eye blink he saw that there was no corn in the field, saw the dangers of the road to his east and west, then turned and slogged through the woods toward the fence he'd seen.

Stepping over the rusting barbed wire he emerged cautiously from the safety of the woods, made his way in the direction of the house. He knew certain things and it was not part of his character to question how he knew there was a horse or horses pasturing close by, that traffic would be a light but continuous presence on the gravel road, that nobody else was in the house. He moved into the treeline that bifurcated the two fields and walked slowly toward the home, favoring his sore ankle a little.

There was a snow fence behind the barns, where a leaky-looking rowboat and an ancient privy rotted away, and he was behind the fence and sensed something, stopped, stood very still, slowing his vital signs to a crawl. Freezing motionless for no apparent reason.

"Oh, that's *real* great," the man was telling the woman in the truck, who whined.

"I'm sorry, I'd didn't *mean* to leave it, I didn't do it on purpose." She had left her grocery list and her money in the kitchen.

"If ya hadn't been runnin' your mouth," he started to say; but he just let it trail off and slammed the gearshift into reverse, backing out of the turn row. Just my luck, he thought.

"We goin' *back?*" the kid hollered at his dad, who ignored him, put it in drive and started back in the direction of their house. The man was disgusted.

The beast knew the people were returning. He felt it and then, a beat later, saw the pickup coming back up the gravel road. He was in a vile mood and his ankle was bothering him and he knew he would enjoy taking them all down. He was very hungry, too, so it would be easy for him to do very bad things to this family of humans.

"I'm goin' to the john," the man told his wife as they went back into the house. "You goin' to be ready to go?"

"I'll be ready," she said, and went into the kitchen. The kid was sitting on the tailgate as Bunkowski walked into the yard. The dog barked at him, the kid told it to shut up.

"Howdy," the huge man said.

"Where'd *you* come from?" the kid asked him. Chaingang thought how easily he could go over and twist the boy's head off. It would be like snapping a pencil in two.

"Over yonder," he said. "Your folks home?"

"Yeah," the kid said.

"Yes?" a woman said through the partly open back door.

"Ma'am. I was hitchin' a ride and this guy's car broke down and I been walkin', quite a way. I was wonderin' if you folks would mind if I rested in your yard for a while?" He could easily pull the door open and knock her out. Go in and chainsnap the man. Come back and get the boy. He was about to make a move, but she said,

"You just sit down and rest yourself. Make yourself to home." And she started asking him where the car had broken down and did he want a lift back to the car and did he want to call somebody, and he kind of got taken off his stride and so he went and sat on the steps.

"You from around here?" the boy asked. The beast only shook his head.

Inside the house he heard the man say something and she said . . . "broke down back over . . ." (something he couldn't make out) and the door opened behind him and the man said,

"You need a ride?"

"Well, I don't mind if it's no bother," Bunkowski said pleasantly, thinking he'd go ahead and make the move now.

"It's no trouble. You can ride into town with us. If you don't mind sittin' back there with the boy." The man said it without any undue emphasis.

"I'd be real grateful."

"No problem," the man said, stepping around the huge bulk that filled his back steps.

The last place where he'd come upon a family, he'd killed everybody in the house. Three people. Man and wife and a son—just like this. The kid, as if reading his mind, moved over out of the way, back into a far corner of the truck bed.

"Get over here, Punk," the boy said to the dog, who wagged and obeyed. "Don't worry," he sneered. "He don't bite."

"What's his name? Punk?" Chaingang sat on the cold steel. Shifted his weight slightly so as not to break the tailgate off, and the truck rocked like a safe had been dropped into it.

"Little Punk." The kid scratched the dog. "We found him starvin' over on the dump. Somebody dropped the fucker. He didn't look like nothin' but a punk." The dog licked the kid's face once and he pushed it away. "Fuckin' Punk."

"Looks like a good dog," the huge man said.

"He's awright."

"You ready?" the man said to nobody in general, and he and the wife got into the truck and they drove off down the rode, Chaingang Bunkowski bouncing along in the back of the truck.

When the beast had been a child, a dog had been his only companion and friend. He loved animals. Watching the boy with the dog had calmed him down, but he wasn't sure what he would do yet. He might take them all down anyway.

When the pickup reached the crossroads of Double-J and the levee road, Chaingang banged on the window and asked the man to stop. He got out, walked around by the driver. There were no other vehicles in sight.

"Doncha wanna go on to town?" the man asked him. Bunkowski fingered the heavy yard of the tractor-strength safety chain in his jacket pocket. Three feet of killer snake were coiled in the special canvas pocket. He thought how easy it would be to take them, now.

"I guess not. This'll do." He nodded thanks to the driver, who shrugged and started off. Chaingang stood there and watched the luckiest man in the world drive away with his family.

The Boneless Doll

Joey Froehlich

The boneless doll
Is small
And she carries
It, yea—
Wherever she goes,
Just a little girl
Happy with this
Doll without bones
(Cloth)
Not flesh all bunched
Up and writhing
When it falls
On the twigs
Of another bruised
Existence lost.

The Skull

Diane Taylor

I never really lived with him. They got divorced when I was three. But Momma always sent me to visit in the summer. Whenever I asked questions, she would say it was all too complex for a child to understand. At the time I didn't think fourteen was a "child."

I begged Momma not to send me again that summer, to let me go to camp instead or work at McDonald's. When she asked why, I couldn't answer. I didn't know why then. So she got my suitcase out of the attic and tossed my tickets on top. "Your plane leaves tomorrow morning," she said. "Nine o'clock."

She had always been a good mother, but not a happy one. I knew she wasn't sending me away to get rid of me. She simply wanted me to spend time with my father. She still loved him. And she wanted me to love him, too.

She never would come right out and say it. She wouldn't talk about him at all. But I could tell by the way she dusted his picture—not real fast with one big swish like I did, but slowly around the edges of the frame, carefully under the crack of the metal casing, and finally the glass, stroking his face softly with her rag.

All she said when she dropped me at the airport that morning was "Have yourself a good time," and "Kiss your daddy for me." I hugged her good-bye, hoping I'd get a window seat.

That afternoon as the plane taxied up to the airport, I saw him standing outside the terminal. He wasn't real tall, just medium, but he looked strong and solid—as if he had grown up out of the concrete. He still had that habit of pushing his hair back with his hand, even though it was too short to be in his face.

I was one of the first ones off. He smiled and waved when he saw me coming down the steps of the plane. I ran over to him and we hugged. Right then, I couldn't imagine why I didn't want to come.

"Sorry you had to wait so long, Dad. We had to change planes in Denver. Something about the hydraulic system."

He didn't say anything, just held my head in his hands. I could feel those hot, enormous hands covering my whole head—palms over my ears, fingers touching the back of my skull, and thumbs outlining my eyebrows. I remembered an Oral Roberts TV show, the preacher yelling, "Heal, heal!" Then Dad kissed me.

He stepped away, pushed his hair back and said, "I almost didn't recognize you, Ronnie. You're getting prettier each time you come."

"And you're looking more and more like Bruce Springsteen," I said, jerking the bandanna from his hip pocket and tying it around my neck. "Great jacket. I know some kids at school who'd *die* for a leather jacket like that."

"It's just my old flight jacket. One of the few things that came out of Nam in one piece. Haven't worn it in years." His hand started up toward his head, but I caught it. We held hands all the way to the Jeep.

It was an hour's drive from the airport to Dad's cabin in the mountains, but the time flew. We sang songs to a Golden Oldies radio station: "I can't get no-o/sat-is-FAC-shun-un." We laughed at the end of every song.

"How do you know all these words?" he asked. "You're too young for this stuff."

"Momma has the records. But she never sings along, like you do. How do *you* know all the words?"

"It's what kept me alive over there. I'll never forget the words." After a few more songs and a news report, we were home. Before going in, we stood for a minute on the porch of his cabin and listened to the night sounds from the woods all around us. He put his arm around me and I could smell him now in the wilderness air—the leather jacket, gasoline from the Jeep, soap.

"Hungry?" he asked.

"Starved! I could eat a horse."

"Would you settle for a cheese sandwich and pickles?"

"Sounds great."

His cabin only had a bathroom and then one big room where everything just kind of blended together. Dad set my suitcase and sleeping bag down in my corner. He slept on the couch, angled toward the TV. The dining room was a wooden block in another corner, and the kitchen area was next to it.

There were a fireplace and a huge bookshelf, an awesome stereo—all being stared at by dozens of pairs of lifeless eyes. I hardly noticed the animal heads anymore. They'd become a natural part of things. Only the soldier's skull still bothered me, hanging above the fireplace, a place of honor. That big room always felt hot and cold to me at the same time. It reminded me of chemistry lab—I loved it, yet I was afraid I was going to blow myself up.

We ate our sandwiches off paper plates, then stretched out on the floor in front of the fire, talking about school, boys and dating, his latest job. I'd lost count of those.

"Why don't you ever go out, Dad? You're so good-looking."

"Not interested, Ronnie. I like things the way they are."

He glanced over at me, eyes heavy from the fire. Then I realized I was getting sleepy, too. I looked up at the animals and had to shut my eyes when I got to the skull.

I remembered the first summer he'd put it up. I couldn't

have been more than four or five. The room was dark; we were curled up together on the couch in front of the fire. Dad was reading me a story called "The Nightingale." I stared up and saw the skull, glowing in the firelight.

At first I was too scared to say anything, even though I didn't even know what a skull was. Dad asked me what was wrong. I pointed to it and whispered, "What's that?"

"Oh, it's okay. That won't hurt you. It's just a trophy, like the others." He held up the book we had been reading. "Do you think the nightingale will save the Emperor's life?"

"No," I said, staring at the skull. "I think the Emperor was very mean to the nightingale. He should die." I looked at Dad and asked, *"Did* somebody die?"

"That story isn't for little girls," he said.

I begged and begged him to tell me, so he did. I guess he figured I wouldn't remember it at that age. Maybe he just needed to tell it to someone; anyone.

His voice was soft when he started but distant, not as if he were reading a fairy tale at all. "It happened in Vietnam," he began. "That's where Daddy went to fight. Me and my co-pilot Frank were flying our helicopter into the jungle to bring out some wounded. It was a hot LZ. We took some heavy fire in the tail rotor and went down, hard. Me and Frank made it out somehow, but everybody had scattered and we were on our own. We were trying to get back to the base when we came to this rice paddy we had to cross. No sooner than we stepped out of the bush, a sniper opened fire on us."

Dad's face perspired with the heat of the jungle as he told the story, and I saw the reflection of the fire in his eyes. His hand pulled his hair back, again and again.

"At first I didn't hear anything. Frank's head just suddenly blew apart. I felt it splatter on me. That's when I heard the little 'pop, pop, pop.' I caught a round in the shoulder and was knocked down. It's funny but I remember thinking, I'm shot. But it's not so bad. It only stings. I looked over at what was left of Frank's head, not really feeling anything at first, not really believing what I was seeing. Then something snapped inside me. I went kind of crazy, I guess.

"I got up and ran at the sniper, all the way across that field—firing my pistol, screaming, not really caring if I shot him or he shot me. I only knew *something* had to die. When I got to the other side, I found him lying in the grass. I'd shot him in the throat. But I couldn't stop, I didn't want to stop."

Dad was suddenly silent as he stared up at the skull. He was breathing hard.

"I stabbed him over and over with my knife. Then I cut off his head." There was no emotion in Dad's voice. "His for Frank's, to even the score. To make it right." He looked away. "I still had it with me when I walked out of that jungle a week later. I kept it. Some guys over there carried around a necklace of ears. I had a head. And as long as I had it, I knew no one could touch me."

He looked down at me, back in this world. "Now I've put it up there with the rest of the animals; that's all. It's just a memory, and memories can't hurt you—can they, pumpkin?" He smiled and brushed back my hair. "You don't understand, do you?"

I never did get to hear the end of "The Nightingale" that night, but I've always remembered his story. Since then there's been so much that I haven't understood. Like how I could love him and fear him at the same time, my own father, this man who was lying on the floor next to my sleeping bag, his eyes bright with fire.

Dad brushed my forehead—just as he'd done that night he'd told the story of the skull. "Are you sleepy, Ronnie?" he asked.

I smiled, shook my head. I saw by the way he said it that he loved me so much. He ran his hand through his hair as he looked down at me, stared into my eyes.

I turned away, shut my eyes tight. Then my mind was sending paragraphs in single sentences. *Don't do this. I don't want to. I love you. Go away.*

And then, as always, it was happening. But not to me.

Never, to me. It was always someone else. My eyes were shut and I was far away, waiting for it to be over.

When I went to the bathroom to get ready for bed, I remember thinking how the steam from the shower was like tears running down the walls. A cabin with crying walls. I closed my eyes and pushed my hair back under the hot, hot water. I pushed my thoughts back, too.

"All you need is *love!*" The stereo jerked me out of sleep.

I could see Dad in the kitchen beating some eggs with a fork in rhythm to the song. The smell of burned toast was making its way over to my corner of the room.

"Hey, Dad. Smells great! What's for breakfast?"

By now smoke was seeping out of the oven and I knew the bread had to be black. I jumped up and ran in to open the oven door. Smoke poured out. When he turned around, Dad seemed more shocked to see me than the smoke.

"Morning, Dad." I turned on the Vent-a-Hood. The fan motor sounded as loud as a helicopter. He just stood there looking at me, gripping the fork in his fist. Sweat was rolling off his forehead, and smoke was everywhere. He looked like someone who'd just woken up from a nightmare.

I took the charred bread out of the oven. "Don't you know you cook out all the nutrients when you do this?"

He wiped his forehead with the back of his hand, looked away and tried to grin. Then he pulled a can of biscuits out of the fridge. "Here," he said, tossing the can to me. "Let's see if you're a better cook than your old man." He went back to his eggs.

I peeled off the wrapper and tapped the seam of the can lightly against the counter. Once, twice. That can reminded me of him that morning—ready to explode.

During breakfast we didn't look at each other or talk hardly at all, just listened to the music. Then he went for a walk while I cleaned things up and watched TV. By lunchtime Dad was back and pretty much himself again. He asked me if I was ready for some decent food. I didn't want to seem too excited. I thought it might hurt his feelings about his cooking.

"Sure."

"Well, let's go," he said, pulling on his flight jacket.

"But I have to change clothes."

"Wouldn't you rather have a new dress?"

This time I *did* get excited. "Sure!" I said and raced him to the Jeep.

We drove down the mountain to town. I had to try on several dresses from the incredibly wide selection at Candy's Fashion Scene before I decided on a short pink one. It was a lot shorter than Momma would've ever let me buy. I really didn't expect Dad to let me either. To be honest, I tried it on just to see if he would say anything. All he said was. "I think that color looks good on you."

After the dress, we drove to the town's new restaurant for lunch. The Mountain Inn didn't look like a restaurant at all. It was just a big blue rectangular building with a gaudy neon sign mounted on the back of a trailer. And I thought, *What a waste of a new dress!*

I guess Dad could tell by my face I was disappointed because he said, "Things aren't as fancy in this part of the country. But the food's good."

I got mad at myself for acting childish and said, "I'm starved." When we sat down, a waitress plopped two plastic menus in front of us. She had on a name tag that said "Wyoma" and a face that said she knew Dad. Her uniform was a pair of tight jeans and a T-shirt with the slogan "Blondes Do It Better." She looked at me, then said to Dad, "Good to see you, Gary. It's been a while."

"Been busy," Dad said. He asked me what I'd like and he ordered the same.

Wyoma asked, "Would you like for me to cut the little girl's meat for her, or is she old enough to handle a knife by herself?"

Dad laughed when I said, "I can cut my own meat, thank you."

"Spunky little thing, ain't she?" Wyoma gave me a fake grin.

"Takes after her father," Dad answered.

Wyoma looked at Dad to see if he was serious, then hit his arm with her order pad. "I could kill you, Gary Fenster! Teasing me like that."

When Wyoma left, I asked Dad, "Wonder what it is she does better?"

Dad's lips moved a little to the side as they always did when he was thinking something funny. "Well, I know she makes better toast than I do," he said, and we both laughed so loud that people turned around and looked at us.

I whispered, "I think she likes you."

"She likes anything with a deep voice and pants," Dad said, and we laughed out loud again.

When Wyoma brought our order over, she asked, "You two hiding a joke book under the table?"

Dad and I couldn't stop giggling. You know how it is when you get really tickled at something? Things aren't even funny anymore, but you keep laughing anyway.

Wyoma tore our check out of her order pad, slapped it upside down next to Dad's plate. "She seems a little too innocent for *your* jokes, Gary." Then she pushed a pencil behind her ear and went to pour coffee for customers sitting at the counter.

That night, Dad surprised me by taking me to an outdoor concert. It was country/western music—not exactly my favorite, but it was okay. Toward the end of the concert, the band started playing a really fast song and everyone hopped up, clapping and dancing. Before we knew it, we were dancing too—swinging, dipping, kicking. As the music sped up, we did too, dancing faster and faster. I felt my new dress swish high around my thighs. I'd never felt so wonderful, so free.

The song stopped suddenly and we fell to the ground, too

out of breath to say anything. We lay there, chests moving up and down, hair wet with sweat. I could have stayed in that same spot all night, staring up at the stars, feeling the earth spin.

Dad held my hand all the way home that night. He didn't even let go to shift gears. It felt so good having someone care that much about me. Momma loved me, but not like Dad. The rhythm of the road and the breeze against my eyes put me to sleep, my head still spinning.

I didn't wake up until Dad was carrying me inside the cabin. I was still half asleep when I felt him put me gently on my sleeping bag and kiss my cheek. He kissed me again on my other cheek. He brushed my bangs back and kissed my forehead. I told myself to calm down. He's your father. He loves you. He wouldn't do anything to hurt you. *He's not like that.*

I opened my eyes. Dad's face was close to mine, and behind him I saw the skull. It glowed in the firelight, the flames dancing in its empty eyes. I wanted to go away again, let it happen to someone else; but the skull face wouldn't let me. I was caught between sleeping and waking, not knowing what was real and what was a dream while he stared down at me, stroking me. I closed my eyes, tried to go away, but I could still feel him on me. "Dad . . ." I started to say. But when I looked, it wasn't him anymore. It was the skull's face, lit by the fire, staring down at me, grinning. It moved closer, that awful mouth opening and closing as it whispered over and over, "I love you, Ronnie, I love you."

I screamed.

I screamed so loud, I scared myself even more. Then I couldn't stop screaming. I screamed at the skull, I screamed at him, I screamed at the dark woods around us. All the ugly pictures flashed through my head, one after the other, blending into each other like the rooms in this cabin, like his face and the skull's face; with no beginning and no end. Then I was crying and shaking so hard, I could barely breathe.

Dad held me down. He was saying over and over, "Ronnie, I'm sorry, I'm sorry. Ronnie, don't cry. Please don't cry."

When I finally got calmed down, he tried to take me in his arms to comfort me, like only a father could. I jerked away from him, said, "I want to go home." I knew it hurt him, but I didn't care.

I stayed awake all night, waiting for the sun to come into the room. I thought it would be better then. But it was worse. Everything was so much more real. I still had on the pink dress. It seemed cheap and dirty, and I hated it.

Dad sat motionless in the chair across the room. He'd been awake all night, too.

I asked if we could get ready to leave and he asked if I was hungry. I shook my head, knowing I would choke if I tried to swallow anything. I changed clothes and packed.

The drive to the airport was silent—no talking, no music. Dad took care of changing the ticket for me.

"Any problem?" I asked when he handed it to me.

"No problem," he said. He backed up a few feet, stared at me. He ran his hand through his short hair. "Except now I wish I had been killed over there and I wouldn't have hurt you like this."

Standing away from me like that, he didn't seem so handsome anymore. He stuffed both hands in his pockets, said, "Tell your mother I'm moving. Tell her I'll . . ." He shifted his weight from one foot to the other. "Straighten things out. I'll make them even." He cleared his throat. I could tell this was tough for him, but I still didn't care. "And I want you to be honest with her. Tell her the truth."

I nodded. Just wanted to get away from there. Away from him. I wondered if I would ever stop hating him.

When the announcement was made to board the plane, I practically ran. I didn't say good-bye or even turn around to look at him. From my window seat, as the plane taxied, I watched him disappear into the terminal, head down and his hands buried in his flight jacket.

That was the last time I ever saw him. No one knows

where he is or even if he's still alive. Momma and I don't play the music anymore. Sometimes I really miss it. Sometimes.

On 42nd St.

William F. Nolan

He hadn't been to New York since he was a kid, not since his last year of high school. That had been his graduation present: a trip to the Big Apple. He'd bugged his parents for years about New York, how it was the center of everything and how not to see it was like never seeing God. As a kid, he used to think of New York as the god of the U.S. He read every book he could find about it at his local library in Atkin.

His parents were quite content to stay in Ohio, in this little town they'd met and married in, where he'd been born and where his father had his tool business. His parents never traveled anywhere, and neither had he until he took the train to New York that summer when he was eighteen.

The city was hot and humid, but the weather hadn't bothered him. He'd been too enchanted, too dazzled by the high-thrusting towers of Manhattan, the jungle roar of midtown traffic, the glitter of Fifth Avenue, the pulse of night life on Broadway—and by the green vastness of Central Park, plunked like a chunk of Ohio into the center of this awesome steel-and-concrete giant.

And by the people. Especially on the subways; he'd never seen so many people jammed together in a single place. Jostling each other, shouting, laughing, cursing. Big and small, rich and poor, young and old, black and brown and yellow and white. An assault on the senses, so many of them.

"The subways are no good anymore," his friends now told him. "They've got graffiti all over them and you can get mugged real easy on a subway. Cabs are your best bet. Once inside a taxi, you're safe . . . at least until you get out!"

And they had also warned him, all these years later, to stay away from 42nd Street. "Forty-second's like a blight," they declared. "New York's changed since you were a kid. It can get ugly, *real* ugly."

And they'd talked about the billions of cockroaches and rats that lived under the city and in it, how even in the swankiest apartment on Fifth Avenue they have cockroaches late at night, crawling the walls . . .

So here he was, Ben Sutton, thirty-eight, balding and unmarried, on a plane to Kennedy—returning to the Apple after twenty years to represent the Sutton Tool Manufacturing Company of Atkin, Ohio. His father, Ed Sutton, who had founded the company, was long dead. Now Ben owned the business, because his mother had died within a year of his father. Over the past decade, he'd been sending other company employees to the National Tool Convention each year in New York, but this time, on a sudden impulse, he'd decided to go himself.

His friends backed the decision. "'Bout time for you to stir your stumps, Ben," they told him. "Take the trip. Get some *excitement* into your life."

They were right. Ben's life had settled into a series of dull routine days, one following another like a row of black dominos. By now the business practically ran itself, and Ben was feeling more and more like a figurehead. A trip such as this would revitalize him; he'd be plugged into the mainstream of life again. Indeed, it *was* time to "stir his stumps."

Kennedy was a madhouse. Ben lost his baggage claim check and had a difficult time proving that his two bags really belonged to him. Then the airport bus he took from

Kennedy to Grand Central suffered some kind of mechanical malfunction and he had to wait by the side of the highway with a dozen angry passengers until another bus arrived a full hour later.

At Grand Central a gaunt-bodied teenager, with the words "The Dead Live!" stitched across the back of his red poplin jacket, ran off with one of Ben's suitcases while he was phoning the hotel to ask for an extension on his room reservation. A beefy station cop grabbed the kid and got the suitcase back.

The cop asked if he wanted to press charges, but Ben shook his head. "Let somebody else press charges when he steals another suitcase. I can't get involved."

The cop scowled. "That's a piss-poor attitude, mister." He glared at the teenager. "This little dickhead ought to be put away."

When the cop finally let him go, the kid gave them both the finger before vanishing in the crowd.

"You see that?" asked the cop, flushed with anger. "You see what that little shit did? I oughta run him down and pound him good. An' I got half a mind to do it!"

"That's your choice, Officer," Ben declared. "But I have to get a cab to my hotel before I lose my room."

"Sure, go ahead," said the cop. "It's no sweat off my balls what the hell you do."

Well, thought Ben, they warned me things could get ugly.

The convention hotel was quite nice and his room was pleasant. His window faced Central Park and there was a wonderful view of the spreading greenery.

The bellhop nodded when Ben told him how much he liked the view. "Yeah—maybe you'll get to watch an ol' lady being mugged down there." He chuckled, then asked if Ben was "with the convention."

"Yes, I'm here from Ohio."

"Well, a lot of the convention people are boozin' it up at the bar. Maybe you'll make some new friends."

The bellhop's words were prophetic.

After he had showered and changed into fresh clothes, Ben took the elevator down to the bar (called The Haven), and he had not been there for more than five minutes when two men sat down on stools, one to either side of him.

"So, you're a tool man, huh?" asked the fellow to Ben's left. Bearded, with large, very dark eyes and a lot of teeth in his smile.

"Correct," said Ben. "How did you know?"

"Lapel," said the other man, the one on the right. He was thin and extremely pale with washed-out blue eyes behind thick glasses.

Ben looked confused. "I don't—"

"That pin in the lapel of your coat," the bearded man said. "Dead giveaway."

Ben smiled, touching the bright metal lapel pin which featured a hammer, wrench, and pliers in an embossed design above the logo: "Sutton's—Tools You Can Trust."

"Are you two gentlemen also here for the convention?" Ben asked.

"You got it," said the man in glasses. "I'm Jock Kirby, and this bearded character is Billy Dennis."

"Ben Sutton."

They shook hands.

"Us, we're local boys, from the core of the Apple," said Billy Dennis. "Where you hail from?"

"Atkin, Ohio."

"Akron?" asked Jock. "I know a tire man from Akron."

"No, *Atkin*," Ben corrected him. "We're a few hundred miles from Akron. People tend to get the names mixed."

"Never heard of it," said Billy.

"It's a small town," Ben told them. "Nothing much to hear about."

"What you drinking?" Jock asked.

"Scotch and water," said Ben.

"Great. Same for us." Kirby gestured to the bartender, raising Ben's glass. "Three more of these, okay?"

"Okay," nodded the barman.

"So," said Billy Dennis, running a slow hand along his bearded cheek, "you're an Ohio man. Not much pizzazz back there, huh?"

"Pizzazz?" Ben blinked at him.

"He means," added Kirby, "you must get bored out of your gourd with nothing much shaking in Akins."

"Atkin. It's Atkin."

"Well, whatever," Kirby grunted.

Their drinks arrived and Dennis shoved a twenty-dollar bill toward the barman.

"What do you do for kicks back in Ohio?" asked Kirby.

"I watch television," Ben said, sipping his Scotch. "Listen to music. Eat out on occasion. Go to a movie when there's one I really want to see." He shrugged. "But, frankly, I'm not much of a moviegoer."

"Boy," sighed Billy Dennis. "Sounds like you have yourself a blast."

"Fun time," said Jock Kirby.

Ben shifted on the barstool. "I don't require a whole lot out of life. I guess I'm what you'd call 'laid back.'"

Billy Dennis chuckled, showing his teeth. "Take my word, Bennie, it's better gettin' laid than bein' laid back!"

"Fuckin' A," said Jock.

Ben flushed and hastily finished his drink. He wasn't accustomed to rough language and he didn't appreciate it.

Dennis gestured to the barman, making a circle in the air. "Another round," he said.

"No, no, I've really had enough," Ben protested. He was already feeling light-headed. He'd never been a drinker.

"Aw, c'mon, Bennie boy," urged Jock Kirby. *"Live* a little. Take a bite out of the Big Apple."

"Yeah," nodded Billy Dennis, his dark eyes fixed on the Ohio man. "Have another shot on us."

And each of them put an arm around Ben Sutton.

* * *

The walk down Broadway was like a dream. Ben couldn't remember leaving the bar. Had they taken a cab here? His head seemed full of rosy smoke.

"I think I drank too much," he said. The words were blurred. His tongue was thick and rebellious.

"Can't ever drink too much at a party," said Billy Dennis. "An' that's what we got goin' here tonight!"

"Fuckin' A," Jock said. "It's party time."

"I've got to get back to the hotel," Ben told them. "The convention opens at ten tomorrow morning. I need sleep."

"Sleep?" Dennis gave Ben a toothy smile. "Hell, you can sleep when you're dead. We're gonna show you a fun time, Bennie."

"Sure are," agreed Jock Kirby. "Make you forget all about Ohio."

"Where are we going?" asked Ben. He found it difficult to keep pace with them, and the lights along the street seemed to be buried in mist.

"Forty-second is where," nodded Kirby. "Jump street."

Ben stopped. He raised a protesting hand. "That's a dangerous area," he said thickly. "My friends warned me to avoid it."

"*We're* your friends now," said Billy Dennis. "An' *we* say it's where all the action is. Right, Jocko?"

"Fuckin' A," Kirby said.

A street bum approached them, his clawed right hand extended. Ben dug out a quarter, dropping it into the scabbed palm. "Bless you," said the bum.

"Butt off," said Kirby.

The bum ignored him. He gestured to the sacks of garbage stacked along the curb, black-plastic bags swollen with waste. Roaches and insects burrowed among them. He nodded toward Ben. "Don't step on the maggots," he said.

And moved on up Broadway.

"I'm not so sure about this," Ben told them. "I still think I should take a taxi back to the hotel."

"The friggin' hotel can wait," said Kirby. His pale skin seemed to glow in the darkness. "Hotel's not goin' anywhere."

"Right," agreed Billy Dennis. "Stuck in that hotel, you might as well be back in Elkins."

"Atkin," corrected Ben. His head felt detached from his body, which floated below it.

"Hey, we're here," grinned Jock Kirby. "Welcome to sin street!"

They had reached Forty-second and Broadway. The intersection traffic throbbed around them in swirls of moving light and sound. Neons blazed and sizzled. The air smelled of ash.

Ben blinked rapidly, trying to sharpen his focus.

"I think I'm drunk," he said.

"No, man," Jock assured him. "You've just got a little *glow* on is all. Go with it. Enjoy."

Billy Dennis held Ben's left elbow, propelling him along Forty-second. Ben felt weightless, as if his body were made of tissue paper.

"Where . . . are you taking me?"

"To a special place," said Billy. "You'll really dig it. Right, Jocko?"

"Fuckin' A," said Kirby.

Ben struggled to get a clear visual fix on the area. His senses recorded a kaleidoscope of color and noise. The walk swarmed with pimps and prostitutes, beggars and barkers, tourists and heavy trippers. Movie marquees bloomed with light, a fireworks of neon. Souvenir shops and porno peep shows gaudily competed for attention. A sea of disembodied voices poured over Ben as he walked; faces drifted past him like a gallery of ghosts.

"I'm dizzy," he said. "I've got to sit down."

"You can sit down when we get inside," Kirby told him.

"Inside where?"

"You'll see," said Billy. "We're almost there."

They stopped at a building of bright-flashing lights with a twenty-foot female nude outlined on its facade in twisting snakes of color. GIRLS . . . NUDE . . . GIRLS . . . NUDE . . . flashed the lights.

A feral-faced barker in a soiled white shirt and worn Levi's gestured at them. His eyes were bloodshot.

"Step right in, gents, the show's ready to start. The girls are all absolutely naked and unadorned. They'll tease and titillate, delight and dazzle you."

Ben's new friends marched him inside the building, one to each elbow, up a flight of wide, red-painted stairs to a landing illuminated by bands of blue fluorescent tubing, and down a hallway to a room in which a series of plastic stools formed a large circle. All very surreal, dreamlike. And, somehow, threatening.

Each stool faced a window, shuttered in gleaming red metal, with a coin slot at the bottom. The other stools were unoccupied, which Ben found odd.

"You're just in time, brother," said a tall beanstalk of a man with badly pitted skin. "Show's about to begin. Ten minutes for a quarter. And the feels are free."

"Open your fingers, Ben," said Jock Kirby—and he put several silver quarters into Ben's hand. "Just pop one in at the bottom," he said. Then he grinned. "Nothin' like this back in Ohio!"

Ben Sutton obeyed, numbly slotting in the first coin.

Now he waited as, slowly, the metal shutter rolled up to reveal a large circular platform bathed in a powdery blaze of overhead spots.

A thick-faced, sullen-eyed woman stepped from an inner door. She wore a dress of red sequins and a cheap red wig. She looked at Ben.

"Welcome to the Hellhole," she said. "You're right on time." Her smile was ugly.

Ben kept expecting to see other windows opening, but he

remained the only customer. Not much profit in this show, he thought dully.

"We herewith present, for your special entertainment, the Flame of Araby."

The thick-faced woman pressed a button by the side of the platform and, to a burst of pre-recorded drum music, a long-limbed blonde stepped through the doorway.

She was wearing several gauzy veils which she quickly began discarding. Young and full-figured, she was attractive in a vulgar sense as she whirled and twisted to the beating drums. Her glittery eyes were locked on Ben, who sat numb and transfixed at the window. Kirby was right; he had seen nothing like this in Ohio.

Now the final veil whispered from her hips and she was, as the barker had promised, "absolutely naked and unadorned."

In all of his thirty-eight years, Ben Sutton had never seen a totally nude woman. Linda Mae Lewis had allowed him to see her left breast under the dim illumination of the dash lights in Ben's old Pontiac convertible when he was in college, and a waitress at the Quick-Cup coffee shop on the outskirts of Atkin had once let him place his hand under her uniform—and he'd been able to view her upper thigh—but that was the full extent of Ben's sexual experience with females.

Thus, he was truly dazzled by the curved, shimmering white body writhing just inches in front of him.

"Go ahead, sweetie, touch one," the girl said in a husky voice, aiming her naked buttocks at Ben. "Go for it!"

Trembling, Ben reached out to touch the naked slope of a mooned buttock; the flesh was marble-smooth and seemed to vibrate under his fingers.

Then, at that moment, the red-metal shutter began sliding down. Ben jerked his hand back with a groan of frustration. His ten minutes had expired.

Frantically, spilling several coins to the floor, Ben slotted in another quarter—and the shutter rolled slowly up again.

But the platform was empty.

The girl was gone.

The music had stopped.

Ben spun around on his stool to ask his two friends why the show had ended, but the room was deserted.

Ben stood up. "Hello! Anybody here?"

No reply. Just the muted sounds of street traffic, punctuated by the thin wail of a distant police siren.

Ben walked into the hall.

"Kirby? . . . Dennis? . . . You out here?"

No reply.

He moved toward the stairs. Or that was the direction he intended to take. Obviously, he had gone the wrong way because the hallway twisted, leading him deeper into the building.

The passage seemed dimmer, narrower.

Ben heard laughter ahead of him. A door opened along the hall, flooding the area with light.

He walked to the open door, looked in. The thick-faced woman and the blond dancing girl were there, with Jock Kirby and Billy Dennis. They were all laughing together, with drinks in their . . . in their . . . their . . .

Not hands. Dear God, not hands!

"Hi, Ben," said the Billy-thing. "We're celebrating."

"Because of you, chum," said the Jock-thing. "Meat on the hoof!"

"Yeah," nodded the blonde, running a pink tongue over her lips, "even maggots hafta eat."

Ben stared at them. His stomach was churning; a sudden rush of nausea made him stagger back, vomiting into the hall.

Inside the room, the four of them were discarding body parts . . . limbs . . . ears . . . noses . . . their flesh dropping away like chunks of rotten cheese.

Ben allowed himself one last, horror-struck backward glance into the room as he turned to run.

The things he saw were like the maggots and roaches in

the swollen bags of trash along Broadway, but much larger, much more . . . advanced.

Ben Sutton ran.

He couldn't find the stairs. The hall kept twisting back on itself—but if he kept running he'd find a way out.

He was *sure* he would find a way out.

Safe

John Maclay

Perhaps, as you said, doctor, this will help. I know that your methods are unorthodox, but I've been to everyone else, and I'm willing to try anything. So I'll just sit here in this light, with the pad and pen you've given me, and write, openly, about my worst fear. The one that, if I don't get help soon, will surely kill me.

It's not strictly claustrophobia, as you know. I've never minded being shut up in a room, no matter how small. It doesn't even matter whether it's light or dark—one time I stood for twenty minutes in a closet, waiting for a friend who was brought late to a surprise party, with no ill effects. And you know, I think I could be a coal miner, bent over in those endless, low tunnels, without any fear. Even an astronaut, in that tiny capsule, provided there was a window. Though only in that situation, not the closet or the mine, would I need one—and even then, it could be light or dark, so long as I knew I was looking out into space.

We're getting somewhere, aren't we, Doctor? My great fear, apparently, is this: *being shut up in a small, window-less place much lower than my head.*

Did I write "apparently?" Oh, my God . . .

The first time I can remember is when I was nine. A playmate of mine lived in a Victorian house with a lot of nooks and crannies, and one day he showed me his new hideout. It was under the back stoop, where a little door led to a closed place probably meant for storing garden tools. He'd rigged up a light bulb from an outlet in the house, smoothed down the earth floor, and tacked up posters of old cars. It looked fine to me.

But then he led me inside. And slammed the door.

It wasn't the lack of air, the dank smell—it's never been that. And I knew, in that situation, that I could leave at any time. As it turned out, I should have, right away—but kids are kids, and not only did I not want to spoil my playmate's fun, I couldn't let him see my fear.

So I sat there cross-legged, feeling the rough ceiling brush my hair—and the sweat started to bead on my forehead. Listening to my friend talk happily about Model As and Model Ts. Watching him point casually to his posters—

Until his voice was drowned out by the pounding of my young heart. Until his image blurred—because I was looking past him, at the tight walls, which seemed to be closing in, *in* . . .

The last thing I remember about my companion—after that, he wouldn't see me anymore—was the shocked look on his face. As I *screamed,* shoved open the door, and *ran.*

Well, that's the childhood memory, Doctor. The one your kind always wants to drag out of me, since presumably the telling will break the spell. But in my case, of course, it hasn't. So let's go on . . .

Movies. I've always loved them. They've provided escape, which is something I've needed, especially of late. And I've always been drawn to the old macho adventures—they seemed to give me strength against my fear. Wayne. Cooper. Bogart. Bogart. Which brings up Cagney. Cagney. And Robinson. Robinson . . .

But—oh, God. That brings up the *scene* . . .

It's one of those black-and-white prisons of the 1930s. Hard enough, with those cold cell blocks, Spartan mess halls, and inmates with knives around every corner. But those things don't frighten me—because, although I'm locked in, at least I can stand erect, even plot with Jimmy and Eddie to escape. Until . . .

We're caught. And then, it's the *Hole*.

Anything, anything but that. That low, narrow cage made of boiler plate. That steel door closing, as I kneel inside. That window, yes, which opens once a day, as the guard hands in my bread and water—but it's not enough, not nearly enough. Because in the meantime, as I try to stand upright, even try to stretch my body out horizontally, pretend to stand—

I slowly go mad.

Please don't laugh when you read this, Doctor. You really shouldn't—because that scene, at the wrong time, cost me my first love. It was like this: we were relaxing on the sofa, watching an old movie, when suddenly . . .

The look on her face was the same as my childhood playmate's. When I screamed again—and *ran*.

But I got over that, too. Found other women. Still enjoyed the movies. Though I chose them carefully—didn't even look at the previews of *Papillon*. I was doing fine—after all, there aren't that many tiny, enclosed places in this great world. And as time went on, I was almost able to relegate those two horrible events into the past, where I thought they belonged. But then . . .

I was a senior in college and had signed up for Art Appreciation. A pleasant course, and easy, with its thrice-a-week lectures that consisted mostly of slides. We were up to eighteenth-century England that day, that awful Wednesday. I was leaning back in my chair, enjoying the work of Kneller and Constable, half-dozing . . . when suddenly a very different picture flashed on the screen.

William Blake. *The Grave*.

I tried to control myself, and I succeeded. No screaming this time—no running. I was older now, and I was proud. And mercifully, the professor's voice droned on, and the slide changed.

But as I walked back to my dormitory room in the beautiful sunlight, I still couldn't get that image out of my mind. So, in an attempt to purge myself of it—you know about that, don't you, Doctor?—I stopped at the library, and took out a book on Blake.

. . . It's late that night. I'm lying motionless on my bed, hypnotized, staring at that picture. The cold, heavy, overarching stone ceiling, even more menacing in black-and-white line engraving. The human figures—lying there frozen, but so, *so* lifelike. Their eyes . . . open. In that constricted, exitless space, the ceiling pressing down, down—and suddenly, I'm *with* them—*in that place which is lower than my head.*

I suppose it's been downhill since then, Doctor. And, I might add, an open book to my few friends. How I had my first nervous breakdown, and didn't graduate with my class. How my marriage broke up: When I was alone at our home in the country, a tiny electrical fire started in the crawl space—something that only needed a squirt of the extinguisher—and I let our new house burn to the ground. (My wife later ran off with one of the firemen—it would be funny, if it weren't so sad.) How I've always steered clear of any . . . place . . . like that, or any image of it, however brief. (I lost another friend, recently, by being unable to ride in the back of his windowless van.) And how I've had the *nightmares—of* ever-increasing frequency and intensity, making sleep impossible, threatening my health.

And yes, how I've become one of those strange people who make, uh, special arrangements. Because, you see, my coffin is already picked out—and wired with a signaling device, in the event I'm buried alive.

Burial—you know, Doctor, we really may be getting somewhere despite all my previous failures. The writing—and what you've done to me—may actually have helped. I'll admit I was terrified at first, but knowing you're there has enabled me to control that.

My playmate's hideout . . . . the Hole in the prison films . . . Blake's tomb—especially, the tomb . . .

It's all the fear of being *trapped,* isn't it? Being *alive* but trapped, unable to stand up, move off, look out—a *death-in-life?*

... Well, Doctor, I've finally had it. I'm tired of living another kind of death-in-life—being thought strange, losing opportunities—because of that fear. I think I'll concentrate, now, on the wonderful world outside—

Knowing, despite those awful experiences, or any others that may come my way—

That when I'm dead and in my tomb, I will be . . . *dead.* Unable to know where I am, or care. Or even if I do know, that I'll draw comfort, instead, from those tight walls, that low ceiling. As they envelop me—especially if it's dark—in *nothingness,* and sleep.

... I have a sense of time passing, Doctor. And it's a bit difficult to breathe—but that's due to a sense of elation at my wonderful breakthrough, isn't it? Also, there's the light—it hurts my eyes. But, in certain . . . situations . . . I've never minded its absence, have I?

So I think I'll turn it off. Yes, that's better. Though I'll have to stop writing, since I'm only guiding the pen, by feel, across the paper . . .

The darkness seems to enclose me now . . . *enfold* me . . .

BALTIMORE (AP)—In a bizarre circumstance, a psychiatrist and his patient were found dead today.

According to notes found by police, Dr. Bertram Mankin, 59, locally known for his unusual forms of therapy, had locked James Ridgley, 33, in a large old safe in his Tower Building office.

The patient, a lifelong sufferer from a form of claustrophobia, had been given a flashlight, pen, and paper, and been told to write of his fear. Apparently, the doctor had intended to release Mr. Ridgley after ten minutes, before lack of air became a problem.

However, when Dr. Mankin's secretary, Bernice Watson, 42, entered the office approximately one hour later, she found the doctor dead in his chair of a massive coronary. She then called police and para-medics who, acting upon the notes, immediately opened the safe, and discovered Mr. Ridgley to be dead of suffocation.

"The funny thing," paramedic John Magruder said, "aside from the whole weird situation, was the look on the guy's face.

"Usually, when they're trapped, you'll find an expression of struggle or horror, like the person just got done screaming.

"But this guy had a sort of peaceful smile."

The secretary, Ms. Watson, is under heavy sedation.

All But the Ties Eternal

Gary A. Braunbeck

All waits undream'd of in that region . . .
Till when the ties loosen,
All but the ties eternal, Time and Space,
Nor darkness, gravitation, sense, nor any bounds
bounding us.

—Walt Whitman
"Darest Thou Now O Soul"

Afterward she spent many hours alone in the house for the purpose of making it emptier; it was a game to her, like the one she'd played as a child, walking on the stone wall of the garden, pretending it was a mountain ledge, not wanting to look down for the sight of rocks below, knowing certain death awaited her should she slip, a terrible fall that would crush her to bits, walking along until her steps faltered and she toppled backward, always thinking in that moment before her tiny body hit the ground: *So that's when I died.*

She had always laughed then, as a child, sitting ass-deep in mud and looking at the wall.

Now all the house had was the hole Daddy left behind, and there was no laughter remaining.

Yolanda stood looking at the small hole in the living-room wall, wondering when it would start bleeding again. It only bled at night, at twenty minutes past twelve, the same time her father had—

—A stirring from the bedroom. She listened for Michael's voice. He would have to wake soon; he always did when she got up. She peered into the darkness as if it would warn her when he awakened, perhaps split down the middle like a razor cut and allow some light to seep through; and in that light she would see her father's face, winking at her as he'd often done before letting her in on a little secret.

He'd let her in on all his little secrets, except the one that really mattered. She found it hard not to hate him for it.

Nothing came at her from the darkness. She turned back, stared at the hole. It was so tiny; silent.

The digital clock blinked: 12:19.

She took a breath and watched as the numbers changed—
—then looked at the hole.

It always began very slowly, like the trickle of water dripping from a faucet not turned completely off: one bulging droplet crept to the edge and glistened, then it fell through and slid down the wall, dark as ink.

She watched the thin stream crawl to the floor, leaving its slender thread path for the others to follow. And they did.

Pulsing out in streams heavier, thicker, they spread across the wall in every direction as if from the guts of a spider until she was staring into the center of a web, admiring patterns made by the small lines where they dripped into one another like colors off a summertime cone. Strawberry; vanilla.

A soft groan from the bedroom, then: "Yolanda? Yo? Where are you?"

She looked once more at the dark, shimmering web, then went to the bedroom where Michael was waiting.

He saw her and smiled. She was still naked.

"Where were you? Come back to bed."

"No," she said. "I want you to come into the living room and see it for yourself."

"See *what* for—? Oh, yeah. Right."

"Please?"

He sat up in bed and rubbed his eyes. "Look, Yolanda, I've been telling you for days—you've *got* to get out of this house! Your father's dead, there's nothing you can do about it. You've no reason to stay here. The sooner you get over this, the sooner you can get on with your life."

"I thought you left social work at the office."

"I only mean—"

"Goddammit, stop patronizing me, Michael! Get your ass up and *come look at this!*"

The anger in her voice made him do as he was told.

When they walked into the living room, she saw the last of the web slip into the hole and thought of how her father used to suck in the last string of spaghetti.

As the last of the streams pulled back in, she gripped Michael's arm and pointed. "Did you see it? *Did* you?"

He placed his other arm around her bare, sweaty shoulder, pulling her close. "Take it easy, Yo. Look, it's been a rotten time for you, I know that. It's why I came over and—"

"I didn't *ask* you to come over!"

"I know, but, Jesus, you haven't even called for *ten days!* I figured you'd need a little time to yourself, but I never thought you'd start to . . . to . . ."

She pulled back, slapped his arm away. "Don't you dare talk to me like that! I am *not* one of your screwed-up runaway teenagers who only needs a shoulder to whine on!"

"I was only—"

"I know what you were 'only,' thank you. I'm not one of your fragile children who might shatter if pushed—and I am *not* imagining things." She crossed to the hole and stuck the tip of her middle finger in, feeling the moisture. She pulled it out and felt the trace of a smile cross her lips: there was a small droplet of blood perched between her nail and the flesh of the quick. She faced Michael, offered her evidence.

"Look for yourself. Blood."

He lifted her hand closer to his face, squinted, flipped on a small table lamp.

For a moment she saw him hesitate.

There was, indeed, blood on her fingertip. He stared at it, brushed it away. "You cut your finger on the plaster."

"I most certainly did *not*."

"You did," he said. "Look." He turned her hand back; she saw the small gash in her fingertip.

Something pinched in her stomach. Her eyes blinked. Her arms began to shake. She swore she wouldn't start crying.

Making no attempt to touch her, Michael said, "If you insist on staying here, why don't you just *fix* the hole? That might take care of . . . *help* things, anyway."

She took a breath and wiped something from her eye. "It's not that big. It's just not . . . that big."

"You must be joking, right?"

She stared at him.

"It's not 'that big'?" he said. "Christ, Yo, I could stick a *pool cue* inside that thing!" He pointed and she followed with her gaze—

—remembering she'd only been able to press her fingertip against the hole before, never *in* it, never—

He was right.

The hole was bigger. Not much, less than a quarter inch in circumference, but bigger.

She stared. Her voice came out in a whisper. "I remember thinking it *should* have been bigger. I mean, he used a bullet with a hollow point, right? He sat in his favorite chair, put the gun in his mouth and . . . and the hole was so small. The sound was so loud. It was like the whole ceiling turned into thunder. I was in my bed, I heard Dad mutter to himself, and . . ." She took a small breath. "When it was over and the sound stopped ringing in my ears, I . . . came out here."

"Yeah?"

She stared hard at the hole. "I didn't look at him. I looked at the hole. It was all I could see. It looked like a mouth. It was . . . *eating*, everything."

She stood, transfixed, hugging herself. "The blood, the tiny pieces of his skull and brain—the *hole* pulled them in. It was like watching dirty dishwater go down a drain. It all swirled up around the hole, got closer and closer till there should have been nothing left—but it was still there on the wall, his blood and brains, all the pieces were still *there* and—"

"Yo, c'mon."

". . . Wanna know why he did it, Michael, if I did something to upset him—but I don't think I did. I loved him a lot, but that wasn't enough. I guess he missed Mom too much. I told him it wasn't our fault that she walked out, that she didn't love us back. He didn't ask me for much, he never did, he always gave, and I wish he had—I wish he would've asked me for help, *said* something, because he was always there for me, and when *he* needed someone, I was . . . was—"

"Yo, you need to rest."

She felt the hot tears streaming down her cheeks, but she didn't care.

". . . Because I just want him back! I want my father back, and all I've got is this fucking *hole* that took him away from me. It sucked him in, left me alone, and it's . . . not . . . *fair!*"

She buried her face in her hands and wept, feeling the fury and sorrow mix, feeling a bellyful of night making her shudder. She hated it, wanted to destroy it.

Before she knew it she was against the wall, pounding with her fists, feeling the force of her blows rip through her arms but she didn't care, she kept pounding as if Daddy would hear her and call out from the other side.

Then Michael was behind her, his arms around her, easing her away; she didn't want him to, so she whipped around to slap his face, lost her balance, suddenly falling from the garden wall again, her arms flailing to protect her from the rocks below as she fell against the wall—

—and saw the hole swallow four of her fingers.

It was still getting bigger.

Then Michael was all over her, picking her up as if she were some helpless, pathetic, frail child. She swatted at his face because he wasn't looking at the hole, he didn't *see* the small globule of blood peek over the edge as if saying, *Wait till next time . . .*

Once in bed, she fell asleep immediately.

Then woke, Michael at her side.

Then slept. And woke. And slept.

And woke—

Daddy was there, just between the beams of moonlight that slipped through the window blinds, smiling at her, his mouth growing wide as he stepped closer to the bed, whispering *It's the family comes first, you and me, that's all, honey, because family ties are the most important ones.* Then he was bending low, his mouth opening into a pit, wide and deep, sucking her in—

She slept—

No sense to her dreams, no rhythm to the words spoken to her there by figures she didn't recognize, moving slowly past her like people on the street; no purpose, no love, no reason, empty here, this place, yet so full of people, and place and time going somewhere but she couldn't tell, wouldn't tell—

And woke—

—massaging her shoulders, Michael, his hands strong, warm and comforting, his voice near, tender. "I'm not going anywhere, Yolanda, I love you, just sleep, *shhh,* yeah, that's it," like talking to a frightened child; she loved him but when would he start treating her like an adult?

She balanced on the edge of sleep, sensing her father. And the ceiling. And walls.

And the hole.

She felt it growing, slowly sucking air from the room, Daddy's voice on the tail of moonbeams *most important because they're the ones that last . . .*

Finally the darkness swirled up to take her where there was only safe, warm peace. She slept without dreams.

When she woke it was still night. But deeper. The covers were moist and warm. She moved back to press her shoulders into Michael's chest and—met cold space.

She blinked several times to convince herself she was awake. "Michael?"

No answer. She turned on her side. The cold space grew. Michael was gone. The ceiling rumbled. The other side of the bed looked so *vast.*

Maybe he'd gone for a drink of water; *she* often did that in the night.

She pulled the pillows close, waited for him to return. The clock ticked once, then again.

She called, "Bring me some water too, please." There was no response. The gas snapped on. Something cold trickled down the back of her neck. The ceiling rumbled again.

A slight breeze drifted by the bed, tickled her shoulders, went toward the open bedroom door, through the corridor—

Into the living room. The beams of moonlight pressed against the foot of the bed to tip it over and send her sliding down to the floor. She closed her eyes, felt the tightness of her flesh.

"MICHAEL!" Her voice reverberated off the walls, left her ears ringing. He *had* to have heard that.

No answer.

Maybe he'd slipped out, thinking she'd be embarrassed when she woke in the morning because of her behavior; yet he had said he *loved* her, wasn't going anywhere. (But how many times had Dad said the same thing?)

The force of the breeze increased.

She rose, put on her nightgown, shuffled into the corridor.

The breeze grew stronger.

Once in the living room, she refused to look at the hole; that's what it *wanted,* for her to stand staring as the streams flowed out and—

There was a stain on the carpet, a dark smear that hadn't been there before. She stared at it.

Was it really moving as she thought? Perhaps it was just a trick of the moonlight casting her shadow, for it seemed to grow larger, then smaller in an instant . . .

The stain kept moving. Slowly. Back. As if dragged.

She put a hand to her mouth, breathed out, reassured by her warm breath; then she snapped on a light.

She remembered a prank she'd played as a child on a neighbor who'd sent a dog to chase her from the yard. She had come home and cleared the vegetable bin of all the tomatoes Daddy had bought at that market he and Mom used to love shopping at and *thrown* them against that neighbor's house, laughing when they splattered every which way, the seeds, juice, and skin spattering, widening with each new throw and moist *pop!,* some of the skin sliding off to the ground.

The living-room wall looked like the side of that house.

Only the skin was crawling along the floor, being sucked back into the hole—which was so much bigger now, so much wider; she could probably shove her entire arm through up to the elbow.

The breeze grew violent, edging her toward the wall.

She saw Michael's Saint Christopher medal still on its chain, near the wall. He loved that medal, always wore it, wouldn't even take it off to shower.

The breeze increased, becoming wind.

The ceiling rumbled.

The hole was swirling under the seeds and skin and juice, opening wide with Daddy's smile on the tail of moonbeams . . .

Yolanda turned, caught a glimpse of herself in the mirror over the fireplace. She nearly shrieked, thinking how right her father had been:

She looked a *lot* like her mother.

The stain backed toward the base of the wall, near the hole.

She could easily stick her head through it now.

The wind almost knocked her off-balance—but she held firm, knowing something about feelings and night, love and tears: all of them could only be judged by what they drew from suffering.

So long as that suffering never drew them back.

—and if you can leave through a hole you can *come back through one,* even if it's one piece at a time. But she loved him—and weren't you supposed to help the one you loved put the pieces back together?

She ran to the wall, called his name into the aperture, watched as it gulped everything in like a last breath before dying. She jammed her hand through, hoped he might reach out to take it and come back—leave all the memories and pain behind like Mom had left them, without a backward glance of regret.

She pushed in deeper, felt something close round her wrist; so very strong, yet so gentle and loving.

Suddenly the pressure of the grip turned to the prick of razors and sucked her arm in up to the shoulder.

The ceiling started to thunder.

She yanked back again, knowing one of them would weaken soon because the stain and pieces were nearly gone now, and when they *were* gone the hole would . . . would . . .

. . . would keep growing until it had *her,* would still send the wind and thunder and memories and—She wrenched away with all her strength—

—and felt herself pull free.

Yolanda fell back-first to the floor but didn't wait to catch her breath, didn't look at the hole; she sprinted out of the room, knowing how she could get him back. She couldn't do it with her hand, didn't dare try that again, yet she *could* make the hole bigger—and Michael would see the way out, he'd come back to her because he loved her, didn't want her to be alone, never again. *I'm sorry, Daddy, that you missed Mom so bad, but Michael is my family now, all I've got left—*

She darted through the kitchen, into the bathroom, unlocked the door to the basement, flipped on the light, took the stairs three at a time.

The shotgun. She hadn't told the police about Daddy's shotgun, they'd only taken the pistol, but that was fine because she *needed* the shotgun now, for Michael and—

—she ripped open the door to her father's work cabinet and found the twelve-gauge under a sheet of canvas. She grabbed the shells and loaded the gun, smiling as she pumped back—

—ch-chick!—

—and felt the first one slide securely into the chamber.

Back upstairs. Fast. Into the living room.

In the mirror she saw the reflection of her mother gripping the gun that had killed Daddy. She tried to work up enough saliva to spit in Momma's face but her mouth was too dry so she hoisted the shotgun, pressed the butt against her shoulder, pulled the trigger—

The ceiling thundered again as Momma shattered into a thousand glittering reflections. Yolanda looked down and saw how small the woman looked, staring up from the floor, shiny, sharp, and smooth, and empty-eyed *pitiful*.

She readied herself—

—ch-chick!—

—and aimed at the hole.

The wind slammed against her with angry hands, but it would not stop her. Nothing would.

Again and again and again the ceiling thundered as she blew the hole apart, her shoulder raw from the pounding of the butt, her chest full of pain and fear; but she kept firing until the force of the blasts weakened her, knocked her from the garden wall.

She dropped to the floor, gazing at the hole.

Wide, dark, bloodied inside. She peered deeper into the mouth of the web and saw *forms* moving within—like people passing on the street—and she listened for Michael's voice but there were others, *different* voices beckoning to her: *Empty here, so empty without you, I love you I miss you I want you back please come—*

The hole was beginning to close.

She tried to rise because *they* were in there, Daddy and Michael; but she was too spent, hurt, too weakened. She fell back, saw a thousand reflections of her mother's face, glaring up at her—

—and knew what to do.

"Wait for me," she said. Whispered. Weakly.

She wanted to be in there with them—away from the draining strength of suffering and the memories whose warmth was tainted by it. She fell forward, groped with shaking fingers for the shotgun and dragged it toward her, sat up.

The hole was small, now—tiny—one shimmering globule was on the edge, winking at her, hurry, *hurry,* get across the ledge.

She propped the shotgun up between her knees—

—*ch-chick!*—

—and shoved the barrel deep into her mouth.

The globule smiled, then winked, like Daddy letting her in on some little secret. *That's my girl, just get over the mountain, don't fall off and I'll tell you something special, because you were brave, you made it back to me—*

From the corner of her eye she saw a thousand images of her mother, all of them screaming.

Then Daddy's voice again. *Almost there, honey, keep your balance, don't slip, don't fall away like Mommy did because I'll never leave you like she did, I'll always be here, I'll be right here waiting for you and always—*

—the ceiling thundered one last time, and a new web spread across the wall—

—*love you.*

Pop Is Real Smart

Mort Castle

Lonny gazed at Jason. He loathed him with all the egoistic hatred of which only a five-year-old is capable. He was supposed to be happy he had a new brother. He was supposed to love him. Oh, sure. Right. Damn.

Lonny's eyes measured the baby's length and studied the pink fingers curled in tight fists at the top of the blue blanket. He watched the fluttery beating of the soft spot on Jason's head as, under skimpy down, it palpitated with the tiny heart.

"Damn," Lonny said. Pop said "Damn" a lot, like when he was driving and everybody else was driving like a jerk, or when he was trying to fix a leaky faucet or something.

And "damn" is just what Lonny felt like saying whenever he looked at Jason. The only thing the baby could do—his ookey-pukey brother!—was smell bad. Jason always smelled, no matter how often Mom bathed him or dumped a load of powder on him.

Jason wasn't good for anything!

Now Scott, down the block, Scott was lucky. Scott had a *real* brother, Fred, good old Fred. Yessir, Fred was a fun kid. You could punch Fred real hard and he wouldn't even cry. And Fred didn't go running to tell, either. Uh-uh. But Fred had these clumpy cowboy boots, and if you punched him, then he would just start kicking you and kicking, and maybe *you* would be the one who wound up crying!

Fred, that was the kind of dude you wanted for a little brother.

Not Jason. This damn baby, hey, he couldn't do anything.

And this was the kid Lonny had helped Mom and Pop choose a name for? Jason. That was a good name for a good guy. Damn! Jason—*this* stupid thing with that stupid up-and-down blob on its head going thump-a-thump, thump-a-thump. No way, José!

Somebody must have fooled Mom. When she'd gone to the hospital, Mom had somehow got stuck with this little snot instead of a good brother for him.

Lonny wondered how Mom could be so damn dumb. Well, she was a girl, even if she was a grown-up, and girls could be pretty dumb sometimes. But damn, how did they put one over on Pop? Pop was real smart.

Lonny reached through the crib slats. He lightly touched Jason's soft spot. At the pulse beneath his fingers, he yanked back his hand.

Damn, this baby was just no good. No good.

He left the room. There had to be some way to get rid of Jason. He would ask Mom to take the baby back to the hospital, tell her she'd made a mistake. Oh, he'd have to say it just the right way so she didn't get pee-owed, but he'd figure it out. Then she could go get him a really good brother, like Fred.

Yeah! He knew just how to say it. He'd talk to Mom right now. "Mom!" he hollered, running down the stairs. He hoped he would wake the baby.

Mom did not answer. Jason did not cry.

"Mom!" Lonny went to the kitchen. The linoleum buzzed beneath his Nikes and he heard the muffled thud of the washing machine in the downstairs utility room.

Mom was doing the wash. Damn, it was never a good

idea to talk to her about *anything* when she was into laundry.

Lonny decided he might as well make himself a sandwich or something. He dragged a chair from the table over to the cabinets. He climbed up and took down the big jar of peanut butter. He got the Wonder Bread from the bread box.

He set the bread and peanut butter on the table. He hoped he could open the new jar by himself. No way did he want to ask Mom for help when she was doing the laundry.

Okay! The lid came right off. "Yeah," Lonny said. "She's gonna have to take it back. It's no damn good, and if it's no good, you just take it back."

Hey, sometimes he wondered how a smart guy like Pop got stuck with Mom, anyway. For real, it was *Pop* had the brains.

Like once Lonny had goofed it. He had spent his birthday money on a rifle at Toys-R-Us and damn! It was wrong. It wasn't a Rambo assault rifle. It was a stupid Ranger Rock rifle. No way did you want a Ranger Rock rifle. Who ever heard of Ranger Rock?

So he and Pop took it back to get the Rambo rifle. "No refunds on sale items, sorry." That's what this real dipstick at the store had to say.

Then Pop showed him how you couldn't even pull the trigger and the way the plastic barrel was all cracked and everything.

No problem, man! They got back his birthday money, went to another store, and bought the Rambo rifle.

And you know what? That nerd at Toys-R-Us never even had an idea that Pop had busted up the stupid Ranger Rock rifle himself! That's how smart Pop was.

With his first finger, Lonny swirled out a glob of peanut butter. He popped it into his mouth. Yeah, peanut butter was great. He could live on peanut butter all the time. He'd make a nice, open-faced sandwich, and then maybe Mom would be done with the laundry and he could talk to her about getting rid of smelly Jason.

He went to the drawers by the sink. He opened the top one.

Mom always spread peanut butter with a dull knife.

It was the sharp knife that caught Lonny's eye.

When the Wall Cries

Stanley Wiater

Tears scorch her porcelain white face with the severity of a Madonna's, but Margarita can no longer taste them, nor waste the time to wipe them away from her quivering lips. Her hands clutch the cold, moist sides of the toilet's rear basin as she focuses her attention on a discolored blotch on the wall.

Standing over the open bowl, knees bent, legs spread unnaturally wide, Margarita cries. And waits. And cries. The pain begins below the pit of her belly, running back and forth on her spine to scrape ultimately behind her eyes like a rat trying madly to escape. It's too late for prayers, yet pray she must to keep from blacking out as she waits for thickly clotted blood and unformed tissue to drop from between her slender, trembling legs.

"Dios te salve Maria, Llena heres de gracia el Señor es contigo . . ."

The teenager's body is a palsied depository of warm liquids and cold moistures as tears linger, then stickily mix with sweat. Margarita throws back her head to try and fling off the long black hair falling repeatedly over her face like a torn and itchy hood. Her recent breakfast of Twinkies and a bowl of Cap'n Crunch cereal, threatening to spray up through her tightly clenched lips, reminds her she mustn't look down when it's over.

If it's ever going to be over.

No matter what she hears or feels, she knows she has to flush the toilet before she can open her eyes again. She can look down only after . . . after it's gone. Gone from her life. Out of any life.

The last convulsion grabs up inside her like heated pliers, then abruptly releases with the unmistakable sensation of flesh being torn from her body. Margarita bites into her lower lip until she tastes blood as a mass of lumpy fluids suddenly voids and splashes loudly into the open bowl. Her legs still shaking violently, she blindly flushes the silver-colored handle a dozen times before somehow pushing herself away from the unending, rust-stained swirl.

Nearly falling, she grabs an unused white towel from the neat pile kept beneath the sink. Margarita hurriedly rolls it into a cocoon and thrusts it beneath her dripping thighs like a diaper. Leaning against the plastic clothes hamper for support, she reaches out to turn on the cold-water tap. With her right hand pressing the towel more firmly between her legs, Margarita splashes the soothing water against the upper half of her body. The soiled cotton nightgown clings like a soaked dishrag as she quickly turns her head and glances back. The terrified girl moans in despair even before she can focus her vision, smelling the fresh blood lingering in the air.

Yet the toilet bowl is finally silent, its cleansing waters no longer disturbed. She starts to make the sign of the cross, then stops herself before it's complete.

Margarita realizes she should take a bath immediately, but first she has to get out of the same room where such an unforgivably sacrilegious act has just been performed. If she had any friends in this strange land, they would tell her she should first rest, try and get some sleep, then maybe she'd be able to face the world again. More important, she could now explain to Junior why she had been acting so strangely

these past several weeks. However, just the slightest suggestion she might be *encinta* made him smash his way out
of their basement apartment in a speechless rage a full three
days ago.

Three empty nights ago.

The towel still between her legs, Margarita slowly moves
out of the bathroom. She wipes the tears from her face with
the back of one hand, thinking of what she has done to keep
the man she loves.

Junior *has* to come back soon. Not only did the owner
of this welfare hotel accept them as a married couple, he
was willing to employ them both as a housekeeper and assistant maintenance man. But she doesn't think Mr. Gonski
will accept another day of her being away from work, while
her "husband" has supposedly gone off to visit a very sick
relative. The few skills they have to offer are far from
unique, though Margarita suspects from the unsettling way
Mr. Gonski smiles that if they ever complain, he has more
in mind for her than bending over to clean toilets or scrub
floors.

Green cards are a luxury neither can yet afford.

Sitting on the edge of a chair in the combined kitchen-
and-living-room area, Margarita takes a deep breath and
slowly removes the towel. Spreading her thin legs wide, she
hesitates at examining herself any further. The bleeding
seems to have stopped, and she whispers another prayer that
tonight there won't be any more stained sheets. At least she
no longer has to hide the symptoms of morning sickness
from her man.

If the subject is brought up at the right moment, she
hopes Junior will take her to the free health clinic always
mentioned on the radio station that broadcasts in their na-
tive language.

When he returns.

If he returns.

Shedding the sticky nightgown like a useless second skin,
Margarita fills a deep pan with warm water from the kitchen

sink. Finding a clean sponge near a tray of unwashed dishes, she whimpers quietly and gives herself an improvised bath. She just *can't* go back into that room until more time has passed. The stabbing pains inside her belly finally subside. Pressing an open palm between her unnaturally tender breasts, her heart beats so feebly she imagines it was also flushed away.

Shuddering, Margarita wonders what she might have done to her soul by not giving another eternal soul a chance to live.

The washing completed, she drops the sponge on the Formica-top table next to the bloody towel. Making her way to the bedroom, she sits naked on the unmade bed, reassuring herself she won't faint as long as she doesn't make any sudden movements. Margarita wishes she could stay here forever. Yet one of the other hotel employees had warned her last night that if she or Junior wasn't seen working today, they'd be back on the streets again. A phone call to the Man might be made. Or Mr. Gonski might find something else for her to do repeatedly on her hands and knees.

Shuffling along to the single walk-in closet, Margarita takes from her own side of the metal rod the blue housekeeper's uniform she must wear. It is permanently discolored along the hem while the lacy trimmings at the collar and cuff have been crudely picked at and discarded like wings from a captured bird. But just as long as the uniform and the person who wears it are relatively clean and neat, Mr. Gonski is satisfied. He has more important items to spend his money on than the working people in his hotel.

Putting on a Stayfree sanitary pad and two pairs of faded cotton panties, Margarita then slips the uniform over her head and ties the attached apron sash behind her slim waist. Finding the matching sneakers beneath a chair, she dons them, then turns to regard herself in the peeling bureau mirror. Combing back her long shiny hair, she applies blusher to disguise how pale her skin appears, then bright scarlet lipstick to her colorless slash of a mouth. She wonders who the young clown is who's staring back at her with the painted smile.

Closing her eyes to suffocate the emerging tears, Margarita has never felt this alone in her entire fifteen years of existence. Her hands shaking, she closes the bedroom door and heads toward the gas stove. There she fumbles for the set of keys which will open all the necessary doors in the ten-story Blodgett Hotel before leaving the apartment.

Not that there is anywhere she can hide.

But when she arrives at the maintenance closet on the first floor, Margarita is struck immediately by how unusually quiet the building is. Then she remembers the holiday, what the radio had reported about the festivities; a big parade downtown. There are no signs of the other housekeepers, even though their cleaning carts are still there. Perhaps they were given the day off?

Someone always has to be on duty at the front desk, plus the two old *cabrones* who, as the hotel's "security force," would still be making their rounds. If they weren't already passed out drunk on the roof. Someone will report her to Mr. Gonski, of that she has no illusions.

While checking the contents of her multi-shelved metal cart, Margarita heads for the nearby service elevator. According to the schedule, the main tasks today will be to go to "the apartments" and check on the fresh linen and toiletries furnished for each tenant. No one would be the wiser if she went through the motions of checking only a few rooms on each floor. Regardless, she *has* to spend a few hours at her job in order to be seen, so that a favorable report can be made to her boss. What otherwise will happen with her life tomorrow is a hardship not worth considering.

The gray metal doors of the service elevator pull themselves apart and wait silently to suck her in.

Margarita knocks at the door of Room 504, receives no answer, then unlocks it and cautiously walks in. Although she has been working here nearly three months, the unkempt and filthy condition of more than a few of the rooms still disgusts her. The reek of vomit and unwashed clothing in some of the so-called apartments is enough to make her gag just thinking of it.

A sixty-second check of the linen shelves in the bathroom indicates that 504 doesn't need her services today. As she's closing the door behind her, an unexpected sound issues faintly from the bathroom. She stops to listen for a moment. Her mother had eight children; Margarita, the third-born, can never forget the only source of such a sound.

It comes from the lungs and throat and mouth of a newborn *bebe*.

"*Dios mio. . .*" Margarita can't bring herself to go in there again—not after what happened this morning in her own squalid little bathroom.

Leaning against the outer wall, she places a fluttering hand against her bosom and waits for the heartbeats to stop hurting. Waiting, too, for the awful, maddening sound to begin again. But all she hears is the rasping of her own shallow breath. Margarita swallows dryly and closes her eyes for a few peaceful seconds. It's only natural she should have babies clogging her thoughts today—*Bebes muertos*.

Dead babies.

A moment later she is moving down the hallway like someone who has heard a dozen smoke alarms go off. She knows she must keep moving. Always to live with the knowledge of what she has done to herself and her unborn child is a sin she isn't yet prepared to suffer. The dull, throbbing pain returns; Margarita clutches her belly, her other hand grasping the side of the cart for support. Her mouth makes weak, meaningless sounds, uncomfortably similar to those she has just heard.

Margarita blinks her eyes rapidly to keep the tears under control. The teenager isn't sure if she should be pleased or worried that she has seen no one on her rounds. The empty corridors don't seem to have heard the sound of footsteps or voices for many years. Looking down their length as she turns a corner, she cannot avoid the sensation of some subtle warping of the walls, the ceiling. The doors appear unevenly matched in size and dimension. The frayed carpeting stretches unendingly like a diseased tongue, the material stained and threadbare. Like the service elevator, the closed doors are hungry mouths waiting to be opened. Waiting to be fed.

Margarita stops the cart's roll outside Room 515.

She listens there for a few moments after knocking at the door to see if anyone is inside. Silence.

Taking a deep breath, she unlocks it and steps inside, leaving the door open wide. She moves quickly through 515. She checks the linen shelves in the bathroom and efficiently deals with the items that must be replaced.

Silence.

Leaves Room 515. Carefully locks the door as if she's never going to return there.

The thought is permitted only after she's around the corner again: *No noises came from the bathroom.* No old foundation settling. No rusty pipes shrieking. Nothing. It's the same situation on the next three floors, where Margarita checks a total of nine rooms. She doubts that, if it weren't for the holiday, so many of the rooms would be unoccupied. There is no one to disturb while getting drunk or shooting up.

Chewing nervously at her thumb, Margarita moves along a corridor that's a drab twin to the previous one. Certainly *someone* will see her before she collapses from nervous exhaustion!

Arms aching, she drops off bundles of sheets and towels in four other rooms before unlocking 208. On a few other occasions, she has met the young family of six who presently resides here. Like everyone else, they have apparently gone outside to watch the parade. The quiet surrounding her becomes increasingly unsettling.

Placing her hand on the doorknob to shut the door after her routine is again completed, Margarita hears something. In the bathroom. She doesn't want to listen, but can't help hearing it.

Cries. Much like a newborn baby's crying. Yet so loud it's as if the very walls were pleading to be heard by someone who gives a damn.

"Dios mio, ayudame! Dios mio!" she screams back, clutching the doorknob as if she might use it to turn off what she's hearing.

As if triggered by the pitiful cries, Margarita is stricken by a new wave of cramps that rise up inside her belly. The intense wails make it difficult for her to think clearly; they virtually rise and fall with the rhythm of her own heartbeats. Gasping, she rushes from 208 and slams the door shut with a force that startles her. But before she can move far enough away, the young woman overhears the old toilet flushing, gurgling unnaturally loud and long. Cleansing and swirling sounds.

Swirling and drowning.

Drowning.

Then the cries are no more.

Too nauseous to return the cart to the floor station, Margarita finds herself suddenly afraid to take the service elevator. Hands pressed against her damp forehead, she considers all the countless secrets within the rooms of this crumbling welfare hotel. Memories which are so intensely painful that they can never be swept away, lingering like the rectangular traces of the framed paintings that once hung in the barren hallways.

Crazily, Margarita recalls how, when she first arrived here, a goldfish was given away to her and Junior at a pet-store opening. How the tiny creature died right after she had brought it back in the water-filled sandwich bag. And how no one had thought anything the matter as the beautiful, shiny little life was unceremoniously flushed away. Now she understands.

Hotel bathrooms possess their own dirty secrets that no

one wants to remember. Now the traces of their sins are finally calling out, though no one wants to hear.

Twisting a handkerchief around sweating hands, Margarita listens fitfully to the sobs issuing faintly from Room 110. And from Room 114. *Doesn't anyone hear them?* Worse, there's something strange in the way the cries come, as if from mouths that aren't yet fully formed. Just fleshy, tiny holes. She spins in a circle as the wailing grows louder still, like a boom-box being thoughtlessly turned up to the max.

Stifling a scream, Margarita runs to the end of the hall and down the two flights of stairs to the basement and the sanctuary of her own squalid apartment. The lighting is out again over one section of the stairwell, forcing her to hold out her arms to grope along the wall. At this level, the handrails broke off years ago and were never replaced. The walls are pimply, warm in the dark, like the skin of some exotic animal Junior couldn't identify for her when they once visited a zoo. The wall feels ready to give away at any instant, its moist surface almost indented by the pressure from her sweating hands.

She slips over something soft yet bulky lying in a corner where another section of stairs begins. The released fetid smell is nearly overpowering. Momentarily losing her balance, Margarita falls against the darkened wall. Some skin scrapes off her fingers; it feels like removing a glove that is lined with dull razors. The unseen object had vaguely felt like a stuffed toy as it gave way under her foot. Another discarded plaything, left to rot where no one will see.

Like so many unwanted things in this hotel.

As she finally reaches the fire door, her sneaker slides across a substance as warm and slimy as the inner walls. She tells herself it's only some drunk's fresh vomit as the heavy metal door opens sluggishly, its weight almost too great for her to force in her weakened condition. The reinforced glass window in its center is blacked out with dirt and grime, but Margarita knows the apartment is on the

other side. It slowly pulls open with a rusty screech—
sounding too much like her own voice should she lose all
control and start screaming again. Then, at last, she's
through.

And now the smell of fresh blood and new flesh is everywhere.

Rushing blindly into the apartment, Margarita lurches toward the bedroom and collapses on the still unmade bed. No
odors. No noises here. In a few moments she realizes she is
safe, if still alone. It was simply too much to hope that Junior might be there, waiting for her to return to him. The
thought begins to creep into her mind that he just might
never come back.

Shooting pains stab between her legs when she tries to
get off the bed.

Biting her lower lip, Margarita can only lie quietly and
pray that the pain won't worsen. She reaches up to pull a
lumpy pillow under her head. Flat on her back, her pain sub-
sides slightly when she spreads out her legs. She doesn't
dare touch herself now, though her underwear is soaked
through; the sticky wetness seeps into it. She knows she
should bathe somehow, but it's so hard just to keep her pale
brown eyes open.

A huge plastic crucifix looks down at her from over the
headboard of the bed, seeming to share her suddenly re-
newed agony.

Hours appear to have passed. A different kind of dull
ache tells the girl she must use the toilet or stain the sheets
once more. At least the hot needles in her belly have departed. Pulling herself up, she considers using the
employees' rest room on the first floor. But with legs as stiff
as the bed, she can't possibly make it in time.

"Estaba soñando, solamente soñando," she whispers
over and over to try to reassure herself. Hoping desperately

that, when he does return, Junior will take her to the free clinic just to make sure everything is all right inside her.

He has to come back! Junior has to or she'll—

Margarita's head jerks around as she hears noises suddenly from outside the bedroom. Crouching on the edge of the bed, she is unable to recognize them, though they're obviously increasing in both intensity and number. One sound, however, is unmistakable: the toilet flushing.

Junior—has he finally come home? Or is it just the cold, rusty water giving back its unwanted wastes? Her ninety-pound body shudders violently; she starts to weep again.

Margarita realizes she must still be sleeping.

This guilty imagining of sounds that several unborn infants would make if gathering together in a brood. Why, she can even visualize clearly their tiny little hands— hands not yet completely formed in their various fetal stages—pulling in unison to move aside the tremendously heavy bathroom door. Then slowly, painfully, crawling across the cracked and warped linoleum floor on their way into the bedroom.

In the dream, they are leaving behind a trail of bright scarlet mucus like a multitude of snails in their search, their minute eyes not yet capable of seeing a world that didn't want them to be born. Crawling from a moist, filthy blackness, unable to shed tears for those who didn't wish ever to have to see them return, ever to acknowledge that— even in this sluglike form—they still exist; can still cry out for another chance at love, until finally heard by someone who understands what it means to be completely undesired.

While the drenched, fragile hands complete their task at the bedroom door, Margarita's own mouth opens wide to lead the others in their unending, wailing chorus. Then at last, at long last, she feels the smallest, freshest one grasp her bare ankle and begin instinctively to ascend toward her inner thigh. The tears stop falling from her eyes.

"*Bienvenida, pequeña, bienvenida a esta casa,*" she says,

smiling down at him benevolently as the floor is covered in a dripping, stinking mixture of red and black and pink. While the others, no longer alone and no longer crying, slide over one another in fervent search of her open legs.

Impatiently awaiting a second chance.

Return to the Mutant Rain Forest

Bruce Boston and Robert Frazier

Years later we come back to find the fauna and
   flora
more alien than ever, the landscape
   unrecognizable,
the course of rivers altered, small opalescent lakes
springing up where before there was only
   underbrush,
as if the land itself has somehow changed to keep
   pace
with the metaprotean life forms which now inhabit it.

Here magnetism proves as variable as other
   phenomena.
Our compass needle shifts constantly and at random,
and we must fix direction by the stars and sun alone.
Above our heads the canopy writhes in undiscovered
   life:
tiny albino lemurs flit silently from branch to
   branch,
tenuous as arboreal ghosts in the leaf purple shadow.

Here time seems as meaningless as our abstracted
     data.
The days stretch before us in soft bands of verdigris,
in hours marked by slanting white shafts of
     illumination.
At our feet we watch warily for the tripvines of
     arrowroot,
while beetles and multipedes of every possible
     perversion
boil about us, reclaiming their dead with voracious zeal.

By the light of irradiated biota the night proliferates:
a roving carpet of scavenger fungi seeks out each kill
to drape and consume the carcass in an iridescent
     shroud.
A carnivorous mushroom spore roots on my exposed
     forearm
and Tomaz must dig deeply beneath the flesh to
     excise
the wrinkled neon growth which has sprouted in
     minutes.

We have returned to the mutant rain forest to trace
rumors spread by the natives who fish the white water,
to embark on a reconnaissance into adaptation and
     myth.
Where are the toucans, Genna wonders, once we
     explain
the cries which fill the darkness as those of panthers,
mating in heat, nearly articulate in their complexity.

Tomaz chews stale tortillas, pounds roots for
     breakfast,
and relates a tale of the Parakana who ruled this land.
One morning the Chief's wife, aglow, bronzed and
     naked
in the eddies of a rocky pool, succumbed to an attack

both brutal and sublime, which left her body inscribed
with scars confirming the bestial origins of her lover.

At term, the massive woman was said to have borne a
child
covered with the finest gossamer caul of ebon-blue
hair.
The fiery vertical slits of its eyes enraged the Chief.
After he murdered the boy, a great cat screamed for
weeks
and stalked about their tribal home, driving them
north.
His story over, Tomaz leads our way into the damp
jungle.

From base camp south we hack one trail after another
until we encounter impenetrable walls of a sinewy
fiber,
lianas as thick and indestructible as titanium cables,
twining back on themselves in a solid Gordian
sheath,
feeding on their own past growth; while farther
south,
slender silver trees rise like pylons into the clouds.

From our campo each day we hack useless trail after
trail,
until we come upon the pathways that others have
forged
and maintained, sinuous and waist-high, winding
inward
to still farther corrupt recesses of genetic abandon:
here we discover a transfigured ceiba, its rugged
bark
incised with the fresh runes of a primitive ideography.

Genna calls a halt in our passage to load her
    Minicam.
She circles about the tree, shrugging off our
    protests.
As we feared, her careless movement triggers a
    tripvine,
but instead of a hail of deadly spines we are
    bombarded
by balled leaves exploding into dust—marking us
    with
luminous ejecta and a third eye on Genna's forehead.

Souza dies that night, limbs locked in rigid
    fibrogenesis.
A panther cries; Tomaz wants us to regroup at our
    campo.
Genna decides she has been chosen, scarified for
    passage.
She notches her own trail to some paradise born of
    dream
hallucination, but stumbles back, wounded and
    half-mad,
the Minicam lost, a cassette gripped in whitened
    knuckles.

From base camp north we flail at the miraculous
    regrowth
which walls off our retreat to the airstrip by the river.
The ghost lemurs now spin about our heads, they
    mock us
with a chorus as feverish and compulsive as our
    thoughts.
We move relentlessly forward, as one, the final
    scenes
of Genna's tape flickering over and over in our
    brains.

In the depths of the mutant rain forest where the water
falls each afternoon in a light filtered to vermilion,
a feline stone idol stands against the opaque foliage.
On the screen of the monitor it rises up from
  nowhere,
upon its hind legs, both taller and thicker than a man.
how the cellular accretion has distended its skull,
how the naturally sleek architecture of the
  countenance
has evolved into a distorted and angular grotesquerie,
how the taloned forepaws now possess opposable
  digits.
In the humid caves and tunnels carved from living
  vines,
where leprous anacondas coil, a virulent faith calls
  us.
A sudden species fashions godhood in its own
  apotheosis.

The Willies

James Kisner

Ron stood at the window, looking down on the crowded streets of the city. His office was located on the third story of the building, so he had a clear view of the different varieties of humanity out and about on this pleasant autumn day.

He liked watching people and amused himself by imagining who and what they were. Most of the persons he saw in the streets below were obviously young businessmen like himself, caught up in the electric pace of the metropolitan hustle—going to lunch, discussing market projections, and making dates for golf before the weather turned too cold. Yes, Ron thought, people just like me. They've got their act entirely together. Upwardly mobile. *Sharp* guys. Born to succeed.

Weaving among the businessmen (and women, Ron amended mentally) were shoppers, schoolchildren playing hooky, street kids with ghetto blasters, and working stiffs, some of whom (Ron imagined) were going to the unemployment lines at the state office building the next block over, or perhaps to the police station to pay traffic fines and plead innocent to various misdemeanors.

All these people seemed to Ron to have purpose, no matter how trivial they might be in the overall scheme of things.

And Ron approved of that, because he believed a being without purpose was the most worthless thing imaginable.

That's why the winos bothered him so much.

A withered man was slumped in an alley not far away. He sat on the rough pavement with his arms wrapped around his knees, mumbling through fragments of memories and luxuriating in the warmth of his piss-stained trousers. He could have been thirty-five or seventy, depending on the light he was seen in. Most of the time, though, he avoided being seen at all, preferring the almost perpetual, dim twilight of the alley.

A few minutes each day, when the sun was directly overhead, the man would look up and vaguely wonder who he was and what exactly had happened to him. He couldn't remember at what point he had ceased being whoever it was he had been and had become what he was now, which was still, at bottom, not much of anything; and sorting through all the imprints in the few (scant few) brain cells he had left yielded very little to which he could append a definite identity, nor any shred of certainty.

After the sun had passed over, he would settle down again and not worry about anything other than panhandling to get enough money for a jug, which he'd do when the urge came over him, usually later in the day.

And as he turned his face back to his knees, hugging himself a little tighter perhaps before shrinking down into inertia, he comforted himself with the old one-and-three axiom he had formulated long ago to propel him through life. The old one-and-three consisted of one thing he *suspected* was true, and three things of which he was almost abso-goddamn-lutely *certain*.

The one thing he suspected was that he had tuberculosis.

The three things of which he was certain were: that *one*, he was a man (though—he inspected his withered tool, a sort of homuncular duplicate of his face—only on rare occasions); *two,* he was a wino; and *three,* his name was Willie.

All winos are named Willie, just as all bulldogs are named Spike.

It was a breezy day in the city, but not unpleasantly so. There was just enough wind to carry shapeless things.

Shapeless invisible things that nevertheless had purpose.

"Ready to go to lunch?" Bill asked.

Ron turned from the window slowly, reluctant to give up his people-watching.

"Sure." He sighed heavily. "Where to?"

"Let's walk somewhere. It's such a nice day out, you don't even need a jacket."

"Okay," Ron said. "Let's go over to the deli."

The wind bristled the hairs on Willie's ears, and he ached suddenly for the comfort of a jug. He ordered his mind to relay a message to his limbs that it was time to stir— lunchtime, guys, when a lot of people are out and it's a little easier to mooch a few quarters for a bottle. The cells in Willie's body responded eventually to the mental imperative and he unfolded himself and lurched into a standing position, moving awkwardly and with great uncertainty, like a crude figure in an old cartoon movie.

Life *was* a cartoon sometimes, for people like Willie. Maybe most of the time.

Standing as erect as he could, Willie still resembled a question mark. He had developed the habit of constantly peering down, because he knew no one cared really to look him in the eyes. Most people just wanted to be rid of him, and the easiest way was to shove him four bits or a dollar, generally holding the money out in such a way as to avoid being touched by his smelly presence.

He brushed off his colorless clothes with the palms of his hands, pausing here and there to rearrange a wrinkle or change the direction of the nap on the corduroy jacket that once had been brown. His trousers had been charcoal-gray, and his plaid shirt had once been predominantly blue. There was a woolen tie he never wore stuffed in one pocket and an obscenely snot-and-mucus-encrusted handkerchief in another pocket. In the back pocket of his trousers was a battered suede cap, which he thoughtfully removed and arranged on his head at a slight angle.

Now ready to meet the public, Willie walked slowly out of the alley and onto the sidewalk. There certainly *were* a lot of people out today; it should be easy to make a touch.

Spare change, mister? Can you spare a dollar for a jug, mister? Jeez, mister, I really *need* a jug. Got a quarter for a cup of coffee? Spare four bits for a guy that really needs it?

No use rehearsing, Willie decided at last. It didn't matter what you said. They either gave you some goddamn money or they didn't.

He moved through the crowds on the sidewalk at a leisurely, almost lackadaisical pace, managing to beg seventy-five cents by the time he traveled the half block from the alley to the corner. Not bad, but not enough. He turned the corner and paused to stare at a newsstand where the latest men's magazines were on sale. He blinked at the cover of a *Penthouse* from which a nearly nude woman seemed to be smiling at him. The way the artful camerawork hid her obvious sexual characteristics was admirable. Even Willie could appreciate it.

A wind came up and flipped the cover slightly, creating an illusion that taunted Willie. As the sun played on the moving, glossy surface, the woman was suddenly animated, not alive but just seeming to *be:* a cartoon woman for a cartoon man like he was. Like Willie was.

Hot damn!

Willie's withered brow wrinkled.

He hadn't had a woman in years, and even the most worn-out old hooker would turn him down now; but something strange stirred deep down inside him, perhaps a vague memory, a stray hormone wiggling through his brain reminding him of what once was, and how it had been for him as a younger man, before he became Willie and just about everything in him had turned off; not even latent any more, but almost absolutely dead.

There are absolutes, even in a cartoon universe.

When they sat across from each other in the deli devouring sloppy sandwiches, Ron and Bill were almost mirror images. They both wore crisp white shirts with button-down collars, striped rep ties, and slacks with the proper creases. Their faces were smooth and framed with neatly styled light-brown hair.

"Pass the spice," Ron said.

Bill reached for the shaker of ground oregano and dried hot peppers, handed it to Ron.

Ron opened his sandwich and liberally sprinkled the spice over its steaming contents. "Great lunch."

"Think I'll have another iced tea."

"Should we have some dessert?"

"Sure," Bill said. "Let's try that cannelloni stuff."

The tips of Willie's fingers itched and his chest ached when he recalled the feel of warm flesh against his own, and, for a fleeting second, he thought he felt a little lead in his pencil.

Then he shut the feeling off, abruptly, deciding it was unseemly after all and that he had better things to worry about than the raw longing for a goddamn woman.

He didn't need a woman, neither to look at nor to touch. They were just too much trouble for what you received in return from them, and they wasted money that was better spent on a jug.

Wine never let you down like any female would, like every woman he'd ever known had done. Wine never broke its promise of sweet relief from the past, of numbing the senses for the present, and the surcease of sorrow from the already moribund future.

He continued down the block, seeking enough hard cash to buy the jug that now seemed especially important. Wine made all the difference in life. Sweet wine. Not women.

Goddamn *Penthouse* anyhow.

Goddamn women.

Pure evil is a potent force to be admired, and pure evil rode shapelessly on the wind, seeking something.

It had no words with which to think, no brain cells in which to store memories, no substance, no organs of any kind, nor any function to worry about.

It was an essence only. Pure. Driven. Its substance—that is, its absolute ethereal essence—was animated by a singular purpose: find its ultimate victim.

And though the shapeless thing had no reason, it sensed somehow—in the striations of its invisible gossamer vapors—that there was poetry in its purpose.

Very few things, living or dead, purposeful or purposeless, have poetry in them.

"Yeah, you're right, that was a great lunch," Bill said as he and Ron left the deli.

"Okay, I guess," Ron said. "I think I ate too much, though. Those meatball sandwiches are real belly bombs. And, Lord, what was *in* that cannelloni?"

"A little bit of everything, but mostly sugar." Bill glanced at his watch. "Hey, it's already after one. We'd better get back to the office on the double, or we'll really get our asses chewed out."

"Hey, I'm not worried."

"We've been late getting back twice this week already."

"Oh, all right. Let's cut down this alley."

Willie stood in the alley, propping himself against the brick wall with one hand while urinating. He glanced down at himself and grimaced. His old wrinkled penis had no shine to it at all. It was a dull piece of meat that knew nothing and sensed only the most basic biological imperatives. Willie cursed at it, tucked it back in and zipped up; then he folded himself in a crouching position against the opposite wall.

He had a bottle of cheap wine, still in its brown paper bag, tucked under one arm. He had purchased it only a few minutes ago and had drunk almost all of it. Now he held the bottle up to his lips and finished it off, chugging it noisily. Then he hugged the empty to his body for a while, as if he might refill it with wishes, then sighed and tossed it away.

Damn.

It wasn't quite enough to wipe him out. At least it took the edge off his senses, which was all he needed to settle into his afternoon stupor.

"Life sucks," he mumbled through purple, wine-stained lips, then smiled crookedly.

The wind whipped through the alley, stirring up the little wads of trash, causing dust to whirl in tortuous little dances, and giving Willie a bit of a chill that was somehow soothing.

He spat out a whimpering little sound as something settled in him.

"Oh, hell," Ron said as they neared the end of the alley, "would you look at that? A goddamn wino."

"So just walk by him," Bill said. "He's harmless."

"Winos aren't harmless! They're a drain on society."

"Don't be so heavy, Ron. We have to get back to—"

"What purpose do they serve? None. Just derelicts. They occupy space, that's all. They ought to round them all up and *shoot* them!"

"Come on, Ron. The poor old guy will hear you."

"Let him."

Ron stopped directly in front of Willie and looked down with evident scorn. "What a mess." He started to turn away.

That was when Willie grabbed him.

"Hey, you old rummy, let go! Let go before I kick your teeth in."

"I'll handle this." Bill leaned down to pull the wino's hands from Ron's legs. He tugged at the bony fingers with all his strength, but he couldn't pry them away.

Then he found himself up in the air.

Then he was back on the pavement about ten feet away from his friend and the wino.

He tried to get up and discovered his left leg was broken. Strangely, it didn't hurt much.

Ron stared down at Willie. "What the hell did you do?" He turned. "Bill?"

"I can't move." A gasp. "Leg's broken, I think."

Ron snarled, "You old *bastard*. Now I *will* give you a going-over."

Willie's head snapped back abruptly. He glared up at Ron.

Ron desperately tried to look away, but couldn't. Willie's eyes were red with tiny yellow snake-slit pupils that tore into Ron's brain. Reflected in those eyes were miniature screaming things.

And tombstones.

Ron panicked, tried to pull away again and realized the wino's fingers had sprouted razorlike claws that were cutting into his calves. He bent over to beat the wino on the top of his skull, but some force shoved him back; the only thing that prevented him from falling was the claw grip on his legs.

Ron screamed—but the sound died quickly in the alley, as if muffled by an unseen force. Then he realized he could say or do nothing to escape what was happening. He was frozen in time for a moment, completely awestruck by the sudden transformation of the withered man, viewing it with a kind of fleeting detachment that reason could not alter:

The top of Willie's head had split open and became a huge mouth ringed with rows of pointed fangs, and out of this gaping red orifice came a stench of alcohol, blood, and piss that stung Ron's nostrils so badly they began to bleed.

The mouth-thing wasn't finished growing, though. It ripped down the center of Willie's body, stopping at his groin, and it grew more teeth and stank more and rippled obscenely.

Then it was feeding time.

Later, Bill couldn't remember if he had passed out because of the pain in his leg or because of what he had seen.

It didn't matter. No one seemed to believe his story and there was very little evidence of what had happened; only a few nondescript stains and an old wino's cap.

Perhaps people would be more inclined to believe Bill later. Later, when more guys like Ron disappeared. Later, when more absolutes met more ultimate victims.

Because there were more shapeless things in the wind, and a lot more Willies haunting the streets and alleys.

Soon all the Willies would have a purpose.

The Drinking Party

K. Marie Ramsland

Amniotic. That's how the place felt. Warm and oozy, concealed in membrane—so damp it made your bones swell. I licked my lips, tasting salt, trying to focus on what we were there for.

We'd let ourselves in, which I thought odd; but Frank, who claimed to know our host well enough, had insisted. The odor of sodden earth assailed us at once, as if we'd entered the late summer lair of a listless newt. Candles burned on either side of several doorways in what appeared to be some sort of sparsely furnished waiting room. The windows were round, small and few, like portholes on a ship. A faint background bubbling reminded me of the job I'd once held and quickly lost at an oceanography lab. Glancing around, I shrugged against underwear that suddenly seemed too tight. Or too loose. Or something. I wanted to get out or get started—anything to slip out of the cloying skin of that unwelcoming room. But our host had not yet begrudged us an appearance.

Frank, younger than my forty years by half a decade, nudged me, pointing.

"Say, look at that!"

He walked toward a shadowy wall to our right. For the first time, I noticed a huge aquarium stretching across five feet of wall space—as tall from the floor as a man of average height. That explained the bubbling. Thrown back to the false but seductive promise of my days as a biology graduate student, I joined Frank beside it. Moments later, I was sorry I had.

The filmy glass container seemed more a captured swamp than an exotic aquarium. It smelled of stale neglect. Amid slimy, strangling weeds, a large frog straddled murky water at eye level. It stared, its eyes dull. I waved my hand but it didn't even blink. I felt invisible. Then I realized what had drawn Frank's attention.

The frog was disappearing—right there in front of us!

Well, not disappearing exactly, but *changing*—as if it were being devoured from *inside*. The skin sagged and crumpled into something like the formless folds of a shirt dipped into a washtub. The amphibian flattened out. Something drained from its eyes, some life force bade farewell; blinked out. The frog dropped lower, shrinking, emptying backward into its former tadpole state. The once-taut skin drifted to the brackish surface, blending into tiny islands of curdled scum.

Frank looked at me. *What the hell . . . ?* his eyes asked.

I shrugged, bewildered, then glanced again at the gruesome, floating bag. It began to sink. That's when I saw the shadow.

A thing dark and oval scooted away, as if the frog's own astral projection were swimming free of its visceral cage! I stepped closer, squinted. I'd heard of this marvel but had never witnessed it: the feeding habits of a subaqueous beetle, paralyzing its prey before turning bones, muscles, and organs into a siphonable juice. I strained to recall the scientific name.

"A water bug," came a voice from behind us. I jumped as if I'd been swatted, and made my first visual acquaintance with our host.

"Oh, geez, Leth!" Frank exclaimed—"You scared the bejiminies out of us."

I was glad Frank'd spoken. I'd lost my voice.

Leth was unlike anyone I'd ever seen. A bald head of brownish skin and small watery eyes topped an obesely bulbous body. I'd heard from Frank that this guy was a former bartender who'd won enough money from outdrinking everyone who wagered on it to have quit his job altogether. He claimed he'd never lost.

That's why we were there, to take up Leth's challenge. But I saw immediately what such a degenerate life had done to the man: I could almost hear the liquid sloshing around inside him, and not just in his belly—in the whole, bloated trunk of his disgusting body.

He turned dark eyes on me. I stepped back, involuntarily touching the cold glass of the aquarium. I thought of the frog and drew away. Leth extended his hand, a stubby thing with several fingers cramped arthritically inward. Frank was introducing us, so I swallowed and allowed my palm to slip quickly across the one extended to me. I didn't quite catch his last name. It sounded Irish: O'Serus, or something like that. It didn't matter. He was clearly a foreigner.

"I'm glad you came, Victor," he said. "Frank has impressed me with your capacity to stay sober."

I swallowed. Suddenly the whole thing seemed like a bad idea, an adolescent game. But I couldn't back out—not with him looking at me like that, gloating, ready. I thought of my cut of the money we'd get if I stayed—and if I won.

"Let's begin," I said.

Leth gestured toward a doorway. I strode boldly into the next room, almost as dark and humid as the first save for two candles burning in the center of a splintering table, and two at each of three doorways.

I took a seat. Frank sat to my left, eyebrows raised. His fleshy chin quivered below pale lips. Clearly, I was not the only one who wished we hadn't come.

Leth set a bottle of Jack Daniels—my request—and three glasses on the table. Then he slapped down a shabby deck of cards. Poker was not the point, we all knew that; we simply had to pass the time somehow.

"Let's get one thing straight," piped up Frank. His voice was raspy, taut with nerves. "I'm betting on Victor here. Are we settled on the stakes?"

"We're settled," the brown man replied.

I glanced at Frank through narrowed eyes. I knew only what he had to gain—a great deal of money with which to shovel himself out of debt; Frank hadn't told me what he—*we*—had to lose. He winked to reassure me. I shrugged and went along.

Leth filled our glasses equally, then handed the bottle to Frank, who acted as referee. It didn't seem fair to Leth, actually. Frank had something to gain by cheating. But the idea was that we'd all be sober enough to recognize cheating if it happened; so it didn't much matter who poured.

While Leth dealt cards, I studied him surreptitiously. He was an odd one, no doubt. To boost my own confidence, I envisioned him caught in a sticky web, bleating "Help me" in a pathetic voice. It didn't work. The web would have to be enormous because he was at least six feet tall. I glanced to Leth's misshapen hands—thick, stubby paws, with hardened skin. It reminded me of a snake I'd seen once, about to shed its lifeless shell. I grimaced.

Leth caught my eye. He grinned. Too much liquor had rotted his teeth into a dark, cavernously empty mouth. I concentrated on my cards.

The game went on as we continued to drink. Frank watched me closely. He seemed nervous. I thought of his wife and two-year-old son, hoped he hadn't gambled with their security the way I had once with my own family, losing them with the house. Long since, I had substituted a debilitating drinking habit for a promising career in science, but the work was a negligible loss compared to never seeing my wife and two children again.

Scratching the back of my neck, my hand came away— shockingly—with a live *roach!* I flung it to the stone floor, froze.

"I'm not much of a housekeeper," Leth said. "I suppose

I like having the critters around." He took another drink. I swallowed, mentally nodded. The guy liked bugs? It made sense. People who look like bulldogs bought bulldogs.

Frank filled my glass. I held the gaze of the brown man opposite me, tried in vain to read his thoughts. If there was anything swimming around behind those liquid eyes, it was neatly hidden from my perception.

"You okay?" Frank asked. Beads of sweat had popped out on his brow. I frowned, lit up a cigarette, casually replaced the pack in my shirt pocket.

"I'm fine," I replied, "Got a long way to go."

But I didn't; not really. One had to stay in control to win such games, and I was getting rapidly digested in the stomach of apprehension. The third empty bottle quivered before me. Empty. I caught the hard, smirking eyes of my host.

Also empty.

Swollen air pressed my clammy shirt to my back. I took a deep breath, licked the sting of whiskey off my mustache. Frank poured another round. It struck me he was somehow acting out a part. The room seemed to brighten. I wanted to puke.

I'd experienced a similar sense of unanchored floating when my wife had announced her intention to divorce me, to leave me with my debts, my isolation, my habits. I'd gasped then for air too thin to sustain consciousness, swaying with the surreal force of her verbal blow: "You won't see me again."

Frank nudged me. My eyes had closed. I snapped to attention, a wayward schoolboy. The "teacher" across the table eyed me with a Mona Lisa grin.

"Shit, Victor," Frank exclaimed, "you done better than this before! What's with you?"

He was right. Something was seriously wrong. I filled my lungs, clenched my teeth for control.

Abruptly, I simply didn't care enough. I didn't need money *that* badly. I wanted out, no matter what it cost. It was Frank's fault if he'd gambled everything away. I pushed back from the table. "That's it." My tongue was thick, my brain battered seasick by booze. "I concede."

Frank jumped up. His chair crashed to the floor.

"Concede?" he screamed. "You *can't!* I *bet* on you!"

I shrugged. "Sorry. Y'win some, ya lose some." I needed a place to vomit.

Frank grabbed me by my jacket lapels. "You don't get it, Vic!" he shrieked, his control gone. "You lose *this* one, there won't be no chance to win *anything else!* Ever!"

I jerked away, urgently ill.

Leth leaned forward, his smallish head on crusty hands. His face was expressionless. Yet I had the distinct impression he was savoring his easy victory. I wasn't sober enough to be sure, but he seemed not the least bit affected by his own fast intake of alcohol.

Out of one eye, I saw Frank run to the door. Leth made no move to stop him.

The door was bolted.

"Let me out!" screamed Frank. He pounded on the solid wood, hysterical. I began to understand that Frank's fear implied more than financial collapse. He was trapped—*we* were trapped.

Frank groped his way along the darkened wall to another door and I stood up. "Frank, get hold of yourself!" I called shakily.

He pushed open the door. Flinging a desperate look toward me, he grabbed a candle and ran.

And turning to Leth, woozily, I got it through my head *that I was alone with him!*

Nausea braided into panic. I dared not look at Leth's face, sensing his expression would somehow be terrifying. Mumbling about assisting Frank, I staggered to the door through which he'd disappeared. I called out, heard nothing, then felt along a descending corridor so slick with moisture I surmised we'd meandered into an underwater tunnel. Outside, I hadn't noticed water, but it had been dark. Muggy, bubbling queasiness fused my senses.

Hearing a noise, I turned. The light from the room I'd just left was extinguished by the closing door. I gasped aloud. Had our repulsive host locked us in? *Why?* Did he intend to keep us there until we paid our debt, whatever it was?

I thought of the roach. Leth liked bugs. What would I encounter farther into his damned tunnel? Movie images of screaming people covered with ants, being devoured bite by little bite, crawled into my thoughts.

And then I realized a more horrifying possibility.

Perhaps Leth'd locked himself in with us!

I forced myself to stay calm. What could he do, anyway? I'd aged, yes, my belly was bloated—but I was fit enough to take on Leth, even with the disadvantage of inky darkness.

So I waited, listened, heard no sound, not even my friend somewhere ahead of me. Slowly, cautiously, I pressed numbed fingertips along the roughened stone wall, moving farther from the room where I'd drunk myself into the first stages of a perceptual haze. Toward what I moved I had no idea.

A sound. I stopped, listened with acute awareness. Something dragging, scraping, clawing. Did Leth have a weapon? Did he want to *kill* us?

I took a few more steps, found a doorknob, let myself noiselessly into an equally lightless room. I shut the door, moved to the side. If anyone opened it, then I'd have the advantage.

Nothing happened.

Something rotten stank nearby. Whatever it was, I hoped to God it wasn't alive. I remembered slipping a book of matches into my cigarette cellophane, safe and dry in my shirt pocket. Seconds later, holding the lit match high, I scanned the small room.

It was a cell of some kind, without furnishings, but it had the ubiquitous porthole window. A pile of rancid clothing lay in one corner, heaped against the wall. I went closer, but the match burned out.

A sound, outside the door, startled me. I waited. Then I

lit another match. I moved closer to examine the lumpy, smelly material. I poked around gingerly. Several black shapes skittered out of the folds. It was not someone's discarded suit. Grayish in color, it looked more like a stiffened vinyl garment bag.

I don't think I understood that it had been human until I saw an eyeball dangling from a stiff, dark hole. It took me a moment to figure out, like a perceptual illusion coming into focus, that I was kneeling next to a sack of skin . . .

With a howl, I jumped back, burned my finger on the match, slammed myself against the wall. Breathing hard, I tried to steady my swimming senses. The gorge boiled into my throat. I had to get out, get away from that reeking thing. My God, what had *happened* here? Who was this Leth O'Serus?

I stopped, straightened. I knew at that moment where I'd heard the name. Yet it was no wonder I hadn't made the connection earlier. It had been part of . . . all *that!*

A piercing scream ripped into my slowly understanding brain. *Frank!*

I flew to the door, jerked it open. Frank's candle, thrown aside, illumined an expected but incomprehensibly freakish sight.

Frank struggled with our host, shrieking, his eyes turned to me, pleading. But there was nothing I could do, just as there'd been no way to assist the wretched frog back in the tank. I watched in stunned helplessness—unable even to run—as Leth held Frank in a vampire-like grip, his beetle mouth pressed to Frank's chest—injecting him, I knew, with paralyzing serum. *Preparing Frank for a grisly evening meal!*

Leth O'Serus; lethocerus. *Lethocerus americanus.*

I'd never thought of it before, never wondered how really huge they might get. *Giant water bugs.* I leaned against the frame of the door, laughing weakly at the ironic misnomer. Giant! They'd all been tiny in those oceanography tanks—mere specks compared to the one now munching on the shriveled neck of my friend.

Exactly like the frog, Frank went limp as his bones dissolved into edible mush. He lost the definition of his shoulders at once, then his rib cage; his face melted into an amorphous sack of loosened teeth and unsupported eyeballs. I watched for only a moment more as Frank's shoes fell from his dangling, flattened feet and the pants began to slide from his emaciated waist. Then I turned to flee back into my tiny cubicle.

There seemed only one means of escape: the window. I lifted the latch, pulled. But it wouldn't budge. I had no idea how long it would take that monstrous thing out there to devour Frank, but I thought I had precious little time. No doubt Leth's hunger was as voracious as his thirst. I tried again, wildly.

Water crashed into the room, slapping my face with a force that made me stagger. In moments, I'd lost the support of the floor and I was floating. Somehow I kept my wits enough to hold up my head and tread the water that was quickly filling the room. Something knocked against me. I pushed it away, realized it was the bag of human skin, almost vomited, reflexively. I dived under and kicked my way to the window. It had looked—if I hadn't drunkenly miscalculated—just large enough to pull myself through. I knew I might drown but I had to try.

I found a wall, pushed along it, banged my head, almost breathed in; mentally gasping, I pushed again. My fingers dipped into an unevenness, a depression! The water had balanced itself. I forced my shoulders through the small hole, squeezed up to my cursed beer belly.

But too many years of drinking had taken their toll. *I was stuck.*

I strained, desperately needing air, tightly maintaining control, thought of the supping water bug, perhaps finishing up—and still hungry. I gripped the outside wall and strained harder. Something tugged at my shoe. I kicked out, felt the sharp puncture of my toe. That was enough to send me through!

* * *

I awoke in daylight, half-submerged in a watery ditch. Sitting up was too quick for my expanding head and I turned, lost it. Vomited. Groaning, I tried to recall just how I had gotten there. I felt my swollen nose and it all came back.

Leth. Frank. The drinking party. I was sick again.

Somewhat composed, then, I sat up and glanced around. There was no sign of a lake, pond, or river, as I'd expected—nothing from which I might have emerged when I swam to freedom. Had I imagined the whole thing? For a long time I sat in muck, rocking myself against all the numbing possibilities, nauseous and uncertain, sliding between visions of Frank's shrinking, beseeching face and my own disgraceful alcoholic history.

My foot hurt. I'd lost a shoe. And I'd been bitten.

It could have been a snake, or a snapping turtle in the ditch. I might have banged my nose in another drunken tumble. There were simple explanations, if I wanted them. Perhaps the ditch water had nurtured a harrowing hallucination neurotically formed by deeply suppressed guilt over my lost career.

With some difficulty I got to my feet. The countryside looked perfectly normal. Stepping away from the muck, I heard *ker-plunk*. A frog, startled in its morning hunt. We peered fleetingly at one another, both hesitant, both wanting to go our own way and forget the other.

The frog. Frank. It all seemed too vivid for some pie-eyed delusion. I walked around all that day searching in vain for the dreadful house, Frank's remains, *anything* that might provide assurance that my mind hadn't simply snapped under the weight of boomeranging self-laceration.

No luck.

I've stopped drinking now. For good. I couldn't look a bartender in the eye without wondering whether he might have another life, another shape . . . whether he was eyeing me for some predaceous purpose. It seems ridiculously clear at times that I simply went too far, drank too much. Saw the dreaded "pink elephant." Perhaps that's all it was. I don't really know.

But the fact is, I never saw Frank again.

Chosen One

G. Wayne Miller

Her voice was silky. So incredibly silky. That was the only reason she'd been able to come on to him successfully, that extraordinary voice.

He remembered how it used to be. Late at night—her time to rule the airwaves—he'd lie back, smoke a joint, close his eyes and listen to that voice, fantasizing what she looked like. Blond, he imagined. A Nordic face, with high cheekbones and ice-blue eyes. Blush-red lips that pursed perfectly for every word. A body to make a man a kid again, like the first time in the backseat of his daddy's car. If he felt bad about anything, that was it: that someone with a voice so magical, so powerfully seductive, had to be destroyed.

But it was a fact of life now. Her blood had to be splattered, pooled in pretty red patterns across the floor. Maybe before it dried he would dip his finger into it, then put his finger to his mouth, savoring victory at last. Maybe that would be most fitting.

He hadn't set out to be a hero. He'd only meant to survive. That's why, early on, he'd lined the walls of his apartment with aluminum foil. That's why he'd bricked up the windows, sealed the bathroom ceiling vent, disconnected the phone, pulled out the wall switches, the TV cable, those two tiny wires that went to the doorbell. Anything—

anything at all—that might conduct electromagnetic radiation, the means she used to get inside his head.

How silly it had been. He knew that now.

Because nothing kept her away, not for long. Such meticulous precautions and her voice was still strong and clear inside his head. Cajoling him to surrender, pleading with him to give in and join her in conquering the world . . . before drastic steps became necessary.

Only now was he in true awe of her power.

No question, he thought, feeling his bulletproof vest, fingering the .44-caliber Magnum he'd bought from a sunglassed dude who did business out of a Cadillac trunk. *It's past the crisis stage. Stop her tonight, or there will never be another chance.*

Mankind will be lost.

Already it may be too late.

It had taken almost a year to get to tonight.

In the beginning, there was only a new show, a new disc jockey, an exciting new voice. It was inevitable they'd get together. He was a late-night person, a Pink Floyd fan, a thinker, philosopher, a loner with a master's in computer software. She was a companion. A *friend.* She understood the cruel things girlfriends and bosses had done. She understood the terrible odds men like him labored under, making their way through the heartless world.

More than that, she *agreed.*

It's not you, she assured him on an early visit inside his head. *It's them. Let's be friends. Us together, the rest be damned.*

Beguiled by that audio silkiness, he welcomed her. And at first, they got along swimmingly. A purely platonic relationship, two soulmates helping each other through the long, lonely night. Even when she was off the air, she'd sometimes seek him out. In the company men's room, on the subway, on his noontime walks through Central Park, she would drop in to chat. How thrilling, being singled out like that. How special he felt.

He remembered the first danger sign.

It was a Saturday, the day she discovered the Dirty Thoughts he'd begun to have. There he was in the privacy of his own bathroom, kneeling by the mirror, towel in one hand, violent erection in the other. He was thinking about her. Thinking about having her from behind, where you wouldn't have to look into the depths of those ice-blue eyes. Thinking how he would blindly cup her breasts, kiss her neck, ease slowly inside, the passion escaping like steam . . .

In the sharpest of terms, she'd told him how disappointed she was, finding those Dirty Thoughts. He tried to explain that his thoughts were meant as tribute. What higher compliment was there than showing how desperately he wanted to merge their flesh, their souls, by taking her from behind?

Get rid of them, she ordered, her disgust tearing through him like shrapnel.

He had tried. For a day or two, they were gone. But the Dirty Thoughts always came back, stealing into his head like rats through a darkened alley. She began to use the power of her voice to nudge them out. Sometimes—most times—she succeeded. The thoughts faded. In their place was black, hollow pain that Tylenol with codeine couldn't touch.

It wasn't long before he understood: she was no different than the rest. She didn't want to share; she wanted to control. A simpleton could see the distinction.

Of course, Krystal discovered *that* thought, and when she did, she came clean: *Perhaps sharing secrets is better than angry tirades to make an ally out of such a fine, strong man. I am not a DJ,* she admitted. *I am an extraterrestrial, beamed down to begin my species' takeover of the world.* The first phase, she informed him, was subjugation; that would be followed by colonization. Electromagnetic radiation—a refinement too complex for humans to comprehend—was their secret. And while it took time to deploy such an awesome weapon, Central Control had no doubt victory would be theirs.

Once Krystal clued him in, he had seen things in a whole new light. Where once he was scornful of his fellow humans, he saw them now as innocent victims, deserving of pity and salvation. Through no fault of their own, they were being conscripted into Krystal's army—an army of zombies. Now he understood that you didn't have to tune in to her show to be taken over. If that were the case, you could simply have turned your radio off. No, she was infinitely more clever. Electromagnetism—in the air, passing effortlessly through walls, silent, damn near inescapable—was how she worked.

Now do you comprehend the true nature of her threat? he wrote in the diary he prayed would be cherished someday by millions.

Now do you understand why I had to act so drastically? Now will you thank me?

Over the next week, he did what any good citizen would do: he called the police. He typed long, fact-filled letters to the White House, the governor, Congress, NASA, the FBI, the Air Force. "For humanity's sake," he ended each letter, "Krystal must be stopped."

He received several responses. Someone identifying himself as an agent of the Secret Service called, asked a stream of highly personal questions. Someone else in the governor's office chatted amicably for over ten minutes. But nothing changed. No one arrested her or canceled her show or blew up her station or set out to find her spaceship. It made him realize how deeply she'd infiltrated the fabric of society.

It was only then that Apocalypse occurred. One night, alone in his apartment, another voice—a voice he'd never heard before, would never hear again—announced that he had been Chosen.

"Go on and laugh," he wrote the next morning to the editor of *The New York Times*. "Get it out of your system, then listen carefully. The hour is late. But there's still hope. I am Chosen . . ."

The letter wasn't published.

His arrest was next.

It came comparatively late in the game, but before he understood what radical measures had to be taken. He was still leaving his apartment, making the rounds of politicians and agencies, trying desperately with a sandwich board, a bullhorn, and pamphlets to get his message out. That is not to say he was entirely reckless. He knew enough to wear a lead bib he'd stolen from a hospital. To protect his head, he wore a football helmet customized with asbestos and foil.

He was dressed that way the afternoon he attacked a remote-broadcast van belonging to Krystal's station. He spotted it there in Washington Square, a crowd of zombies gathered around. Wielding a baseball bat, he'd smashed through the windows and was bloodying a zombie-technician by the time the cops dragged him away.

In jail, a zombie-cop gave him a tranquilizer, a zombie-sergeant read him his rights, a zombie-matron tried to make him eat zombie food. He was taken in handcuffs to district court, where a zombie-judge released him to the custody of a mental health center.

Why you? one bespectacled little zombie-turd wanted to know.

It wasn't ego, he explained calmly. It was part of a larger plan. He had been anointed, if you wanted to look at it like that. Chosen. No one might ever know why it had been he and not, say, a gas jockey from Perth Amboy or Larry Bird. If you knew anything, you knew that was sometimes how it happened. Look at Joan of Arc. Who, back then, would ever have guessed a milkmaid would be a Chosen One?

Why can't she conquer you as easily as other people?

He almost laughed, that was so stupid.

But he didn't. Patiently, he explained that it was a tribute to his strength of character that she couldn't succeed behind his back. *He* had to be faced. *He* was the enemy, her most formidable enemy.

By now, almost certainly, her final one.

Because I am anointed. I am The Chosen One.

That's what The True Voice said.

Praise The Voice.

Hallelujah.

In the end, he was no fool. He allowed them to give him any intramuscular shot of Thorazine. He signed the form agreeing to return voluntarily in two weeks for another one.

He didn't, of course.

He vowed not to leave his apartment until he had a plan. How long that might take, he had no idea. He'd devote every waking hour, but it could be days . . . months. An awesome responsibility saving his people.

In the meantime, there was no choice but to go full battle alert. He stockpiled food and bottled water. He lined his apartment with a second layer of aluminum and brick, and a third, and a fourth. He started drawing a half-pint of his blood every day, storing it in bottles in his refrigerator, which he kept packed with dry ice. The blood was for contingencies; exactly which contingencies, he didn't know yet. But it was better to be overprepared than caught short. Any soldier worth his salt would tell you that.

It was 2:15 A.M. now. A Tuesday morning. Twelve floors below him, the streets of lower Manhattan slumbered.

Krystal had been on the air two hours and a quarter.

He hadn't been listening.

He'd learned, through the most incredible concentration, that he could keep her out of his head for as much as an hour or two. He'd been very careful in drafting his plan. Careful never to think of the great task ahead of him without first blocking her out. He prayed it had worked.

He fingered his handgun, patted his bulletproof vest and ammo belt. It might get very ugly in there. Krystal had confided that twenty-four hours a day she surrounded herself with security forces armed with Uzis. The standing orders were shoot first, ask questions later—if any were to be asked.

Again, he thought of the risk. There was every chance he was going to get his guts sprayed all over the walls before the night was done. Any other man would say it was 99.9 percent certain that's how it was going to go down. What gave him strength was knowing that any other man would have backed out by now.

Suddenly, a knock on the door. A voice said he was from the mental health center's mobile crisis team. Could it possibly be coincidence? Or had Krystal succeeded in reading his thoughts after all? Was closing in at the zero hour?

"We know you're in there," the voice repeated. "Neighbors have been calling."

He didn't move.

"We only want to talk."

He didn't answer.

"You missed your appointment. Can't we just talk? We won't harm you. I promise."

Any second he expected the firing to start. He fingered his gun. They wouldn't get him without a fight.

"If we have to come back with the police, we will."

No answer.

And then, retreating footsteps. A trap? Minutes passed. The pounding in his head built to thunder level. He felt dizzy, hot.

Finally, he had no choice. The night was getting away from him. He cracked the door and peeked up and down the corridor. It was deserted. Gingerly, he stepped outside.

* * *

It must have been luck.

Finally, a well-deserved stroke of luck! Using alleys, he made it to the station without being seen. Jimmied the lock to the door without being seen. Up the elevator without being seen. Past corporate offices without being seen.

He was crouched outside her studio now, squinting through the glass door. From somewhere, he heard a janitor vacuuming.

She was alone.

She doesn't know, he dared think, giddy with the thought. *I've been able to keep her out!*

He stared, transfixed. She was smaller than expected, but in every other respect exactly what he'd imagined. Her hair was blond, straight, sweeping down over her shoulders. High cheekbones. Steely blue eyes. Perfectly round lips.

And her body . . . The sight of that body took his breath away.

He walked on sneaker-silenced feet through the glass door.

"Krystal," he said.

She turned but didn't answer. For a moment, her face was blank; then an expression—a mixture of surprise and fear—crossed it.

"Who are you?" she demanded. "How did you get in?"

"You know who I am," he said.

"I've never seen you before in my life."

"Don't play games with me," he shouted. "You *know* me. You've been inside my *head.*"

"I . . . I don't know what you're talking about."

"No games, Krystal." He moved toward her. "It's over."

"W-what do you want?"

"You know what I want."

"Is it money?" She reached for her pocketbook. "Here, take it all, take the credit cards, take—"

"DON'T MOVE!" he shouted. He was too supercharged to notice her foot, making contact with the emergency button under the console.

"Please don't hurt me," she whimpered.

"Back away from the console!"

Trembling, she did.

"Put your hands on your head."

She did. Her hands were shaking; she could not control them.

"Now walk toward me. *Slowly.*"

She started toward him.

"Turn around. Back into me."

She hesitated.

"AGAINST ME OR I SHOOT."

She made contact. Her body recoiled in disgust. He ran his fingers through her hair and the first tears fell.

"I wouldn't have thought it was possible anyone could be so beautiful."

"Please . . ."

He was tempted. The Dirty Thoughts eddied and swirled, beating against the inside of his skull. She was in there with them, stoking them. He felt her then, her last-gasp shot at defeating him. Such sweet promise, taking her from behind, she allowing him, encouraging him . . . His head began to pound.

"Please don't hurt me," she pleaded.

Grunting, he pushed the Dirty Thoughts away. "Before I end it," he said, "I want you to apologize. Apologize to the people."

He forced her to the boom mike. She began sobbing.

"Apologize and set them free!"

He didn't see the back door open. He didn't see the guard come in. He didn't see the guard draw a bead on him with an Uzi.

"Say *'I'm sorry.'*"

"I . . . I'm sorry," she cried.

"*. . . for enslaving my people.*" He squeezed her violently. "Go on—say it."

"F-f-for enslaving my—"

The bullets traveled through his head on a line between his

ears. Blood gushed. His grip on Krystal loosened. She wriggled free as the gun tumbled harmlessly to the floor. No more Dirty Thoughts now, nothing about salvation, only a kaleidoscope of white noise and pain. He collapsed to the floor as if deboned.

The only sound was the turntable, spinning emptily.

Krystal slumped into her chair. The tears were flowing freely.

With effort, she brought herself to look at him.

There was nothing left of his ears or the sides of his head, just mangled gray tissue and matted strands of hair. His body spasmed and a crimson froth decorated his lips. His chest heaved as he drew his last breath. His eyelids fluttered and were still. She noticed a sudden purplish tinge to his cheeks, and wondered if that was normal under the circumstances.

She stared up at the security man. "I don't know how to thank you," she said. "You saved my life."

"It's my job," he answered.

The tension started to drain away. Krystal would have nightmares for ages, but life would go on.

Her show would, too.

She gazed at his body again. She couldn't help herself. The final death twitches had passed. The joints already were stiffening, his temp dropping. Around the studio, his blood was splattered in pretty red patterns. Krystal dipped her finger into it, then brought her finger slowly to her mouth. She hesitated, then licked it.

Then smiled.

It was an irony Krystal knew wouldn't have escaped him.

She wiped her finger on her pants, then bent over the console to punch up the right frequency. She leaned into the microphone.

"Central Control," she said. "Colonization may begin."

Them Bald-Headed Snays

Joseph A. Citro

After the cancer got Mom, Dad took me way out in the Vermont countryside to live with my grandparents.

"I'll come back for you, Daren," he said. His eyes looked all glassy and sad. I bit my top and bottom lips together so I wouldn't cry when he started home without me. Sure, he'd come back, but he didn't say when.

Before that day I'd never seen too much of my grandparents. They'd come to visit us in Providence once, right after Mom got sick. But that was years ago, when I was just a kid. I remember how Dad and Grampa would have long, quiet talks that ended suddenly if Mom or me came into the room.

After that they never came to visit again. I don't think Mom liked them, though she never said why. "Their ways are different from ours," that's all she'd say.

And they sure weren't the way I remembered them! Grampa turned out to be sort of strange and a little scary. He was given to long, silent stretches in his creaky rocking chair. He'd stare out the window for hours, or read from big, dark-covered books. Sometimes he'd look through the collection of catalogs that seemed to arrive with every mail delivery. My job was to run to the bottom of the hill and pick up the mail from the mailbox. There were always the catalogs, and big brown envelopes with odd designs on them. There were bills, too, and Grampa's once-a-week newspaper. But there was never a letter from Dad.

"Can we call Dad?" I asked. Grampa just snorted as if to say, *You know we ain't got a phone.* Then he turned away and went back to his reading. Sometimes he'd stand, take a deep breath, and stretch, reaching way up toward the ceiling. Then he'd walk—maybe to the kitchen—bent over a little, rubbing the lower part of his back.

Grampa didn't talk to me much, but Gram was the quiet one. She'd move from room to room like a draft. Sometimes I'd think I was all alone, then I'd look over my shoulder and Gram was sitting there, watching me. At first I'd smile at her, but soon I stopped; I'd learned not to expect a smile in return, only a look of concern.

Sometimes she'd bring me a big glass of greenish-brown tea that tasted of honey and smelled like medicine.

"How you feeling today, Daren?" she'd ask.

"Good," I'd say.

"You drink up, now." She'd nod, pushing the glass toward me. "You'll feel even better."

When I'd take the glass away from my mouth she'd be gone.

Every other Friday, Grampa went into town to get groceries. After I'd been there about a month, he took me along with him. And that was another odd thing about him: he had a horse and buggy when everybody else had cars. I felt embarrassed riding through the downtown traffic beside an old man in a horse-drawn wagon.

Grampa said his back was acting up real bad, so he made me carry all the bags to the wagon. Then he told me to stay put while he made a second stop at the liquor store.

I didn't, though. I took a dime from my pocket and tried

to make a collect call to my father. The operator said our number was no longer in service.

Grampa came back with his bottle before I'd made it back to the wagon. He yelled at me, told me he'd tan me brown if I ever disobeyed him again.

I'd lived in Stockton, Vermont, about two months before I saw Bobby Snay.

I was playing in the barn, upstairs in the hayloft, looking out the loading door toward the woods. I saw him come out from among the trees. He swayed when he walked, moving with difficulty, as if a heavy wind were trying to batter him back to where he'd come from.

He continued across the meadow, weaving through the tall grass and wildflowers until he came to the road that ends in Grampa's dooryard. When he got closer I saw how funny he looked. His skin was the color of marshmallows, his eyes so pale it was impossible to say if they were blue or brown.

And it looked like his hair was falling out. Maybe it wasn't really, but it wasn't very plentiful. It looked limp and sparse and stuck out here and there in little patches, making his head look like it was covered with hairy bugs.

Back home he would have been the type of nerdy kid we'd picked on in school. But here, well, he was the only other kid I'd seen for a long time.

"Hey!" I called, "hey! Wait up!"

I dodged back into the barn and jumped down into the pile of hay below. I sneezed once, then made for the door, ran after him. But I didn't need to; he was in the barn waiting for me.

All of a sudden I wasn't so eager to say hi. In fact, I was kind of scared of him. He was taller than I, but he was spindly, weak-looking. I wasn't afraid he was going to beat me up or anything. It was something else. Maybe it was the way he had crossed the dooryard and entered the barn in less time than it took me to jump out of the loft. Maybe it was the way he stared at me as if there was no brain behind his washed-out eyes.

Or maybe it was the smell.

I didn't realize it at the time, but now I think that strange odor was coming from him.

It was like the odor of earth, the strange scent of things that were once alive—like rotting squirrels and leaves mixed with the smell of things that would never live. Like water and stones.

"I . . . I'm Daren Oakly."

"Bobby," he said. "Bobby Snay." His voice was windy-sounding, like air through a straw.

"Where you going?" I couldn't think of anything else to say.

"Walkin', jes' walkin'. Wanna come?"

"Ah . . . No. Grampa says I gotta stay here."

"You don't gotta. Nobody gotta. Nobody stays here."

It was warm in the barn. The smell seemed to get stronger.

"Where d'ya live?"

He pointed with his thumb, toward the woods.

"You *live* in *the woods?* "

"Yup. Sometimes."

"How old are you?"

He blinked. I hadn't noticed till then, but it was the first time he'd blinked since we stood face to face.

"I gotta go now," he said. "But I'll come again. I always come 'round when ya need me."

I watched him walk away, lurching, leaning, zigzagging through the field. He had no more than stepped back into the woods when I heard Grampa's wagon coming up the hill.

"You ain't to do it again!" Grampa raged. "I won't have it. I won't have you keepin' time with them bald-headed

Snays! Not now, not till I tell ya. You don't know nothin'
about 'em, so you stay clear of 'em, hear me?"

"But—"

"You see them around here again, you run an' tell me.
That's the long an' short of it."

"But Grampa—!"

It was the fastest I'd ever seen him move. His hand went
up like a hammer and came down like a lightning bolt, striking my cheek.

"An' that's so you don't *forget.*"

Anger flared in me; adrenaline surged, uselessly. Then
fear settled over everything. I couldn't look at Grampa. My
nose felt warm. Red drops splatted on the wooden floor like
wax from a candle. I bit my lips and fought away the tears.

Later, I heard him telling Gram, "They're back. The boy
seen one of 'em just today." Grampa sounded excited—almost happy.

I woke up to the sound of shouting. Outside my bedroom
window, near the corner of the barn, two persons were fighting. One of them, the one doing the hollering, was Grampa.

"I don't care *who* you come for, I'm the one's got you
now!"

Grampa pushed the other away, butted him with his
shoulder against the open barn door. The door flapped back,
struck the side of the building like a thunderclap.

I could see the other person now. It was Bobby Snay.

Grampa hit him in the stomach. Bobby doubled up. Puke
shot out of his nose and mouth.

Grampa lifted a boot and Bobby's head jerked back so
hard I thought his neck would snap. He tumbled sideways,
slid down the barn door and curled up on the ground.

Grampa stomped hard on his head, once, twice. Every
time his boot came down he'd yell, "YEH!"

There was a big rock near the barn. Grampa kept it there

to hold the door open. It was about the size of a basketball, yet Grampa picked it up like it were weightless.

I was surprised how easily Grampa lifted that rock all the way to his shoulders. Then he did something crazy: he let it drop. Bobby lay still after it had smashed against his head.

Grampa turned and walked toward the house. He was smiling.

All the rest of the day I tried to pretend I hadn't seen anything. I knew I couldn't tell Grandma, so I actually tried to forget how weird Grampa was acting. But I couldn't forget; I was too scared of him.

It was then I decided that staying clear of him wouldn't be enough. I'd have to sneak off, run away. Then I'd find my father and things would be pretty much the way they used to be.

Gramma watched me force down a bowl of pea soup at the silent dinner table. Then I got up and started toward the back door. My plan was to run through the woods to the main road, then hitch a ride.

When I opened the door, Grampa was in the yard. He stood tall and straight, hands on hips. That arthritic droop to his shoulders was gone now. His face, though wrinkled as ever, seemed to glow with fresh, pulsing blood. He was still smiling.

I knew he could tell by the terror on my face that I'd seen everything. "Get dressed," he said, "you got some work to do."

I thought he was going to make my bury Bobby Snay's body. Instead, he made me go down to the cellar to stack firewood he handed to me through a window. We did that all afternoon. After about an hour my back was hurting something awful, but Grampa never slowed up. Now and then he'd stand straight and stretch his arms wide. He'd smile; sometimes he'd laugh.

I didn't dare say anything to him.

I could hardly eat supper. I was tired and achy and I wanted to take a nap. Grampa wasn't tired at all. He ate lots of beans and biscuits, even carried on a conversation with Gramma. "I feel ten years younger," he said.

The next day Grampa went into town again. I asked him if I could go too. I wanted to get at least that far in the wagon, then . . . well, I wasn't sure. I'd go to the police, or run away, or something.

He said, "No. I'm goin' alone. I want you *here.*"

I was sitting on the fence by the side of the barn, trying to decide what to do, when Bobby Snay stepped out of the woods.

I couldn't *believe* it.

As he got closer, I saw what was really strange: he wasn't bruised or cut or anything. I mean, I was sure Grampa had killed him, but here he was, without any trace of that awful beating.

He walked closer, weaving this way and that, as if one of his legs was shorter than the other. When he was near enough to hear me, I forced myself to ask, "Are you okay?"

He stopped walking. His eyes were pointed in my direction but I didn't feel that he saw me. "Yeah," he said, "yeah, sure, 'course I am."

Then he lurched to the right as if someone had shoved him, and he continued on his way.

I watched him go, not believing, not knowing.

Should I tell Grampa Bobby was okay? Should I talk to the law? Keep quiet? Or what? I had to decide; I had to do something.

Friday at supper Gramma had a heart attack.

She was spooning stew onto Grampa's plate when she

dropped the pot. Grampa's hand went up like he was going to smack her. Then he saw what was happening.

She put both her hands on the tabletop, trying to steady herself. Her knuckles were white. Sweat popped out all over her face. "I . . . I . . . I. . . ." she said, as if her tongue was stuck on that one word.

Then her knees folded and she dropped to the floor.

Grampa said, "Jesus, oh Jesus . . . oh *God*."

But instead of bending over and helping Gramma, he did something awfully weird: he grabbed his shotgun and ran out the door.

Left alone with Gramma, I didn't know what to do. I knelt over her and tried to ask how I could help. I was crying so hard I was afraid she couldn't understand what I was saying.

Now her skin turned completely white; her lips looked blue. Her whole face was shiny with sweat. She whispered something: "Go get me a *Snay*, boy. Go quick."

I didn't argue. I ran toward the door.

Maybe Mr. Snay was a doctor, a preacher, or something, I didn't know. Whatever he was, Gramma seemed to need him. Somehow, I guessed, he'd be able to help her.

Quickly finding the path Bobby Snay had taken earlier, I entered the woods. Almost at once I heard noises. Grunting sounds Soft *thupps*. Cracks and groans.

It was Grampa and one of the Snays—not Bobby this time, but surely one of his relatives. It was a girl. She had the same tall, frail body, the same mushroom-white complexion, the same patchy growths of hair.

Grampa was smashing her with a piece of pipe that looked like a tire iron. The Snay didn't fight back, didn't scream, she just stood there taking the blows. I saw Grampa jab at her with the flattened end of the metal rod. It went right through her eye, sinking halfway into her skull. She fell backwards, sat on the ground. Grampa jerked the rod up and down just like he was pumping the blood that spurted from her eye socket.

I couldn't look and I couldn't run away. "Grampa," I shouted "stop it! You gotta *help Gramma!*"

Grampa finished what he was doing and looked up. His eyes were bright, fiery-looking. Then he took a step toward me, squeezing the bloody pipe in his slimy red hand.

He looked wild.

I backed away from him, thinking, He's going to brain me with that thing.

Then my heel hit something.

The shotgun!

I picked it up from where Grampa must have dropped it. I guessed he wanted to do his job by hand. I guessed he enjoyed it.

I pointed the gun at him.

"Put that down, boy!" His voice was as gruff as I'd ever heard it. When he stepped toward me I stepped backward, almost stumbled. I had the gun but that didn't keep me from being afraid.

"Put it *down.*" He waved the tire iron, gesturing for me to drop the shotgun. Tears blurred my vision; the gun shook in my hands.

"Listen to me, boy . . ." His hand was reaching out.

I looked around. The Snay wasn't moving. There was no one to help me.

Grampa took another step.

"I'm *tellin'* you, boy—"

Closer.

I cried out and pulled the trigger.

If I hadn't been shaking so much, I might have killed him straight off. As it was, his shirt tore away and red, slimy skin exploded from his left side.

We both fell at the same time, me from the recoil, Grampa from the shot.

I stared at him. A white, red-glazed hipbone showed through his mangled trousers. Broken ribs bit through the shredded flesh.

"Daren," he said. This time his voice was weak.

I couldn't move. I couldn't go to him. I couldn't run away.

"Daren, you don't understand nothin'."

I could barely hear him. "The Snays," he said, "you gotta give 'em your pain. You gotta give 'em your troubles. You *can't* hurt 'em. You can't *kill 'em*. They jest keep comin' back . . ."

I found myself on my feet again, moving closer to Grampa dragging the shotgun by the barrel.

Suddenly, I was standing above him.

"You shot me, boy—but you can make it right. You gotta *do* one of 'em. You gotta do jes' like you're killin' one of 'em. Then I'll be all right. You gotta kill one of 'em, for me."

"But what about Gramma?"

"Please, boy . . ." His voice was weak. I could barely hear him. He lifted his finger toward the Snay with the ruined eye. "See that? I got to her in time. Your gramma's all right."

I needed proof, wanted to run back to the house to see for myself, but there was no time. And Grampa was dying.

The mangled Snay was moving now. She was using the tree trunk to work her way back up to her feet.

"See there, boy," Grampa wheezed. *"Get* her, boy, shoot her. Hit her with the gun!"

I lifted the shotgun, braced my shoulder for another recoil.

"Hurry, Daren, 'fore she gets away."

My finger touched the trigger. I was shaking so much the metal seemed to vibrate against my fingertip.

"Please, boy . . ." Grampa was propped up on his elbow. He watched the Snay lurch, stumble toward the shadowy trees—

"Now, boy, *NOW!"*

—and disappear.

Grampa collapsed on the ground. He was flat on his back, head resting on an exposed root. Now his eyes were all cloudy-looking. They rolled around in different directions.

I was still posed with the gun against my shoulder. When he tried to speak again, I just let it fall.

I had to kneel down, put my ear right up next to his mouth, to hear what the old man was saying.

"You shoulda *shot,* Daren . . ."

"I couldn't, Grampa." I was blubbering. "I can't shoot nobody . . ." My tears fell, splattered on his face.

"You *gotta,* son. Your daddy, he never had no stomach for it neither. Couldn't even do it to save your mama. That's why he brung you here. He knew old Gramp would know what to do. That cancer that got your mama, boy—that cancer that killed her? Well, Daren . . . you got it, too."

His words stopped in a gag, his eyes froze solid, and he was dead.

I looked up. Looked around. The Snay was gone. The birds were quiet. I was alone in the woods.

Motherson

Steve Rasnic Tem

Joel found Samson in a freight car. Or Samson found him. In any case, both would have been hard to miss.

Joel was a runaway. One of his many social workers said he was becoming a "chronic" runaway, whatever that meant. All he knew was he had to run away all the time. *Had* to. How else was he going to find his own true mother?

Joel's mother had abandoned him when he was just a year old. Or at least that's what the social workers told him. But everybody knows social workers are liars, so he had no idea if that story was true or not. The social workers really liked to tell the story, though, and that made him suspicious. They made it sound like an adventure.

A woman from their agency had just gotten off the plane from a two-week vacation in the Bahamas. She was in the airport rest room when she heard a soft crying sound. She looked everywhere, even in the toilets, but she couldn't find a thing. But she knew that somewhere a baby must be in terrible trouble, so she kept looking.

Finally she thought to lift the lid of the trash can, and there was Joel, all wrapped in a blanket. They said he must have been crying for a very long time because his face was bright red and he had trouble catching his breath. He'd even thrown up on the blanket, he'd been crying so hard.

So she called the police and brought Joel to the agency. The social workers were always telling him how cute he was then, and how all of them wanted to take him home with them, especially the lady who had "saved" him, but unfortunately it was against agency policy to place a child with someone who worked there.

That was a big lie. None of them had really wanted him. Joel was ugly. His face wasn't red just from crying. He had a big strawberry birthmark covering the right side of his face. It looked as if he had been left under a sunlamp too long on one side. And when he got mad the mark got redder and redder, until it almost looked like his face was on fire, that he'd burn you if you touched him. He'd watched himself in the mirror, made himself get mad just to watch the birthmark flame. That wasn't hard; there were a lot of things that made Joel mad, and all he had to do was think about any one of them.

He'd been in six or seven foster homes, and three "adoptive placements." They hadn't wanted him either—they just said they did so they could brag to their friends and neighbors about what good people they were. Nobody wanted a kid with that kind of face, and Joel made sure that the families who took him in finally realized that fact.

He remembered the first place they'd sent him to. He had a little brother, five years old. The kid had a white puppy. The parents didn't want Joel to feel jealous, so they let him feed the puppy sometimes. Joel didn't feel jealous at all, but adults always thought they knew everything you were thinking. So he went along with them and fed the dog. Except one day he just added a little broken glass to the high-priced dog food they always bought.

Joel used to tell the social workers he only wanted to find his *real* mother and go back to her. They always told him she must not have been able to take care of him because she'd just abandoned him like that, but they didn't know that. They'd never even talked to her.

Sometimes Joel imagined his mother must be somewhere

crying over him, wondering what could have possibly happened to him. Maybe she'd been sick, or knocked unconscious. Or maybe someone had kidnapped him and left him in that bathroom. Maybe even that social worker who said she had found him had actually stolen him out of his mother's front yard. Maybe the whole agency had been part of the crime. *Anything* might have happened.

Sometimes Joel could hear his mother inside his head, telling him to get out of whatever house and family the social workers had put him into and go find her. She needed him; they belonged together. Joel wondered if she had a big red mark on her face, just like his.

But that wouldn't be right. His own true mother was beautiful.

This last time Joel had run away from a foster home. They were nice-enough people; at least they didn't bother him with a lot of family-togetherness crap. But his mother told him it was time to leave. She told him to go to the railroad yards, where the freight trains go through. Maybe she was going to meet him, or tell him which train to take when he got there.

His mother told him to crawl into a certain freight car. *Go to sleep,* she said. That wasn't hard to do—Joel always felt tired when his mother was talking to him. And the steady rocking of the train was about the finest thing Joel had ever felt.

When he woke up, the car was all red inside. Without thinking, he touched his face, wondering what was wrong. He'd been dreaming of fire, of burning up, and for a moment he wondered if he might still be dreaming. He turned his head in nervous little jerks.

The freight car was full of straw and empty cloth sacks. Most of the sacks were gathered in a big bundle at the shadowy other end of the car. The sliding door to the car was cracked a little, and it was there all the red was coming from. Joel staggered to his feet and went to take a look outside.

It was the most beautiful dawn Joel could remember. The

sky was a gorgeous crimson, like it was on fire; but a nice fire. It warmed his birthmark pleasantly. He touched his face, helpless to prevent the smile he felt coming.

Nice, huh?

Joel stiffened. "Mother?" He turned and peered back into the darkened interior of the car. His eyes had to adjust again; he could barely see.

The bundle of empty sacks began to rise on two enormous legs.

"What you mean, boy?" The sacks parted to reveal the wide, bearded face. "You lost or something?"

Joel stared at the man standing among the discarded sacks. He was incredibly tall, with matted black hair and beard, and he wore a huge black overcoat that hung past his knees. It was hard to judge the man's width because of the bulk of the coat, but Joel figured he must have weighed well over three hundred fifty.

"I asked you a question, son."

Whoever he was, he was an adult, and not to be trusted. "I'm *not* your son," Joel said. "And I'm not lost."

The man tilted his head awkwardly, like as if he was stiff or something. Joel had a thought that the man might be crippled, but he couldn't imagine where that idea came from. The man coughed a little, and Joel wondered if the man might be laughing at him.

"Well, you must be somebody's son," the man said. "I heard you asking for your mama."

"Don't you talk about my mother!" Joel felt his birthmark beginning to burn.

It's all right, son. Don't upset yourself so.

"What, what did you say?" Joel raised his fists. He suddenly felt confused, like he wasn't fully awake yet.

"I didn't say anything uh . . . what's your name, anyway?"

Joel just looked at him. "Joel," he finally said, not sure why he was telling him.

"No last name?"

"No. Not one that belongs to me, anyway."

"Well, that's okay. My name's Samson. No last name for me, either." They stood like that awhile, awkward with each other. "Nice sunrise," Samson said a couple of times, and Joel simply nodded. After a while Joel sat down, watching the countryside roll past the door. "You hungry . . . Joel?" Samson held out something wrapped in brown paper.

Joel took it, examined it. It was a candy bar. "Thanks," he said, feeling a little more relaxed.

"No problem." Samson was squatting now. Joel stared at the big man's coat. It creased funny. He turned away again, afraid to look too closely.

They said nothing for several miles. The train seemed to change direction in a switching yard. For some reason Joel felt nervous. He didn't know why. "I've never done this before," he said. "I don't even know where this train is going."

It's all right, baby. Everything's going to be fine.

Joel stared at Samson's beard, searching for signs of movement.

"Nothing to worry about, Joel," Samson finally said, facing him, his mouth moving distinctly between the rolls of greasy dark beard. "I've been doing this for years. Perfectly safe. Where you off to, anyway?"

"I'm looking for my mother." Joel felt foolish for having told him, but he was scared now, he needed for this man to help.

I'm here. I'm here, baby.

Joel shook. He rubbed his hand back and forth in the hay, wishing she would stop, wondering where she was.

"Well, that's just fine. Mothers are *real* important. Ol' Samson *knows.*"

Joel couldn't understand how the man could look so calm.

It's me, baby. Mama's right here.

Joel closed his eyes tightly, then opened them again. Samson was staring right at him. He wondered if his birthmark was glowing. It burned his face just thinking about it. "What you looking at?" he muttered between clenched teeth.

"Nothing, Joel. Not one thing. We gots lots in common, you know?"

Joel felt like laughing. "Like what?"

"Mothers, for one. We're both our mother's son and that's real important. And we ain't got no last names. My mama never told me hers."

Come here, baby.

Joel bit the inside of his mouth. "Where is your mother now?"

Samson grinned. He had no teeth. "Oh, here, there, everywhere."

Everywhere . . .

Joel started to cry.

Don't cry . . .

"Oh, don't cry, Joel. I didn't mean nothing."

Baby, don't cry . . .

"I want my mama."

"I know. We all want our mamas. And it's like . . . it's like all mamas are the *same,* even when they're not the same person, you know?"

"She didn't mean to leave me behind. They're all liars!" Joel began to wail.

"That's a fact, son. They'll lie every chance they get. You don't have to tell ol' Samson about social workers."

"But how did you know . . ."

"I tell you, I've had more than my share of social workers in my time."

Baby . . .

Joel felt something. Joel felt inspired, and he risked a silly, crazy question: "Is your mother my mother?"

Samson chuckled. "No, no, that's not it at all. You're looking for your mama. My mama understands that, and she just appreciates how you feel. Yes, indeedy, she *does* appreciate it. That's what got her interested in you; that's what brought you here. Like a moth to a burning fire." Samson's head fell back and the close air filled with his deep-throated laugh.

Joel hesitated. Then he felt it all rush out of him. "She must have been sick. Something *bad* must have made her leave me!"

"I believe you." Samson crawled across the rocking floor and looked Joel in the face. "Mamas go through a lot. My mama got her belly *cut open* giving birth to me. And she *died* for her trouble!"

I did it for you, baby. I'd do anything for you.

Joel stared at Samson. The huge man looked even more grotesque, splayed across the shaking, rocking floor of the freight car. The vibrations of the moving car made his loose overcoat move and bend in strange ways, as if it had a life of its own.

Come to me, son. I'm here for you.

Joel scooted back until he was leaning against the metal wall. Samson looked exhausted, his mouth open and eyelids half-lowered. He turned over awkwardly, lumping the straw together to make a cushion for his back.

"I'll help you find her, Joel. Least I can do. 'Cause I know how you feel."

One of the shiny black buttons holding Samson's coat together had pulled off.

"You owe it to your mama to keep looking."

Something gray was falling into the gap in the coat left by the missing button.

"I thank my own mama every day for what she did for me—giving me life like that."

More buttons popped from the coat as the gray skin pressed away from Samson's body. Joel could see hair, and white bonnet

My baby . . .

Joel rose up on his knees, leaned forward to get a closer look.

"Your mama'll do anything for you, you know that?"

Joel rose to unsteady feet. The coat was almost completely open now. Something was dropping from its hidden folds to the freight car floor.

"My mama, now, she suffered *bad.*"

For you, son . . .

Joel bent over, his hand on Samson's overcoat.

My baby . . .

Joel began to lift one side of the heavy coat.

"They shouldn't have cut her open like that! Weren't even proper hospital!"

Something flopped forward onto the floor, grinning up at him.

My son . . .

"Why, that woman was just a midwife! Not no proper doctor." The operation just didn't work out!"

Joel stared down at the shriveled woman's corpse.

Mama's boy . . .

"But she never left me, my mama. That ol' midwife couldn't keep us apart. So that crazy ol' midwife just kept us together. Raised me up, all by myself in that little attic room, still in my mama's arms. My mama dearly loved me. Couldn't give me up."

Mother's son . . .

Joel stared down at Samson's hips, where the emaciated man's body joined his mother's broken frame. The woman's empty eye sockets stared up at him, her mouth fallen open.

Joel could barely contain his rage. He wanted to kick through the twisted joining of mother and son, shatter the point where Samson's narrowed, deformed torso emerged from female, skeleton thighs. He wanted to smash apart all the marbled surfaces where living flesh and old bone had blended into one. It wasn't fair.

Joel had never had his mother. Samson had never lost his.

Motherson . . .

Kill for Me

John Keefauver

Now, the gun is aimed at him as he sleeps so peacefully there, and all I have to do is pull the trigger and the whole horrible thing will be finished. Finally finished. Years of it, over. And I'll be the only one left. Not that I deserve to be the one surviving. But if Irene had told me what she was going to do, there would have been two of us left. I would have killed him then instead of now.

In a way, of course, she's the one who will be killing him. Not that she would want it that way. Still, there's the irony of it. Her note to me after I found her: "Tell him you did it, that it was your idea. He will think I'm the 'somebody' and he will stop. He will be satisfied . . ."

Satisfied? *Him?* Him, stop? Whatever possessed her to think that he'd stop! Why should he stop after all these years? To my mind he's just getting started. A bullet will be the only thing that will stop him.

She was always the optimist, though, Irene. She always said he would grow out of it. From the very beginning, she was the one who gave in to him, thinking he'd stop. And what she has just done was her final giving-in. Not that I didn't think the same way she did, too, at first, that it was simply a baby thing on his part. After all, don't all babies go into a tantrum at some time or another, at least once, in order to get their way? Like holding their breath until you give them whatever they want. Like he did, although I don't remember what it was he wanted anymore. But that was the beginning. And I suppose if we hadn't given in to him then, and all the childhood years afterward, I wouldn't be standing here now in his bedroom with a gun aimed at his head, my finger on the trigger. Can I really do it? If I hadn't lived through it, I would think of myself now as a monster. Can I really do it?

It's not a matter of whether I can, but that I must do it. For Irene's sake. And for all the others he will destroy if I don't destroy him. I won't give in to him again. If I—and Irene— had only stopped years ago. If we'd let him hold his breath until he turned blue. He couldn't hurt himself—we knew it then—but he scared us and we gave him what he wanted. Scared us . . . Little did we know.

That time when he was six or seven and he wanted to see that movie and we wouldn't let him and he said he was going to jump out of a tree if we didn't let him go. We wouldn't, and we found him not long afterward with a broken leg at the foot of the elm in the backyard. He hadn't made a sound. No screaming or crying, lying there I don't know how long with a broken leg. Just lay there until we found him. All he said then was "I demand to be allowed to go to all the movies I want to go to." Demand. Allowed. That was the way he talked, even then. As if he was reading the words out of a book.

So from then on we let him go to the movies he wanted to. Wouldn't you? No?

That started it, anyway. We were afraid, although Irene for a long time didn't entirely come to stop believing that he simply had fallen out of the tree. She asked him more than once about it, at first: "Now, Billy, you *must* have fallen out of that tree." He'd simply say, "I jumped. I deliberately jumped." I believed him. After all, hadn't he been building up to it with his other threats from the time he'd learned to talk? The time he said he was going to burn himself with the birthday candles if he didn't get a bicycle for his birthday. Not a small boy's bike; a big one, one he couldn't possibly ride. Of course, he didn't get it—and he deliberately waited until it was time to blow out the candles, and we were all watching, to stick his hand over the flames and hold it there until Irene jerked it away. I felt sorry for the kids at his party. Of course, that was before we stopped inviting his friends to the house. He didn't mind. It wasn't long after that that he didn't have any friends, not at school or anywhere. He didn't care.

Even Irene had to admit that he had deliberately burned himself, since it happened right in front of her eyes that way. I think he did it in front of her to make her understand that it couldn't possibly have been an accident—especially when, about a year earlier, he'd fallen down the cellar steps after we wouldn't let him go ice-skating one day. (He had a bad cold.) Even I thought it had been an accident. He was furious with us for thinking he had simply fallen. "I told you I was going to do it!" he kept yelling. When he jumped out of the tree, I guess he just got tired of waiting for us to come out and watch him. He claimed he had yelled for us to "come see." We didn't hear him.

He got his bike, and when he eventually asked for another one, an expensive racer type, we gave it to him, even though he couldn't possibly ride it. He told us he would drown himself if he didn't get it. What would you have done? Irene was very frightened. She kept saying that he "might accidentally drown himself." I argued against it because I could see what was going to happen to us for the rest of our lives if we didn't take a strong stand, although I admit I never thought it would come to this. I told her there wasn't any body of water large enough for him to drown himself in for miles around. How could he get to it? (He was only seven or eight.) Then she mentioned our bathtub . . .

When I heard him running the water for his bath that night, on his own, I gave in. Especially considering that we'd always had to drag him to the tub.

From then on we gave in to all his demands that were halfway reasonable. When we balked on some of the more outlandish ones, he threatened to do himself bodily harm. Always bodily harm. I began to dread hearing him open his mouth for fear of another demand. He got everything he wanted.

Three or four years went by like this. Why didn't we take him to a doctor, a psychiatrist? We tried to. We told him he was going to the "doctor for a checkup." He thought he was going for a physical examination—until, unfortunately, he saw the word "psychiatrist" at the entrance to the doctor's office as we walked up to it. He darted from us, pulled a penknife out of his pocket, and told us he would stick it in his stomach if we didn't promise never to try to make him see a psychiatrist again. Or any kind of a doctor. Or—he was a smart one—if we ourselves ever tried to see a doctor *about* him.

The worst thing, for then, was when a year or so later he told us he was going to jump in front of a car if we didn't buy him one—a VW. "A car!" I yelled at him. "You're only twelve years old!"

"I *demand* a car. Do you think I'm only a child because I'm twelve?"

We argued about it until he made me so mad that I told him he could jump in front of cars for the rest of his life before I'd ever buy a twelve-year-old kid an automobile.

I had no sooner said that than he ran out of the house. I went to the door, but I didn't realize he was running toward the highway until he was too far away to hear me. I screamed then that he could *have* a car and began to run after him. From a distance, still screaming, I saw him reach the highway, wait a moment, then jump right in front of an oncoming sports car.

I had the VW waiting for him when he got out of the hospital—a new one. That's what he'd demanded.

I'd hoped that he'd be content just to own the car, to sit in it, to pretend he was driving it. But as soon as he was recovered enough, he demanded that Irene or I drive him wherever he wanted to go whenever he wanted to. We did. Wouldn't you? I was particularly anxious not to displease him. Irene had told me that if I ever did anything again that might cause him to do something on the order of jumping in front of a car, she would leave me. I also felt guilty about causing his injuries, if you can believe it.

He soon tired of being driven, though, and demanded that we buy him some property, a field large enough for him to drive the car in himself. He wasn't old enough to drive legally on public streets, of course, and the fact that he insisted on not breaking the law amused me in an ironic way—until I came to the conclusion that he was not really interested in not breaking the law, or even in driving. His interest lay in making another, a larger, demand on us. He well knew that I couldn't afford to buy a field. But I did it.

He'd had the VW less than a year when he told us that he'd cut his finger off if we didn't buy him a Porsche. I borrowed on the house for it.

I thought he was tiring of the game when he didn't make a major demand—there were many minor ones—for more than a year. Then out of the blue he said that unless we swore to give him anything he wanted for the rest of his life—*anything*—he would kill himself.

We agreed—what else was there to do?—and he said the first thing he wanted was for us to kill somebody for him.

He said this at dinner. Sitting at the head of the table, saying it very calmly, as if he were asking for the mashed potatoes (which he liked very much and which we therefore had every day), very composed, his face calm. He's a skinny, pimply kid, hardly someone who looks forceful. Yet right then he spoke with the assurance of a President of the United States—a mad president. And very seriously, just as he always was, incidentally, in asking for the potatoes.

In the morning, I thought, I'd go to the authorities and commit him to a mental institution. He was still a minor.

"Kill somebody for you?" I was afraid to look at Irene.

"That's what I said."

"Why?"

"Because I demand it."

"Well, then, who?"

"Anybody. It makes no difference. I demand that you kill for me."

"When?" I had to have until morning.

"Within twenty-four hours. If you don't, I'll kill myself."

There was no doubt in my mind that he would carry out his threat. And there was also no doubt in my mind that if we killed once for him, he would demand that we kill again—and again. How far could he go? To, indeed, the President of the United States?

With that, he rose and we were dismissed.

That night in our bedroom I told Irene about my plan to go to the authorities in the morning. In fact, I told her a number of times; she seemed so numb, so uncomprehending, so withdrawn, that I didn't seem to be getting through to her. She never answered me. She made no reply—except for a low moaning sound. As I tried to go to sleep I kept hearing her moan. She wouldn't let me hold her. And she wouldn't take a sleeping pill.

Toward dawn I awoke to find her gone from the bed. There was a light coming from our bathroom, and when I went in, there she was lying on the floor, dead, an empty bottle of sleeping pills beside her. The bottle had been nearly full.

Beside the bottle was a note: "Tell him you did it, that it was your idea. He will think I'm the 'somebody' and he will stop. He will be satisfied. It will shock him into sanity." And then a P.S.: "Hide the pills. Say you suffocated me with a pillow. Put me in bed."

Wild grief first. Then a fury. Calling the police simply wasn't enough.

I went into our bedroom and got my gun. Then, into his bedroom.

The gun, aimed at his head. What could be more fitting

than that he be the 'somebody,' that within the time specified his last demand be fulfilled?—by me, as always.

Now that the police and everybody else have gone, I suppose I ought to tidy up a bit. If nothing else, clean up the blood. That's what Irene would do, God bless her soul. (Oh, God, how will I ever get along without her?) At least I got her into bed before the police saw her—she wouldn't have liked to be seen on the floor—although I didn't do anything else for the rest of the day except wait for dinnertime. I wasn't up to it. I thought a lot, though—about not killing "somebody" for him, putting it into the right words. And once more I thought about all of his threats, especially the last one, and how he'd followed through on every one of them. Had I made the right decision? Including telling him the truth about Irene, that she had committed suicide?

I had. He'd done exactly what I knew he was going to do. As soon as the twenty-four hours were up, at dinnertime, and I'd said, I-don't-know-how-many times, that I hadn't killed "somebody" and that I wasn't about to, he'd taken the gun I'd offered him—the same one I was going to shoot him with until I came to my senses, and thinking of his final threat, changed my mind just before I pulled the trigger—and he'd blown his own brains out.

Shave and a Haircut, Two Bites

Dan Simmons

Outside, the blood spirals down.

I pause at the entrance to the barbershop. There is nothing unique about it. Almost certainly there is one similar to it in your community; its function is proclaimed by the pole outside, the red spiraling down, and by the name painted on the broad window, the letters grown scabrous as the gold paint ages and flakes away. While the most expensive hair salons now bear the names of their owners, and the shopping-mall franchises offer sickening cutenesses—Hairport, Hair Today: Gone Tomorrow, Hair We Are, Headlines, Shear Masters, The Head Hunter, In-Hair-itance, and so forth, ad infinitum, ad nauseam—the name of this shop is eminently forgettable. It is meant to be so. This shop offers neither styling nor unisex cuts. If you hair is dirty when you enter, it will be cut dirty; there are no shampoos given here. While the franchises demand fifteen to thirty dollars for a basic haircut, the cost here has not changed for a decade or more. It occurs to the potential new customer immediately upon entering that no one could live on an income based upon such low rates. No one does. The potential customer usually beats a hasty retreat, put off by the too-low prices, by the darkness of the place, by the air of dusty decrepitude exuded from both the establishment itself and from its few waiting customers, invariably silent and staring, and by a strange sense of tension bordering upon threat which hangs in the stale air.

Before entering, I pause a final moment to stare in the window of the barbershop. For a second I can see only a reflection of the street and the silhouette of a man more shadow than substance—me. To see inside, one has to step closer to the glass and perhaps cup hands to one's temples to reduce the glare. The blinds are drawn but I find a crack in the slats. Even then there is not much to see. A dusty window ledge holds three desiccated cacti and an assortment of dead flies. Two barber chairs are just visible through the gloom; they are of a sort no longer made: black leather, white enamel, a high headrest. Along one wall, half a dozen uncomfortable-looking chairs sit empty and two low tables show a litter of magazines with covers torn or missing entirely. There are mirrors on two of the three interior walls; but rather than add light to the long, narrow room, the infinitely receding reflections seem to make the space appear as if the barbershop itself were a dark reflection in an age-dimmed glass.

A man is standing there in the gloom, his form hardly more substantial than my silhouette on the window. He stands next to the first barber chair as if he were waiting for me.

He is waiting for me.

I leave the sunlight of the street and enter the shop.

"Vampires," said Kevin. "They're both vampires."

"Who're vampires?" I asked between bites on my apple. Kevin and I were twenty feet up in a tree in his backyard. We'd built a rough platform there that passed as a tree house. Kevin was ten, I was nine.

"Mr. Innis and Mr. Denofrio," said Kevin. "They're both vampires."

I lowered the *Superman* comic I'd been reading. "They're not vampires," I said. "They're *barbers.*"

"Yeah," said Kevin, "but they're vampires too. I just figured it out."

I sighed and sat back against the bole of the tree. It was late autumn and the branches were almost empty of leaves. Another week or two and we wouldn't be using the tree house again until next spring. Usually when Kevin announced that he'd just figured something out, it meant trouble. Kevin O'Toole was almost my age, but sometimes it seemed that he was five years older and five years younger than I at the same time. He read a lot. And he had a weird imagination. "Tell me," I said.

"You know what the red means, Tommy?"

"What red?"

"On the barber pole. The red stripes that curl down."

I shrugged. "It means it's a barbershop."

It was Kevin's turn to sigh. "Yeah, sure, Tommy, but why *red?* And why have it curling down like that for a barber?"

I didn't say anything. When Kevin was in one of his moods, it was better to wait him out.

"Because it's blood," he said dramatically, almost whispering. "Blood spiraling down. Blood dripping and spilling. That's been the sign for barbers for almost six hundred years."

He'd caught my interest. I set the *Superman* comic aside on the platform. "Okay," I said, "I believe you. Why is it their sign?"

"Because it was their *guild sign,*" said Kevin. "Back in the Middle Ages, all the guys who did important work belonged to guilds, sort of like the union our dads belong to down at the brewery, and."

"Yeah, yeah," I said. "But why *blood?*" Guys as smart as Kevin had a hard time sticking to the point.

"I was getting to that," said Kevin. "According to this

stuff I read, way back in the Middle Ages, barbers used to be surgeons. About all they could do to help sick people was to bleed them, and . . ."

"Bleed them?"

"Yeah. They didn't have any real medicines or anything, so if somebody got sick with a disease or broke a leg or something, all the surgeon . . . the barber . . . could do was bleed them. Sometimes they'd use the same razor they shaved people with. Sometimes they'd bring bottles of leeches and let them suck some blood out of the sick person."

"Gross."

"Yeah, but it sort of worked. Sometimes. I guess when you lose blood, your blood pressure goes down and that can lower a fever and stuff. But most of the time, the people they bled just died sooner. They probably needed a transfusion more than a bunch of leeches stuck on them."

I sat and thought about this for a moment. Kevin knew some really weird stuff. I used to think he was lying about a lot of it, but after I saw him correct the teachers in fourth and fifth grade a few times . . . and get away with it . . . I realized he wasn't making things up. Kevin was weird, but he wasn't a liar.

A breeze rustled the few remaining leaves. It was a sad and brittle sound to a kid who loved summer. "All right," I said. "But what's all this got to do with vampires? You think 'cause barbers used to stick leeches on people a couple of hundred years ago that Mr. Innis and Mr. Denofrio are *vampires?* Jeez, Kev that's nuts."

"The Middle Ages were more than five hundred years ago, Niles," said Kevin, calling me by my last name in the voice that always made me want to punch him. "But the guild sign was just what got me thinking about it all. I mean, what other business has kept its guild sign?"

I shrugged and tied a broken shoelace. "Blood on their sign doesn't make them vampires."

When Kevin was excited, his green eyes seemed to get

even greener than usual. They were really green now. He leaned forward. "Just think about it, Tommy," he said. "When did vampires start to disappear?"

"Disappear? You mean you think they were *real*? Cripes, Kev, my mom says you're the only gifted kid she's ever met, but sometimes I think you're just plain looney tunes."

Kevin ignored me. He had a long, thin face—made even thinner-looking by the crew cut he wore—and his skin was so pale that the freckles stood out like spots of gold. He had the same full lips that people said made his two sisters look pretty, but now those lips were quivering. "I read a lot about vampires," he said. "A *lot*. Most of the serious stuff agrees that the vampire legends were fading in Europe by the seventeenth century. People still *believed* in them, but they weren't so afraid of them anymore. A few hundred years earlier, suspected vampires were being tracked down and killed all the time. It's like they'd gone underground or something."

"Or people got smarter," I said.

"No, *think*," said Kevin and grabbed my arm. "Maybe the vampires were being wiped out. People knew they were there and how to fight them."

"Like a stake through the heart?"

"Maybe. Anyway, they've got to hide, pretend they're gone, and still get blood. What'd be the easiest way to do it?"

I thought of a wise-acre comment, but one look at Kevin made me realize that he was dead serious about all this. And we were best friends. I shook my head.

"Join the barbers' guild!" Kevin's voice was triumphant. "Instead of having to break into people's houses at night and then risk others' finding the body all drained of blood, they *invite* you in. They don't even struggle while you open their veins with a knife or put the leeches on. Then they . . . or the family of the dead guy . . . *pay* you. No wonder they're the only group to keep their guild sign. They're vampires, Tommy!"

I licked my lips, tasted blood, and realized that I'd been

chewing on my lower lip while Kevin talked. "All of them?" I said. "Every barber?"

Kevin frowned and released my arm. "I'm not sure. Maybe not all."

"But you think Innis and Denofrio are?"

Kevin's eyes got greener again and he grinned. "There's one way to find out."

I closed my eyes a second before asking the fatal question. "How, Kev?"

"By watching them," said Kevin. "Following them. Checking them out. *Seeing* if they're vampires."

"And if they are?"

Kevin shrugged. He was still grinning. "We'll think of something."

I enter the familiar shop, my eyes adjusting quickly to the dim light. The air smells of talcum and rose oil and tonic. The floor is clean and instruments are laid out on white linen atop the counter. Light glints dully from the surface of scissors and shears and the pearl handles of more than one straight razor.

I approach the man who stands silently by his chair. He wears a white shirt and tie under a white smock. "Good morning," I say.

"Good morning, Mr. Niles." He pulls a striped cloth from its shelf, snaps it open with a practiced hand, and stands waiting like a toreador.

I take my place in the chair. He sweeps the cloth around me and snaps it shut behind my neck in a single fluid motion. "A trim this morning, perhaps?"

"I think not. Just a shave, please."

He nods and turns away to heat the towels and prepare the razor. Waiting, I look into the mirrored depths and see multitudes.

* * *

Kevin and I had made our pact while sitting in our tree on Sunday. By Thursday we'd done quite a bit of snooping. Kev had followed Innis and I'd watched Denofrio.

We met in Kevin's room after school. You could hardly see his bed for all the heaps of books and comics and half-built Heath Kits and vacuum tubes and plastic models and scattered clothes. Kevin's mother was still alive then, but she had been ill for years and rarely paid attention to little things like her son's bedroom. Or her son.

Kevin shoved aside some junk and we sat on his bed, comparing notes. Mine were scrawled on scraps of paper and the back of my paper-route collection form.

"Okay," said Kevin, "what'd you find out?"

"They're not vampires," I said. "At least my guy isn't."

Kevin frowned. "It's too early to tell, Tommy."

"Nuts. You gave me this list of ways to tell a vampire, and Denofrio flunks *all* of them."

"Explain."

"Okay. Look at Number One on your stupid list. 'Vampires are rarely seen in daylight.' Heck, Denofrio and Innis are both in the shop all day. We both checked, right?"

Kevin sat on his knees and rubbed his chin. "Yeah, but the barbershop is *dark,* Tommy. I told you that it's only in the movies that the vampires burst into flame or something if the daylight hits them. According to the old books, they just don't *like* it. They can get around in the daylight if they have to."

"Sure," I said, "but these guys work all day just like our dads. They close up at five and walk home before it gets dark."

Kevin pawed through his own notes and interrupted. "They both live alone, Tommy. That suggests something."

"Yeah. It suggests that neither one of them makes enough money to get married or have a family. My dad says that their barbershop hasn't raised its prices in years."

"Exactly!" cried Kevin. "Then how come almost no one goes there?"

"They give lousy haircuts," I said. I looked back at my list, trying to decipher the smeared lines of penciled scrawl. "Okay, Number Five on your list. 'Vampires will not cross running water.' Denofrio lives across the *river*, Kev. I watched him cross it all three days I was following him."

Kevin was sitting up on his knees. Now he slumped slightly. "I told you that I wasn't sure of that one. Stoker put it in *Dracula,* but I didn't find it in too many other places."

I went on quickly. "Number Three—'Vampires hate garlic.' I watched Mr. Denofrio eat dinner at Luigi's Tuesday night, Kev. I could smell the garlic from twenty feet away when he came out."

"Three wasn't an essential one."

"All right," I said, moving in for the kill, "tell me *this* one wasn't essential. Number Eight—'All vampires hate and fear crosses and will avoid them at all cost.'" I paused dramatically. Kevin knew what was coming and slumped lower. "Kev, Mr. Denofrio goes to St. Mary's. *Your church, Kev.* Every morning before he goes down to open up the shop."

"Yeah. Innis goes to First Prez on Sundays. My dad told me about Denofrio being in the parish. I never see him because he only goes to early Mass."

I tossed the notes on the bed. "How could a vampire go to your church? He not only doesn't run away from a cross, he sits there and stares at about a hundred of them each day of the week for about an hour a day!"

"Dad says he's never seen him take Communion," said Kevin, a hopeful note in his voice.

I made a face. "Great. Next you'll be telling me that anyone who's not a priest has to be a vampire. Brilliant, Kev."

He sat up and crumpled his own notes into a ball. I'd already seen them at school. I knew that Innis didn't follow Kevin's Vampire Rules either. Kevin said, "The cross thing doesn't prove . . . or disprove . . . anything, Tommy. I've been thinking about it. These things joined the barber's guild to get some protective coloration. It makes sense that they'd try to blend into the religious community, too. Maybe they can train themselves to build up a tolerance to crosses, the way we take shots to build up a tolerance to things like smallpox and polio."

I didn't sneer, but I was tempted. "Do they build up a tolerance to mirrors, too?"

"What do you mean?"

"I mean I know something about vampires too, Kev, and even though it wasn't in your stupid list of rules, it's a fact that vampires don't like mirrors. They don't throw a reflection."

"That's not right," said Kevin in that rushy, teacherish voice he used. "In the movies they don't throw a reflection. The old books say that they avoided mirrors because they saw their *true* reflection there . . . what they looked like being old or undead or whatever."

"Yeah, whatever," I said. "But *whatever* spooks them, there isn't any place worse for mirrors than a barbershop. Unless they hang out in one of those carnival fun-house mirror places. Do *they* have guild signs, too, Kev?"

Kevin threw himself backward on the bed as if I'd shot him. A second later he was pawing through his notes and back up on his knees. "There was one weird thing," he said.

"Yeah, what?"

"They were closed Monday."

"Real weird. Of course, every darn barbershop in the entire *universe* is closed on Mondays, but I guess you're right. They're closed on Mondays. They've got to be vampires. 'QED,' as Mrs. Double Butt likes to say in geometry class. Gosh, I wish *I* was smart like you, Kevin."

"Mrs. Doubet," he said, still looking at his notes. He was the only kid in our class who liked her. "It's not that they're closed on Monday that's weird, Tommy. It's what they do. Or at least Innis."

"How do you know? You were home sick on Monday."

Kevin smiled. "No, I wasn't. I typed the excuse and signed Mom's name. They never check. I followed Innis around. Lucky he has that old car and drives slow, I was able to keep up with him on my bike. Or at least catch up."

I rolled to the floor and looked at some kit Kevin'd given up on before finishing. It looked like some sort of radio crossed with an adding machine. I managed to fake disinterest in what he was saying even though he'd hooked me again, just as he always did. "So where did he go?" I said.

"The Mear place. Old Man Everett's estate. Miss Planlunen's house out on 28. That mansion on the main road, the one the rich guy from New York bought last year."

"So?" I said. "They're all rich. Innis probably cuts their hair at home." I was proud that I had seen a connection that Kevin had missed.

"Uh-huh," said Kevin, "the richest people in the county, and the one thing they have in common is that they get their haircuts from the lousiest barber in the state. Lousiest *barbers*, I should say. I saw Denofrio drive off, too. They met at the shop before they went on their rounds. I'm pretty sure Denofrio was at the Wilkes estate along the river that day. I asked Rudy, the caretaker, and he said either Denofrio or Innis comes there most Mondays."

I shrugged. "So rich people stay rich by paying the least they can for haircuts."

"Sure," said Kevin. "But that's not the weird part. The weird part was that both of the old guys loaded their car trunks with small bottles. When Innis came out of Mear and Everett's and Plankmen's places, he was carrying *big* bottles, two-gallon jars at least, and they were *heavy*, Tommy. Filled with liquid. I'm pretty sure the smaller jars they'd loaded at the shop were full too."

"Full of what?" I said. "Blood?"

"Why not?" said Kevin.

"Vampires are supposed to take blood *away*," I said, laughing. "Not *deliver* it."

"Maybe it was blood in the big bottles," said Kevin. "And they brought something to trade from the barbershop."

"Sure," I said, still laughing, "hair tonic!"

"It's not funny, Tom."

"The heck it isn't!" I made myself laugh even harder. "The best part is that your barber vampires are biting just the rich folks. They only drink premium!" I rolled on the floor, scattering comic books and trying not to crush any vacuum tubes.

Kevin walked to the window and looked out at the fading light. We both hated it when the days got shorter. "Well, I'm not convinced," he said. "But it'll be decided tonight."

"Tonight?" I said, lying on my side and no longer laughing. "What happens tonight?"

Kevin looked over his shoulder at me. "The back entrance to the barbershop has one of those old-style locks that I can get past in about two seconds with my Houdini Kit. After dinner, I'm going down to check the place out."

I said, "It's dark after dinner."

Kevin shrugged and looked outside.

"Are you going alone?"

Kevin paused and then stared at me over his shoulder. "That's up to you."

I stared back.

There is no sound quite the same as a straight razor being sharpened on a leather strop. I relax under the wrap of hot towels or my face, hearing but not seeing the barber prepare his blade. Receiving a professional shave is a pleasure which modern man has all but abandoned, but one in which I indulge myself every day.

The barber pulls away the towels, dries my upper cheeks and temples with a dab of a dry cloth, and turns back to the strop for a few final strokes of the razor. I feel my cheeks and throat tingling from the hot towels, the blood pulsing in my neck. "When I was a boy," I say, "a friend of mine convinced me that barbers were vampires."

The barber smiles but says nothing. He has heard my story before.

"He was wrong," I say, too relaxed to keep talking.

The barber's smile fades slightly as he leans forward, his face a study in concentration. Using a brush and lather whipped in a cup he quickly applies the shaving soap. Then he sets aside the cup, lifts the straight razor, and with a delicate touch of only his thumb and little finger, tilts my head so that my throat is arched and exposed to the blade.

I close my eyes as the cold steel rasps across the warmed flesh.

"You said two seconds!" I whispered urgently. "You've been messing with that darned lock for *five minutes!*" Kevin and I were crouched in the alley behind Fourth Street, huddled in the back doorway of the barbershop. The night air was cold and smelled of garbage. Street sounds seemed to come to us from a million miles away. *"Come on!"* I whispered.

The lock clunked, clicked, and the door swung open into blackness. *"Voilà,"* said Kevin. He stuck his wires, picks, and other tools back into his imitation-leather Houdini Kit bag. Grinning, he reached over and rapped "Shave and a Haircut" on the door.

"Shut up," I hissed, but Kevin was gone, feeling his way into the darkness. I shook my head and followed him in.

Once inside with the door closed, Kevin clicked on a penlight and held it between his teeth the way we'd seen a spy do in a movie. I grabbed on to the tail of his windbreaker and followed him down a short hallway into the single, long room of the barbershop.

It didn't take long to look around. The blinds were closed on both the large window and the smaller one on the front door, so Kevin figured it was safe to use the penlight. It was weird moving across that dark space with Kevin, the penlight throwing images of itself into the mirrors and illuminating one thing at a time—a counter here, the two chairs in the center of the room, a few chairs and magazines for customers, two sinks, a tiny little lavatory, no bigger than a closet, its door right inside the short hallway. All the clippers and things had been put away in drawers. Kevin opened the drawers, peered into the shelves. There were bottles of hair tonic, towels, all the barber tools set neatly into top drawers, both sets arranged the same. Kevin took out a razor and opened it, holding the blade up so it reflected the light into the mirrors.

"Cut it out," I whispered. "Let's get out of here."

Kevin set the thing away, making sure it was lined up exactly the way it had been, and we turned to go. His penlight beam moved across the back wall, illuminating a raincoat we'd already seen, and something else.

"There's a door here," whispered Kevin, moving the coat to show a doorknob. He tried it. "Drat. It's locked."

"Let's go!" I whispered. I hadn't heard a car pass in what felt like hours. It was like the whole town was holding its breath.

Kevin began opening drawers again. "There has to be a key," he said too loudly. "It must lead to a basement; there's no second floor on this place."

I grabbed him by his jacket. "Come on," I hissed. "Let's get out of here. We're going to get arrested."

"Just another minute . . ." began Kevin and froze. I felt my heart stop at the same instant.

A key rasped in the lock of the front door. There was a tall shadow thrown against the blind.

I turned to run, to escape, anything to get out of there, but Kevin clicked off the penlight, grabbed my sweatshirt, and pulled me with him as he crawled under one of the high sinks. There was just enough room for both of us there. A dark curtain hung down over the space and Kevin pulled it shut just as the door creaked open and footsteps entered the room.

For a second I could hear nothing but the pounding of blood in my ears, but then I realized that there were *two* people walking in the room, men by the sounds of their heavy tread. My mouth hung open and I panted, but I was unable to get a breath of air. I was sure that any sound at all would give us away.

One set of footsteps stopped at the first chair while the other went to the rear hall. A second door rasped shut, water ran, and there came the sound of the toilet flushing. Kevin nudged me, and I could have belted him then, but we were so crowded together in fetal positions that any movement by me would have made a noise. I held my breath and waited while the second set of footsteps returned from the lavatory and moved toward the front door. *They hadn't even turned on the lights.* There'd been no gleam of a flashlight beam through our curtain, so I didn't think it was the cops checking things out. Kevin nudged me again and I knew he was telling me that it had to be Innis and Denofrio.

Both pairs of footsteps moved toward the front, there was the sound of the door opening and slamming, and I tried to breathe again before I passed out.

A rush of noise. A hand reached down and parted the curtain. Other hands grabbed me and pulled me up and out, into the dark. Kevin shouted as another figure dragged him to his feet.

I was on my tiptoes, being held by my shirtfront. The man holding me seemed eight feet tall in the blackness, his fist the size of my head. I could smell garlic on his breath and assumed it was Denofrio.

"Let us go!" shouted Kevin. There was the sound of a slap, flat and clear as a rifle shot, and Kevin was silent.

I was shoved into a barber chair. I heard Kevin being pushed into the other one. My eyes were so well adjusted to the darkness that now I could make out the features of the two men. Innis and Denofrio. Dark suits blended into black, but I could see the pale, angular faces that I'd been sure had made Kevin think they were vampires. Eyes too deep and dark, cheekbones too sharp, mouths too cruel, and something about them that said *old* despite their middle-aged looks.

"What are you doing here?" Innis asked Kevin. The man spoke softly, without evident emotion, but his voice made me shiver in the dark.

"Scavenger hunt!" cried Kevin. "We have to steal a barber's clippers to get in the big kids' club. We're sorry. Honest!"

There came the rifle shot of a slap again. "You're lying," said Innis. "You followed me on Monday. Your friend here followed Mr. Denofrio in the evening. Both of you have been watching the shop. Tell me the truth. *Now!*"

"We think you're vampires," said Kevin. "Tommy and I came to find out."

My mouth dropped open in shock at what Kevin had said. The two men took a half-step back and looked at each other. I couldn't tell if they were smiling in the dark.

"Mr. Denofrio?" said Innis.

"Mr. Innis," said Denofrio.

"Can we go now?" said Kevin.

Innis stepped forward and did something to the barber chair Kevin was in. The leather armrests flipped up and out, making sort of white gutters. The leather strops on either side went up and over, attaching to something out of sight to make restraining straps around Kevin's arms. The headrest split apart, came down and around, and encircled Kevin's neck. It looked like one of those trays the dentists puts near you to spit into.

Kevin made no noise. I expected Denofrio to do the same thing to my chair, but he only laid a large hand on my shoulder.

"We're not vampires, boy," said Mr. Innis. He went to the counter, opened a drawer, and returned with the straight razor Kevin had been fooling with earlier. He opened it carefully. "Mr. Denofrio?"

The shadow by my chair grabbed me, lifted me out of the chair, and dragged me to the basement door. He held me easily with one hand while he unlocked it. As he pulled me into the darkness, I looked back and caught a glimpse of my friend staring in silent horror as Innis drew the edge of the straight razor slowly across Kevin's inner arm. Blood welled, flowed, and gurgled into the white enamel gutter of the armrest.

Denofrio dragged me downstairs.

The barber finishes the shave, trims my sideburns, and turns the chair so that I can look into the closer mirror.

I run my hand across my cheeks and chin. The shave was perfect, very close but with not a single nick. Because of the sharpness of the blade and the skill of the barber, my skin tingles but feels no irritation whatsoever.

I nod. The barber smiles ever so slightly and removes the striped protective apron.

I stand and remove my suitcoat. The barber hangs it on a hook while I take my seat again and roll up my left sleeve. While he is near the rear of the shop, the barber turns on a small radio. The music of Mozart fills the room.

The basement was lighted with candles set in small jars. The dancing red light reminded me of the time Kevin took me to his church. He said the small red flames were votive candles. You paid money, lit one, and said a prayer. He wasn't sure if the money was necessary for the prayer to be heard.

The basement was narrow and unfinished and almost filled by the twelve-foot slab of stone in its center. The thing on the stone was almost as long as the slab. The thing must have weighed a thousand pounds, easy. I could see folds of slick, gray flesh rising and falling as it breathed.

If there were arms, I couldn't see them. The legs were suggested by folds in slick fat. The tubes and pipes and rusting funnel led my gaze to the head.

Imagine a thousand-pound leech, nine or ten feet long and five or six feet thick through the middle as it lies on its back, no surface really, just layers of gray-green slime and wattles of what might be skin. Things, organs maybe, could be seen moving and sloshing through flesh as transparent as dirty plastic. The room was filled with the sound of its breathing and the stench of its breath. Imagine a huge sea creature, a small whale, maybe, dead and rotting on the beach for a week, and you've got an idea of what the thing itself smelled like.

The mass of flesh made a noise and the small eyes turned in my direction. Its eyes were covered with layers of yellow film or mucus and I was sure it was blind. The thing's head was no more defined than the end of a leech, but in the folds of slick fat were lines which showed a face that might have once been human. Its mouth was very large. Imagine a lamprey smiling.

"No, it was never human," said Mr. Denofrio. His hand was still firm on my shoulder. "By the time they came to our guild, they had already passed beyond hope of hiding amongst us. But they brought an offer which we could not refuse. Nor can our customers. Have you ever heard of symbiosis, boy? Hush!"

Upstairs, Kevin screamed. There was a gurgle, as of old pipes being tried.

The creature on the slab turned its blind gaze back to the ceiling. Its mouth pulsed hungrily. Pipes rattled and the funnel overflowed.

Blood spiraled down.

The barber returns and taps at my arm as I make a fist. There is a broad welt across the inner crook of my arm, as of an old scar poorly healed. It is an old scar.

The barber unlocks the lowest drawer and withdraws a razor. The handle is made of gold and is set about with small gems. He raises the object in both hands, holds it above his head, and the blade catches the dim light.

He takes three steps closer and draws the blade across my

arm, opening the scar tissue like a puparium hatching. There is no pain. I watch as the barber rinses the blade and returns it to its special place. He goes down the basement stairs and I can hear the gurgling in the small drain tubes of the arm-rest as his footsteps recede. I close my eyes.

I remember Kevin's screams from upstairs and the red flicker of candlelight on the stone walls. I remember the red flow through the funnel and the gurgle of the thing feeding, lamprey mouth extended wide and reaching high, trying to encompass the funnel the way an infant seeks its mother's nipple.

I remember Mr. Denofrio taking a large hammer from its place at the base of the slab, then a thing part spike and part spigot. I remember standing alone and watching as he pounded it in, realizing even as I watched that the flesh beneath the gray-green slime was a mass of old scars.

I remember watching as the red liquid flowed from the spigot into the crystal glass, the chalice. There is no red in the universe as deeply red, as purely red as what I saw that night.

I remember drinking. I remember carrying the chalice—carefully, so carefully—upstairs to Kevin. I remember sitting in the chair myself.

The barber returns with the chalice. I check that the scar has closed, fold down my sleeve, and drink deeply.

By the time I have donned my own white smock and returned, the barber is sitting in the chair.

"A trim this morning, perhaps?" I ask.

"I think not," he says. "Just a shave, please."

I shave him carefully. When I am finished, he runs his hands across his cheeks and chins and nods his approval. I perform the ritual and go below.

In the candlelit hush of the Master's vault, I wait for the Purification and think about immortality. Not about the true eon-spanning immortality of the Master . . . of all the Masters . . . but of the portion He deigns to share with us. It is enough.

After my colleague drinks and I have returned the chalice to its place, I come up to find the blinds raised, the shop open for business.

Kevin has taken his place beside his chair. I take my place beside mine. The music has ended and silence fills the room.

Outside, the blood spirals down.

The Orchid Nursery

Amanda Russell

In this humid artificial tropic,
Images of lust are grown in pots.
For sixty-five dollars,
One can buy a leering maniac
With a greasy green face
Spotted in bloody purple.
"An excellent breeder," says the tag.
He has the prognathous jaw
Of a later Hapsburg emperor,
But his line will grow stronger
With each succeeding generation.
On the next table
His courtesans await him,
Tiny and delicate beauties
Of pure white, yellow, and lavender.
Their waxen faces
Reveal only a hint of insane passion,
Like a women in a Goya tapestry.

Of Absence, Darkness, Death: Things Which Are Not

Ray Bradbury

Of absence, darkness, death: things which are not
Each unshaped shape resembles
Some midnight soul
That "with Nothing trembles."
Blind skies, cloudless dimensions;
Do smother souls
Whose nameless apprehensions
Go unborn; all's diminution;
No spirit-fire flares, no apparition
Leans forth its faceless face from looking-glass
Or windowpane.
The rain wears only wind, while wind wears rain,
And when the wind with winter-white bestows
A-spectral ice, there no ghost goes.
All attics empty, all breezeways, bare,
No phantom, prideless, restless, drifts his dustprints
   there.
The autumn round all dreamless goes; no seamless
   shrouds,

No palaces of callous stars, no marble clouds,
The earthen basements drink no blood,
All is a vacuumed neighborhood,
Not even dark keeps dark or death hides death,
And sightless pulse of panics keep their breath.
Nor does a ghostless curtain pale the air
All absence is, beyond the everywhere.
Then why this unplumbed drowning-pool of fear?
My soul dissembles
Like unit candles blown down-wind where nothing
    trembles
With bloodless, lifeless snowchild's seed
Miscarried by nobody's blood and need,
No moans, no cries
No blizzard mourns of silent celebration
Whose tongueless population
Stays unborn-dead.
But in my mindless marrow-bed:
Fears unremembered
How then forgot? Yet:
Absence, darkness, death: things which are not.

The Pack

Chet Williamson

They didn't remember rising. They were just dead one
minute, up and around the next. Those whose noses were
crushed were the lucky ones. They couldn't smell the others, and they couldn't smell themselves. That was the worst
of it for those whose noses were still working.

Rusty's nose worked just fine, and the stench annoyed
him. He didn't know if he'd ever be able to get it out of his
nostrils, ever be able to scent game again. The leader ought
to be able to scent the pack's prey. And he was the leader,
there was no doubt of that. He was the biggest, for one
thing. A mutt, to be sure, but there was a lot of German
shepherd in him, and his thin, taut frame indicated that either a Great Dane or a Doberman had participated in a train
pulled on his mother or grandmothers. He was also in the
best condition of the motley crew gathered around him,
which wasn't saying a whole hell of a lot.

Jesus, Rusty thought, they looked like shit. Fluffy in particular, one of the few he knew. He had humped her damn
near every time she'd been in heat, but had never connected
well enough to impregnate her. She was a mutt too, a small,
yellow, long-haired bitch who had always carried her tail up
and waving, as if to advertise the availability of her
hindquarters. Now that tail was matted and askew, the

hindquarters grotesquely large and swollen by the compression of her stomach where the 4 x 4 had mashed her. Her rear had had no choice but to split apart, and what Rusty remembered as tight and hot organs had given whelp to strands of dirt-caked gut on which she sat, resting her unbroken forepaws on a thick loop of her intestine.

Rowdy was the only other he knew, an old, old dog who had been dead a long, long time. He'd been run over many times, left to be simmered by hot summer rains and fried in the skillet of high noon asphalt. He lay on the grass more like a well-used welcome mat than a dog. It seemed that only the hemisphere of his skull had not been flattened, and dry, puckered little things that Rusty figured were eyes watched him from that mass of fur and splintered bone, and waited for him to offer a plan.

For a plan was what was needed. There had to be a purpose in what had happened, in what had drawn them all here together.

A plan. Rusty shivered at the thought. And then he shivered again at the thought of *thought*. His mental processes seemed so complex now, and he could tell that those of the others were similar. There had been such *simplicity* before the awakening—looks and growls and barks and motions that indicated all the necessities of canine existence:

Play!

Eat!

Shit!

Roll in it!

Fuck!

But now there was far more than could be communicated by *You smell my asshole, I'll smell yours.* Now there was memory and subtlety and, at long last, understanding of everything Rusty had seen and heard while he lived with the people who had called themselves his family. He knew what family was now, understood it. Males who fucked, bitches who whelped, them and the pups living together, enslaving the dogs, making them trade their freedom for food from cans (vomitous horsemeat shaped like a fat cylinder, the rings of the lid impressed upon the first bite), making them give up the heritage of the pack for a stroke once or twice a day, a walk on the end of a leash, an occasional flight of liberty when a bitch in heat might be fucked, a pile of dung might be rolled in, a wounded rabbit tormented and eventually killed.

And what response from the humans when these joys were over? A newspaper on the nose, the end of a leash across the hindquarters, stinging the anus, burning the balls. Torture, pure and simple. And then at last, after a lifetime of cowering and cringing and tail-wagging and licking the hand of the goddamned male and his bitch and their pups, after *years* of that, when the only thing you want to do is lie and rest, then the final visit to the Great Devil in his white coat, the spurt of the needle, the ultimate injection, oh yes, he knew, he'd lain by the fireplace many times while the "family" watched that show on the television (television— Christ, he even knew its name now! And *Christ,* he could even curse like the humans had!). He had seen the actor pretend to be the vet and kill the dogs with sorrow on his pasty, blotchy face, and Rusty's "family" had watched too, snuffling, the bitch wiping away tears and the male blinking, pretending his own tears weren't there, when all the time they knew that when Rusty got old and tired, they'd take him to the *real* Great Devil as soon as he sneezed, or puked on the carpet, or shit in the house.

And if not the Great Devil, then dogs died as Rusty and all who now surrounded him had died—crushed, battered, squashed, splattered by the cars, the trucks, the great, stupid machines that carried the humans everywhere because their legs were so weak, so slow.

"Did they ever try to stop?" Rusty clearly wondered, and the thoughts were like words to the others. They heard, and thought, and he heard in return.

"Stop?" The word came from Rowdy, and in Rusty's mind it was festooned with ornaments of flayed fur. It sounded like Rowdy looked. "They *tried* to hit me. And they did. Too old to get out of the way. Just crossing the road. Just wanted to get to the cool of the oak trees and take a good long piss against them. Took me down. One great flash of yellow fire, and that was all. Next thing I remember, I'm crawling here, moving like a rug, dragging myself along like nothing's ever moved before, like nothing should be *able* to move. And why? There's got to be a reason why. I'm older than you, seen more, heard more, maybe now I understand more. But I don't understand why. There's got to be a reason."

"There's a reason," said a young but twisted thought, and the pack turned what was left of their heads and looked with what was left of their eyes at another dog. Sparks was the name his "family" had given him. He had enough eyes to serve all of them. They had been pushed from their sockets by whatever vehicle had struck him. One looked one direction, one the other, so that his ovoid gaze seemed all-encompassing. "There's a *good* reason. To devour what devoured us. To eat what ate us away."

The thought struck a flame in Rusty, and he licked his chops with a caked tongue. "The family," he thought. "Humans."

The compressed muscles of Sparks's haunches pulsed in a futile effort to wag his tail. "Humans."

Rusty looked around the ring of broken creatures. Dry, parchment tongues panted in agreement, those tails wagged that could, heads nodded, even one that dangled from a thick strand of neck muscle that was barely visible beneath the sheep dog's shaggy hair. "It must be," Rusty thought. "Why otherwise would we have been given life once more, given knowledge, understanding, the complexity of thought necessary to finally realize the perfidy of our persecutors?"

"There may be no reason like that," stated a broken-faced dachshund, its jaw and snout poking at right angles to each other. "It may rather be a situation akin to the kind of entertainment that the 'families' watch on the television—

radiation, chemicals, nitrates from manure on the farms oozing out of the soil and into . . . the soul. There may be no purpose at all, merely a random chain of events."

"I for one," thought Sparks, "do not believe in a purposeless cosmos."

"You believe in God then?" inquired the dachshund.

"I believe in *Dog.*" Sparks grinned, and Rusty thought the effect was hideous.

"Fuck your palindromes, and fuck your philosophy," mentally growled a junkyard dog whose middle resembled a veterinarian's anatomical chart. "All I know is that I'm back and I'm pissed and though I don't have much of a stomach to digest it with, I want to tear out some human guts, and get a little back."

"I did not say," clarified the dachshund, "that I did *not* want that as well. I simply feel there may be no moral or theological justification of such acts. But whether there are or are not, I'd like to rip some humans myself. 'Wiener,' they called me. 'Little Wiener.' And that was only the first of many injuries, both mental and physical."

"Whatever the reason," thought Rusty, "we have all returned, and we all have the same basic drive—as Sparks so eloquently put it, to devour what devoured us. We are a pack, and together we can triumph."

Fluffy resettled her forepaws on her filthy bowels. "They may come after us, try to kill us."

"We're already dead, bitch," thought Sparks. "If we're moving around in *this* condition, bullets aren't going to be too effective, do you think?"

"But in this condition," she replied, "do you think we'll be able to pull down humans? I mean, look at Rowdy."

"It's true," Rowdy thought, "I'm not as spry as I used to be. But I do have means of locomotion, albeit slow. If the more active of you can bring our prey down, I can still participate in the final rending. Pieces of teeth remain in here, sharp, capable of cutting." And a mass of compressed fur rose up so that Rusty and the others could see smooth bits of yellow beneath. Rusty's newfound imagination could not, however, conceive of those pitiful bits of enamel abrading human flesh, if, indeed, they were still attached to what remained of Rowdy's jaw. Still, Rowdy was one of the pack.

This last thought he communicated to the others, and they agreed that the stronger would pull down the prey, but not finish it until all were there to share in the death and the eating.

"Can we eat?" wondered a desiccated terrier.

"We can try," Rusty thought. "Perhaps it will pass through us, perhaps it will be only symbolic. But still, this should be the law of the pack—to devour what devoured us."

Rusty lifted his head and tried to catch the sound of traffic to determine the whereabouts of a road. To scent gasoline or exhaust would have been impossible with the stench of carrion in his nose. Finally, from far away he heard the sound of an engine. "Come. Let's hunt."

The pack began to move in the direction of the road, but quickly learned that they would make dreadful time if they waited for Rowdy. So Rusty and Sparks got on either side of the irregular disc of leather and fur, dug their fangs into the mass, and hauled their companion along. The dog had been dead so long that Rusty tasted only the ghost of vileness. Once or twice Rowdy's matted hair got caught on roots and in branches, but the old dog writhed and twisted while the young ones tugged, until they reached a state game trail.

On the way, Rusty's eyes (still sharp, despite yellowing of the white and minor leaking of the vitreous fluid) discerned a rabbit standing in darkness next to a stump. Although his first reaction was to immediately drop Rowdy's fur pie and race after the creature, something made him hesitate. He thought at first that it might be increased intelligence, that the mental maturity he and his cohorts had achieved had shown him the futility of chasing rodents. But as the stump and the creature that stood next to it retreated in his peripheral vision, he realized that there had been something dreadfully *wrong* with the rabbit, if rabbit it was. It had seemed terribly thin, reduced in girth beyond the effects of emaciation. He had seen rabbits like that before, but where? . . .

He nearly damned himself for being so obtuse. Roadkill. Of course. He had seen rabbits that had been hit right across the torso by cars, their spines splintered, their innards smashed into one another so that their heads and hind legs looked perfectly natural, but what lay in between could have been slipped under a door. It was just like the dried up terrier's guts, the terrier who, like all of them, had been born again into this world.

And if a terrier, why not a rabbit? Why not cats, for Christ's sake? And turtles? And deer and squirrels and mice? Rusty had always liked to chase animals smaller than himself, though he hardly ever caught them. But he did not think he would like to chase the rabbit he had seen, and he wondered what its own prey might be.

The thoughts were blotted out by the sound of an engine idling, and Rusty saw a wooden bar ahead, the gate that kept vehicles out of the game trail. A car was next to that gate, perhaps fifty yards back from the main road, in the small parking area bounded by trees. Through the open windows of the car he could hear strains of that abysmal music that still drove spikes into his sensitive ears.

The pack crept closer to the car on splintered limbs, some of them trailing strands of gut like bridal trains behind them. Rusty heard voices now, one pleading, one protesting, and then the engine went dead, the music stopped. The pack froze in an instant, and the only sound was the soft clack of the dachshund's misaligned jaw as he excitedly tried to moisten his tongue.

Rusty and Sparks opened their own jaws then, letting Rowdy's ragged edges flop quietly to the earth, and looked at each other. Sparks's dueling eyes were wild with anticipation of the kill, and his legs trembled. The other dogs were ready too, their tongues hanging from their mouths like dry leaves.

"Wait," thought Rusty. The pack looked at him curiously and, he felt, angrily, as if frustrated at being heeled. But he was the leader, and the leader had a plan. "Let's get them out. Out in the open."

The pack pictured it in their minds and found it good. After a moment of plotting, Fluffy dragged herself to where the bitch inside could see her, while the others went to the front and back of the car. Lying on her mass of gut, she began to whimper, softly and pitifully.

"Ben . . ." came the bitch's voice. "Ben, there's something out there . . . "

"Come on, it's just an animal or something. Forget it."

"No, it's . . . a *dog.*"

Fluffy increased the volume now. It sounded, Rusty thought, like when she'd been mated a few times and was begging for more, and he gave a dog smile in the darkness.

"Oh, it *is,* it's a little yellow dog, and it looks hurt, the poor thing." The door opened, the bitch got out and knelt next to Fluffy, who was trying her damnedest not to let a loop of intestine pop out from between her forelegs. "Oh, Ben, come quick . . . "

Come quick, Ben, Rusty thought to himself.

Ben came quick, heaving a sigh of annoyance and frustration, opening the door, stepping out, and Rusty the first, around the side of the car, battering into the male snout first, burying his fangs in the midsection, through the shirt, the soft, yielding skin, into the guts, like the guts the humans so gaily and thoughtlessly scattered on their moonlit roads, the guts of the pack. And now others were on the male, and from the passenger side Rusty heard the squeal of the bitch as Fluffy and the junkyard dog, the terrier and the dachshund brought her down.

Rusty buried his snout in the male's viscera, bit and bit again, tasted the chunks his sharp teeth detached, spit, shook them out, bit again, ripped more soft gut, heedless of the fists of the man raining down on his back, on his skull already broken, fists driving shards of white bone deeper into his brain, his brain that thought more clearly than it ever had before. He felt the others beside him, ripping, snarling, taking the man to pieces more surely than tires and metal underbodies had rended those of the pack, pressing them down into the asphalt, making them one with the road, and Rusty thought of Rowdy, then thought, *"Stop!"*

They did. It was as though they shared a mind, shared a will, and their bloodied snouts, bent jaws, dripping teeth came up from both the male and the bitch.

"The bitch?" Rusty thought, and Fluffy's thought came back to him, "Dead."

He looked down at the male. The chest was still rising and falling, though the stomach was torn wide open, the bowels flopping over the edge of the bloody pool. Rusty looked at Sparks, who was chewing vigorously on a dripping piece of meat. "Rowdy."

Sparks nodded, spat the chunk away, and padded toward the matted pile of dog. Together he and Rusty dragged what was left of Rowdy over to the male, and set the old dog down so that the edge of Rowdy touched the male's forehead. Rowdy pulled himself over the male's face by short jerks, unseen pieces of claw dragging the mat up and over until the male's panting face was hidden. Then the mass quivered, shook, and Rusty saw the dome of Rowdy's skull move up and down, up and down, until the dog's hair turned red with the blood it soaked up. When Rowdy finally slid off, the male's face was stripped of all its skin, and most of its muscle. The chest no longer rose and fell.

"Rowdy has fed. Now devour what you will," thought Rusty, and sank his fangs into the male's windpipe, feeling the blood, still warm, burst into his mouth, run down his chin.

The dachshund ripped with crooked jaws at the front of the male's pants, tearing away the fabric with difficulty, and finally gnawing at the shriveled pouch of flesh until it came off, and he chewed with satisfaction. "Family took mine long ago," he thought gleefully, and Rusty laughed, then stopped, feeling pity for the dachshund.

He sat up, felt the warm blood running down his jaw, watched the dogs greedily burrowing into the body of the male, then went to the other side of the car. Fluffy was chewing happily on the bitch's thigh, and the junkyard dog was gobbling pieces of gut. He stopped, stretched, and rolled over in the puddle of blood so that Rusty could see the pieces of bitch flesh pressing against the lining of the dog's exposed stomach. Then Rusty looked at the nearly decapitated sheep dog. The jaws of the dog's head, hanging from a strand of muscle and skin, laboriously worked at tearing away a hunk of the human bitch's bowels, but when the dog swallowed it, the meat merely crawled through its severed esophagus and dropped onto the dirt. The sheep dog turned, angled itself so that the jaws could grasp the morsel again, the throat could swallow again. But the esophagus excreted again, and the dog picked it up, swallowed, over and over.

Rusty, saddened nearly beyond the capacity of a dog to feel sorrow, turned away, walked to the front of the car, listened to the feast, of dead meat filling dead meat.

Days passed, and the dogs continued to hunt. Fewer cars drove through the woods now, but the pack had learned new ways to take their prey. The cars had to pass through several hollows, and Rusty and Sparks, the two most vigorous of the pack, would stand on the rocks at a level just above the car windows. Then, when a vehicle passed, they would leap through the windows into the car, and savage the humans within. The cars crashed, the humans (if they had not already been killed by the dogs) injured or made insensible, and the pack fed. If the windows were rolled up, it made no difference, for the skulls of the dogs, already broken, shattered the glass, allowing entrance.

Then, one night, a car filled with policemen parked by the side of the road near the rocks. The pack killed them all. Their bullets went through the dogs, spitting away only small pieces of meat the dogs could do without. The blast from a shotgun, however, did shear off Sparks's left front foreleg, which, after the slaughter, they retrieved and re-attached. It was a bit tricky. Rusty held the leg in his jaws while Sparks pushed his stump against it. Somehow the crevices wedged together firmly enough so that the limb remained in place, though Sparks used it as little as possible, and it became more of a liability to locomotion than an aid.

Three days after the devouring of the policemen, more humans came to the edge of the woods. They were armed with shotguns, and had dogs on leashes. But the living dogs refused to go among the trees, and sat and howled and cowered, until the humans, cursing and scowling, put the dogs back into their trucks and cars and drove away, glancing out their windows in discomfort. Though the pack's nostrils were caked with decay, they could still scent the humans' fear on the wind, and they laughed.

And continued to laugh and hunt and prey until the day Sparks disappeared. Or rather, until most of him disappeared. The left foreleg remained, the limb that had become not so much a part of him as a prized possession, like a shit-caked rag or a rotting rabbit carcass would have been when the pack lived.

The pack remained together most of the time, but, as dogs will, they would go off by themselves from time to time, or in a pair or a trio. One night Sparks went off alone, just for a trot, to make the motions of pissing against a tree to mark territory (though none of them were any longer capable of producing urine. If they drank, it merely flowed through and out of them, so the pissing motion was now more symbolic than ever). The longest any of the dogs had ever been gone before was an hour at a time, so when nearly the entire night passed without his reappearance, the pack began to worry, and went to look for him.

They found only the pitiful left foreleg, in which no life remained. That, and some fragments of bone that appeared to have been shattered by remarkably strong teeth. There was no blood on the ground (Sparks and the other dogs had emptied their blood on the roads long before), but the brush was torn up as though there had been a tremendous struggle, and broken branches showed where a large body, no doubt the same creature that had devoured Sparks, had crashed through it.

The pack was silent, keeping its individual thoughts to its separate selves. The dogs poked about with dead noses, trying to catch a scent, something that would tell them what it was that had cut out a member of their pack. For a moment, Rusty thought he caught a trace of something familiar, something large and gross and dimly remembered, but then it was gone, and would not come again, and he was unable to recall it strongly enough to claim the memory he was sure was there.

By the time they gave up, it was morning, and they crept, crawled, and slid silently back to the lair they had found in the shelter of two fallen trees. They lay there on the thick carpet of dead pine needles and leaves, lay and rested, though none of them was capable of sleep.

"Was it a monster?" the dachshund thought, and Rusty knew the query was directed to him alone.

"I don't know," Rusty replied. "I thought *we* were the monsters, and now . . . "

"Another pack?"

"No. You saw how high the branches were broken. Not a dog. Or dogs."

The dachshund grinned lopsidedly. "God then."

"And not God."

"What would you call something that can devour one of us? Give us long enough and we'll be gods to men—or demons. They'll come to fear us and avoid us. They'll make these woods forbidden—sacred, if you will." The dachshund gave a thoughtful whine. "Funny how things come around. Men were gods to us. They crushed us, devoured us, and now we devour them. What were *we* Gods to, Rusty? What did *we* devour?" He thought silently for a moment. Rusty concentrated on a solution, remembering that he was the leader. "Could it have been man?" the dachshund asked.

"There were no gunshots. And men would not have devoured Sparks. Not in that way."

Rusty, unable to come up with an answer, brooded, and was still brooding when night fell again. It had begun to rain, but none of the dogs were bothered by it. The drops merely matted their fur a little more, beaded on their exposed viscera, pooled in the hollow pouches of their rotted flesh, so that every now and then they would have to twist one way or the other to let the malodorous water run out onto the forest floor.

Rusty mentally inquired if the others were ready to hunt, but he felt only mild interest in return. Their last few nights of hunting had been unsuccessful. Humans hardly dared to travel the road anymore, and when they did they drove so fast that Rusty and Sparks found it difficult to leap at the windows. Indeed, on the last attempt, while Sparks was still alive, Rusty had landed on the car's trunk and slid right off, while Sparks had missed the vehicle completely.

Something else interested the pack tonight. Fluffy, the only female among them, had somehow gone into something that passed for estrous, despite the mutilation of her sexual organs. She dragged her posterior along the ground, whining and moaning, her vegetation-coated insides roiling behind her like thick, drunken serpents. The males crowded around her, sniffing futilely, but recalling the scent, and what remained of their penises left their sheaths reluctantly, as if sheer will rather than blood engorged them, making them a sickly yellow rather than the thrilling pink of former matings.

Rusty ignored them. His equipment would have functioned better than any, but he wasn't in the mood, and wondered how the others could be. He felt no sexual stirring whatsoever, and suspected that the pack was planning to rut (or attempt to rut—what could they really *do* with that conglomeration of bowels and fissures that used to be Fluffy's slit?) more for the sake of nostalgia than out of any real lust.

For a while he sat there, watching the others follow the bitch through the woods. Soon they were out of sight, and he sighed for the lost times that would not come again, and thought about taking the pack elsewhere, away from the woods where prey no longer came, perhaps into the cities, from which humans could not flee. The dogs could hide there almost as easily as in the woods, and the supply of prey would never run low.

Rusty trotted back to the shelter, crawled in, and lay down, his head on his forepaws. He could hear them now, and guessed that they were a half mile or more away. He heard the feigned yaps of anger as the males fought for dominance, then Fluffy's rather unconvincing yowl as something Rusty didn't care to think about was penetrated, then a long period of silence, during which, he surmised, a mere charade was performed for old time's sake.

Screams shattered the silence—authentic, sincere cries, yelps, growls that Rusty took at first to be the vocal outbursts of passion, and, upon hearing them, forgotten lust launched itself in his haunches, engorged his rod with memory alone, pressing it from its sheath. Aroused, he stood, drinking in what he took to be the sounds of hot, wet sex, until he realized that such could not take place in cold, dry bodies.

The screams were screams of pain, of terror.

But what could terrorize the dead?

Rusty launched himself toward the sound. He was supposed to have been the leader, and he cursed himself for not going with them, as he thought of what it could have been that had taken Sparks. He pushed himself through the brush, taking the most direct route to the sounds of his shrieking pack. There was no moon, and the darkness was thick and blinding. Several times he battered his already crushed forehead against the trunks of trees, but it had no more effect on him than if he had been wearing a helmet. He simply righted himself, aimed himself in the direction of the sounds, and charged once more, bouncing, ricocheting off oaks, maples, pines, until he broke through a final thicket whose thorns and brambles tore at his scraggly coat like sharp wires, one of them piercing his eye and holding him captive until he wrenched himself away from it, ripping the eyeball, leaving half of it hanging on the thorn, and entered a small clearing.

With his one remaining eye, Rusty saw the carnage that had been his pack. He saw Fluffy's head lying on the leaves, the jaw flapping up and down, trying to drag it toward the mud-yellow body from which great chunks of dead meat had been chewed away; saw the junkyard dog, his middle bitten through so that only a rod of spine connected the two halves, trying to push himself to his feet like a broken bridge in a windstorm; saw the dachshund's short legs swinging at something that towered above it, a deeper darkness against the dark of night, and that darkness detaching itself, falling toward the dog and entrapping his pointed head in blackness. There was a thick crunch, and the dachshund's head vanished in a cacophony of splitting bones and tearing gristle. The legs of the headless body continued to jerk, but with no sense of balance, no eyes to guide it, no ears to hear, it could do no more than wait to join its cicerone in the maw that had stolen it. With the next bite it was divided once more, then, with the last, was reunited with its other pieces.

Whether it continued to live in the stomach of its devourer was a possibility that occurred only dimly to Rusty. Such metaphysical thoughts on the afterlife of the afterlife were far from his mind now. The destruction of his fellows had maddened him, returned him to that state of canine savagery to which rational thought was a stranger, and he thrust himself at the greater darkness over the bits and pieces of the pack. Something sharp-edged and brutal battered him, hurling him to the side and against a tree whose trunk cracked his spine. Then that something pressed against his chest like God's hammer, pinning him to the ground, and Rusty heard a snort, but saw no breath steam from the creature's nostrils. It was as dead as Rusty, but not as dead as the pack.

The horse's head came down, buried itself in Rusty's guts, and chewed. Its teeth and jaws were strong, even stronger than the musky, tinny taste of its fellows' canned flesh that Rusty had wolfed down a thousand times. And as Rusty watched himself entering the horse's dead mouth bite by bite, he wondered with his recently-found imagination what would devour the horse? Then his head was taken, the brain smashed, swallowed, and the thoughts ceased.

Grain? thought Rowdy, continuing Rusty's thought. Dead oats? Dead apples come alive again? And what would they do? Bounce up the road on which they fell and were run over? Fruit roadkill? But how could they bounce if they were squashed? And how could oats devour, or hay destroy, or clover hate? But hell, there'd be *something*.

Rowdy shook the half dome of his skull. The thoughts were too much for him, and he lay still while the horse finished its meal, going from chunk to chunk, its grinding teeth preparing the flesh for its ruminant stomach, unused to meat and bone. The feast would kill it, Rowdy thought, if it weren't already dead.

It came up to Rowdy, and he saw the great rift in its once proud neck where the car or truck must have struck it and killed it. It sniffed at Rowdy for a moment, but Rowdy remained still. It was easy for a dead thing to pretend to be dead.

The horse moved on then, and Rowdy waited until it was gone, then examined the small remnants the beast had left. Nope. They twitched and moved, but they weren't worth a bitch's spit. He'd have to find another pack, and he would. He moved slowly, but he had time. Yep, time was all he had. What kind of creature, dead or alive, would bother a ratty old hunk of kitchen carpet like him?

He had scarcely traveled ten yards when he felt the first flea bite him. And him without a leg to scratch with.

"Fool: it is you who are the pursued, the marked down quarry, the destined prey."
—George Bernard Shaw, *Man and Superman*

Children

Kristine Kathryn Rusch

Bear Trap Lake
June 17, 1987

McIntyre leaned forward as he pushed his paddle in the water. The muscles in his arms ached. He didn't know how much longer he could keep rowing the canoe.

He shot a quick glance over his shoulder. The swimmer still hounded him. The whole afternoon had the feel of a nightmare; the growing panic, the illogical but certain knowledge that the thing which pursued him was evil, and the utter, ruthless determination of the swimmer. The swimmer had grabbed McIntyre's canoe twice, and only luck and a good sense of balance had kept him from capsizing.

Splashes echoed behind him, and he braced himself for another hit. But nothing happened. The swimmer glided up beside him and McIntyre screamed. He yanked his paddle out of the water and swung it like a sword. The paddle slapped against the swimmer's skull, slicing through the skin. McIntyre leaned over the side of his canoe, and watched the bloody bubbles rise as the child sank beneath the waters.

* * *

Madison, Wisconsin
May 4, 1969

Shouts and the tinkle of breaking glass woke him. He lay for a moment on the stained mattress, his legs trapped under Patty's, listening, before he realized that another riot was going on. He tried to remember if he knew of any action that day, but he thought of nothing.

Patty sat up and pushed her hair out of her face with one hand. "W-what's that?"

McIntyre shook his head.

Downstairs a door banged and Jason screamed, "Piiigs!"

McIntyre heard footsteps on the stairs and suddenly the bedroom door swung open. Patty grabbed for her dress. Jason looked in.

"Hey, man," McIntyre said as he reached for a sheet to cover his nakedness. Something crashed beneath the window.

Jason didn't even notice. His thin face was flushed. "You gotta see this," he said. "It started on State Street, but they brought it down here"

"What happened?" Patty asked. She had pulled her dress on. It pooled around her legs, but her buttocks were still visible. McIntyre felt her growing excitement.

"I don't know, but it's a mess. You gotta see it." Jason ran down the hall to the other rooms, flinging the doors open so hard that they banged against the wall.

Patty stood up and McIntyre handed her a pair of underwear. He slipped into some cutoffs and shoved his feet into his sandals. Patty had already started for the door.

"Wait," he said, and closed the windows. Immediately the shouting became muffled. "Last time they used gas. We want to sleep here tonight."

She nodded. He took her hand and together they ran down the worn stairs and out the front door. On the sagging porch, they stopped. Kids filled the street, screaming, yelling, some holding rocks, others with the tattered remains of signs. Cops were using nightsticks to move the crowd forward.

McIntyre took a step back. He didn't want to be part of that scene; it looked too dangerous to him. But Patty loved danger. She pulled him forward and rather than lose her, he followed her into the street.

The air was thick with the smell of sweat and fear. McIntyre coughed and brought an arm up to his face. Somehow Patty's hand slipped through his and he watched her run to the other curb. She was yelling something or maybe she was screaming. He tried to reach her—after what he had done two days before, he was scared to let her do anything alone—but he kept colliding with other bodies that pushed him forward in a wave. A woman brushed past him. She was moaning and blood was running from her left ear. Patty stood at the fringes of the crowd. As she waved her arms above her head, the motion hiked her dress up to show the edges of the underwear he had given her a few moments before. Then he lost sight of her. He finally made it to the curb as Patty crumpled onto the grass.

By the time McIntyre reached her, blood covered her face. He touched the sticky wetness. "Patty?" he said, but couldn't hear himself over the noise.

A car window shattered beside them. He thought he saw her eyelids flicker, although he wasn't sure. But he did know the exact moment she died. One moment, she was in her body, regulating its breathing, making its heart pump, and the next minute, she had left. And that was when he started to scream.

Bear Trap Lake
June 17, 1987

He pulled the canoe up onto the shore and winced as the aluminum scraped the sand. Then he grabbed the rope, made sure it was firmly tied to the bow and tied the other end to an oak. He staggered across the sand and collapsed on the grass. The rich smell of the land filled his nostrils.

"Dad?"

The shout came from the cabin. McIntyre didn't move. He was too tired. His limbs hurt and the skin on his back was beginning to throb. He must have gotten too much sun.

"Dad?"

The call was closer. Sean knelt down beside him.

"I thought that was you. You okay?"

"I'd like a beer." McIntyre's voice scraped sandlike against his throat.

"Okay, you got it. Looks like you need some lotion too."

"Yeah." McIntyre breathed the word and the blades of grass in front of his face moved. He rested, almost dozing, as images of the afternoon ran through his mind.

He had decided to take a leisurely trip around the lake. Bear Trap was small, with five cabins and lots of open water. On weekdays, he and Sean were the only ones there. Seeing the swimmer dive in at the public landing had surprised him. It hadn't been until he had realized that it was one of the children paddling at him that he had grown frightened.

Cold, wet goo spurted on his back and McIntyre jumped.

"Sorry," Sean said as he rubbed the lotion in. "You really got fried. Why didn't you come in sooner?"

McIntyre shrugged. He imagined himself trying to explain what had happened to his son: Well, Sean, I had to kill a kid before I could get off that lake. But don't worry about it. I've killed kids before.

The lotion soaked into his back, easing the burn and stinging at the same time.

"I got you the beer, too."

McIntyre pulled himself up. He was going to be sore for days. Sean handed him the beer and McIntyre poured it into his mouth, not caring that some ran over his lips and dribbled off his chin. The icy coldness made his throat ache.

After he finished half the can, he stopped, wiped his face with the back of his hand and took a deep breath.

Sean smiled. He had his mother's smile, crooked, whimsical, and fey. Sometimes, McIntyre felt that he touched her through their son.

"Help me inside," he said to shake that lonely thought.

Sean pulled him up, and together they walked to the cabin they had finished building the summer before.

Highway 53
April 2, 1983

The extension course had gone well. Even after two sessions, McIntyre still didn't believe the enthusiasm that a group from Solon Springs, Wisconsin, showed in learning how to trace their family histories. He remembered that excitement from tracing his own history, but he had thought that was due to the peculiarity of his family background.

He steered the car carefully onto the highway. The road was thick with early April ice and slush. As he headed into the darkness, he felt a presence. He flicked on the brights and searched for deer in the trees.

Something thudded against the passenger side and he looked sharply. A packed wad of snow slid down the window. It had probably fallen from one of the branches above. The Oldsmobile swerved slightly and he righted it when a body slammed into the windshield.

McIntyre drew his breath in sharply and pumped the brakes. Then he looked up and found himself face to face with one of the children.

Children had been his grandfather's word, but it only described their general shape and form. The eyes were hollow, dark, lacking whites, but reflecting light like a cat's. The creature pressed its face against the window and McIntyre could see its gray skin. Its hands were splayed, the long fingernails tapping like claws against the glass.

The car swerved again, but this time McIntyre couldn't see. The back end fishtailed on the ice. McIntyre struggled to straighten it. The creature seemed to be laughing. It slid its hands up to the top of the windshield, stretched its body along the glass and pulled, McIntyre stared for a moment at its shrunken penis, and the long, lean bones sliding into its pelvic girdle. He had learned over the years just how strong these things were. It would break in. And then it would kill him.

He made himself look away from the creature and out the windshield. The car was heading straight for the trees. He tried to turn the wheels, but they slipped on the slush. He had promised himself when Carol had died in January that he would let the next child go. But he couldn't. He pulled his foot off the brake and stepped on the gas. The car lurched forward, slipping in the muck and finally slamming into an old pine. The creature flew back in a crunch of metal and glass, and hit its head on the tree trunk.

McIntyre shut off the ignition and shakily let himself out of the car. The front end was damaged beyond repair, but he seemed unharmed. He stepped around the wreckage and looked down. The body was twisted between the tree and the car. Bone shards and bits of brain tissue hung from the flayed skin at the back of its skull. He leaned against the passenger door to catch his breath before taking the shovel out of the trunk. He tried to ignore the blood that slowly stained the snow red.

Bear Trap Lake
June 17, 1987

Sean cooked dinner that night. McIntyre had a thudding headache and his back burned so badly that he couldn't lean against a chair. He sat on a stool and watched his son throw strips of chicken breast into the wok.

"The weirdest thing happened to me today," Sean said.

He scraped the utensils against the pan as he stir-fried the meat. "Just after you went out canoeing."

McIntyre rubbed his hand against the back of his neck. The smell of cooking chicken made his stomach growl. "Oh?"

"Yeah. I had made myself some ice tea and I was heading out to the hammock when this thing ran through the kitchen."

McIntyre looked at his son. Sean kept his face averted as he added onions, bamboo shoots, water chestnuts and snow peas to the wok. "Then what?" McIntyre said.

"It was little, you know. And at first I thought it was a naked child. But it didn't look like a child." Sean laughed nervously. He shot a glance at his father. "I really did see this."

"I know," McIntyre said. "Tell me what happened."

"Nothing really. It just looked at me and then it scampered out through the living room door. By the time I got there, it was gone." Sean poured sauce over the entire mixture and stirred it. "Weird, huh?"

McIntyre didn't say anything. The first time he had seen one of the creatures had been on the day his father had died. McIntyre had been sixteen, like Sean.

"Dad?" Sean stopped stirring.

"I don't know what it is, Seanie. But if it's any consolation, I saw it too."

Sean grabbed a potholder and spooned the contents of the wok into a bowl. He placed rice in another bowl and brought them both to the table. "It scared me, Dad."

"It should." McIntyre grabbed a bowl and put food onto his plate. "They're dangerous."

Madison, Wisconsin
August 18, 1971

Books, papers, dirty dishes and empty Coke cans covered the kitchen table. McIntyre was lost in a physics problem, deep within the spiral of numbers, all interconnected and beautiful, when Sharon set the baby in his lap.

Seanie drooled on the page. McIntyre looked up. Sharon smiled in a way that always made him smile back.

"I just realized I have to do a textural analysis of Elizabeth Barrett Browning's work, too. I didn't read the last question on the take-home."

McIntyre wiped the baby's spit off the page and then rubbed Seanie's mouth. "And you don't have the poems."

"Not a one."

He sighed. He wouldn't be able to concentrate on his physics again until after Sean went to sleep. "I suppose it can't wait until tomorrow."

"Oh, it could," she said. "But I'd flunk. The test is due at my 7:50."

"Who's going with you?"

"You worry too much."

"Who?"

"I'll stop at my sister's on the way."

"All right." He set his physics book on top of the page he had been working on. "But you owe me."

She shrugged, then bent down and kissed him. Her skin smelled like sunshine and perfume. She ran her hand on the baby's bald head, then grabbed a notebook off the table and let herself out the back door. As the screen banged shut, she turned around and waved. He watched her walk through the trees lining Vilas Park.

When McIntyre no longer saw her blonde hair flowing out behind her, he pulled a book on Celtic mythology out from under a stack of papers. He cradled the baby in one arm and thumbed through the copy, searching for a familiar child-like form. The book said that the children were rare, that they haunted families for generations because of simple things, mistakes long gone. McIntyre hoped that the book had the secret to ending the curse. But then Seanie choked, coughed and started to wail. McIntyre placed the book back in its hiding place.

The baby continued to cry for most of the evening, until McIntyre cuddled with him on the living room floor in front of the television.

The shrill ring of the phone woke McIntyre up. The tv was broadcasting static. Sean was asleep on his back. The grey light of dawn filtered in through the uncurtained windows. McIntyre wondered where Sharon was. He grabbed the screaming phone and rubbed the sleep out of his eyes.

"Yes?"

"Is this Sharon Blason's residence?"

"Yeah "McIntyre came fully awake. The voice sounded official.

"This is the Madison Police Department. Are you her husband?"

"Sort of."

"We have a situation down at Camp Randall. A squad will be at your home shortly to pick you up."

McIntyre felt cold. The demonstrations had slowed down. And Sharon hadn't been involved with the movement anyway. "What kind of situation?"

"It's better that the officers tell you in person, Mr. Blason."

"What kind of situation?" The panic in his voice woke up the baby. Seanie whimpered.

"I'm sorry, sir. But your wife is dead. The squad will take you down to the morgue to identify her body."

"No," McIntyre said. He watched Sean grab the edge of a blanket and fall back into sleep. "I want to see her now."

"Mr. Blason, it's not a good—"

"I don't care." He set the receiver down, got up and washed his face in the kitchen sink. Then he called Mike, his upstairs neighbor, and asked him to come down and watch Sean. Mike arrived at the same time the squad car did.

McIntyre didn't remember getting into the squad or driving the short distance to the stadium. But he did remember watching the iron gates rise in front of him, and passing the two obscure Civil War soldiers decorating the archway. He hadn't known that Sharon crossed behind the stadium on her way home. If he had known that he would have insisted on walking with her. He explained that to the officers, over and over. They said nothing as they led him to her.

She lay beneath one of the tall old trees decorating the path. Her shoes were missing and her dress was ripped. Her long blonde hair was tangled and black with matted blood.

"It's Sharon," he said calmly enough. He had seen death before. He was getting used to it.

But that afternoon, when Seanie had smiled his first real smile, sweet, whimsical and fey, McIntyre had started to cry.

Bear Trap Lake
June 17, 1987

"Dad?"

Sean's whisper echoed across the darkness. In the silence between his question and McIntyre's answer, something fell in the kitchen.

"What?"

"Hear that?"

McIntyre sat up in bed. The moonlight outlined Sean standing in front of the window. The house was quiet. The woods were quiet. All McIntyre heard were the waves lapping against the shore. "No."

"There's something downstairs."

"It's probably a raccoon."

"Yeah, probably."

McIntyre lay back down, wishing Sean would leave so that he could investigate. Below them, a chair scraped across the linoleum.

"Whatever it is," Sean whispered. "It sure wants to get caught."

McIntyre frowned and rolled out of bed. He padded barefoot across the hall and grabbed the hunting rifle. The gun wasn't loaded, but no one had to know that. It was big enough to scare a person, and his presence was enough to frighten a raccoon. He didn't want to think about the possibility of the noise being anything else.

He started down the spiral staircase. Sean was right behind him. "No," McIntyre whispered. "I'm going alone."

"No, you're not," Sean said. He followed his father down the iron stairs and into the kitchen. Nothing moved in the darkness. McIntyre flicked on the light.

The screen door stood open and the garbage pail had been tipped over. Garbage covered the floor. McIntyre relaxed. "We've got to find a better way to store that shit."

He turned toward Sean. His son was staring at the refrigerator. There was a tiny, bloody handprint on the freezer door.

Elmira, Wisconsin
October 20, 1976

"I wonder which one of us it's come for," McIntyre's grandfather said. He stuck a finger in the footprint. "Blood's still wet."

McIntyre started up the porch steps. Grandfather grabbed his arm. "Don't tell me you haven't seen 'em, Davie. They come after a McIntyre has his first woman and they stay with him until he dies."

McIntyre wrenched his arm free. The children he had seen over the years—and killed—had been nightmares. Figures of his imagination taking form in the daylight.

"Running from me won't help either of us, Davie. They may kill our lovers, but it's the McIntyres they want."

McIntyre turned. His grandfather stood beside the bloody footprint. The old man's eyes still twinkled with intelligence.

"What do they want us for?" McIntyre whispered.

"I never took the time to ask one of them." The old man pulled himself up the porch steps. "But they've been there ever since I slept with Tina Wood sixty years ago. And I know your daddy started seeing 'em after he started seeing your ma. And I don't know about you. You kept it real quiet and if you hadn'ta run right now, I would have guessed you hadn'ta seen 'em at all."

"What are they?"

His grandfather shrugged. "Children. I think they're just children."

"It makes no sense."

"Maybe not. But they follow rules, Davie. They hunt alone. If you kill one of theirs, they kill one of yours. If you don't kill them, they kill you. Either way, you don't win."

McIntyre frowned. "You ever tried letting them be?"

"No." The old man took a deep breath. "But I think your daddy did."

The thought made McIntyre ache. He opened the door and let himself inside. His grandfather's house smelled like leather and old books.

"Davie," his grandfather said. "We got a better chance together than we do by ourselves."

"I'll be right back," McIntyre said. He ran toward his grandfather's bedroom, opened the closet and pulled out the old deer rifle. He had to dig for the bullets. He loaded the gun and then ran back for the porch. When he reached the dining room, he heard a scream and a thud. Gingerly he opened the door. His grandfather's heels rested on the top step. His grandfather's head lay in a pool of blood on the concrete sidewalk.

Bear Trap Lake
June 17, 1987

"You know what these things are, don't you, Dad?"

McIntyre didn't answer. He grabbed Sean's elbow to keep them together. "We're going to go back upstairs and get the bullets," McIntyre said. "This time we're going to do it right."

"Dad?"

Metal clanged in the utility room. Suddenly McIntyre knew where the creature was. Sean yanked his arm free and ran in the direction of the noise. Then the lights went out.

"Sean?" McIntyre's voice sounded hollow in the quiet room. He heard a rustle off to his left.

"It's okay, Dad. I'm coming back toward you. Just stay still, okay?"

"All right, Sean."

McIntyre was holding his breath. As his eyes adjusted to the darkness, he could see Sean make his way across the kitchen floor. Behind the boy, a shadow moved. McIntyre opened his mouth to shout a warning, but Sean screamed first. McIntyre started toward his son, thinking that they couldn't kill Seanie. It wasn't fair that they killed Seanie. McIntyre couldn't have protected himself from them this long only to have them kill his son.

Something leaped onto McIntyre's back. Sharp claws digging into his sunburn made him cry out. He whirled, trying to shake the thing off of him, catching its slightly musty odor every time he moved. He slammed into the counter and the creature let go. McIntyre turned and the creature reached for his face, its claws narrowly missing his eyes. McIntyre grabbed the creature's arms, squeezing them until he felt bones snap. The creature screamed, and McIntyre dropped it. It landed heavily on the floor and then ran out into the darkness.

"Sean?" McIntyre called.

He saw his son in the moonlight, lying in the same position they had found his mother in.

"Seanie?"

McIntyre knelt beside Sean and touched his face. McIntyre's fingers came away sticky with blood. Goddammit, he thought. He had let that one go free, and Seanie was still dead.

* * *

Fond du Lac, Wisconsin
February 26, 1966

McIntyre's father knelt beside the crumpled body. McIntyre stood beside him.

"I can only tell you this once, Davie," his father said. "You see one of these, you leave it alone. You don't touch it. After tonight, the score will be even. And if one comes after you, you let it. You may not save yourself, but you'll save a lot of others. You understand me, David?"

McIntyre looked at his father's face. The older man was serious. "Yeah, Dad," McIntyre said. "I understand."

His dad went to the shed to get a shovel so that they could dispose of the creature. McIntyre knelt beside the tiny body and noted how the skin along the back of its head flapped open, how the bones splintered and mixed with its grey brain tissue, how its blood melted the snow. He memorized the details because he knew he would never see anything like it again.

Sea Gulls

Gahan Wilson

I have been sitting here, throughout this entire morning, watching the gulls watching me. They come, a small group at a time, carefully unnoticeable, and squat on various branches of a large tree opposite the hotel veranda. When each shift of them have gaped their fill of me, they fly away and their places are taken at once by others of their disgusting species.

Outside of their orderly coming and going, the deportment of these feathered spectators of my discomfort has been calculatedly devoid of anything which might excite the attention of anyone lacking my particular and special knowledge of their loathsome kind. Their demeanor has been more than ordinarily ordinary. They are on their best behavior, now they have sealed my doom.

I stumbled on their true nature, and I curse the day I did, by a complete fluke. It was, ironically, Geraldine herself who called my attention to that little army of them on the beach.

We had been sitting side by side on a large, sun-warmed rock, I in a precise but somewhat Redonesque pose, Geraldine in her usual, space-occupying, sprawl. I was deep in a poetic revery, reflecting on the almost alchemical transition of sand to water to sky while Geraldine, my wife, was absorbed in completely finishing off the sumptuous but rather over-large picnic the hotel staff had prepared for our outing, when she abruptly straightened, a half consumed jar of *paté* clutched forgotten in her greasy fingers, and suddenly emitted that barking coo of hers which has never failed to simultaneously startle and annoy me throughout all the years of our marriage.

"Hughie, look!" she cried. "The gulls are marching!"

"What do you mean, 'marching'?" I asked, doing what I could to conceal my annoyance.

"I mean they're marching, Hughie," she said. "I mean they *are* marching!"

I looked where she pointed, the *paté* jar still in her hand, and a vague complaint died unspoken on my lips as I observed that Geraldine had been scrupulously correct in her announcement. The gulls were, indeed, marching.

Their formation was about ten files wide and some forty ranks deep, and it was well held, with no raggedness about the edges. A line of five or so officer gulls marched at the army's head, and one solitary gull, I assumed their general, marched ahead of them.

The gull general was considerably larger than the other birds, and he had an imposing, eagle-like bearing to him. His army was obviously well drilled, for all the gulls marched in perfect step on their orange claws, and seemed capable of neatly executing endless elaborate maneuvers.

Geraldine and I watched, fascinated, for as long as ten minutes, observing the creatures wheeling about, splitting and rejoining, and carrying out whole routines of complicated, weaving patterns. The display was so astoundingly absorbing that it took me quite some time to realize the fantastic impropriety of the whole proceeding, but at last it dawned on me.

"This will never do," I observed in a firm, quiet tone, and carefully placing my cigar on the edge of the rock, I selected a large, smooth stone and hefted it in my hand.

"Hughie!" Geraldine cried, observing the rock and the

look of grim determination on my face. "What are you planning to do?"

"We must discourage this sort of thing the instant we see it," I said. "We must nip it in the bud."

I shot the stone into their midst and they scattered, squawking in a highly satisfactory fashion. I threw another stone, this one rather pointy, and had the pleasure of striking the general smartly on his rear. I turned to Geraldine, expecting words of praise, but of course I should have known better.

"You should not hurt dumb animals," she said, regarding me gently but mournfully as a mother might regard a backward child. "Look, you have made that big one limp!"

"Gulls are birds, not animals," I pointed out. "And their behavior was far from dumb. It was, if you ask me, altogether too smart."

My cigar had gone out so I lit another one, using the gold lighter she had given me a day or so before, and I was so piqued at her that I was tempted to ostentatiously throw it away as casually as I would a match, but she would only have forgiven me with a little sigh and bought me another. I would only be like an infant knocking objects off the tray of his high chair, its bowls and cups replaced with loving care. I had learned, through the years, that there really was no way to get one's rage through to Geraldine.

That night, as we were having dinner on the terrace of the hotel, Geraldine stared out into the darkness and once again drew my attention to an odd action on the part of the gulls. This time her tiny little bark caught me with a spoonful of *consommé* halfway to my lips, and when I started at the sudden sound, a shimmering blob of the stuff tumbled back into the bowl with a tiny plop.

"The gulls, Hughie," she said, in a loud, dramatic whisper as she reached out and tightly clutched my arm. "See how they are staring at you!"

I frowned at her.

"Gulls?" I said. "It's night, my dear. One doesn't see gulls at night. They go somewhere."

But then I peered where she had pointed, and I saw that once again she was right. There, in the branches of the tree which I have mentioned before, were in view perhaps as many as thirty gulls staring at us, or more precisely at me, with their cold, beady little eyes.

"There must be hundreds of them!" she whispered. "They're everywhere!"

Again she was quite correct. The creatures were not only in the tree, they were perched on railings, stone vases, the heads of statues, and all the various other *accoutrements* with which a first-class, traditional French seaboard hotel is wont to litter its premises. They were all, to the last gull among them, staring steadily and unblinkingly at me.

"Do you think," I whispered very quietly to Geraldine, "that anyone else has noticed?"

"I don't believe so," she said, and turned to openly study the people sitting at neighboring tables. "Should we ask them if they have?"

"For God's sake, no!" I said, in a harsh whisper. "What do you think it looks like—being singled out by crowds of gulls to be stared at? How do you think it makes me *feel?*"

"Of course, Hughie," she said, loosing her hold on my arm and patting my hand. "Don't you worry, dearest. We shall just pretend it isn't happening."

Halfway through the wretched dinner the gulls flew off for mysterious reasons of their own, and when it was through I made my excuses and left my wife to attend to herself while I took a thoughtful little stroll.

I had some time ago sketched out the broad design of what I intended to do during our visit to this hotel; had, indeed, begun to plan it the very day Geraldine suggested we come here to celebrate our wedding anniversary, because it had dawned on me even as she spoke, fatally and completely and quite irreversibly, that we had already celebrated far too many anniversaries and that this one should definitely be our last.

But now it was time to put in the fine details, the small, delicate strokes which would spell the difference between disaster and success. Eliminating Geraldine would serve very little purpose if I did not survive the act to enjoy her money afterwards.

I wandered down to the canopied pier where I knew the hotel moored several, brightly-painted little rowboats, and even a couple of dwarfish sailboats, for the use of their guests. I knew full well that the sailboats would strike Geraldine as being far too adventurous, so I concentrated on examining the rowboats.

I was pleasantly surprised to discover that they were even more unseaworthy than I'd dared to hope. I quietly tested them, one after the other, and found that the boat at the end of the pier, a jaunty little thing with a puce hull and a bright gold stripe running around its sides, was especially dangerous. I felt absolutely confident the police would have no trouble at all in convincing themselves that any drowning fatality associated with this highly tippy boat had been the result of a tragic accident.

Just to make sure—I have been accused of being something of a perfectionist—I climbed into the tiny craft, pretended I was rowing, and then suddenly made a move to one side. The boat came so close to capsizing that I had considerable difficulty avoiding unexpectedly tumbling out of it then and there! I exited the craft carefully, with even more respect for its deadliness, and started walking up the path leading back to the hotel, whistling a little snatch of a Chopin mazurka softly to myself as I went.

The path took a turn by a kind of miniature cliff which concealed it from almost all points of view and when I reached this point the mazurka died on my lips as I saw that the ground before me was lumpy and grayish in the moonlight as though it was infested with some sort of disgusting mold, but then I peered closer and saw that the place was horribly carpeted with the softly stirring bodies of countless sea gulls.

They were crowded together, so tightly packed that there was absolutely no space between them, and every one of them was glaring up at me. The menace emanating from their hundreds of tiny eyes was, at the same time, both ridiculous and totally terrifying. It was also positively sickening, and for a brief, absolutely ghastly moment I was afraid that I would faint and fall and be suffocated in the soft, feathery sea of them.

However, I took several very deep breaths and managed to still the pounding in my ears and to steady myself. With great casualness, very slowly and deliberately, I reached into my breast pocket and withdrew a cigar. I lit the cigar and blew a contemptuous puff of smoke at the enormous crowd of gulls at my feet.

"You have exceeded your position in life," I told them, speaking softly and calmly. "You have overstepped your natural authority. But I am on to you."

I drew on the cigar carefully, increasing its ash, and when I'd produced a good half inch, I tapped the cigar so that the ash fell directly and humiliatingly on the top of the head of the remarkably large gull standing directly in front of me. Of course I had recognized him as the general. He did not stir nor blink, nor did any of the others. They continued to glare up at me.

"Whereas you are merely birds," I continued, "and scavenger birds at that, *I* am a human being. I am not only smarter than you are, I am stronger. If you attack me, I will simply shield my eyes with my arm and walk away, and soon other humans will see me and come to my aid."

I took another long pull at my cigar and looked away from them, as if bored.

"I guarantee you," I went on, "that I will not panic. I will survive, merely scratched, to see that you, and a great number of your kin, pay dearly for attacking your betters. Pay painfully. Pay with your lives."

I paused a little in order that my words might sink into their reptilian little heads, and then I began to walk casually along the clearing path, gazing upwards and smoking dreamily as I did so. I did not even watch to see how they slunk, in cowed confusion, out of my way.

The next morning, during breakfast, while I was having my second coffee and Geraldine her second herbal tea, I proposed brightly that we take a short row in the cove. I approached the whole thing in a very airy, casual fashion, but made it clear I would be saddened and a little hurt if she did not accept my whimsical invitation. Naturally I knew the whole idea would strike her as childish and that she would do it only to indulge me. She, herself, would never dream of instigating anything childish, of course. That, in our marriage, was understood to be my function.

To my relief—one never knew with Geraldine—never—she accepted with almost no perceptible hesitation. She even suggested we do it without further ado, seeing as how the sun was bright and the waters of the cove presently smooth and placid. We rose from the table and went directly to the gaily beflagged pier.

We were the first arrivals for water sports that morning and the little puce boat with its gold stripe bobbed fetchingly as it waited for us in the water. In a rather neat piece of seamanship, I managed to get both Geraldine and myself aboard it without her realizing how tiltable a craft it was. Smiling and chatting about how extremely pleasant everything was, I rowed us to an isolated part of the cove behind a rise of the shore which put us out of sight of our fellow vacationers.

Once I had reached this point I let go of the oars, took firm hold of the sides of the boat, and gave it the tipping motion I had practiced with such great success the night before. I was highly discomfited to discover that the little craft had somehow achieved a new seaworthiness.

"Hughie," she asked, "what on earth are you trying to do?"

I looked up at her, perhaps just a little wild-eyed, and suddenly realized that it must be Geraldine's considerable bulk which was stabilizing the boat. I would have to exert a good deal more effort if I was to upset it successfully. I began to shake the boat again, this time with markedly increased determination. I was uncomfortably aware that I had begun to sweat noticeably and that damp blotches were beginning to spread from the armpits of my striped blazer.

"Hughie," she said, a vague alarm starting to dawn in her eyes, "whatever you are doing, you must stop it now!"

I glared at her and began to shake the boat with a new energy verging on desperation.

"I've asked you not to call me Hughie," I told her through clenched teeth. "For *years* I've asked you not to call me Hughie!"

She frowned at me, just a little uncertainly, and had opened her mouth to say something further when, with a gratifyingly smooth, swooping motion, the little golden boat finally tilted over.

For a moment all was blue confusion and bubbles, but then my head broke water and I saw the boat bobbing upside down on the sparkling surface of the cove a yard or two away from me. There was no sign whatsoever of Geraldine so I ducked my head down under the water, peered this way and that, and was pleased to observe a dim, sinking flurry of skirts and kicking feet speedily disappearing into the darker blues far below the bright and cheery green hues flickering just under the surface.

I swam up to the little inverted craft, took hold of it, surveyed the coastline to see if it was empty of witnesses, and saw that this was, indeed, the case. Several gulls were circling overhead, but when I glared up at them and shook my fist in their direction, they flew away with an almost furtive air. I cried for help once or twice for effect, then pushed off from the side of the boat and swam for the shore where I staggered, gasping, up onto the hotel grounds into the view of my astonished fellow guests.

At first the investigation proceeded almost exactly along the lines I had envisioned it would. The general reaction toward me was, of course, one of great pity and everyone, the police included, treated me quite gently. It never appeared to occur to anyone that the business was anything other than a tragic accident.

But then things began to take an increasingly odd turning as the authorities, after a highly confident commencement, found themselves unable to locate Geraldine's cadaver, and by the time I was judged able to sit warmly wrapped on the veranda and overlook their activities, they had become seriously discouraged.

I watched them as they carefully and conscientiously trailed their hooks and nets up and down the cove and in the waters beyond, observing their scuba divers bob and sink repeatedly to no effect, and seeing them all grow increasingly philosophical as Geraldine's large body continued to evade them. There was more and more talk of riptides and rapid ocean currents and prior total vanishments.

Towards the end of this period I was on the veranda consuming a particularly subtle *crêpes fruits de mer,* and rather regretting it had almost come to an end, when the chain of events began which have led to my present distasteful predicament.

Startled by a sudden flurry of noise, I looked up to see a large bird perched on the railing which I had no difficulty in recognizing as the general of the gulls. As I gaped at the creature, he hopped from his perch over to my table, gave me a fierce glare, dropped something which landed with a clink upon my plate, and then flew away emitting maniacal, gullish bursts of laughter.

When I saw what the disgusting beast had dropped amidst the remains of my *crêpes* my appetite departed completely and has not, to be frank, ever been quite the same since. I recognized the object instantly for what it was—the wedding ring I had given my late wife—but to be absolutely sure, I rubbed the ring's interior clear of sauce with my napkin and read what she had caused to be engraved there years ago: "Geraldine and Hughie, forever!"

I carefully wiped the remaining sauce from the ring, and deposited it in the pocket of my jacket. I heard another burst of crazed, avian laughter and, looking up, observed the general of the gulls leering at me from a far railing of the veranda. I determinedly returned to my *crêpes* and made a great show of appearing to enjoy the remainder of my dinner, even to the extent of having an extra *café filtre* after dessert. I then strolled in a languid fashion down to the beach for a little constitutional before retiring.

It was a quiet, clear night. The Mediterranean was smooth and silvery under the full moon, and its waves rolled softly and almost soundlessly into the sand. I gazed up at the sky, checking it for birds, and when I was absolutely sure there were none to be seen, I threw the ring out over the water with all the strength I could muster.

Imagine my astonishment when with a great rush of air the general of the gulls soared out over my shoulder from behind me and, executing what I must admit was a remarkably skillful and accurate dive, reached out with his orange claws and plucked the ring from the air inches above the surface of the water. Emitting a final, lunatic laugh of triumph, he flew up into the moonlight and out of sight.

That night I was awakened from a very troubled sleep by a sound extremely difficult to describe. It was a soft, steady, rhythmic patting, and put me so much in mind of a demented audience enthusiastically applauding with heavily-mittened hands that as I pushed back my covers and lurched to my feet in the darkness of my room, my still half-dreaming mind produced such a vivid vision of a madly-clapping throng in some asylum auditorium that I could observe, with remarkable clarity, the various desperate grimaces on the faces of the nearer inmates.

I groped my way to the curtains, since the sound seemed to emanate from that direction, and when I pulled them aside and looked out the window a muffled shriek tore itself from my lips and I staggered back and almost fell to the carpet for I had suddenly given myself all too clear a view of the source of that weird, nocturnal racket.

There, hanging in the air in the moonlight directly outside my window, was the large, sagging body of my wife, Geraldine. She looked huge, positively enormous, like some kind of horrible balloon. Water poured copiously in silvery fountains from her white lace dress and her bulging eyes, also entirely white, gaped out like prisoners staring through the dark, lank strands of hair which hung down in glistening bars across her dripping, bloated face.

The sound I had heard was being made by the wings of the hundreds of gulls who were holding Geraldine aloft by means of their claws and beaks which they had sunk deeply into her skin and dress, both of which seemed to be stretching dangerously near to the ripping point. She was surrounded by a nimbus of the awful creatures, each one flapping its wings in perfect rhythm with its neighbors in a miracle of cooperative effort.

Sitting on her head, his claws digging almost covetously into her brow, was the gull general. He watched me staring at him and at the tableau he had wrought with obvious satisfaction for a long moment, and then he must have given some command for the gulls began to move in unison and the lolling, pale bulk of Geraldine swayed backwards from the window and then, lifted by the beating of gleaming, multitudinous wings, it wafted upward and inland, over the dark tiles of the roof of the hotel and out of my line of vision.

I had breakfast brought up to my room the next morning for I anticipated, quite correctly as it turned out, a potentially awkward visit from the police and preferred it to take place in reasonably private surroundings.

I had barely finished my first cup of coffee and half a *brioche* when they arrived, shuffling into my room with an air of obvious uncertainty, the inspector looking at me with the downward, shifting gaze which authority tends to adopt when it is not quite sure it is authority.

It seemed that a local farmer hunting just after dawn for a strayed cow had come across the body of Geraldine. It had been tucked into a small culvert on his property and been rather ineffectually covered with branches and leaves and little clods of earth. One particularly unpleasant feature about the corpse was that it had been brutally stripped of the jewelry which Geraldine had been seen to be wearing that morning. Her fingers and wrists and neck had been deeply scratched by the thief or thieves which had clawed her gold from her; the lobes of both her ears had been cruelly torn.

The police could not have been more courteous with me. Their community's main source of income originates from well-to-do vacationers, and the arrest and possible execution of one of them—myself, for instance—because of murder would be bound to produce all sorts of unfortunate and discouraging publicity. They were vastly relieved at the taking of Geraldine's baubles since it suggested not only the sort of common robber they could easily understand and pursue enthusiastically, it gave their imagined culprit a clear motive for spiriting the body away from the water and later trying to hide it.

Taking my cue from them, I confessed myself astonished and saddened to learn that my wife's drowned corpse had been so grossly violated and wished them luck in apprehending the villain responsible as soon as possible. The lot of us, from differing motives, were considerably pleased to have the affair resolved so amicably, and after shaking hands all around and giving them permission to look over my suite—an action understood by us all to be a mere formality—I took my leave of them and assumed my present situation on the veranda.

Just now I've noticed that in the midst of the latest shift of gulls taking their places to observe me from the overlooking tree is the general himself, and since I gather that signifies that something of considerably import is about to transpire, I've cast a sidewise glance at the doors opening out onto the terrace from the hotel's lobby.

Sure enough, I see the approaching police, all of them wearing expressions of unhappiness and great regret. Worse, I see the unmistakable glint of gold in the inspector's cupped hands. The gulls obviously paid another, quieter, visit to my rooms last night in order to leave my dead wife's pretty things behind in some craftily-selected hiding place. Perhaps the general did it personally. It would be like him.

Now I have risen, a *demitasse* held lightly in one hand, and strolled slowly over to the railing of the veranda. There is a considerable drop to the rocks below and if I tumble directly from here to there it will surely put an quick and effective end to a very rapidly developing unpleasant situation so far as I am concerned.

I have stepped up onto the railing which is a very solid structure built wide enough to hold trays of nightcaps or *canapés* and any number of leaning lovers' elbows. The police are calling out to me in rather frantic tones and I hear the soles of their large shoes scuffling and scraping on the stones of the veranda as they rush desperately in my direction.

My eyes and the general's are firmly locked as I step out into space. He lifts his wings and, with an easy beat or two, he rises from his branch.

Our paths cross in midair.

He can fly, but I can only fall.

The Coming of Night, The Passing of Day

Ed Gorman

Penny knew Mr. Rigler's schedule pretty well. After all, Mr. Rigler's eleven-year-old daughter Louise happened to be Penny's best friend.

So Penny knew just when to do it, just when to walk down the alley, just when to climb the slanting covered stairs that led up to the rear apartment, just when to find Mr. Rigler in the wide, sagging double bed where he slept off the hangovers he inflicted on himself after working the night shift at Raylon Manufacturing.

Penny—dressed in a white blouse and jeans and a pair of Keds (Mom always saying "Jesus Christ, kid, you think I'm made outta fucking money?" whenever Penny brought up the subject of Reeboks)—Penny moved through the noon-day heat, pretty and shy as one of the soft blue butterflies she liked to lie on the grass sometimes and watch.

On her back was the red nylon pack she carried to school every day. Inside it smelled of the baloney sandwiches and Ho-Hos Mom always packed for her lunch.

She turned off the gravel alley and into the small junk-yard of rusting cars that belonged to Mr. Rigler. He was always promising his wife and daughter that he was going

to clean up the back yard someday—"Get ridda them eyesores once and for all"—but that was sort of like his
promise that he was someday going to stop beating his wife
and daughter, too. He hadn't kept that promise, either.

A week ago Mr. Rigler had broken Louise's arm in three
places. He'd first hit her in the mouth with his fist and then
shoved her over an ottoman. She'd tripped and smashed the
arm. Mr. Rigler was pretty drunk, of course. There was so
much shouting and yelling that half the block ran into the
alley to see what was going on and then two cop cars came
screaming down the street and the cops jumped out and they
pushed Mr. Rigler around pretty hard, even though he was so
drunk he could hardly stand up; and then Mrs. Rigler (who'd
been screaming for them to arrest him) started crying and saying how it was all an accident, and the cops looked real
frustrated and mad and said you mean you aren't going to
press charges, and Mrs. Rigler kept crying and holding on to
her husband like he was some kind of prize she didn't want
to lose and saying no, she wouldn't press charges because it
was all an accident and if those fuckin' cops knew what was
good for them they'd get off her fuckin' property and right
now. So the cops had left and Mrs. Rigler had taken Louise to
the emergency ward.

Next day, Louise came over and showed Penny her cast and
talked about how weird it felt to have something like this on
your arm and how much her arm hurt and how she'd had to
get five different X-rays and how cute the young doctor was.
Then she'd started crying, the way she usually did after her father had beaten her or her mother, started sobbing, and Penny
had taken her in her arms and held her and said over and over
that sonofabitch that sonofabitch, and then Louise had said
Why couldn't something happen to *her* father the way it had
to Mr. Menetti, who used to beat his wife and child just the
same way. But then one day they found Mr. Menetti burned
char black in his bed. Seems he'd been drunk and smoking

and had dropped his cigarette and the whole bed had gone up in flames.

Fortunately, the afternoon with Louise had gotten a little better. They both liked to smoke cigarettes so Penny got out the Winston Lights she stole one-at-a-time from her mother and they sat in front of the TV and watched MTV and drank Pepsi and told kind of semi-dirty jokes and laughed and gossiped about boys at school and generally had a good time until Bob came home.

Bob was Mom's newest boyfriend. He'd lived with them for a year now. He was a used car salesman, one of the few men on the block to wear a necktie to work, which Mom thought was real cool for some reason. He had black wavy hair and very white teeth and you could tell by the way he looked at you that he really thought he was pretty hot stuff. On all his sport coats you could see a fine white powder of dust from walking around the car lot all day.

Penny hated Bob but Mom loved him. After she'd been dumped by her last boyfriend, Mom had tried to kill herself with tranquilizers. She'd ended up getting her stomach pumped and staying in a mental hospital for three weeks while Penny lived with her aunt. Mom hadn't really snapped out of it for a whole year, till she met Bob. Now Mom was her old self again. "Oh, hon, if Bob'd ever leave me, I just don't know what I'd do," Mom would always say after she and Bob had had a fight. And Penny would get scared. Maybe next time Mom actually would kill herself.

She thought of all these things in an instant as she watched Bob's slow, sly smile.

Now, he stood there staring down at Penny so long that Louise finally got up and said it was time she git and so she got, and Bob said then, "Your Mom's not gonna be home for another couple hours."

But Penny didn't want to think about Bob now. She wanted to think about Mr. Rigler. The way she'd thought about Mr. Menetti before him and Mr. Stufflebeam before him (Mr. Stufflebeam was another who frequently used his fists on his family).

She went up the rear stairs quickly.

The covered porch smelled of heat and spaghetti from last night. From the downstairs apartment came the sounds of dorky country music and a little baby crying. In this kind of heat, babies usually cried.

At the screen door, Penny knocked once and then listened very carefully. She didn't hear anybody talking or moving around. Louise, she knew, was across the city at a movie with her cousin. Mrs. Rigler was at the restaurant where she was a short-order cook.

And Mr. Rigler was sleeping off his drunk. He'd get up at two, shave, shower, fix himself something to eat, and then head for the factory in an old Ford that was nearly as junky as those dying beasts he kept in the backyard.

"Mr. Rigler?" she called.

She could hear a window air-conditioner roaring and rattling in the distance. But nothing else.

"Mr. Rigler?"

She waited a full two minutes and then went inside.

The apartment smelled of cigarettes and beer and spaghetti. Dirty dishes packed the sink. Without both arms, Louise could hardly do housework.

Penny went through the kitchen into the living room where aged overstuffed furniture was all covered with decorator sheets so they'd look newer.

The bedrooms and the bathroom were down a hall.

She was halfway down the hall when she picked up his snoring. He was really out.

When she reached the door, she peeked in and saw him on the bed. He wore a sleeveless T-shirt. You could see his huge hairy belly riding up and down beneath it as he breathed. His face was dark with stubble. The panther tattoo on his fleshy right arm looked as faded as the flesh itself. He smelled of beer and onions and cigarettes and farts. Penny's stomach grabbed momentarily.

She stood watching him. Just watching him. She wasn't even sure why.

She thought of Louise's arm. The way it must hurt. She thought about the time Louise's Mom had gotten her collarbone broken. And the time he'd given her not one but two black eyes.

He was the same kind of man Mr. Menetti had been. The same kind of man Mr. Stufflebeam had been.

"You sonofabitch," she said to the man who lay there in the silence of the bedroom. "You fucking sonofabitch."

Then she got to work.

Penny was back in her apartment watching a *Happy Days* rerun—she dreamed of a world as nice as the one Richie Cunningham lived in—when she heard the fire truck rumbling down the brick street, siren singing.

They'd hurry in there with their axes and their hoses, but it would be too late. Just as it had been too late with Mr. Menetti and Mr. Stufflebeam. "Asphyxiation" was the word that had been in all the newspaper articles.

After a time, she went out on the fire escape and looked across five back yards to where the two red fire trucks filled the alley. Maybe as many as forty or fifty neighbors had come out to watch.

The ambulance came next, a big white box, two attendants rushing over to the back stairs.

After more time, Penny went in and opened a Pepsi and turned on MTV. She really liked the new Whitney Houston video. She hoped they'd play that before three o'clock, which was when she had to be out of the apartment. Before Bob got home.

At two-thirty, she was in the bedroom, tugging on a fresh Madonna T-shirt, when she heard the front door open and shut.

It could have been Mom but she knew better.

She knew damned well who it was.

By the time she was finished pulling on the T-shirt, he was leaning in the doorway, a smirk on his mouth and a cigarette in his hand.

"Hey, babe, how's it goin'?"

"I'm on my way out."

"Oh, yeah? To where?"

"The park."

"Your Mom don't like for you to go to the park."

"Yeah," Penny said, staring right at Bob and knowing he'd get her meaning. "She's afraid a child molester will get me."

He was still smiling, even when he took two quick steps across the room to her, even when he slapped her hard across the mouth.

"That crack about the child molester s'posed to be funny, you little bitch?"

She fought her tears. She didn't ever want him to see her cry. Ever.

"Huh? That s'posed to be funny?"

She didn't want to say anything, either, but she hated him too much and words were her only weapon. "I could tell her. I could tell her what you been doin' to me in the bathroom."

At first, Bob visibly paled. This was the first time she'd ever threatened him this way. And there was great satisfaction in watching him lose his self-confidence and look scared.

But he quickly recovered himself. She could see cunning now in his stupid blue gaze; he was Bob the used car salesman once again.

"You know what she'd do if you told her about us?"

"She'd throw you out," Penny said. "That's what she'd do."

"Yeah. Yeah, she probably would. But you know what she'd do then?"

He drew a long, white finger slowly across his throat. "She'd kill herself. 'Cause I'm the only hope she's got. The only god-damned hope she's got in the whole wide world.

She's never had no other man stay with her as long as I have, not even your old man, that sorry sonofabitch."

She started to say something but he held up his hand for silence.

"I'm goin' in the bathroom and I want you in there in five minutes."

"No."

He stared at her. "Five minutes, you understand me, you little bitch?"

She shook her head.

He grinned. He was the old Bob again. "Five minutes, babe. Then I'll take you out to the mall and buy you a new blouse. How'd that be?"

She had the satisfaction of watching him panic again.

She'd taken three steps back to the nightstand and picked up the phone.

She didn't threaten, this time. She simply dialed her Mom's work number, and before he could slap the phone from her hand, she said, "This is Penny Baker. I'd like to speak to my mom please. Thank you."

"You little bitch—"

"Hi, Mom."

She almost laughed. Bob nearly looked funny. He'd totally lost it. Was starting to pace back and forth, running a trembling hand through his hair.

"Hi, honey, everything all right?"

"I just wanted to talk to you, Mom."

"Hon, I'm kinda busy right now. Is it real important?"

"It's about Bob."

He made a big fist and shook it at her.

"Bob?" Mom said. "What about him, hon?"

"Just that—"

But Mom didn't wait. "Nothin' happened to him, did it?"

"No, Mom, I—"

"Oh, God, hon, I have nightmares all the time about somethin' happening to him. Getting hit by a car in a crosswalk or gettin' mugged somewhere or—"

Penny heard the need then, heard it more clearly than ever before, the childlike need her mother felt for Bob. Bob hadn't been exaggerating when he'd said that her mother would kill herself if he left.

"You gonna tell me, hon?" Mom said, still sounding crazy with fear.

"Tell you?"

"Why you called, hon? Jesus, Pen, this is scaring the shit out of me."

"I just called to—"

"—yes?—"

"Tell you that Bob—"

And now Bob moved closer. She could smell his sweat and his aftershave. And in his eyes now she could see pleading; *oh, please, Penny, don't tell her; please don't tell her.*

"Tell me what, hon? Jesus, please just *say* it."

"That Bob's going to take me to the mall."

And then Mom started laughing. "God, hon, that's what you wanted to tell me?"

Bob knew enough not to approach her. He just stood there a few feet from her and held his hands up to God as if in supplication and gratitude.

"That's all you wanted to tell me?"

"Yes," Penny said. "That's all I wanted to tell you."

A few minutes later, Bob was in the bathroom. The water running and the medicine cabinet closing. He liked to get himself all cleaned up for her down there, he always said.

Penny lay on the bed. She listened to a distant lawn mower on the summer afternoon.

The water in the bathroom stopped running.

After a time the door opened and he said, "You can come in here now."

She didn't get up. Not at first.

She lay there for a time and thought of Mr. Rigler and Mr. Menetti and Mr. Stufflebeam.

The smoke and the fire and the too-late screams.

She saw Bob lying on such a bed now. And heard his own too-late screams.

"You don't want to keep the old Bob waitin' now, do you, babe?" he called again.

Oh, yes, someday it would happen; somehow. Bob on the bed with his too-late screams.

And then she got up and went into the bathroom.

Please Don't Hurt Me

F. Paul Wilson

"Real nice place you've got here."

"It's a dump. You can say it—it's okay. Sure you don't want a beer or something?"

"Honey, all I want is you. C'mon and sit next to me. Right over here on the couch."

"Okay. But you won't hurt me, will you?"

"Now, honey—Tammy's your name, isn't it?"

"Tammy Johnson. I told you that at least three times in the bar."

"That's right. Tammy. I don't remember things too good after I've had a few."

"I've had a few too and I remember your name. Bob. Right?"

"Right, right. Bob. But now why would someone want to hurt a sweet young thing like you, Tammy? I told you back there in the bar you look just like that actress with the funny name. The one in *Ghost*."

"Whoopi Goldberg."

"Oh, I swear, you're a funny one. Funny and beautiful. No, the other one."

"Demi Moore."

"Yeah. Demi Moore. Why would I want to hurt someone

who looks like Demi Moore? Especially after you were nice enough to invite me back to your place."

"I don't know why. I never know why. But it just seems that men always wind up hurting me."

"Not me, Tammy. No way. That's not my style at all. I'm a lover, not a fighter."

"How come you're a sailor, then? Didn't you tell me you were in that Gulf War?"

"That's just the way things worked out. But don't let the uniform scare you. I'm really a lover at heart."

"Do you love me?"

"If you'll let me."

"My father used to say he loved me."

"Oh, I don't think I'm talking about that kinda love."

"Good. Because I didn't like that. He'd say he loved me and then he'd hurt me."

"Sometimes a kid needs a whack once in a while. I know my pop loved me, but every once in a while I'd get too far out of line, like a nail that starts working itself loose from a fence post, and then he'd have to come along every so often and whack me back into place. I don't think I'm any the worse for it."

"Ain't talking about getting 'whacked,' sailor man. If I'd wanted to talk about getting 'whacked' I woulda said so. I'm talking 'bout getting *hurt*. My daddy hurt me lotsa times. And he did it for a long, long time."

"Yeah? Like what did he do to hurt you?"

"Things. And he was all the time making me do things."

"What sort of things?"

"Just . . . things. Doin' things to him. Things to make him feel good. Then he'd do things to me that he said would make me feel good but they never did. They made me feel crummy and rotten and dirty."

"Oh. Well, uh, didn't you tell your mom?"

"Sure I did. Plenty of times. But she never believed me. She always told me to stop talking dirty and then *she'd* whack me and wash my mouth out with soap."

"That's terrible. You poor thing. Here. Snuggle up against me now. How's that?"

"Fine, I guess, but what was worse, my momma'd tell Daddy and then he'd get mad and *really* hurt me. Sometimes it got so bad I thought about killing myself. But I didn't."

"I can see that. And I'm sure glad you didn't. What a waste that would've been."

"Anyway, I don't want to talk about Daddy. He's gone and I don't hardly think about him anymore."

"Ran off?"

"No. He's dead. And good riddance. He had an accident on our farm, oh, some seven years ago. Back when I was twelve or so."

"That's too bad . . . I think."

"People said it was the strangest thing. This big old tractor tire he had stored up in the barn for years just rolled out of the loft and landed right on his head. Broke his neck in three places."

"Imagine that. Talk about being in the wrong place at the wrong time."

"Yeah. My momma thought somebody musta pushed it, but I remember hearing the insurance man saying how there's so many accidents on farms. Bad accidents. Anyway, Daddy lived for a few weeks in the hospital, then he died."

"How about that. But about you and me. Why don't we—?"

"Nobody could explain it. The machine that was breathing for him somehow got shut off. The plug just worked its way out of the wall all by itself. I saw him when he was just fresh dead—first one in the room, in fact."

"That sounds pretty scary."

"It was. Here, let me unzip this. Yeah, his face was purple-blue and his eyes were all red and bulgy from trying to suck wind. My momma was sad for awhile, but she got over it. Do you like it when I do you like this?"

"Oh, honey, that feels good."

"That's what Daddy used to say. Ooh, look how big and

hard you got. My momma's Joe used to get big and hard like this."

"Joe?"

"Yeah. Pretty soon after Daddy died my momma made friends with this man named Joe and after a time they started living together. Like I said, I was twelve or so at the time and Joe used to make me do this to him. And then he'd hurt me with it."

"I'm sorry to hear that. Don't stop."

"I won't. Yours is a pretty one. Not like Joe's. His was crooked. Maybe that's why his hurt me even more than Daddy's."

"How'd you finally get away from him?"

"Oh, I didn't. He got hurt."

"Really? Another farm accident?"

"Nah. We weren't even on the farm no more. We was livin' in this dumpy old house up Lottery Canyon way. My momma still worked but all Joe did was fiddle on this big old Cadillac of his—you know, the kind with the fins?"

"Yeah. A fifty-nine."

"Whatever. He was always fiddlin' with it. And he always made me help him—you know, stand around and watch what he was doin' and hand him tools and stuff when he asked for them. He taught me a lot about cars, but if I didn't do everything just right, he'd hurt me."

"And I'll bet you hardly ever did everything 'just right'."

"Nope. Never. Not even once. How on earth did you know?"

"Lucky guess. What finally happened to him?"

"Those old brakes on that old Caddy just up and failed on him one night when he was making one of his trips down the canyon road to the liquor store. Went off the edge and dropped about a hundred feet."

"Killed?"

"Yeah, but not right away. He got tossed from the car and then the car rolled over on him. Broke his legs in about thirty places. Took awhile before anybody even realized he was missin' and took almost an hour for the rescue squad to get to him. And they say he was screamin' like a stuck pig the whole time."

"Oh."

"Something wrong?"

"Uh, no. Not really. I guess he deserved it."

"Damn right, he did. Never made it to the hospital though. Went into shock when they rolled the car off him and he saw what was left of his legs. Died in the ambulance. But here . . . let me do this to you. *Hmmmmmmm.* You like that?"

"Oh, God."

"Does that mean yes?"

"You'd better believe that means yes!"

"My boyfriend used to love this."

"Boyfriend? Hey, now wait a minute—"

"Don't get all uptight now. You just lie back there and relax. My *ex*-boyfriend. *Very* ex."

"He'd better be. I'm not falling for any kind of scam here."

"Scam? What do you mean?"

"You know—you and me get started here and your boyfriend busts in and rips me off."

"Tommy Lee? Bust in here? Oh, hey, I don't mean to laugh, but Tommy Lee Hampton will not be bustin' in here or anywheres else."

"Don't tell me he's dead too."

"No-no. Tommy Lee's still alive. Still lives right here in town, as a matter of fact. But I betcha he wishes he didn't. And I betcha he wishes he'd been nicer to me."

"I'll be nice to you."

"I hope so. Tommy and Tammy—seemed like we was made for each other, don't it? Sometimes Tommy Lee was real nice to me. A *lot* of times he was real nice to me. But only when I was doin' what he wanted me to do. Like this . . . like what I'm doin' to you now. He taught me this and he wanted me to do it to him all the time."

"I can see why."

"Yeah, but he'd want me to do him in public. Or do other things. Like when we'd be driving along in the car he'd want me to—here, I'll show you . . ."

"Oh . . . my . . . *God!*"

"That's what he'd always say. But he'd want me to do it while we were drivin' beside one of those big trucks so the driver could see us. Or alongside a Greyhound bus. Or at a stop light. Or in an elevator—I mean, who knew when it was going to stop and who'd be standing there when the doors open? I'm a real lovable girl, y'know? But I'm not *that* kind of a girl. Not ay-tall."

"He sounds like a sicko."

"I think he was. Because if I wouldn't do it when he wanted me to, he'd get mad and then he'd get drunk, and then he'd hurt me."

"Not another one."

"Yeah. Can you believe it? I swear I got the absolute worst luck. He was into drugs too. Always snorting something or popping one pill or another, always trying to get me to do drugs with him. I mean, I drink some, as you know—"

"Yeah, you sure can put those margaritas away."

"I like the salt, but drugs is just something I'm not into. And he'd get mad at me for sayin' no—called me Nancy Reagan, can you believe it?—and hurt me something terrible."

"Well, at least you dumped him."

"Actually, he sort of dumped himself."

"Found himself someone else, huh?"

"Not exactly. He took some ludes and got real drunk one night and fell asleep in bed with a cigarette. He was so drunk and downered he got burned over most of his body before he finally woke up."

"Jesus!"

"Jesus didn't have nothin' to do with it—except maybe with him survivin'. Third degree burns over ninety per cent of Tommy Lee's body, the doctors at the burn center said. They say it's a miracle he's still alive. If you can call what he's doing livin'."

"But what—?"

"Oh, there ain't much left to him. He's like a livin' lump of scar tissue. Looks like he melted. Can't walk no more. Can barely talk. Can't move but two or three fingers on his left hand, and them just a teensie-weensie bit. Some folks that knew him say it serves him right. And that's just what I say. In fact I do say it—right to his face—a couple of times a week when I visit him at the nursing home."

"You . . . visit him?"

"Sure. He can't feed himself and the nurses there are glad for any help they can get. So I come every so often and spoon feed him. Oh, does he hate it!"

"I'll bet he does, especially after the way he treated you."

"Oh, that's not it. I make *sure* he hates it. You see, I put things in his food and make him eat it. Just yesterday I stuck a live cockroach into a big spoonful of his mashed potatoes. Forced it into his mouth and made him chew. Crunch-crunch, wiggle-wiggle, crunch-crunch. You should have seen the tears—just like a big baby. And then I—

"Hey. What's happened to you here? You've gone all soft on me. What's the matter with—?

"Hey, where're you goin'? We were just starting to have some fun . . . Hey, don't leave . . . Hey, Bob, what'd I do wrong? . . . What'd I say? . . . *Bob!* Come back and—

"I swear . . . I just don't understand men."

Splatter Me an Angel

James Kisner

The angels came that morning for Ed.

He was lying face-down on the sidewalk in a pool of his own blood and vomit, waiting for them.

Before he walked down the tunnel towards the light, he asked the angels for a little time to think things over. The angels told him time was meaningless now. He could have as much as he wanted.

Ed thanked the angels.

He began to think.

Why am I here? was his primary thought. Then he remembered:

It was summer, perhaps a couple of years ago. Years were mere blips in his consciousness as he considered time past. Micro-blips. He could view a year in a microsecond. A nanosecond. Whatever increments smaller than that he could not comprehend.

But it wasn't much more than a couple of years; he was sure of that. He saw a woman getting down from the bus, as he sat on a bench watching. Her legs were clad in dark nylon, her knees covered by a swaying dress which the wind threatened to whip up around her thighs. That didn't happen, no matter how hard Ed wished for it.

He was between women at the time. Actually, he had not been between any woman for a long time. His luck with the ladies was never too great. He had two failed marriages to confirm that, plus a less than exciting dating life. He spent a great deal of time in the bar on 32nd Street, a semi-respectable joint called Lou's Diamond Bar, where women came in frequently.

Mostly, the women patrons ignored Ed, though he was not unattractive. He had dark hair, a strong, square chin and dressed neatly, and he was only thirty-five. Maybe he was just too ordinary. Perhaps he lacked charisma. Or maybe it was because he wanted a woman so much that his desperation kept them away. Or maybe he just didn't know the right moves; he often observed other men who seemed to have a different woman every night. Some of these guys were butt-ugly and had foul habits. Ed couldn't figure out their secret.

There *had* to be a secret.

Being in a womanless state, as could be expected, honed Ed's desire for women to a fine edge, to the brink of a vast despair which seemed more awesome with each passing day. He wasn't sure how much longer he could endure.

So he watched them.

As the woman now in his sights finished her descent from the bus and walked, high-heeled, down the boulevard, prim and precious, Ed suddenly was filled with a revelation:

Women are disposable.

His mind almost caved in on itself as the underlying meaning of that concept rushed in to fill the spaces between his beleaguered brain cells. It was a concept, Ed quickly grasped, that could change the face of the world, and Ed had thought of it on his own, right there in the middle of the afternoon, while watching women get on and off the busses.

It was a concept destined to jerk him up out of the funk in which he languished.

Women being disposable, he didn't need to consider them human beings any longer. He didn't need to consider them at all.

With this revelation simmering in his mind, Ed's life changed entirely.

So many women walked the streets, just going from one place to another, probably not contemplating sex.

Ed would sit in the bar, waiting for them to approach him. And as soon as he had realized they were disposable, he found that many more women came to him, as if they *wanted* to be used like tissues. As if they were content to be mere depositories for Ed's teeming sperm.

Ed treated them like dirt. He made them do nasty things. He made them squeal like pigs. He cursed them for whores. He pissed on them. He refused to wear condoms.

They loved it.

For once in his life, Ed had all the women he needed; more than enough. It was like—when he was sitting in a bar, just smoking a cigarette and drinking a beer—like they sensed his disdain for them. His indifference was like a magnet.

After a while, Ed even grew tired of women, eventually developing a mild distaste for the opposite sex. He swore off women for a couple of weeks.

They still flocked to him, offering to buy him drinks, offering to give him blow jobs right there in the bar, offering to do threesomes with other women, giving him autographed pornographic pictures of themselves.

Ed fended them off. He blew smoke rings of disgust in their direction. He quaffed beer and belched loudly to ward them off. He stopped bathing and shaving.

Nothing kept them away. But Ed refused to participate.

The magical purpose of the universe which Ed had absorbed in that single instant on the bench kept asserting itself, however:

Women are disposable; *use* them.

Ed stayed away from Lou's for a few days and returned to sitting on the bench at the end of the day, watching women getting on and off the bus.

He was not even mildly aroused by the sight of a tightly-clad thigh in nylon, the thrust of a pair of aerodynamically superb breasts, the perfectly pert embouchure of pouting crimson lips, or the glitter in the eyes of the most sparkling blonde.

Life had become dull.

Repetitive.

Redundant.

With knowledge had come the responsibility of knowing. Some things, once learned, could not be pushed aside; they festered forever in the mind, like the multiplication tables, or one's Social Security number, or like an embarrassing moment from childhood.

With responsibility also came duty. Duty demanded that a man who had knowledge make use of it.

But, Ed reasoned with himself, he was not content. That women were disposable had been the most staggering revelation of his life so far, but, like anything of a revelatory nature, its novelty had worn off. You could only get saved once; you could only lose your virginity once; you could only grasp a particular staggering concept once.

Ed realized the underlying problem. There were too many things that you could do only one time. The second time was always different; so was the third, the fourth, and, so on, until the end.

Never, Ed thought, do anything for the first time.

* * *

Days passed. A discontented Ed spent most of his spare time feeling sorry for himself, sitting on the bench. Sometimes he sat there late into the evening, until the busses stopped running. People in the street would pass by him, regard him with scorn or pity, as if he were a vagrant, then go on.

Ed ignored them.

He was in stasis. He was, in fact, ignoring the universe.

Then one night, an angel appeared, floating just a few feet above the ground.

Ed yawned.

"I have come," the angel said, "to show you The Way."

Ed barely moved his eyes. He could see the angel well enough. It had an epicene, fey look about it. Its wings were so obviously for effect and not function. Its long white robe was so obviously part of the stereotype, as was the musical voice.

"I have no religion," Ed said.

"Even as I manifest before you?"

"An angel? Give me a break. If I'm going to go crazy, I think a bug-eyed monster would be more in order. Don't you?"

"I don't know what a bug-eyed monster is," the angel said in its lyrical, all-too-soothing voice.

"I get a *dumb* angel on top of it all. Why don't you go away? Send me a devil instead."

"You don't mean that."

"Goodness is boring. You should know that. That's why people don't believe in angels any more. They'd rather believe in bad things. Bad things you can understand. Good things are just plain unnoteworthy. Try to sell newspapers with good news and you'll go broke."

"May I tell you, Ed, that you are quite eloquent?" The angel's tone was mellifluous, genuinely admiring.

"Thank you."

"Your eloquence is born of despair, I realize—the despair

that comes from contemplating the nature of the universe—but, still, I have to commend you for it."

"Now that you've admired my eloquence, would you please go away and let me suffer in peace?"

"I can't. I have to show you The Way." The angel pronounced the last two words with inspired emphasis.

"The way to what?"

"I hesitate to say 'salvation,' because that doesn't interest you."

"Too true, bud, or, sister."

The angel didn't flinch; nor did it reveal its sex as Ed hoped it might.

Instead, it shook its head. "You're a hard case."

"Don't I know it."

"You need another revelation, perhaps?"

"What would *you* offer? Some kind of namby-pamby, goody-two-shoes philosophy? Is that what you're peddling?"

"No. Of course not. I wouldn't insult your intelligence."

"Well, I guess I can take another revelation. Why not?"

"You're a troubled man. You need something to live by."

"Well, shoot!"

"What do you mean?"

"Give me the revelation."

The angel fluttered a few inches higher, so it could look down upon Ed with its painfully obvious beatitude. It seemed to be thinking.

Ed couldn't help but cast his gaze upward now. He was merely trying to look up the angel's gown. But, strain as he might, he could see nothing; not even pubic hair. He tried to hide his disappointment by making his face receptive-looking to the angel. After all, the angel did promise to give him a revelation.

Finally, the angel waved its hands, causing a shaft of golden light to fall on Ed from out of the night sky.

"Women," the angel said, "are *prey* "

* * *

As the angel floated away, Ed's brain had intercourse with itself. The right half humped the left half and vice-versa. The two hemispheres did a sixty-nine, throbbing in Ed's skull with cerebral lust. Had he heard the angel right?

Women are prey?

What kind of revelation was that? He compared it to his former revelation.

It made sense.

If women were disposable, then they were not only prey, but the *perfect* prey. Indeed, the first revelation was almost the same as this one; Ed had merely misinterpreted it.

He arose from the bench and walked home, his brain still engaging in lewd acts, while he mulled over the phantasmagorical scope of the revelation.

It gave life a new meaning.

It gave death a new meaning.

It gave Ed a new purpose.

The next day, he returned to Lou's bar.

Less than five minutes after Ed sat down, he was approached by a tall black woman with a bustline that resembled the twin turbines of a science fiction vehicle. She looked like she might be diesel-powered. Her hair was streaked with purple and orange and she had *eight* earrings in each ear.

"Hi," she said, taking the cigarette from between Ed's fingers and inserting it between her thickly-rouged full lips. Her lips were like two disparate beasts, like animated, imaginary things that could perform feats no real lips could. They wrapped around the end of Ed's cigarette so lusciously and with such accompanying movement that Ed was reminded of a tornado.

She opened her mouth briefly, curled her tongue around

the cigarette, flicked it, and, leaning forward, put it in Ed's mouth.

Not many women could do that trick with their *tongues*.

He tasted lipstick on the cigarette. Not a bad taste. A womanly taste. From a tasty woman.

"Hi," he said as the woman leaned even closer to him, almost falling into his lap. She wore a tight tube top through which he could see engorged thumb-sized nipples. She had on tight, shiny black leather slacks with a zipper that went from her navel down through her crotch and came out on the other side at the apex of her butt cheeks.

Despite his disdain for women, Ed found himself interested. The new revelation must be working, though he still doubted any of the old magic could still be there.

Ed sucked on the cigarette, highly aware of her saliva on its end, blew smoke sideways, and said, "I'm Ed."

"Wanda," she replied. "It all right if I sit with you, White Boy?"

"I'm not a boy."

"You like *hot* chocolate?"

"Any marshmallows come with it?

Wanda laughed. "That's the first time anyone ever had a good comeback for that line, mister." She draped her right arm over his shoulder. He ordered her a drink.

"Never do anything for the first time," he told Wanda.

They went back to his apartment. Perhaps in anticipation, Ed had cleaned it thoroughly before going to the bar. The place sparkled like the sheen on Wanda's ass. Even the bed was made.

Ed gave Wanda another drink—she liked gimlets—and sat on the edge of the bed with her and sipped a beer.

"You're not a working girl, are you?"

"Me? Hell, no. Do I *look* like a whore?"

"Well, to be honest, yes."

Wanda laughed. "Okay. Maybe I do dress up too much."

"It's okay with me. I like your outfit."

"Even the pants?"

"Yep. I never saw that kind of zipper before."

"It's made for action, honey. One zip and both sides fall down at once." She stood up. "Wanna see?"

"Sure."

Wanda reached behind her, tugged the zipper down the back of her ass, reached between her legs and pulled it up to her navel. She popped a snap and peeled down one leg of the slacks, revealing a thigh that made Ed think of polished ebony.

She quickly peeled the other leg. She stood there a few seconds, a broad grin on her face. She still had the tank top on, and it seemed to be even sexier with her lower regions on display.

Ed undressed slowly, deliberately. He focused on the black triangle he knew was twitching between Wanda's legs.

He twitched a little himself.

It was pretty good sex. Back before he'd had his first revelation, he would have considered it great sex. But his new awareness had taken the edge off total enjoyment.

Of course, now he had his new revelation to stimulate him, but he was saving it for later.

With a little effort, some imaginative placement of pieces, and a lot of sweat, Ed managed to get all of Wanda into two trash bags.

He took the bags downstairs, one at a time, and deposited them in the dumpster across the street, behind the hardware store. Ed returned to his apartment and cleaned up. The bed was a particular mess. He made a mental note to himself that he would have to buy new sheets.

Cleaning up the kitchen cutlery wasn't that bad, and the blood came up from the kitchen floor with a lot of paper towels. When he was finished, he had another trash bag to carry outside. This one he just left on the curb for the morning pick-up.

As he ascended the stairs the last time that night, he silently thanked the angel for the new revelation.

Life was good.

For the next year or so, Ed experienced the joy of sex again. Women flocked to him. He screwed them. He killed them. He stuffed them in trash bags. He left them in the Dumpster across the street.

He experimented with ways of putting the women in the bags until he found the perfect arrangement for two bags, including the soiled paper towels and sheets. The only real problem with the whole thing was buying so many sheets and trash bags.

No one seemed to notice that women that went away with Ed never came back.

Women were disposable, after all.

Women were prey.

It was a big city. He'd have to dispose of many, many women before their disappearances would be noted. And who would suspect good old Ed, anyhow? He was just an average guy who happened to like having different women two or three times a week. Lots of guys who hung out in bars were like him.

The angel had saved not his life, but the *quality* of his life, which was much more important.

Ed was happy. His brain no longer contorted itself in multiple sexual positions while trying to understand things. He could appreciate the absolute ecstasy of sex again, because he always climaxed twice every time he was with a woman.

The second time was in his head, of course. His testicles couldn't manufacture two wads in an evening. Not any more—not when the second climax—the cerebral one— was so exquisite.

Life was fantastic. The women came to him with little or no effort on his part. They allowed him to do anything.

He sometimes thought they even *knew* how the evening would end, but that they didn't care.

Yes, life was good, fantastic, wonderful, exciting.

But it was becoming boring.

Ed was sitting on the bench as he had before, awaiting a revelation. Had his angel forgotten him? He really needed its help now. What was there beyond the last revelation? How could he ascend to the next rung of enlightenment and spiritual pleasure?

The angel did not come.

Ed was about ready to leave, which meant he was about to give up on life, embrace its boredom and swear off women again.

Then *she* came along.

A woman who even in the dim light cast by the street lamp a half block away was stunning. Her movements were a study in fluid locomotion and the dynamics of kinetic science. Her breasts were two living, separate animals, hunching against the fabric of her white blouse like horny rabbits. Her stomach seemed to undulate in the throes of orgasm even as she walked. Her thighs smacked together like giant lips slurping up every last ounce of a man's seed like a hungry two-dollar whore. She wore black checked slacks. No panty lines. The puff of her bush protruded beneath the fabric. She had five-inch black heels on. She carried a large pocketbook under one arm.

Under the other arm was a whip.

She was like one of those cartoons in the back pages of men's magazines. Her hair was auburn, her eyes impossibly green, her lips magenta.

She sat down next to him.

"Hello," she said, her voice a rasp of lust cutting Ed to the core. For once, Ed was not glib. He merely nodded.

"You want it here, baby?"

"What?" he asked hoarsely.

"Me, of course."

Ed shivered. Of all the women he had possessed the last couple of years he had never encountered anything like her. *She,* he realized, was the revelation.

In the flesh.

It was a quick walk back to Ed's apartment, during which his pants almost exploded. He held her hand all the way there, and it was like holding electricity.

They fucked like quicksilver minks. They twisted in and out of each other. They turned each other inside-out, ass-backwards, willy-nilly, cat-a-corner, upside-down, over and under, inventing new positions to accommodate their lust. Ed's brain was impressed.

Sweat, saliva, the mucilage of love, the fluids of conjunction, the spurts of jetstream jism—all flowed copiously, as if they originated in a bountiful, overflowing fountain that would never empty.

After it was over—or were they merely taking a break?— Ed was hungry for yet more.

He was, he realized in fact and not in fantasy—in love. And he didn't even know her name.

He gasped as she stood up from the bed and used a damp towel to sponge her glistening body.

"That was fantastic," he said weakly, hanging over the side of the bed. He had been drained dry, wrung out by a woman whose body was so different from any he'd ever seen before she could have been an alien. It was so goddamn, fucking, sonofabitching absodamnlutely *perfect.*

"Of course," she said, her voice a rasp that dragged across his spine and made his testicles draw up in anticipation. Her chest was not heaving as Ed's was. She didn't seem a bit tired. "Ready to go again?"

"I don't think I can immediately." He gulped air. "Not right this minute."

"Oh, well," she said. "It doesn't matter."

"It doesn't? You mean you're leaving?"

"No." She rolled him over on his back. "*I* still have to come."

"But, didn't you . . . ?"

"That was orgasm, not coming."

Before Ed could react, she had tied his arms and legs to the four posts of the bed. He didn't put up much of a struggle.

"Kinky stuff," he said lamely. "Maybe that'll work."

"It always works for me," she said. "And *I'm* all that matters." Ed frowned with curiosity. Then he grimaced with pain. He'd forgotten the whip she had been carrying.

That next morning, Ed awoke through a cloud of agony. The woman was gone. So were Ed's private parts. The whip had snapped them off.

As she left, he had barely heard her say the words that now reverberated in his mind:

"Men are prey."

Ed realized the angel was toying with him. Or maybe the angel was playing mind-fuck games with everybody.

He hadn't lost much blood yet. He pulled his pants on, stuffed a towel down the front to staunch the flow, and put on a shirt and shoes.

He stumbled down the stairs to the street. The blood seeped through the front of his pants and, when he saw it, he vomited. Then he fell forward into vomit and blood ran from his mouth. He felt his life float out of him, taking the pain away, and he saw the angels come—

They were the angels of death and sex and taxes and things that go zip in the night and things that lie and fester, and things that just lie, and things that make the hapless brain do flip-flops like a badly adjusted television set.

They had been waiting for him. Now they beckoned to him. They said his time for thinking things over was up.

He started to protest that they had told him he could have all the time he wanted and they said they had lied.

He recognized the angels now. One was the angel of revelation. The other angel had a whip. The third, the last, strongly resembled the woman he had seen step down from the bus that day he received his first self-induced (or so he thought) revelation.

Ed started down the tunnel towards the light, just like in the pages of the *National Enquirer,* he imagined—but he didn't expect Jesus to be at the end.

The angels fluttered before him, beatific, holiest of all the holies there ever were.

Ed was muttering.

"What did you say?" the angel with the whip asked.

"I said I'm so damn pissed."

He threw himself at the middle angel, the angel of revelation, and tore open its back with his hands. He reached in and jerked out angel guts. Before the angel could scream— or make the sound dying angels made—Ed turned and snatched the whip from the second angel. He snapped the whip and lopped off the third angel's head. Angel blood spurted from the stump of its neck. Then he turned on the last angel, the one who had, in her earthly guise, rendered him unearthly, and expertly split her asunder with her own weapon. The two halves of the angel fell aside, and angel stuff oozed and spurted out of them.

That's funny, Ed mused. Angels are destructible. We never learned that in Sunday school.

The remains of the three angels hovered briefly, as if there was life left in them, and exploded. Blood gushed all over Ed and looped around the circumference of the tunnel, transforming it into a crimson corridor. Ed grimly sloshed through the blood, going beyond it, closer to the light.

Before he reached the light, he found his old bench sitting there off to one side, in its own alcove within the tunnel, just waiting for him.

Ed didn't care where the light led now. Where was it written he *had* to go to the light?

Fuck it.

He smiled, settled down comfortably on the familiar bench, and crossed his arms. The blood-drenched whip was clutched in his right hand, prepared for any heavenly bodies that might intrude.

Ed was sure there would be more revelations, and he wanted to be ready for them. In the meantime, he would warn any unwary travelers who came along:

Never—ever—do anything for the first time.

Untitled Still Life with Infinity Perspective

Rex Miller

He was a moderately successful, midlist genre writer, and he was dying. Humorously enough, his metier was bloody suspense books, horror, crime and violence, and a weird sub-genre called dark fantasy/cyberpunk/speculative science fiction, a category so strange that not even those who wrote it were altogether certain what it was. The point being that for a man whose every waking hour was spent immersed in the topic of sudden death, his own sudden death, imminent or otherwise, was an event that found him singularly unprepared.

The curious biochemical anomaly that had been slowly killing him for the last few years produced several interesting side effects, one of them being that some corner of his brain had been unlocked. In a stream-of-consciousness flood he had written nearly forty novels in four years. His publishers would be cranking out his books forever. He would not be around to see it, alas.

In all fairness it had hardly been a sudden death, his impending demise-to-be, since he'd had a good four years to prepare for it. And every morning, like clockwork, he'd been at the keyboard of his word processor pounding out the purple prose. Seven to noon. Break for lunch. One to three. Year in, year out. His agent and his editors were amazed.

Truthfully, he wasn't a writer so much as he was a typist or a clerk. He simply typed onto the screen those dreams that came to him in the night. He always told interviewers who seemed awed by his prolificness, "I'd have written a lot more if I could've typed faster." He'd tried dictating to a speed-typist but that hadn't panned out. And what was the big deal? It would take them years to publish his oeuvre, as it was. Now his illness had progressed to the point where all he wanted to do was quit work and head for a warm, sunny clime. Drink tequila; sit on the beach. But it wasn't going to work that way.

Something was prodding him to write more. To write faster. To write and keep writing and write and never stop until the thing came and smashed him down once and for all. The dreams that had been a godsend for the last four years were now becoming nightmares. He dreamed all night long. Active, turbulent, strange dreams of bizarre characters acting out the weirdest death fantasies.

And in the morning, if he didn't start writing it all down, he'd begin daydreaming—and the daydreams were a thousand times worse than the others—horrible, seamless things that caught him up and imprisoned him inside their crazed storylines. With each successive daydream it was harder and harder for him to escape, to think his way out, to plot his way out of his own scenarios of paranoia and murder.

He'd come to Dr. Kervale to see if there wasn't some new medication he could try that would numb his brain, sedate him to the point where the stories might stop coming, where his ideas would leave him alone. It had become unbearable. It was like being inside one of those infinity drawings where you see a picture of someone looking at a picture of someone looking at a picture of someone looking at a picture of . . . and about the seventh or eighth level of hell, you began to go a little mad. What if there were an infinity picture that never ended, with a subject so mesmerizing it locked the viewer deep inside? That's what the dreams had become.

Kervale was apparently with a patient and presumably had let his receptionist go to lunch. There was no one at the telephone and he didn't see any nurses in sight. He was scarcely in any hurry so he sat in one of the chairs and skimmed through the magazines in the doctor's waiting room.

The thing tugged at him. There was no denying the ideas when they attacked, he'd tried again and again. This time he tried to force his mind to other things, to think about business: he wondered what sort of a cover mechanical they'd produced on *Lured,* the book they were doing as a lead the following month. Without knowing why, he got up, put his magazine down and went over behind the receptionist's desk.

This is absurd, he thought as he removed the cover from the woman's typewriter. His mind fought to regain control but his hands searched for paper in the unlocked desk drawer. It took him only a few moments to insert a sheet into the strange machine and begin looking for the power switch. Within a minute or so he was typing words and phrases on the unfamiliar typewriter in all caps:

NIGHT MAYOR. RAINSTREAKER. DURRELL. HEADRIPPER. THOUGHTGAME. OILSLICK. VENUSIAN BLIND. SEE VENUS AND DIE. MATA MUA. TIME SLIDES DOWN. DURRELL. MUTILATED CLOWN. Without warning he was slipping into the dark folds of the chilling plot, typing "Durrell, the neutered by-product of three confused bondings and eight bewildering cohabitations, is asexual/heterosexual. A burn-out with diagonal burn streaks on the right side of his face, a dead eye—which his triangular one-ways conceal—and no nose. Having only a left nostril and half a nose is not a serious handicap for a tactile audile." He was typing so furiously he didn't hear the doctor come out of the office behind him.

"You all right?"

"Mmm." He didn't bother to shut off the typewriter though he knew he was sliding down.

"Are you *doing all right?*" The doctor was a pleasant man, hair covered, face masked, gloved; plas-net to the breathing mask. So really all you could see were the eyes, slightly myopic through the thick eyeshield, a triangular pair of framed lenses that meshed tightly against the hood, everything in institutional charcoal.

"Fine." Half-five Alpha Durrell-Human, known as Durrell, felt nothing. He waited for the tingling sensation of the probe and the sound of his dreamkey. Knowing now the *real* reason he was there.

"Atta boy," the man said with his jovial workaday smile in place, preparing to look at Durrell's brain.

The probe hit tentatively, professionally centered. He opened the front section of his thoughtshield as he heard the first three words of The Fleetwoods' "Mr. Blue" sound familiarly in his ears.

On the word "STAR" he let the probe track and breathed deeply, smiling reflexively when he heard the doctor's surprised intake of air.

"Holy GOD!" he heard, almost laughing, as "All Along the Watchtower" blew across the eighth pair of cranial nerves, transmitting Jimi Hendrix to the part of his brain not sheathed in thoughtshield.

In the flash of a microtick he dreamthemed an icy moonlet near the blue edge of Triton's shadow, an ancient cornfield and the rusting tin sign "Funk's Hybrid," the whoreband of the same name, and a sidewalk mug joint on the Rue des Jasperjohns, a double-clenched shallop tethered to the balustrades and yawing gently in the petrotide. These were just "kneecaps," involuntary jerks to the non-hostile probe, so he forgot them instantly.

"Nobody told me you were—"

"A braincop?" Durrell chuckled softly, his head in the padded, viselike maw of a NECAP. He couldn't recall just that moment what the acronym represented; the fanciest new neuro-something, something-probe. The operating theatre was one of the finest and there was nothing to fear but the unknown. Nobody kills a galactic-class champion gamer, except maybe another gamer, so he was relaxed and totally at ease.

You die of a killer virus, a spontaneous act of random violence in isolated instances—and old age. Nothing can sneak up on you. No plan to injure you will succeed—because when the perp or perps reach that instant of crystallized thought, you *share* it with them. If a doctor was going to play games with your thoughtshield, the second he even contemplated a hostile mood you'd know it, too, and you could gangslam him braindead before his heart could beat again!

Mindscans were part of the deal, like the dental plan, the annual physical checkup. It paid to take advantage of Uni's resources, the ultimate state of the art in dreamtech sciences; better safe than sorry.

The cartel used them like truth serum. And what the doctor had read off his screen in that flashing microtick when the cop relaxed his brainshield was something that he would have to pass up the chain of command. It fell under the primary dictum, "Report any unusual discrepancies."

In the lightning bolt of electro-scan the machine had photographed a negative fault line cracking down through the braincop's quadruple-thick mindset as he dreamed the probe in for a peek. It wasn't anything major; just a jagged line that would end up on some controller's desk back at Threat Directorate, probably in the Department of Sensorium Analysis—a misnomer if ever there was one.

The doctor did nothing to pass the report up the line. The NECAP unit was programmed to report any unusual discrepancies, and the small, jagged line instantly became spoonfeed.

Deep inside the labyrinth of Uni Central a woman sat watching a bank of consoles. One of them glowed blue. She watched the tiny, negative fault in Half-five Alpha Durrell-Human become hard downlink.

The tech keyed Durrell-Human, ½5 Alpha, hit the Data Transfer, and got DENIED.

Hit a query and got DENIED.

Hit an explain-query denial and got DENIED. Turned it over to her supervisor who contacted *her* supervisor who asked for the same information in a different way and was told—

ACCESS DENIED.

Explain query denial to supervisor?

ACCESS DENIED.

It went on like this until they reached an Assistant Controller in TD-5 who had supersecret security clearance and his screen advised him—

ACCESS DENIED. SUBJECT/PROJECT/PROGRAM UMBRA/ PENUMBRA SENSITIVE.

An umbra/penumbra-cleared executive, who was at home with her family and not at all pleased by being disturbed for something so routine, had to call *her* boss and get him to open his supersecret document vault and trot out the codeword, which in machinespeak was §§§§§§§§§§§§ stroked-ampersand 10 ¶¶¶¶¶¶¶¶¶¶¶¶, followed by the unit or cipher numbers and designations 1191-Y/E-4-91284-Y, and the crypto-brackets which were 7-place KER-prefix nymics, KERATIN/KERZEAL. The program in which Half-five Alpha Durrell-Human worked was locked tightly under the classification crypto KERVALE.

Armed with all of this, the long-suffering executrix accessed the interlink again and saw the following exchange:

CRYPTO	*UNIT NUMBER*
KERATIN	1191-Y
KERBATE	399910-E
KERBIZA	33880-EE
KERCINE	861515-Y
KERCHOY	91-E-4485

KERDART	81831-7Y-3
KERELAN	UTILITY-1Y7
KERFBAT	63518-E-7Y
KERGONE	FEED 7Y-E
KERJURA	66120E-Y
KERKIMO	718518-Y
KERLECH	442-E
KERMESS	101072-Y
KERMOTH	5123E-Y-9
KERNELS	UTILITY-LOCK-Y-2E77
KERNITE	99-99Y-5-3
KEROGEN	E-8245-Y
KERPLOP	E-FEED-1Y8154-E
KERSHAM	Y8117234-E
KERSTOP	6570-E-26
KERTREL7	E-1Y-399-0
KERVONA	588E-2222-Y
KERWAKE	2003-E
KERYGMA	7-E-7-Y-LOCK
KERZEAL	E-4-91284-Y

PROGRAM LOCATE: KER VALE
CLASSIFIED ULTRA MOST SENSITIVE TOP
  SECRET
UMBRA/PENUMBRA EYES ONLY MAX-
GRADE
*UMBRA/PENUMBRA EYES ONLY MAXGRADE
  SEC/CLR*
PROGRAM LOCATE: KERVALE
Entry?
*(A)CODE STAR / 661-33 EDICT COMMCENT/
  CLEAR/*
PRIORITY 1 PLUS/ ACCESS
Access:KERVALE
MAXGRADE SEC/CLR EMPLOYEE HISTORY
Employee Name: ½5 Alpha Durrell-Human
A/K/A: Durrell

ER:	Access: PAYROLL [COALITION]
CODE:	Star/661-33
AUTH:	Edict CommCent
RANK:	Access: UNIWORLD CONTROL
OS:	Enforcement
SI:	491-38-408-689-UNI-A-(OP)
ASSND:	Freelance (GAMER)
DESK:	SSB/Action
PROJECT:	Access: CONTROLLER [COALITION]
CRYPTO:	KERVALE
Status:	Audit
N/C:	A1-30
ASMT:	4410, 5111, 5190-K, 6827, 9901, 9992 10725, 11186, 14833, 14994, 17665, 18322
Uniworld Credits:	Access: BANKING [COALITION]
Emergency Access:	VASTAR SYSTEM
Dreamtheme Keys:	Mr. Blue/All Along the Watchtower
Response Type:	Audile
Termination:	Audit
Languages:	English, Franco, Vorse, Mata, Seblenese

The executrix keyed TRANSFER AND CLEAR and washed her hands of it. Far away, on Santa Satana Breton, a senior controller examined the display and said, "Easy way to fix that. Put him to work." He tapped the photo on his desk.

"You sure?" his colleague asked.

"I *run* Durrell. These two are perfect for each other." He looked into the cold eyes of a beautiful killer mutant.

Back on the home base of Uni Central, the umbra/penumbra-cleared executrix killed power on the interlink unit and left the console, moving down the hallway to her privacy cubicle. She plugged into a thoudiola and instantly relaxed as the opening chords of "Salotenwjopra," the Hotsteel rocker, slammed across the synapses. The second she crossfaded "Since I Fell for You" she heard:

You have accessed a Thought-HOlovid Uniworld Dream-theme Disseminator. Alter reality at will.

And she was blissfully happy once again in the land of the midnight suns, where umbra and penumbra had far different meanings.

Renée was multilingual but she tended to think in Matamuan, so she appreciated the triple-entendre of stovepipe motif on yet another level. They were in front of some of her favorite mug joints along the oil canal and she told the gondolier to stop so she could admire the facades. She knew he would assume she was building a mindset, but Renée was merely admiring the witty facades of Hi Hat, Topper, and Nite Mayor, their three famous 'pipe hats soaring into the Venetian* sky.

The sky itself was a beautiful thought-xparency, which she knew was one-sided; but the Ub Iwerks Dreamtheme—stylized cartoon stars and ringed planets—was the perfect Olden Times backdrop for the clubs and fake painting operations along the canal. An anthropomorphic moon grinned down at her from what she knew to be the floor of the Oysla gray-wheel chamber.

Renée had fled here to the outlaw world of "Venice,"

---

*Venetian is spelled Venusian but henceforward all turvywords will be spelled phonetically. *[He dreamed that he crossed this out. His editors hated footnotes.]*

deep inside the anti-gray popularly called Oilslick. She could blend in and take her pleasures.

The pipes of Hi Hat and the others were as different as up and down: Hi Hat's name only appeared across the very top of the stovepipe so you could identify it from a sky-rocker or metro, but the facade was unmarked, a gently blinking figural of dyracolor thoughtwindows. Inside the fake painting operation it was all endless cake-out-in-the-rain graphics, after the wonderfully funny work of the rocker Ah-Ha. Topper, on the second level, sat above the face of a four-handed counter-clock, and the Mickey hand shot its middle digit in welcome. She pointed toward Nite Mayor and the gondola began to move quietly through the plastic pads.

They stopped against the formex and flexcal steps and she got out gracefully, entering the letter "O" on her eight-inch stiletto fetish heels. The "O" of Mayor was a fanged monster's mouth, the monster's stovepipe rising three levels above the mug-joint, and she walked seductively across the red carpeted tongue as "Schemer for Souls of Glass" roared from the dim recesses.

The sharp edge of Renée's mind pulsated with excitement as she felt herself moistening to the provocative notion of being surrounded by easy, vulnerable targets.

Inside Renée the voice of Linda Logs screeched "Shit Pile Shuttle" and she wet her perfect lips and stepped into the wall of sound.

THIS FACILITY IS FOR ZETA-CLASS ONLY UNI WORLD PROVIDES ADVANCED THOUGHTGAMERS WITH Z-CLONE THOUDD THOUGHTFONES. BRAINALONES PROMOTE SOCIAL SAFETY

Renée laughed in hot anticipation.

On an alien star that was home base for the intelligence and enforcement directorates of the vast coalition owned by Uniworld Petro, a tall, harlequin-masked man in a moderate stovepipe waited to be cleared to Public Information, the huge monolith that housed his employer's headquarters.

Fewer than two day cycles ago he'd been on V-41, in a drugged-out jungle lab near New Orchid City. Now he was cooling his heels in a Pro Dex THT outside the PI building on Santa Satana Breton. It really was a small world.

"Here you are, sir," the young security man said politely, and Durrell thanked him and clipped his breathprint I.D. on.

The pathway to the entrance was marked with the thought-balloon arrows that were the ubiquitous trademarks of a Uni operation. Durrell walked slowly towards the monolith, a tall man in black, face half red-lined in the manner of a half-rainstreaker mutant, black eye triangles over a rough-hewn countenance. He was early as usual.

All the way in he'd played Kenton and his wives: June Christy, Ann Richards, interpolated with backgrounds of Intermission Riff. Dynaflow. Blues in Burlesque. Hallowed sounds from ancient purple discs called 78s, found and restructured for thoudiola. Olden goodes.

Now the ever-present thoudd blasted C-Slash Gamma Utrillo at him, and Durrell hummed along with their big hit, "000-111," in a better mood now and glad to be back on his feet again. His metal-shod cop shoes rang out on the hard surface of the formex as he entered the massive structure. A thoudd lecture to other-worlder children pulled at him as he walked past INDOCTRINATION, and he smiled and thought, why not?—then stepped in to take an alcove and kill some time.

The famous voice of the announcer Free Bird crackled resonantly as Durrell took a comfort recliner and plugged in to the lecture.

"—time had elapsed since the fourth war, and in the parallel Milky Way galaxy, it was discovered that time ran both forward and backward, and spatial relationships varied from system to system and from star to star.

"Following the breakthroughs in neural communication and thought transmission, mankind learned to alter certain physical realities with a type of instantly-induced self-hypnosis or *dreamttheme.* Technological research and development provided industrial, medical, and military applications for these new abilities.

"After the Big War the top thoughtgamers were hired by Uniworld Petro, a multi-planet coalition for restratification, and by employing braincop tradecraft, the law enforcement and intelligence agency set out to restore order.

"Today freelance gainers are engaged to seek out and neutralize criminals and sociopaths who endanger social safety and subvert law and order.

"The most hazardous braincop jobs are those missions to the various satellites of Mata Mua, which means 'In Olden Tymes,' where the worst outlaw mutants gravitate. El-Ones, homicidal brainiacs, Brainfreak tax bandits, severely retarded 'Muans known as walking breadbrains, and other societal rejects populate the dark core-inverts, making such environments ideal camouflage for galactic-class thoughtgamers on the run." *You can say* that *again, Free Bird,* Durrell thought to himself.

"Post-War societies are called straights and anti-grays. The latter are those stars with artificial gravities. These systems allow repopulated worlds to double in size, one class on the surface or within, and one 'gravitating'—up or down—to the reversed polarity. Core-inverts allow racial purification and promote social safety. Typically these environs utilize a petrochemical barrier that both divides the classes and houses the gravity brainwheels. The giant wheels maintain magnetic polarity, axis rotation, inworld ecospherics, and surveillance mechanisms."

Durrell tried to dream *THE END,* a trick he'd attempted before, but it only made the Free Bird narration louder.

"Matamuans and others often appear today in olden tyme regalia. Extremely tall stovepipe hats and rainstreak-motif bow-style ties are considered quite fashionable. Female role-players wear ancient ball gowns, or go nude and half-nude. Male and female roles are mentally, not physically, adaptive. And all three sexes wear triangular one-ways and foot-fetish shoes." The audience laughed as, on screen, a player in high-heeled stilts towered over her dancing partner.

"Languages include English, Franco, Vorse, Mata, and Seblenese. Many coreworlds are thought-xparent, dimensional and real from the outlaw side, but with the dreamthemes transvisible to the obverse. This feature allows such stars to be converted into tourist attractions, and flourishing resorts enable straightworlders to view mutated or outlaw societies in safety and comfort.

"An example of these is the fugitive star Oysla, where such a colony is gravwheeled. Mutants known as 'rainstreakers,' because of their distinctive facial radiation burns, live in a classical Italian-style city of old world architecture and contemporary metroblock, the town built on a spherical plan of interlocking oil canals, and structured inside Oysla's dreamtheme apparatus. The local nickname for the star is 'Oilslick.'

"Rainstreakers work and play in a culture of thoughtgaming, relaxing in mug joint holotechs and turvyworlds constructed to dreamtheme great paintings or famous classical dioramas.

"When the Thought-HOlovid Uniworld Dreamtheme Disseminators, THOUDDs—called 'thoudiolas' popularly—were invented, music was used to key the neural transmission states. Uniworld's Museum of Popular Culture supplied all the two-step masters. Every gamer has his own dreamtheme key, unique to him in all the worlds—a combination of registered melodies recorded between the early 1900s and the Trimillenery. Mine are 'Time Slides Down' by Calico Jack, and Lenny Skinny's four-cycle version of 'Free Bird!'" The audience applauded as the screen displayed the announcer's baroque and audioscopic dreamtheme.

"Uniworld controls every step of thought-holovid gaming from first generation production to management seminars, offering safe applications of the latest dreamtech to major manufacturers such as VisaRama, Universal Control Systems, Imaginex, DreamCorp, and others. The Diorama Mark IV, Uni-9000 Dreamscanners, DreamCorp Interworld's Xparenlator, and NeuroPathic Viewscape machines are just a few examples."

Durrell unplugged and got out of the recliner as Free Bird's dreamtheme dissolved from the screen, and he heard the special track telling other audiles like himself that

THOUGHT-HOLOVID UNI-9000s ARE COMPATIBLE WITH VORSE, MATA, OR SEBLENESE BRAINSHIELD APPARATUS AND CAN BE EXPANDED TO STORE UP TO A VEZILLION ANTI-GRA VS.

Durrell had more time to think on the long walk to the Coalition Controller's office, a small room in an out-of-the-way alcove marked only with an unobtrusively-rendered black infinity sign. He could have ridden the moving walkways, but he preferred to walk and peer into the huge, open rooms. It was immense, the Public Information monolith.

He stopped in front of a room that appeared to have no walls—a room anyone would be afraid to step into—and Carmel Pucker hammered from the thoudiola inside. Durrell examined it for a moment until he assimilated the data: the room's walls were like matte paintings, but you could see through them infinitely and he heard,

YOU HAVE ACCESSED A THOUGHTXPARENCY UNI-WORLD DREAMTHEMES ARE MAINTAINED FOR YOUR PLEASURE. PLEASE REPORT ANY UNUSUAL DIS-CREPANCIES. He glanced at the sign on the doorway. "Journey to the Heart of the Brain." He hurried down the hall, thinking that was the last place he wanted to go.

He saw again the small black infinity sign that always brought a slight pain to his chest, then he walked through the outer alcove.

YOU HAVE ENTERED A UNI WORLD PETRO UNAU-THORIZED AREA. DO NOT MOVE. REMAIN IN YOUR

PRESENT POSITION AND YOU WILL BE REPRO-
GRAMMED. FOR YOUR SAFETY DO NOT MOVE. He
flashed and kept moving past the thoudiola.

Inside the Controller's office it was blazing high noon on
the Western Matamuan desert.

"Nice," Durrell gestured admiringly.

"You like that?"

"I like."

"Thanks. Sit."

"Sure." He took a seat and adjusted the position for his
height.

"You look fit," the Controller said.

"Feeling fine." Durrell knew the man across from him
had scanned his field meticulously. There were few secrets
left unprobed. "So far as I know."

"Mindset-wise, I mean."

"Yeah?"

"I'm just asking if you want to do a piece of work."

"You mean will I be *enthused* about it?" Durrell laughed
as the man in the bow tie and one-ways glowered at him.
"Listen, what I want and what I *have* to have are two different things."

"At least two," the Controller said wryly; "maybe three."

"Right. Sure, boss." They were speaking conversation-
ally, which Durrell found tedious in the extreme; but this
man was not one to forego the polite sociai amenities. Durrell realized he'd scanned a gravisign as he looked into the
reflection of the man's mirrored eye triangles. He flashed on
it and his boss caught the take.

"You're seeing those signs because of the target. Might
as well get you started thinking top-side up right away." He
reached for reprogramming and the western desert dimensional dissolved into a full scale cutaway of an anti-gray.
"This is Oysla; Oilslick, remember?"

"From the first time." Durrell didn't mention his re-
fresher course taken on the way down the long hall. The
realistic cutaway was POV-specific, moving eastward

through the oil pole to the gravity brain-wheels. It stopped
at the Sector Zeta delineation and began to refocus on the
oil canal ring and its Venice Rainstreak Colony coreworld.

"I thought you might. You pulled one of the 5100 numbers in there—right? Well, this ain't no tame duck, kid." A
beautiful, flawless face supered over the legend VENUS.
"This is a Matamuan calling itself Renée MeXXico. Wanted
for Lobotocide One. Alive and well inside the rainstreak
colony."

"Nice mouth," Durrell grunted.

"That's an ARIZONA CLASS 12, sonny boy! It's hiding
in there with a bunch of the Zeta clones and if you go in
after her, you better keep your shit screwed down tight or
that mean Matamuan will have you braindead and floating
under the plastic lily pads in the fucking oil canal!"

"Nice. Pasadena, eh? I'll give this one a wave."

"Up to you, Durrell. There's a trey on it."

"Please?"

"30,000 urt-keys, ace—30,000 Uniworld Tax Credits.
Lordy, Durrell! Let's see . . . that's roughly 90,000 in tax-
free *UP* scrip! You say you'll pass, huh?"

"Did *I* say that?"

"I guess not," and they both laughed. "So. You want this
whore?"

"She know a braincop is coming?"

"Count on it."

Durrell looked at the screen full of history below the mug
shot. *Nationality:* Matamuan. *SI:* R140 something. A 12-
rated Arizona Class killer android! *Man,* he must love
money even more than he thought. "Infiltration?"

"Thought-resistant Corvallis Galileo. Nighttime inser-
tion. You could go right through the East Pole oil lock like
you did before."

"Why me? Not that I'm looking a trey in the mouth,
but—"

"You're part rainstreaker. You were there and you came
out alive, didn't you?"

"Barely."

"Okay." The Controller shrugged, leveled. "You're also the craziest brainman we've got. If that won't make you 101% thoughtproof against a galactic-class freak like little Renée, I don't know what the hell will."

Durrell said no more.

At 02503050 they stood on the blastpad, the Controller's briefing at its end.

"Remember, you want to start retraining your senses for Venice." He didn't mean it in the literal sense. He was an audile like Durrell. "When you go into reversal-inversion your bloodflow will regulate the autonomics, but orbitlag becomes a factor. Now, you only have twenty hours in the day cycle, and at least five of them go dark as you rotate. Oysla itself is on a twelve-day cycle week, Aurelius system—and remember, when you're in Venice, time moves counterclockwise."

"What are the surveillance parameters?"

"The usual shit, turrets and gondolas." Durrell headed toward the metro but the Controller added, "Renée likes to play lame duck, then gangslam you braindead before you can think a shield, so keep a strong thoughtjacket up."

"Yeah. So long."

"If you drop your field you've got *serious pain.*"

"Just deposit the trey," Durrell called back over his shoulder.

The metroliner was an old type, one of the dependable Lindbergh shooters, the U.S.S. George Méliès.

But the in-flight braincop loopner was some silly garbage about dreamtheme brainmanuals. Durrell wiped it in disgust and played Dyna Borzoi all the way to Osyla.

The Méliès landed on a tri-D blastpad with a hologram of the weeping eye moon logo. "Q Phone Suicide Rennaissance" by Botz blasted from the thoudiola and he plugged in, heard: *PREPARE TO BRAINTRAIN IN WORLD. CORE-*

INVERTS PROTECT ECOSPHERICS AND PROMOTE SOCIAL SAFETY.

Durrell nodded, passed through a security thought-field, and instantly felt the old memories of Oilslick wash over him. It was one of the only counterpops within metro shot that still displayed all the old "down is up" stuff. Uniworld Petro, UP on the interstar xchange, owned the satellite which had gone fugitive right at the end of the war. But afterward they kept it for tourist rights and concessions, allowing the renegade in-core to self-regulate. At one time the corporate slogan had been "On Oysla down is up—and if UP ever goes *down,* down goes *under!"*

Oilslick's surface was a beehive of industry. Here the huge cogs that powered the master gravity wheels intermeshed in perpetual motion. Uni's C.O.N.T.R.O.L. offices were here.

The Coalition of Nationalities and Technocracies for Repopulation of the Outer Locales, originally responsible for restructuring the satellites of Mata Mua with cogwheel races, was headquartered on the surface, and used the rainstreak colony as a kind of lab and working model.

Venice specialized in exploded heads, walking breadbrains, braindead, longneckers, and Flemish runners. Rainstreaked outlaws could blend in to this multi-faceted mutant community and leave no trace.

Rainstreakers hated other-worlders and would have loathed them all the more had they realized they were a tourist zoo regularly surveilled from the surface of Oilslick itself. "Recherche" was one of the olden tyme words you heard a lot now, here. Outlaw viewing was chic again.

Durrell was bemused by the stream of skyrockers and streetrockers zooming hither and yon, and the intrepid holo-happy tourists everywhere one turned, tripping out to endless dreamthemes of "Un Viage a la Luna" and "Timeslide." The constant din of the cogwheels and the oiling mechanisms was an incessant background hum against the back beat of Antique Hard Rocque, also. Everywhere on

Oysla the petrochemical stench was overpowering. Durrell's half-nose wrinkled in disgust; he thanked the stars he was an audile.

As soon as he'd obtained clearances he climbed into the Corvallis Galileo, a nifty sub-mariner model, and spent the rest of the day cycle brain-flying and practicing converting the craft to air bathtub.

At precisely 2000:00:00:00 Hawkins Mean he was standing in the industrial oil lock chamber, the large egress area between Tourist Surveillance and Population, looking down through the "sky" xparency. When the timer hit, Durrell climbed into the sleek CG and plugged in.

POLARITY REVERSAL IS IN EFFECT TIME MOVES COUNTER-CLOCKWISE. ADJUST YOUR MINDSET TO THE 20-HOUR DAY CYCLE AND REVERSAL-INVERSION. PROTECT YOURSELF AT ALL TIMES.

Durrell took her straight in, figuring the egress lock would be under the canals like before; but it was an old "breakfront" type, and when the CG hit something solid he knew he was in a spot of trouble.

By the time the next sun cycle broke, Durrell found himself in somebody's scum tree and a good five to ten el-exes from the oil canal. He waited a few hours, then came up properly, his scope between two plastic lily pads.

Now to find Renée. *Don't walk away, Renée,* he hummed as he began his search.

For nearly a week Durrell worked to penetrate the rain-streaker night scene. He managed to befriend maybe a tenth of the Zeta bandit crowd; Ozz, Zebra, Azure, Insane Zane, Zulu. But nobody had seen anyone who looked even remotely like Renée MeXXico. And you didn't blunder around showing somebody's picture in renegade mug joints or mutant mumbo-jumbos unless you were a braincop or somebody very stupid, or both. Durrell knew word would get around.

He paid special attention to the mug joints playing PXL 5Rem stuff. "Mutilated Clown" was Renée's dream-trigger. The words laid an icy finger on him every time he heard—

> ROLLER COAST KILLER DWARF,
> CARNY THRILLER MESOMORPH,
> GHOULIE-RAMA, ULTRA-SLIME,
> HEAVY DUTY COUNTERTIME.
> DON'T BE SHY NOW STEP RIGHT DOWN,
> AND SEE THE MUTILATED CLOWN.

One night cycle he heard about "this girl who's trying to pass." A Z-clone sneered, "The bitch is Matamuan, I'd bet my six on it." And that night Durrell dreamed of a dark gondola archway, number 1872, and an air tub capsized by a mighty oilcruiser, the U.S.S. 1872; and he was in the tub, going down, his lungs bursting; and he screamed "help!" but the thought transposed itself so that the letters became numerals: 1-8-7-2; and then he woke up drenched in the heat of a waking dreamtheme, his mind wrenching itself free of the impending slam.

He found her in a fake-painting operation called 1872— no surprise—after Claude Monet's stolen *Impression: Sunrise,* the most famous holo on Oilslick. It was a murky, single-sun operation, painted in shades of tan, pinkish gray, dark blue-green, and sleitch. Female gondoliers and a nude brainwhore band shook the immense room with noise while Zep's Stairway blasted.

They did a slow touch and took a break, a thoudd booming an invitation to "See El Mirador & Punkster Funkster starting next week at Snotto's, Brighton Canal at 28th!" And Acillatem's Heavy Water Band smashed out of the thoudiola, rocking "Half Red," the half-rainstreaker anthem.

Durrell sauntered across the floor, scanning, singing along with the band. A nude gondolier asked him if he wanted to order but he ignored it, focusing his concentration into the chilly depths of a galactic class thoughtfreak:

Renée MeXXico, wearing cosmetic streaks across half her beautiful kisser, a nipple-clinging silver sweater—and nothing but Last-tan from the plexus down.

Durrell was forming the first thought when her automatic probe hit. He'd forgotten what it was like to get broad-brained like that. It hit like an involuntary dreamtheme, and she almost slipped inside before he could block. It was *clever*. The sort of brain gangslam that swallows you like a thousand vezillion simultaneous migraines and he thought himself going—

"Faut-il croire a une evolution of *mankind presentaient des temps?"*

"Mais, suivant des Malakei Elyon Mitteilugen fuer juedischevarno sakra d'aujourd'hui—(funny you don't LOOK Jewish!)—*qui faveur chez nous des le oder das schaedliche welches ces lointaines cette diffusion dessuffisent a expliquer?" Much* as you might ask "Pardon me, but would you happen to—?" but so clever and quick you think you're listening to a thought; reacting; assimilating; preparing normal response; but you're only dreamtheming gibberish camouflage over a probe.

(1/50th of a microtick, the thing hits; 2/50th, she tries to turn him into a chess piece she can PLAY; 3/50th nearly brainsplits Durrell's halves; and in the DOWN quarter of 3/50th she braingames him with a fucking joke of a half-masked Zorro icon and a snake's head.

(At the instant of 4/50th, going for an inverted thought balloon, she tries to think his arms flexcal, and he reaches toward her and smashes it with his *own* thought, ballooning her back into the snake twist as hard and fast as he can. Everything he has is in it—flat out, foot to the floorboard, *plunging* into the darkness at Mach 100, afraid of nothing— *try or die!*)

Renée was the fastest galactic-class Matamuan still surviving, certainly the most formidable Arizona Class 12 he'd *ever* come down against. His counter made her so ferocious she almost penetrated his thoughtshield.

For the *full mini-micro* of 5/50th Durrell felt himself ballooning as she tried her damndest to gangslam him into a pig. It was all he could do to force-feed her a column of scan digits from the 'droid's own central compu-rig. He was too *old* for this work; the trey waiting for him back on Breton suddenly looked like urtkeys he'd *never* spend.

And she was fighting with *everything* she had! She made him see heads on spikes, disembodied organs, balloon brains baking in bloodbroth. She crucified his image with the window, and hung his shadow upside down in his head; attacked him with a windmill razorman and tried to make his hands and feet decoagulate the way a mutant kid will when it's backed into a corner.

"Sorry, Renée," he thought to her—"I'm a headripper!"

And the full power of his mind rainstreaked her for real right before he carried her twitching body past the Z-clones.

She might have weighed 85 pounds tops.

Durrell buried the remains under the brown mountains of chocolate Sierra Merde, leaving the killer mutant braindead, streaked, and cooling in a cheap thoughtcoffin with the black infinity sign. By the time he'd worked his way back to the little Corvallis Galileo he'd dreamthemed away the trey maybe eight times and he was drag-ass, dead dog *tired*.

The gangslam hit Durrell when he was going through the oil lock—hit him so hard he was braindead before the CG popped through the surface. Oddly, he'd never dreamthemed himself as a liability and the moment he felt it coming, and he understood, it just laid him right out . . .

There was only one way to slam a thoughtgamer the likes of ½ 5 Alpha Durell-Human. You let him wear himself down and hit him when he completely dropped his thoughtjacket. When he knew he was out of danger.

Durrell just had time to see himself reversing his mind-set to Aurelius System, moving away from the little Corvallis Galileo and heading for the brown mounds of Sierra Merde, when he went out altogether. The Coalition stopped him at the thoughtcoffin, naturally. They buried him in the same box with Renée MeXXico, both of them brain-dead, dreamless, and six feet over.

One of his most painful deaths.

With a sigh of relief he typed, *THIS DREAMTHEME IS TERMINATED, so* thankful that, at last, he had pulled out of another one. He'd been typing so furiously he had not even heard the doctor come out of the office behind him.

"You all right?" he heard the doctor say. He recalled the name "Kervale" from the dream. His forthcoming novel, *Lured,* an easy to decode transposition of the name Durel(l). His preoccupation with death, an obvious dream trigger.

"Mmm," he said, noticing his fingers on a typewriter key-board. The keys felt oddly-placed; unfamiliar. On the paper inserted into the machine someone had typed in caps:

UNTITLED STILL LIFE WITH INFINITY PERSPEC-TIVE.

The thing tugged at him again, mercilessly. His mind fought to regain control but his hands hovered over the key-board and his fingers began pecking out the words.

NIGHT MAYOR. RAINSTREAKER. Without warning, he was slipping back down into the dark folds of the same plot.

"Are you *doing all right?*" The doctor was a pleasant man, hair covered, face masked, gloved; plas-net to the breathing mask. So really all you could see were the eyes, slightly myopic through the thick eyeshield, a triangular pair of framed lenses that meshed tightly against the hood, everything in institutional charcoal.

"Fine," he said, waiting for the tingling sensation of the probe and the sound of his dreamkey.

"Atta boy," the man said with his jovial workaday smile in place, preparing to look at Durrell's brain . . . .

Pratfall

John Maclay

My name is Josef Stern. I am seventy-five now, but with my full head of dark hair and my small, wiry body, I could pass for years less. Born in Vienna, I have lived through two world wars, two world peaces, and everything in between. I take things in stride. You see, I am a clown.

It used to bother me some, seeing people laugh as I tramped around the sawdust rings of the great circuses of the world. Berlin, Paris, London, I played them all. Moscow and Washington. I knew that I thought more deeply about things than did the crowds who watched me from above, even the leaders and crowned heads. One has to feel, to be a clown. To create laughter, one also has to cry. I foresaw what havoc Hitler would bring, even before he came to power. I knew that the Cold War would follow. Therefore it seemed ironic that my audience was so secure, while I carried on in such a trivial manner.

But then I came to know that this was exactly my defense, and my victory. My white makeup, my painted smile hid attitudes that might have put me in trouble with the vast, unthinking majority. My polka-dotted suit inspired smiles, instead of the vengeance which always follows the prophet. Nobody kills a clown.

So I was able to do good, in my own small way. I saved

Jews, hiding them in a circus wagon on the road to Berne. Evenhandedly, I later smuggled Germans through the Wall. There was even a young man fleeing the F.B.I. after the events of 1968; America or no, it was all the same.

Yet there was another part of my job which caused me concern. That was the violence, the continual slapping around. Reflecting upon it, I feared it would inspire real anger, real bloodshed, real war.

However, an older clown told me that it served a useful purpose, it was merely relief. By acting out their primitive urges through me, he said, people rendered them harmless. So I went on.

And then, scarcely a year ago, the barriers came down. It did my old, good European's heart proud to see the end of that same Wall, the people surging happily through the streets of the capitals I knew and loved, even the Russians speaking freely in a way I had never known. The American leader had also called for a kinder, gentler time, and I believed that he had the peaceful strength to bring it. In Berlin, I danced, now, for joy.

Such was my feeling, when the circus finished its engagement in Tel Aviv. Such it was, when I set out alone to visit Baghdad.

The war began, as all wars do, with a spark. There was the rape of the tiny country. But then, through intransigence, through the visceral rush of blood, it flared. I have never seen anything to war, no glory or honor. Even the "noble" emotions it inspires are, to me, bogus, given their origin in animal slaughter. War is, in a word, stupid.

Yet I was caught in it, as I had been caught in worse ones. My rented car was diverted from the Amman-Baghdad road, to carry some Iraqi troops to the front. And there I was, invited to share a hole near the Kuwaiti border, in the middle of the desert.

Spirits were high at first, food and water was in good supply, and I spent some of my time entertaining the soldiers. I pulled my age-faded, polka-dotted suit from my trunk, painted my face, and made them laugh heartily at my antics. None of them really wanted to be there, except for a few of the pathological sorts that one finds in any army.

Then the bombing began, the metal death loosed by the swooping eagles and the lumbering cranes that had long since removed war from the hands of man, made it impersonal. The effect, however, was very real, as my ears were deafened and huge geysers of sand rose into the mockingly blue sky. Very real, as a man who had laughed at me a moment ago was surreally torn into four pieces, his mouth now an obscenity, gushing blood. Yes, the sand was red that day, as if from a child's drink spilled on a playground.

There were rumors of peace, and rumors again. But the food stopped, the men grew gaunt, and even the water became nothing but dew collected from spread canvas. I could no longer perform my pratfalls, I could merely survive.

One night, as I lay looking at the stars, I began to think again. Had I been wrong; had the violence in my act truly inspired the portrayal of more, as in the films exported in such quantity from the land of peace? Had these, indeed, become a self-fulfilling prophecy, along with the fervor of those who called upon the Islam God?

But no, I decided. It was unsmiling men who made war, those who followed concepts instead of life, those who could not find humane answers before further evil ensued. Those who were still in thrall to the weapons which had become their masters. Those who had stayed serious during my antics in the ring. Those who, well, had never been clowns.

Still the bombs came. Yet one day, there was silence. I awoke to find my companions gone. And when I poked my head above the sand, I saw two lines of tanks a thousand yards on either side, facing each other, facing me.

I did not know what to do, when the muzzle flashes began. Some rounds fell short, exploding merely a stone's throw away, so I had to decide. I considered running toward one of the lines, waving a flag of peace, but shells were falling even there. I thought to remain in my hole, but it provided little shelter. I did pray to my God.

But then, slowly growing in my old mind, behind the eyes that had seen so much, came the thought. Throwing my wiry body erect, I donned once more my faded suit, bounded up and out into the light.

And I danced there, danced on the desert floor! As the mechanical lines drew closer, as the explosions shook the land, I danced for love and joy! I was giving the performance, perhaps the last, of my long life. I danced against war. I danced!

Do as I do, I seemed to be saying to the men in the machines. Come out now, and dance with each other, dance with Josef Stern. The violence was never meant to be real. This is insane. Paint a smile on, slap yourselves around a bit, but dance! Then go home and tell your leaders, your nations, what you have done.

That was when, as if I had been given preternatural sight, I saw the two projectiles, one from either side. Both headed, unerringly, for me.

What sort of people? I marveled, as my body left the earth.

What sort of people would kill a clown?

The Heart of Helen Day

Graham Masterton

A huge electric storm brewed up as Martin drove out of Tumbleton, in Henry County, Alabama, and fat warm rain-drops began to patter onto the windshield of his rented Pontiac. Over to the east, above the Chattahoochee valley, the sky was so dark that it was purple, and snakes'-tongues of lightning licked the distant hills.

Behind him, to the west, the sky was still clear and serene, and Martin was tempted to U-turn and drive back. But he was expected in Eufaula this evening at six, and he still had a hell of a haul; and he doubted in any case if he could outrun the approaching rainclouds. The wind was rising, and already the bright green sunlit trees were beginning to thrash and dip like panicky women.

He switched on the Pontiac's radio, and pressed "seek." Maybe he could find a local weather forecast. But all he could hear was fuzzy voices. One of them sounded just like his ex-wife nagging. Over and over, *"you bastard, you pre-dictable bastard."* He pressed "seek" again and picked up *"—vorce becomes final today . . . "*

"Divorce"—shit! That was all he wanted to hear. If he hadn't gone to that sales seminar in Atlanta last April . . . if he hadn't picked up that ridiculous ass-wiggling girl in the hotel bar . . . if Marnie hadn't flown to Atlanta to surprise him . . . if life wasn't always so damned grisly and so damned absurdly *un*surprising.

Marnie had always told him that it would only take one act of infidelity to destroy her trust in him; and it had.

She and her lawyers had systematically dismantled his life. She had taken the house, the cars, the paintings, the silver, the savings. She hadn't taken Ruff, his retriever, but the day after the divorce became final, Ruff had slipped the dog-sitter's leash and been fatally injured under the wheels of a van.

Martin was now reduced to old-style town-to-town traveling, the Alabama and Louisiana representative of Confederate Insurance, selling packages of cut-price business cover to one fat, sweaty redneck after another. He could sum up the majority of his customers in just a few words: bald, bigoted, with appalling taste in neckties. But he wasn't complaining. It had been his own choice to travel. He had the experience and the references to find himself a much better job, but (for a while, anyway) he felt like letting the days go by without name or number, and he felt like exploring the South. Days of steamy heat and sassafras; days of rain and bayous and girder bridges; days of small towns melting under dust-beige skies; and deputy sheriffs with mirror-blind eyes.

The rain lashed harder and harder. Martin flicked the windshield wipers to HI, but even when the wipers were flinging themselves from side to side at top speed, they were scarcely able to cope. The evening grew suddenly so dark that Martin felt as if the highway had been overshadowed by the wing of a giant crow. *Just then flew down a monstrous crow, as black as a tar barrel* . . .

He kept driving, hoping that the storm would ease. But after nearly an hour the rain was just as furious, and lightning was crackling all around him like a plantation of tall electrified trees. He had to drive slower and slower, down to 20 mph, simply because he couldn't see where he was going. The ditches at the sides of the highway were gorged with sewage-brown water and the water suddenly began to flood across the blacktop. The Pontiac's air conditioning worked only intermittently and he had to keep wiping the inside of the windshield with his crumpled-up handkerchief. He was terrified that a truck was going to come cannon-balling out of the rain and collide with him head-on. Or—almost as bad—that another truck would rear-end him. He had seen that happen only two days ago, on Highway 331 just a few miles north of Opp. A whole family had been sent careening in their Chevy Blazer right off a bridge and down a steep embankment, where they had lain in individual depressions in the lush green weeds, bleeding, broken, screaming for help.

He had woken up in his motel room the same night and he could still hear them screaming.

Lightning crackled again, followed almost at once by a catastrophic rumble of thunder, real heaven-splitting stuff. If it were possible, the rain cascaded down harder and the floodwaters spurted and bellowed against the Pontiac's floorpan. Martin smeared the windshield with his handkerchief and strained his eyes and prayed for some kind of a turn-off where he could wait for the storm to pass.

Then, through the rain and spray and the misted-up glass of his windshield, he saw a pale illuminated blur. A light. *No*—a sign, of some kind. A green neon sign that (as he slowed and approached it) read "Sweet Gum Motor Court." And, underneath, flickering dully, the word "acancies."

O Lord I thank Thee for all Thy many favors, and in particular for the Sweet Gum Motor Court in Henry County, Alabama, with its acancies.

Martin turned off the highway and down a sloping drive-way that, in this weather, was almost a waterfall. Then ahead of him he saw an L-shaped arrangement of cabins with wooden verandahs and corrugated-iron roofing, and (on one side) an oddly-proportioned clapboard house which at first appeared to be gray but, in the sweeping light of his head-lights, turned out to be pale green. There were lights inside the house, and he could see a white-haired man in a red plaid shirt and suspenders, and (O Lord I really *do* thank Thee) the smell of hamburgs in the air.

He parked as close to the house as he could, then wrenched open the Pontiac's door and hurried with his coat tugged in a peak over his head to the brightly-lit front verandah. Even though the highway had been flooded and his wipers had struggled to keep his windshield clear, he hadn't realized fully how torrential this rainstorm was. In the few seconds it took him to cross from his car to the house he was soaked through, and the new light tan Oxfords that he had bought in Dothan were reduced to the consistency of blackened cardboard.

He opened the screen door but the main door was locked, and he jarred his wrist trying to pull it open. He rattled the doorhandle, then knocked with his wedding band on the glass. Yes, he still wore his wedding band. It gave him a ready-made excuse when pink-lipsticked strumpets slid up onto barstools next to him and asked him in those cheap husky accents if he needed a little friendship, sugar.

He didn't need friendship. He needed hot timeless days, and miniscule communities where it was interesting to watch flies walking up a window, and electric storms like this; the catharsis of being unimportant, and adrift.

The white-haired man in the red plaid shirt came to the door and somehow he was uglier and less welcoming than he had appeared through the rain. He had a face that would have looked better the other way, chinside up, like Old Man Muffaroo. Dull-brown suspicious eyes that reminded Martin of olives left on a lunch counter too long.

"What do you want?" he shouted through the glass.

"What do you think I want?" Martin shouted back. "Look at me! I'm soaked! I need a room!"

The white-haired man stared at him without answering, as if Martin had spoken a foreign language. Then a big henna-haired woman in a green dress appeared behind him, and Martin could hear her say, "What the hell's going on here, Vernon?"

"Fellow wants a room."

"A room?"

"That's what he said."

"Well, for God's sake, Vernon, if the fellow wants a room, then for God's sake open up that door and give him a room. You don't get any damned better, do you? You really don't."

She unlocked the door and held it wide so that Martin could step inside. As he passed her he smelled frying hamburgs, sour armpit and Avon scent.

"Hell of a storm," she said, closing and locking the door behind him. "Come through to the office, I'll fix you up."

Martin followed her along a red-lino corridor flanked with damp-stained posters for Martz Airlines' "Safe Scenic Swift Service" and vacations in Bermuda. In the office there was an untidy desk, a whirring electric fan, and a pegboard with rows of keys hanging on it. There were no keys missing so Martin assumed that he was the only guest. Not surprising, the reception that would-be customers were given by old upside-down-face Vernon.

A ragged-looking brown dog was slumbering on the floor. "Just for the night?" asked the woman, stepping over it.

"That's right," Martin told her. "I was supposed to meet somebody in Eufaula at six, but there's no hope of my getting there now." As if to reassure him that he had made the right decision by stopping here, the rain rattled noisily against the window, and the dog stirred in its sleep. Dreaming of quail, maybe; or hamburgs.

Vernon was standing just outside the office, scratching the eczema on his elbow. "You'll find plenty of peace here, mister. You won't be disturbed."

Martin signed his name in the register. The pages were deckled with damp. "Anyplace I can get something to eat?"

The woman peered at his signature. Then she said, "Used to be a diner down the road about a half-mile did good ribs but that closed. Owner blew his head off with a shotgun. Business being so bad and all."

She looked up at him, aware that she hadn't yet answered his question. "But I can rustle you some eggs 'n' bacon or cornbeef hash or something of that nature."

"Maybe some eggs and bacon," said Martin. "Now . . . maybe I can get myself dried off and use the telephone."

The woman unhooked one of the keys, handed it to Vernon. "Number Two'll do best. It's closer to the office and the bed's new."

She unlocked the front door and Vernon led him out into the rain again. The concrete parking lot was awash with floodwater and bright brown silt. Martin heaved his overnight case out of the trunk of the Pontiac and then followed Vernon across to the first row of cabins. Vernon stood hunched in front of the door with his white hair dripping, trying to find the right way to turn the key. At last he managed to open up and switch on the light.

Number Two was a drab room with a sculptured red carpet and a mustard-colored bedspread. There were two dimly-shaded lamps beside the bed and another on the cheap varnished desk. Martin put down his case and offered Vernon a dollar bill, but Vernon waved it away. "That's not necessary, mister; not here, on a night like this. So long as you pay before you go." It occurred to Martin that—almost uniquely for these days—the woman hadn't taken an impression of his credit card.

"Food won't be long," said Vernon. "You want any drinks or anything? Beer maybe?"

"A couple of lites would go down well."

Vernon frowned around the room. "These lights ain't sufficient?"

"No, no. I mean 'lites' like in 'lite beer.'"

"Lite beer," Vernon repeated, as if Martin had said something totally mysterious, but he was too polite to ask what it meant.

"Miller Lite, Coors Lite; anything."

"Coors Lite," Vernon repeated, in the same baffled way.

He left, closing the door firmly behind him. It had swollen slightly in the downpour and needed to be tugged. With a loud, elaborate, extended sigh, Martin raked back his wet hair with his fingers, lifted off his dark-shouldered coat, and loosened his wet necktie with a squeak that set his teeth on edge almost as much as fingernails on slate.

He pushed open the door to the bathroom and found dismal green-painted walls and a shower curtain decorated with faded tropical fish. But there were four large towels folded up on the shelf, three of them marked "Holiday Inn" and the fourth marked "Tropicana Hotel, Key Largo." He stripped and dried himself, and then dressed in clean pajamas and blue silk bathrobe, and combed his hair. He wished that Vernon would hurry up with that beer: his throat was dry and he felt that he might be catching a cold.

He looked around for the TV. Maybe there was a cable movie he could watch tonight. But to his surprise there was no TV. He couldn't believe it. What kind of a motel had rooms with no TV? The only entertainment available was a pack of sexy playing cards and an old Zenith radio. *Shit.*

He pulled open the cabin door and looked outside. The rain was still thundering down. A rain barrel under the next row of cabins was noisily overflowing and somewhere a broken gutter was splattering. No sign of Vernon. No sign of anything but this shabby huddle of cabins and the dim green light that said acancies.

He wedged the door shut. He thought of all the times that he had cursed Howard Johnson's for their sameness and their lack of luxury. But a Howard Johnson's would have been paradise compared with the Sweet Gum Motor Court. All it was doing was keeping him safely off the highway and the rain off his head.

He sat down at the desk and picked up the telephone. After a long, crackling pause, the voice of the henna-haired woman said, "You want something, mister?"

"Yes, I do. I want to place a call to a number in Eufaula—

Chattahoochee Moldings, Inc. Person-to-person to Mr. Dick Bogdanovich."

"I'm frying your eggs 'n' bacon. What do you want first, your call or your eggs 'n' bacon?"

"Well . . . I really need to make this call. He usually leaves the office at seven-thirty."

"Eggs'll spoil, if they haven't already."

"Can't I dial the number myself?"

"'Fraid not, not from the cabins. Otherwise we'd have guests calling their long-lost sweethearts in Athens, Georgia, and chewing the fat for an hour at a time with their folks back in Wolf Point, Montana, wouldn't we, and the profit in this business is too tight for that."

"Ma'am, all I want to do is make a single fifteen-second telephone call to Eufaula, to inform my client that I shan't be able to make our meeting this evening. That's a little different from an hour-long call to—Wolf Point, Montana." *Thinking:* what on earth had inspired her to say "Wolf Point, Montana?"

"I'm sorry, you can't dial direct from the cabins; and I can smell eggwhite burning."

The phone clicked and then he heard nothing but a sizzling sound. It could have been static, it could have been frying. It didn't much matter. Frying and static were equally useless to him.

His eggs and bacon eventually arrived at a quarter after eight. Vernon brought them across from the office building under a rain-beaded aluminum dish-cover. Vernon himself was covered by an Army surplus parka, dark khaki with wet.

"Rain, rain, goddamned rain," said Vernon. He set the plate down on the desk.

"No knife and fork," said Martin. "No beer."

"Oh, I got it all here," Vernon told him, and fumbled in the pockets of his parka. He produced knife, fork, paper napkins, salt, pepper, catsup, and three chilled bottles of Big 6 Beer.

"Denise fried the eggs over, on account of them being burned."

Martin raised the aluminum cover. The eggs and bacon looked remarkably good: heaps of thin crisp rashers, three big farm eggs, sunnyside up; toast, fried tomatoes, and hash browns; and lots of crispy bits. "Tell her thanks."

"She'll charge you for them, the extra eggs."

"That's okay. Tell her thanks."

After Vernon had gone, wedging the door shut again, Martin propped himself up in bed with his supper balanced in his lap, and switched on the radio. It took a few moments for it to warm up: then the dial began to glow, and he smelled that extraordinary nostalgic smell of hot dust that his grandmother's Zenith had always given off whenever it heated up.

He twisted the brown bakelite tuning knob but most of the dial produced nothing but weird alien whistlings and whoopings, or a fierce sizzling noise, or voices that were so blippy and blotchy that it was impossible to understand what they were saying. As he prodded his fork into his second egg, however, he suddenly picked up a voice that was comparatively crisp.

"*. . . Eight-thirty, Eastern Time . . . and this is the Song O' The South Soda Hour . . . coming to you from the Dauphin Street Studios in Mobile, Alabama . . . continuing our dramatization of . . . 'The Heart of Helen Day'. . . with Randy Pressburger . . . John McLaren . . . Susan Medici . . . and starring, as Helen Day . . . Andrea Lawrence . . . "*

Martin turned the dial further but all he could find were more fizzes, more pops, and a very faint jazz rendition of the old Negro ballad *Will the Circle Be Unbroken*.

"*. . . in the same old window, on a cold and cloudy day . . . I seen them hearse wheels rolling . . . they was taking Chief Jolly away . . .*

He decided that he could do without a funeral dirge, so

he turned back to *The Heart of Helen Day*. This turned out to be a chatty romantic radio-soap about a busybody girl who worked for a tough-talking private detective and kept losing her heart to his clients, even though the tough-talking private detective really loved her more than anybody else.

Martin finished his supper and drank two bottles of beer and listened to the serial in amusement. It sounded incredibly 1930s, with all the actors talking in brisk, clipped voices like *One Man's Family* or the *Chase & Sanborn Hour*.

"*But he's not guilty, I tell you. I just know hers not guilty.*"

"*How can you know? You don't have any proof?*"

"*I searched his eyes, that's all.*"

"*You searched his eyes but I searched his hotel room.*"

"*Oh, Mickey. I looked in his face and all I saw was innocence.*"

"*You looked in his face? That's unusual. I never knew you looked any higher than a man's wallet.*"

This week's episode concerned a famous bandleader who had been accused of throwing a beautiful but faithless singer out of the seventh floor window of a downtown hotel. The bandleader's alibi was that he had been conducting a recording session at the time. But Helen Day suspected he had used a stand-in.

Martin got up off the bed and went to the door, opened it. The room was becoming stuffy and smelled of food. He put his plate out on the boardwalk, where it rapidly filled with rain and circles of grease.

"*It couldn't have been Philip, Philip always taps the rostrum three times with his baton before he starts to conduct . . . and in this recording the conductor doesn't tap the rostrum at all.*"

Martin stayed by the door, leaning against the jamb, watching the rain barrel overflow and the silty mud forming a Mississippi delta in the parking lot, and the distant dancing of the lightning. Behind him the radio chattered, with occasional melodramatic bursts of music, and interruptions for commercials.

"'The Heart of Helen Day' is brought to you by Song O' The South Soda . . . the fruitier, more refreshing soda that makes the whole South sing . . . "

Then it was back to Helen Day. She was talking at a cocktail party about her success in solving the case of Philip the rostrum-tapping bandleader. Martin drank his third and last beer out of the bottle and wondered why the radio station had even considered broadcasting such a stilted, outdated radio soap, when there was *Get a Life* and *The Simpsons* on TV and wall-to-wall FM. Everyplace except here, of course; the Sweet Gum Motor Court, in Henry County, Alabama, in the rain.

"He was so handsome. Yet I knew that he was wicked, underneath."

Suddenly, there was the sound of a door banging in the background. Then the clatter of something falling over. A muffled voice said, "Get out of here, you can't come in here, we're recording!" Then another shout and a blurt of thick static as if somebody had knocked the microphone.

At first, Martin thought this must be part of the plot. But the shouting and struggling were so indistinct that he realized quickly there must be an intruder in the radio studio, a *real* intruder, and that the actors and technicians were trying to subdue him. There was another jumble of sound and then an extraordinarily long-drawn-out scream, rising higher and higher, increasingly hysterical.

Then the most terrible thing Martin had ever heard in his life. He turned away from the open door to stare at the radio with his eyes wide and his scalp prickling with horror.

"Oh God! Oh God! John! John! Oh God help me! He's cut me open! Oh God! My stomach's falling out!"

A noise like somebody dropping a sodden bath towel. Then more shouts, and more thumps. A nasal, panicky voice shouting, "Ambulance! For Christ's sake, Jeff! Get an ambulance!" Then a sharp blip—and the program was cut off.

Martin sat on the bed beside the radio waiting for the program to come back on the air, or some kind of announcement by the radio station. But there was nothing but white noise which went on and on and on, like a bus journey along an endless and unfamiliar highway through thick fog.

He tried retuning the radio but all he got were the same old crackles as before, or those distant foggy Negroes singing. *"I saw the . . . hearse wheels rolling . . . they were taking my . . . mother away . . . "* Did they always sing the same dirge?

Sometime after eleven o'clock he switched off the radio, washed his teeth, and climbed into bed. But all night he lay listening to the rain and thinking of *The Heart of Helen Day*. He guessed if an actress had really been attacked in a radio studio he'd hear about it on tomorrow's news. Maybe it had all been part of the soap. But—up until that moment—it had sounded so normal and correct, even if it had been ridiculously dated. Maybe it had been one of those *War of the Worlds-type* gimmicks, to frighten the listeners.

Or maybe it had actually happened, and Helen Day had really had her heart cut out.

He was awakened at seven o'clock by Vernon tapping at the door. Outside it was lighter but still raining, although not so heavily. Vernon brought pancakes and syrup and hot coffee. He set them down on the desk and sniffed.

"Thanks," said Martin, sleepily smearing his face with his hands. "Don't mention it."

"Hey . . . before you go . . . did you watch the news this morning?"

"The news?"

"The TV news . . . you know, like what's happening in the world?"

Vernon shook his head, suspiciously.

"Well . . . did you hear about any radio actress being murdered?"

Vernon said, "No . . . I didn't hear anything like that. But what I did hear, the highway's all washed out between here and Eufaula, and 54 between Lawrenceville and Edwin's washed out, too. So you'll have to double back to Graball and take 51 through Clio. That's if you're still inclined to go to Eufaula, can't stick the place myself."

"No," said Martin, sipping coffee. "I don't think I can, either."

When he had finished his breakfast Martin packed his traveling bag and looked around the room to make sure he hadn't left anything behind. He stood by the open door listening to the rain clattering from the gutters and stared at the radio. Had he dreamed it? Maybe he would never know.

He put down his bag, walked across to the radio and switched it on. After it had warmed up, he heard a stream of static; but then—so abruptly that it made him jump—an announcer's voice said, *"'—of Helen Day,' brought to you by Song O' The South Soda . . . "*

He listened raptly, standing in the middle of the room with the door open. It was the same episode as last night, the story of the bandleader who didn't tap the rostrum. Then, the same words: *"He was so handsome. Yet I knew that he was wicked, underneath."*

Then again, the door opening. The shouts. The microphone knocked. Scuffles, screams. And that terrible, terrible cry of agony, *"Oh God! Oh God! John! John! Oh God help me! He's cut me open! Oh God! My stomach's falling out!"*

Then, nothing. Only crackling and shushing and occasional spits of static.

Martin swallowed dryly. Was that a repeat? Was it the news? If it was the news, how come there was no commentary? He stood with his hand over his mouth wondering what to do.

* * *

He drove into Mobile late that evening. The sky was purple and there was still a strong feeling of electricity in the air. That day, he had driven on Highway 10 all the way across north Florida, and as he made the final crossing of Polecat Bay toward the glittering water-distorted lights of the docks, he felt stiff and cramped and ready for nothing but a stiff drink and a night of undisturbed sleep. But first of all, he was determined to find the Dauphin Street radio studios.

It took him over an hour. The Dauphin Street Studios weren't in the phone book. Two cops he stopped hadn't heard of it, either, although they asked in a tight, suspicious drawl to look at his driver's license and registration. Eventually, however, he stopped at a bar called the Cat's Pajamas, a noisy, crowded place close to the intersection with Florida Street, and asked the bartender, whose bald head shone oddly blue in the light from the shelves, as if he were an alien.

"Dauphin Street Studios closed down before the war. Nineteen forty-one, maybe nineteen forty-two. But ask Harry. He used to work there when he was younger, studio technician or something. There he is; second booth along."

Harry turned out to be a neat, retired character with cropped white hair, a sallow face, and a whispery way of talking. Martin sat down opposite him. "Understand you worked at the Dauphin Street Studios?"

Harry looked at him oddly. "What kind of a question is that?"

"I'm interested in something that might have happened there."

"Well . . . the last broadcast that went out from the Dauphin Street Studios was March 7, 1941; that was when WMOB went bust. That was a lifetime ago."

"Do you want a drink?" Martin asked him.

"For sure. Wild Turkey, on the rocks."

"Do you remember a soap called *The Heart of Helen Day?*"

There was a long silence. Then Harry said, "Sure I do. Everybody remembers *The Heart of Helen Day*. That program was part of the reason that WMOB had to close down.

"Tell me."

Harry shrugged. "Not much to tell. The girl who played Helen Day was real pretty. I never saw a girl so pretty, before or since. Andrea Lawrence. Blonde, bright. I was in love with her; but then, so was everybody else. She used to get all kinds of weird mail and phone calls. In those days you could still be a radio star, and of course you got all the crank stuff that went with being a star. One day, Andrea started getting death threats. Very sick phone calls that said things like, 'I'm going to gut you, you harlot.' Stuff like that."

Martin said, "It really happened, then? She really was murdered in the studio?"

"Most horrible thing I ever saw in my life. I was only a kid . . . well, nineteen. I had nightmares about it for years afterward. A guy burst into the studio. I never even saw the knife, although the cops said it was huge, a real hog-butchering knife. He stuck it in her lower abdomen and whipped it upwards—so quick that I thought he was punching her. Then her entire insides came out, all over the studio floor. Just like that. I had nightmares about it for years."

Martin licked his lips. He didn't seem to have any saliva at all. "Did they catch him? The guy who killed her?"

Harry shook his head. "There was too much confusion. Everybody was too shocked. Before we knew what had happened, he was gone. The cops went through the city with a fine-tooth comb, but they never found him. *The Heart of Helen Day* was canceled, of course; and after that, WMOB gradually fell apart and went out of business. Not that television wasn't slowly killing it already."

"Was there a recording of that broadcast?" Martin asked.

Harry said, "Sure. We recorded everything."

"Do you think somebody could be transmitting it again?"

"What?"

"I've heard it. I've heard the episode where she gets murdered. I've heard the whole thing . . . even when she says 'Oh God, he's cut my stomach open.'"

"That's impossible."

"I *heard* it. Not just once, but twice."

Harry stared at Martin as if he were mad. "That's totally impossible. For one thing, there was only one recording, and that was my master tape; and my master tape was destroyed in a fire along with all of WMOB's other tapes, in January, 1942. Insurance arson, if you ask me. But I saw the burned spool myself.

"For another thing, I jumped up as soon as the guy came into the studio and accidentally switched off the tape recorder. The actual killing was never recorded. If you heard it, my friend—you were hearing ghosts."

"Ghosts? I don't think so. I heard it clear as a bell."

"Well . . . you're not the only one who's heard stuff from the past. I was reading the other day some guy in Montana picked up his dead mother arguing with his dead father on his car radio whenever it thundered."

Martin had been ready to leave, but now he leaned forward and said to Harry, "Whenever it *thundered?* How?"

"I don't know. It sounds far-fetched. But the theory is that the human brain records things it hears as electrical impulses, right? Normally, it *keeps* them stored. But in certain atmospheric conditions, it *discharges* those impulses . . . so strongly that they can get picked up by a radio receiver. In this case, the guy's car radio. But apparently they have to be real close. Seventy or eighty feet away, not much more."

Seventy or eighty feet away. Who had been seventy or eighty feet away from that old Zenith radio when it thundered? Who had been old enough and unhinged enough to have attacked Andrea Lawrence all those years ago in the Dauphin Street Studios? Who wouldn't have been found in the city because, maybe, he didn't actually live *in the city?*

There was no proof. No proof at all. But apart from the

actors and the radio technicians, only the killer would have heard Andrea Lawrence's last words . . . only the killer would have remembered them. So that one thundery night, nearly forty years later, they would have come crackling out on an old-fashioned radio set. Not a program at all, but a *memory*.

It was late in the afternoon and unbearably steamy when Martin drove his mud-splattered Pontiac back to the Sweet Gum Motor Court. There was a strong smell of drying mud and chicken feed in the air. He parked and wearily climbed out.

He knocked at the screen door. He had to wait a long time before anybody answered. The ragged tan dog sat not far away, and watched him, and panted. Eventually Vernon appeared and unlocked the door.

"You again," he said.

"Is Denise around?"

"What do you want her for?"

"To tell you the truth, it's *you* I wanted."

"Oh yeah?"

"I just wanted to ask you a couple of questions about Andrea Lawrence. You ever heard of Andrea Lawrence? She played Helen Day, in *The Heart of Helen Day*."

Long silence. Eyes dull as olives behind the reflective glass. Then the key, turning in the lock. "You'd best come on in. Go in the office. I won't keep you more 'n a couple of minutes."

The tired-looking redhead took the barrettes out of her hair and shook it loose. On the desk, the remains of her evening meal had attracted the attention of two persistent flies. She picked up the whisky glass and swallowed, and coughed.

She couldn't believe there was no TV here. If it hadn't

been such a stormy night, she would have driven further, to someplace decent. But half the roads were flooded out and she was frightened of lightning.

She switched on the radio. Fuzzy jazz, dance music, some kind of black funeral song. Then two voices in what sounded like a radio play. She lay back on the bed and closed her eyes and listened. If only her husband could see her now.

"You again."

"Is Denise around?"

"What do you want her for?"

"To tell you the truth, it's you I wanted."

The woman sipped more whisky. Outside, the thunder banged grumpily, and the rain started to gush down more heavily.

"I heard something pretty curious on my radio last night."

"Oh yeah?"

"I heard—hey, what are you doing? What the hell do you think you're doing? Get away from—aahh! Jesus Christ! Aaaaggggh! Jesus Christ! You've cut me! Oh Jesus Christ you've cut me open!"

Muffled knocks. A sound like a chair falling over. An indescribable splattering. Then an awful gasping. *"Help me, for Christ's sake. Help me!"*

"Help you what? Help you get me and Denise put away for murder? Or a nuthouse or something?"

"Help me, Jesus, it hurts so much!"

"And didn't it hurt Denise, to listen to that Helen Day every single week, and how Helen Day got men just by winking her eye, and Denise's only fiancé left her high and dry for a girl just like that? Same given name, too—Andrea! Don't you think that hurt?"

"Help me, Vernon."

"Help you nothing. You're all the same. Leaving Denise for your fancy-women."

There was a cry like an owl being dismembered alive by a coyote. Then nothing but white noise, on and on and on.

The woman was already asleep. The white noise continued through the night, like an endless bus journey along an unfamiliar highway, through thick fog.

Nothing But the Best

Brian McNaughton

"You're ugly, you're creepy, you're the filthiest man I ever knew!" Jessica Sexton cried.

"Yes." Ahab Wakefield's head was meekly bowed to hide the fury in his eyes. "But I'm rich."

"And that's the filthiest thing you ever said!"

She flung back his gifts. The emerald necklace bit his cheek. The tiger-skin coat she hurled shrouded him momentarily in the ghost of its original owner's clutch.

"No, please keep them," he said, "they're—"

"Impossible to explain to my husband."

He learned that her laugh could be splendidly scornful. He had possessed only her body, and she had so much more to offer—but it was hopeless.

"Impossible to explain . . . like so much else." Having admitted the futility of his love, he allowed his lips to relax into their most comfortable sneer. "How do you propose to explain why you left him? And what you've been doing all this while?"

"Bruce will forgive me. And even if he doesn't, I can go to any hospital for the criminally insane and find a hundred better men than you'll ever be. You don't know . . . *anything.* Did you really think you could impress me with this?" Her toe, perfect to its pallid lunula, nudged the coat with disdain.

"You deserve nothing but the best."

"Do you know how few of these magnificent creatures are left in the world? To kill one of them for a lousy coat—that disgusts me even more than you do."

Ahab sighed, admitting his miscalculation. The greatest burden of his long life, he often thought, was trying to keep up with current fads.

"But there is only one Jessica." The pain of that truth drove him to his knees.

"Very bad." She spoke with critical detachment. "Sometimes I think you learned how people behave from watching silent movies. What I ever could have seen in you, why I should have left the husband I love so much . . . " She paused, as if realizing that these questions had no sane answers. "This hogwash"—her gesture included ancient volumes on swaybacked shelves, dried herbs and fungi hanging from the ceiling-beams, the uniquely malformed skull on his desk—"it doesn't really *work,* does it?"

He rose deliberately to his commanding height and gazed down on her with less warmth than a corpse from a gibbet. "You will see."

Fright was another emotion Jessica had not shown him, and she expressed it fetchingly. As she fled, Ahab vowed to see more.

He had indulged this folly before, and with the same result. To win a love freely given, he had released Chastity Hopkins, of Portsmouth, N.H., from a similar enchantment in 1652. She had called him a pig-swaying pissabed and scurried off to lodge a complaint of witchcraft. Jessica Sexton had no such recourse. In some small ways, the world had changed for the better.

"When will I learn?"

Thester, the malapert creature that nested in the skull, croaked: "Nevermore."

Ignoring his familiar, Ahab took a knife from his desk

and cut a strip of tiger-skin long enough to bind his cadaverous waist. He had no qualms about ruining the fabulously expensive coat. Cheating fools was his hobby, and he had paid the furrier with illusory cash. That he had not given Jessica an illusory coat proved the depth of his sincerity. It was fitting that the rejected love-token should be his instrument of vengeance.

"Master!" Thester's agitated claws rattled the skull. "Master, give her the pox, give her the flux, afflict her with some cagastrical distemper beyond the skill of the most learned surgeons—"

"Death by dismemberment and ingestion," Ahab said as he assembled further materials, "is beyond their skill."

"Remember what happened in Avignon in 1329?"

"Avignon? My memory . . . "

"That time you turned into a wolf to assassinate Pope John XXII. And the gamekeeper who sold you the wolfhide belt neglected to inform you that the animal had died after chewing off its trapped leg. Whereupon you learned—"

"Yes, yes, yes!" Ahab snapped, having remembered.

"—whereupon you learned that a three-legged wolf is no match for a pack of hounds. You had to spend the Renaissance in bed."

It was true that Ahab would assume the form of the particular beast whose pelt he used. He gave the strip of fur a covert inspection, but it told him nothing. He would have to translate himself to Malaysia to trace the provenance of the hide, and that might take hours. He dismissed Thester's quibbles.

"My dear abomination, a three-legged tiger—even one that's blind and toothless to boot—will be all that's needed for our loving young couple."

"And their dog?"

He winced. Shape-changing was a young man's game, and Ahab was no longer the sprightly bicentenarian who had disported himself as a crocodile among the wading courtlings of Nitokris. He had feared dogs ever since the

Avignon fiasco, but he had forgotten the Sextons' pet, a Doberman pinscher who had in its last life commanded—with notably more audacity than brains—an SS panzer division. Unaware of this background, Jessica had christened it Muffin.

Climbing over the doomed couple's back fence, Ahab was thankful for Thester's reminder. Forewarned, he had rendered himself not just invisible, but inaudible and inodorous. Even so the dog sprang from its doze on the patio and paced the backyard, tunelessly growling the dimly recalled Curse-motif from Wagner's *Ring*. Ahab would never admit to Thester that he'd spared him an embarrassment, but he resolved to find the little horror an especially roly-poly child soon.

He stripped to the furry belt, opened a vein unseen, and made the appropriate symbols in blood on the flagstones of the patio. The dog sprinted and snarled at random shadows as Ahab crouched on all fours and spoke the required words.

Instantly the vigor of a healthy young beast surged through him. The formerly still night echoed with racketing bats and clamorous moths. The neutral smell of the yard was submerged under a canine stench so vivid and frightening that it hurt. It was the memory of Avignon that pained him, of course, potentiated by even the biggest cat's hatred for its old enemy.

As the other enchantments were canceled and Ahab stood revealed in all his fearful symmetry, the stupid dog charged. Ahab's sharper eyes, no doubt, made the puny creature seem like a black and tan locomotive bearing down on him, but he stood his ground and drew back his paw to blast Muffin's bones to gravel.

"What in hell was that?" Bruce Sexton gasped.
"Does it matter?" Jessica tried to draw him down again.

"I guess—" A second piteous cry froze him in the act of being drawn. He tumbled from bed and ran to switch on the patio lights.

"My God! Look—no, *don't* look, Jess. Muffin's got hold of something, a . . ."

"A what?"

Not believing his eyes, he forced them again toward the patio. "It must've been somebody's pet," he said. "But what kind of a nut would dye a rabbit with orange and black stripes?"

Somewhere

Denise Dumars

The grope and blink of sun versus night
is all one, really.
Somewhere it is always midnight
somewhere it is always dawn
somewhere there is always someone
pleading with the gods,
throwing the bone,
scourging the back.

Dogs boil out of the kennel
lights refuse to stop blinking.
So much for the Tarot,
so much for the future,
so much for the reason to raze
the hate from each breast.

Over a field of daisies
an aeroplane falls down.
Heads splat amongst the foliage
in a dewy afternoon,
and sunflowers turn their heads
to the momentary streak of silver
lighting up the sky before the bird descends.

Local women burn the field days later,
and the children who have eaten
of the sunflowers, unbeknownst
to their mothers, begin
to grow extra limbs.

Sitting in the shade
with black glasses on, I drop
my withered hand into the hat.
I draw out two cards, six dice,
and a bundle of dried wheatstraw.
I throw the straw and the wind takes it
and it grows like morning light
and all over the town great shocks of wheat
erupt through gardens and garages,
break the soil and stun like ball lightning.

Everyone who knows me
dons black glasses and
pretends not to see.

Milestone's Face

Gary Brandner

Georgie the makeup man applied sooty smudges under the blazing blue eyes of Stuart Milestone. He thumbed ghost-gray under the cheekbones to impart a hollow look to Milestone's firm, ruddy cheeks. He carefully penciled lines from the flare of the nostrils to the corners of the determined mouth. Finally Georgie stood back, cocked his head, and studied his work.

"It's a real challenge to make you look like a bum, Mr. Milestone."

"Homeless person, Georgie. We don't have bums any more."

"Oh, right. It's still a chore. I mean, even your stubble looks healthy." Milestone flashed the grin that kept The Big Six News at the top of the local ratings among female viewers. "This will be the last time," he said. "We wrap the series today. A week from Monday it goes on the air in time for sweeps month."

"We all think you've got a winner," Georgie said.

"I'd love to see their reaction over at Eyewitness News when we hit them with social consciousness. They're still doing T and A. Times have changed. People want *real*. They want to feel the grit, smell the dirt. That's what we're going to give them."

A short knock at the door of the makeup cubicle, and a tall young man with a long, serious face entered.

"Stuart, I've made a couple of changes in your close for tonight. Want to look it over?"

"What for? Just make sure the cue cards are legible."

The younger man started to leave.

"Oh, say, Alan, I meant to tell you you've been doing a fine job filling for me this week."

"Thanks."

"But don't get too good. I figure I've got a few more seasons before you take over as anchor." Milestone laughed to show he was joking.

Alan Baird laughed because he knew Milestone was serious.

The last day of shooting on Skid Row went without a hitch. The Channel 6 camera van, its logo painted over with a grubby brown, went undetected parked in a loading zone. During the week only one local, a wheezy derelict called Walter, had recognized Stuart Milestone. Fred Keneally, the producer, gave him ten dollars to shut up and go away.

In the cramped interior of the van Keneally and Alan Baird watched Stuart Milestone on the monitor. Camera and Sound concentrated on their equipment while a young production assistant waited for orders.

For this segment Milestone was pretending to be a panhandler. He was not doing well. Real panhandlers knew better than to work a street where there was no money.

"He makes a convincing bum, wouldn't you say?" Alan observed.

Keneally looked at him. "Do I detect a note of jealousy?"

"Not me. We know who the star is. My time will come."

On the monitor screen Milestone turned to face the camera and gave the finger-across-the-throat sign.

"That's it," Keneally said. "Let's go outside and set up for the closing speech. Dexter, got the cue cards?"

The production assistant jumped to attention. "Got 'em, Mr. Keneally."

"Wait a minute, what's he doing?"

Out on the street Milestone saw a woman approaching him. She was a perfect bag lady specimen—eroded face, bent-over walk, stringy hair hanging from a motheaten fedora. She wore several baggy sweaters, a black skirt that hung to her swollen ankles, grubby sneakers. Milestone flashed the sign to the camera van to keep rolling.

The woman walked up close and gave him a blast of winebreath. "You're new on the street, aren't you, honey?" Her voice rattled with phlegm.

Milestone nodded, sinking back into the homeless character he had played over the past few days.

"I'm Jessie. I know about everybody on the street, and I knowed you was new. What's your name?"

"They call me Whitey. I been in town most of a week."

"Where you from?"

"Lots of places. Minneapolis last," Milestone said, using the bio Alan Baird had worked up for his character.

"Cold back there, I'll bet."

"Yeah, cold." Milestone shifted his position so the camera could get an open shot at the women while picking up his best profile. "Tell me about yourself, Bessie."

"That's Jessie." She looked away and back in an oddly girlish gesture. Milestone found her eyes disturbing. Black and lustrous as ripe olives, they did not belong in that wreck of a face. "Ain't much to tell. I been around here most of my life. I do what I can to get along."

"What about your family?"

She gave him a gap-toothed laugh. "Hell, I got no family. The people here on the street are my family. How about you?"

"Nobody," Milestone said, spreading it on. "All alone."

"You don't look like a bad guy, Whitey. You got a place to flop?"

He shrugged. "Just, you know, doorways. The alley. Like that."

"You want to come up to my place? I got a nice room. Stove and sink and everything. You could stay until you get yourself set up."

Milestone bit down on a knuckle, trying to look thoughtful as he fought to keep from laughing. "That's nice of you, Jessie, but I couldn't—"

"Hey, don't worry about it. I got food up there. I'll bet you'd like a hot meal. And I got a bottle of wine. Nearly full."

"That sure sounds good." He pointed at a sputtering neon sign across the street. "How about if I meet you over there at the Horseshoe Bar at, say, eight o'clock?"

The woman's grimy face split in a grin. "Like a date, huh, Whitey? Okeydoke. I'll go on home and get fixed up." She shuffled off down the street, looking back once to flutter her gnarled fingers at him.

Once she had rounded the corner Milestone sat down on the curb and yanked off the stocking cap that had concealed his thick blond hair. He smacked his knee and laughed until tears blurred the dark makeup under his eyes.

Keneally and Alan Baird came across from the van accompanied by young Dexter with the cue cards.

"What was that for?" the producer said.

"It was too good to pass up," Milestone said, getting to his feet, still laughing. "Did you catch that old bat coming on to me? It will make a great scene."

Alan cleared his throat. "Don't you think that's a little cruel? She was just trying to do something nice for you."

"Nice? Bullshit. She wanted my body. *'I got a bottle of wine. Nearly full.'* Can you believe that?"

"I don't like it," Alan said.

"Hey, Mr. Sensitivity, if it will make you feel better I'll slip the old bat a few bucks tonight, okay?"

"Tonight? You're going to keep the date?"

"Oh, hell yes. It will make the party. Picture the look on

the crone's face when she sees me without the tramp getup and realizes she made a date with Stuart Milestone. Beautiful! Fred, tell everybody the crew party will be over there at the Horseshoe Bar. This is going to be priceless."

Alan turned and walked back to the van. Fred Keneally looked after him with a worried expression.

"He'll be all right," Milestone said. "His nose is out of joint because I ad libbed the bit with Jessie. He doesn't think I can talk unless he puts the words in my mouth." He ran a comb through his hair. "Let's shoot the final speech. I want to get cleaned up."

Someone clutched at his jacked and wheezed, "Mr. Milestone?" He turned to see Walter, the bum who had recognized him the first day.

"What do you want? Didn't you get paid off?"

"Oh, yes sir, no problem. I just wanted to tell you that you ought to be, well, careful about fooling with old Jessie."

"Careful? What are you talking about?"

"I heard what you were saying just now, couldn't help it. And you oughtn't to play a joke like that on Jessie. She wouldn't like it."

"So what?"

"She's a witch."

"Hell, I could see that."

"No, I mean she's a *witch*. A real one."

"A witch," Milestone repeated slowly.

"That's right. She doesn't make any trouble for us down here, but I've heard stories. If you go ahead and do her like you were sayin', well . . . " Walter let his voice trail off.

"Gee, thanks a lot for the warning, fella. I'll sure be on my guard." Milestone rolled his eyes and brushed Walter aside to join the others at the van.

The Big Six News took over one end of the Horseshoe Bar for Stuart Milestone's wrap party. They had just watched a tape of Milestone's encounter with Jessie. They looked to the boss for his reaction before venturing their own.

Stuart Milestone, freshly bathed and barbered, laughed. The others, with a couple of exceptions, laughed with him.

"Isn't she marvelous?" he said. "Wait till you see her in person." He shot a cuff to consult his Rolex. "Hey, it's after eight. You don't suppose I've been stood up? Stuart Milestone left waiting at the bar by the ugliest thing ever to put on a skirt. How embarrassing!"

The party people were laughing so hard, again with a couple of exceptions, that nobody saw her when she first stood up from the high-backed booth where she had been sitting. One by one they looked over there, and as they did the laughter died.

Her drab hair was washed and combed straight down. She wore a dress that was thirty years out of date, but clean. There was a dab of rouge on each withered cheek. The black lustrous eyes, the eyes that did not belong in the old face, reached into the soul of each and every one present, settling at last on Stuart Milestone. The silence was deep as a grave. After a long, long minute she turned and walked away from the party and out the door.

For a dozen heartbeats nobody moved. Then Alan Baird stood suddenly.

"Excuse me," he said, and followed Jessie out the door.

"Hey!" Milestone called after him. "Hey, Alan, where do you think you're going?"

The younger man went out into the night without responding.

"Aah, who needs a skeleton at the feast, anyway? Drink up, guys, the boss has deep pockets tonight."

But the fun was gone. The joke was stillborn. After ten minutes even Stuart Milestone heard the false note of his crew's laughter. "Let's call it a night," he said. "This place is depressing."

The Big Six News party straggled out of the bar, paying no attention to the lone figure standing in the shadows. When

Milestone came out she stepped into the light to block his path. The thin old lips with their pitiful dabbed-on color drew back to expose stained and crooked teeth. The black, ageless eyes blazed. In one hand she held a small jar of dark red liquid.

"You didn't want my wine," she said in a dead level voice. "Try *this!*" She splashed the contents of the glass into Milestone's face and vanished into the night.

He staggered back against the building. Half a dozen handkerchiefs were whipped out to wipe away the fluid.

"What is it?"

"Wine?"

"Blood?"

"Get away from me," Milestone ordered. The others backed off and he scrubbed at his face with his own mono-grammed kerchief.

"Are you all right, Stuart?" Keneally asked.

Milestone touched his face gingerly, first on one side then the other. "Yeah, I'm fine. For a minute there I thought the crazy old broad threw acid on me. Come on, let's get out of this sewer."

He slept poorly that night, troubled by dreams of ugly people pursuing him down an endless Skid Row. He awoke Saturday with a sour taste in his mouth and a slight but per-sistent headache. The symptoms were those of a light hangover, though Milestone had drunk nothing stronger than club soda.

He shuffled into the bathroom and began brushing his teeth. In mid-stroke he stopped and leaned close to the glass. Under his neon blue eyes were smudges of brown that definitely did not belong. Leftover traces of makeup? He wiped at his face with a damp cloth. The smudges remained.

Too much time on Skid Row, he decided. He switched his thoughts to the future. Monday he'd be back at the anchor desk, and a week later they'd be showing the homeless spe-cial. Big ratings were assured, and possibly an Emmy. Then he could sit back and wait for offers from the networks.

Milestone went back to bed, slept most of the day away, and felt better when he awoke at dusk. A good dinner with attractive company, and he'd be 100 percent again. He flipped through his Rolodex and chose Chelsea Porter, a bosomy swimsuit model whose dark beauty complemented his blond good looks. Chelsea aspired to a television career and believed Milestone could help her. He did nothing to discourage the idea.

She was ready when he arrived at her apartment. She was stunning, as usual, in a form-fitting blue-black dress. Her smile slipped a notch as she opened the door.

"Something wrong?" he said.

"No, honey, it's just . . . are you okay?"

"Of course I'm okay. What are you talking about?"

"You look kind of peaked, that's all."

He pushed past her to the mirror over the mantel. The bimbo was right. The smudges under his eyes were darker, and the flesh had a puffy look. His overall color was not good despite the thrice-weekly sessions at the tanning parlor. And had the spark dimmed in his eyes?

Chelsea moved up beside him. Comparing her vital young beauty to his new pallor depressed him.

"You've been working too hard," Chelsea suggested.

"Yes, that's it. I had a hard week on Skid Row. What I need is rest. I'll call you next week."

He left Chelsea standing in her doorway wearing the blue-black dress and a puzzled frown. He wanted only to spend the rest of the weekend alone and undisturbed so he would look good for his return to the anchor desk Monday.

"Jesus, Stuart, what *have* you been doing to yourself?" Georgie flitted from one side to the other as Milestone sat rigidly in the makeup chair.

"You got a problem?" The anchor man was in no mood to discuss it.

"Well, *one* of us has. Take a look."

He held the magnifying hand mirror up in front of Milestone's face. In the unfiltered light of the makeup cubicle the flaws were apparent. His eyes were watery with a light crust on the lids. Crow's feet radiated from the outer corners. His jawline was less well defined as the flesh seemed to have loosened. His color was worse than ever.

"Now you tell me if there's a problem," Georgie said.

"Never mind. Just fix me up for the camera."

It took until five minutes before air time for Georgie to restore Milestone to his handsome self. His reading of the news that night was perfunctory, his byplay with Sports and Weather more forced than usual. Not even the promo for next week's homeless series brightened him. After the show he walked off the set and out of the studio without a word to anyone.

He awoke Tuesday from another night of unpleasant dreams. For a long time he lay in his king-size bed, staring up at the beamed ceiling of his bedroom, trying not to think about his face. When finally he could stand it no longer he got up and walked into the bathroom.

After a frozen ten-second look at his image, Milestone brought up a groan. All the imperfections of the day before were there, only deeper, darker, worse. And there was more. Pinches of loose skin drooped over his eyelids. His firm cheeks were sallow and sagging. There were deep wrinkles across his forehead and an angry cleft between his eyebrows. The creases Georgie had last week penciled from nostril to mouth were there now for real.

That night George made no comment as Milestone presented himself in the makeup chair. His frown and his tight little mouth said it all. He worked feverishly on the anchorman right up until air time.

Milestone ignored the startled looks of Sports, Weather, and the crew as he took his place at the anchor desk. He raced through the reading of the news so fast that Sports and Weather had to pad out the close with more inane chatter than usual.

On Wednesday Milestone showed up early in Makeup. All day he had avoided mirrors, but he could feel the scaly patches of skin on his face. He saw in his comb the wads of hair that came away from his crusted scalp without a struggle. The sagging jowls weighed like saddlebags. And on his upper lip something like a cold sore had broken open to discharge a viscous fluid.

Georgie dealt swiftly with him this time. He blow-dried the thinning hair into a semblance of fullness. He spread Tahitian Bronze pancake like frosting, shaded the loose flesh at the jaw, sealed the open sore, and dusted the surface with talc. Without comment he yanked the towel from Milestone's collar and scurried off on some unspecified errand.

The show was a disaster. Milestone's voice cracked. He misread cue cards. The heavy makeup lay on his face like a death mask. No one on the set would meet his eye.

Afterwards, as he was heading for the door, a hand fell on his shoulder. Milestone flinched as though expecting an axe between the shoulder blades.

Fred Kineally said, "Stuart, before you go Mr. Lichty wants to see you."

"I'll call him tomorrow," Milestone said without turning around.

"Now, Stuart." The producer's tone was gentle, but there was an icy core to his voice.

A week ago Stuart Milestone would have told the station manager where and when a meeting would take place. Not tonight.

"Have a seat, Stuart." Norman Lichty—overweight, balding, pockmarked—sat unsmiling behind his power desk. A station executive did not have to look good.

"Can you guess why I asked you up here?"

"I'm in no mood for games, Norman."

"Well, neither am I, so I'll be direct. The Big Six News this week has been deplorable. Tonight's was the worst yet. Your mind isn't on your work, and you look terrible."

"I've been hitting it pretty hard, what with the panhandler series and all—"

"I didn't say tired, Stuart, I said *terrible.*" He adjusted the desk lamp so the light shone full on Milestone's face. "Have you taken a good look at yourself? The switchboard is jammed with calls asking what's wrong with you. What *is* wrong with you?"

Milestone opened his mouth for an indignant reply, but it died in his throat. All he could manage was a shrug.

Lichty turned the light away. "I want you to take some time off, starting tomorrow. Rest up. See a doctor. Do whatever you have to do."

"But the show . . . the homeless special . . . "

"The special is in the can. Alan can handle the anchor desk until you're ready to come back. Believe me, Stuart, this is the best for everybody."

"Oh, sure," Milestone mumbled. "For everybody." He left the building the back way and hailed a taxi.

The next day he sat alone in his apartment with the lights out and the blinds closed. He avoided the mirrors. He knew what he had to do, but not until it was dark. He would not go out on the street looking like something from *Night of the Living Dead*.

When at last the sun was down he pulled a hat low on his head, where the hair now grew only in sparse patches from the liver-spotted scalp. He put on his largest pair of Foster Grants, pulled a coat collar up to his ears, and ventured out.

The bartender in the Horsehoe eyed him coldly. "Jessie? I ain't sure I know the name. Who's asking?"

Milestone pulled a crumpled wad of bills from his pocket and threw them on the bar without looking at the denomination. "Just tell me where she lives. I haven't got time to waste."

The bartender smoothed out the bills one by one and folded them neatly. "Go two blocks to your left, turn right half a block, and you'll see a boarded up store. Jessie lives upstairs in the back."

Milestone covered the distance in a swift walk, holding himself back to keep from breaking into a run. He took the stairs two at a time, raced down a dim hallway and pulled up short before a door at the far end. He drew a deep breath and knocked on the peeling wooden panel. For a heart-stopping moment he thought Jessie might not be home, then he heard her voice from inside.

"It's not locked."

He pushed open the door and entered. The room was what he expected—threadbare carpet, mismatched furniture, peeling flowered wallpaper. A huge new television set looked out of place on a backless wooden chair at the foot of the bed. Jessie stepped from behind a stained green curtain that closed off the kitchen alcove. She wore a faded orange blouse and black skirt with many folds.

She looked at him, saying nothing.

Deliberately Milestone removed the hat and the dark glasses. He turned down the coat collar. "Do you know who I am?"

"I know you, Whitey. What do you want here?"

The words gushed out of him like vomit. "I want my face back. You made me ugly and old. I don't know how, and it doesn't matter. Maybe I had it coming. God knows I'm sorry if I hurt you. I'll make it up to you. Just put my face back the way it was. Please, Jessie!"

She rolled her head slowly from side to side. "Can't be done."

"Don't say that! I'll pay. Anything you say. I've got money. Just tell me how much. Whatever you want to fix my face."

"I don't need your money, Whitey. All I wanted from you was friendship. Now I don't need that either. I've got a friend."

Jessie turned and pushed the curtain to one side. Seated at a rickety wooden table was Alan Baird.

He looked at his watch. "Hi, Stuart. Love to stay and chat, but I've got a show to do. See you later, Jessie."

The new anchor man kissed her withered cheek and walked out the door. The old anchor man felt his face crumble.

Julia's Touch

David T Connolly

Julia spent most of the afternoon decorating the small apartment for her husband's birthday party. She braided crepe streamers and blew up so many brightly-colored balloons that it left her dizzy. She was in the middle of preparing the cheese and cracker plate when she realized she hadn't picked up Robert's cake. This being his thirtieth birthday, she wanted everything to be perfect. Then maybe at least for one night Robert would call a halt to the critical self-examination his approaching birthday had triggered.

Glancing at the clock, Julia saw she had just enough time to get to the bakery and still make it back before Robert arrived. Hurrying, she popped the cheese plate into the refrigerator, wiped her hands and prepared to leave.

She went to the hall closet for a coat and chose the one with the genuine fake-fur collar. The walk would be short but cold. Though Robert worked hard at his job, he earned little and drove their car to work. Because most of the places Julia shopped were close by, she never really felt inconvenienced.

On her way out of the apartment Julia couldn't resist another look over her shoulder at the decorations. Then she checked the deadbolt, walked quietly down the stairway and out onto the crowded sidewalk.

Julia smiled privately, imagining how surprised Robert was going to be! She knew he'd laugh at her for having gone to all this trouble just for the two of them. But she also knew, deep inside, that Robert would be thrilled. And she was happy to be surprising him; after all, Robert had never forgotten *her!*

Of course, this was a lot of trouble to go to just to see a surprised and delighted smile on his face. Nonetheless, Julia knew for a fact her man was worth it.

Wrapped in thought, she never saw the car. It jumped the curb, its drunken driver passed out at the wheel. Striking Julia from behind, the car shoved her through the thick plate-glass window of the florist's shop. The clerk called the ambulance. Julia was pronounced dead at the scene.

Feeling a light tap on his shoulder, Robert turned, surprised to see his shift-foreman standing behind him. Following the man back into the office, Robert was told that he had best sit down. At first the news of Julia's death had no effect. After all, how could it be true? Julia, the only bright spot in his life—*dead?* No, it just wasn't possible. He got back onto his feet and walked out of the office without a word.

Blindly following routine, stared at by his fellow workers, Robert was shutting down the lathe when the police arrived. They asked him to get into his car and follow theirs. It wasn't until he was staring down at Julia's corpse that he truly understood she was gone.

"Is this your wife?" It was a man in a long white coat.

"Yes," Robert answered. The word barely cleared his lips. He felt the word on them, felt it fade away, wanted to take it back. Instead, the tightlipped officers walked Robert back to his car. Slowly then, alone, he drove home.

Entering the quiet darkness of the apartment, his hand went to the light switch. A choked sob pierced the small apartment's silence. He was in the middle of a party for one, prepared by the only woman he had ever loved. Prepared by a woman who lay cold on a slab.

His tear-filled eyes grew redder at the sight of the lovingly draped decorations. Looking from the artfully wound crepe-paper that hung from a bouquet of balloons to the sparkling handmade, "Happy Birthday, Honey" banner, he wiped at the tears with his calloused hand, stopping when he realized the corners of his mouth had pulled back up into a smile—a smile he knew Julia had felt would be worth all her trouble.

Then he felt the smile shatter like a mishandled champagne glass.

He crossed into the kitchen and opened a drawer, withdrew a roll of electrical tape, then a small box of single-edged razor blades. In the living room Robert pulled the album of wedding photos out from underneath the coffee table. Then he took the balloons down from the wall.

He carried his belongings into the bathroom, closed the door behind him.

Quietly, Robert eased down the lid on the toilet and sat, arranging his personal items around him. Tearing off several short lengths of the black plastic tape, he pressed one onto the skin of each balloon. Finished, he set them aside and opened the photo album at his feet.

Squinting down through his shifting curtain of tears, Robert inspected the pictures one by one. In the first photo he was kissing Julia, outside the church where they'd married. The picture had been snapped moments after they went outside; you could just make out the small drifts of rice in the creases of his jacket.

Robert took a blade from the small, red box, peeled off its wrapper.

His tears fell freely, the heavy drops pattering like soft rain on the close-up of the misty-eyed newlyweds. Robert brushed them away; they were quickly replaced.

He reached down to choose a balloon, his damp fingers slipping ever so slightly. He made a tiny incision in the short length of tape. When he'd done that, Julia's captured breath drifted toward his face. Her warm, moist breath slowed his flow of tears, drying them for him as if Julia had never died at all. Very slowly, with infinite care, Robert bled the breath from each bright party balloon—all but one.

Before opening the last, he opened himself. At the wrists.

The rain of tears dropping down onto the newlywed faces was overtaken by a crimson flood.

There was time for the final cut and Julia's breath playing softly on Robert's wet and trembling eyelids.

Savages

Darrell Schweitzer

To Oliver, he was always Billy, never Bill or William, much less Mr. Porter, even after the two of them grew up. To Oliver, Billy was perpetually nine years old, crawling down the embankment behind the old Drake house, under the thick tangle of honeysuckle and briar, completely at his ease under the vaulted arches of the forsythias like something used to all-fours.

"Come on," Billy would say. "I'll show you something *neat.*" And the ritual would begin. Oliver followed him always, breathless with expectation, and sometimes he let his three-years-younger brother Daniel tag along, and maybe Howard Gilmore who lived across the street and down two.

Billy led the way. He was a natural bush-rat, a burrower, able to slip with ease through the tightest hedges, the one who always found the way for the others through the thorn bushes. Down the embankment they went, where their parents had so often forbidden them to go, along the railroad tracks that ran behind the whole neighborhood, then down again, where the hill was so steep they had to take to the trees and lower themselves into a cool, secret place where a stream emerged from a tunnel beneath the tracks.

They had to do it just right, touching all these special places, never revealing themselves to the eyes of others, creeping like Wild Indians through the undergrowth along the edge of the St. David's Golf Course when it would be so much easier just to walk across the grass. If they did it right, if they all ran like startled deer across Lancaster Pike when there were no cars coming and quickly regained the safety of the shrubbery on the other side; if they made their way from there deep into Cabbage Creek Woods with its soapy-smelling skunk cabbages, braving the mud and mosquitoes and stinging nettles that grew by the edge of the stream there; if they did all these things as Billy directed, they would come to a path where the land rose into a gravel heap near the abandoned trackbed of the P&W line and come to Billy's fort: a kind of cave supported by logs, dug deep under the old rail ties.

You could never get there without him. No one else could find the way. And, if by chance you did, there would be Billy's anger to contend with, and he was just too strange, too wild. Even from the beginning, everyone was just a little bit afraid of Billy.

Oliver would always remember Billy that way, his incongruously tubby form able to squeeze through the tightest opening with natural ease, almost always barefoot and shirtless, smeared with dirt, his hands and feet almost black from the dirt and cinders along the railroad embankment.

Billy would take the others into his confidence and show them something "really neat," which might really *be* neat: a Nazi dagger somebody's father had brought home from the war, an amazing collection of firecrackers, baseball cards, a golf ball he'd sawed in half with no apparent ill effects, monster magazines, what seemed to be a real revolver, several pet snakes he swore were poisonous and only Billy would touch—

For long afternoons every summer they'd sit there around a smoldering fire—there always had to be a fire inside the fort; it was part of the magic—and as shadows lengthened and evening came on, Billy would tell them the stories of the Blood Goblin who had been a medicine man, centuries ago, with the disconcerting habit of lifting his head from his shoulders till his spine and his guts dangled in the air. Then he would fly through the night, shrieking, his eyes burning red, his teeth distended into enormous fangs with which to rip out the throats and drink the blood of passers-by.

He was still here, too, Billy said. His body had been stolen and burned while he was away, so he couldn't leave. Once in a great while a kid disappeared. You'd hear he'd been kidnapped. The police would search and search but never find him, because the Blood Goblin had found him first.

Only Billy had seen him and lived to tell about it, because Billy was magic. He was at home there in those woods, clad only in a ragged pair of shorts, so dirty he looked more like an animal than a human. Everyone's parents went on about how poor Billy was, how neglected, but that was precisely why Oliver, Daniel, and the rest envied, all but worshipped him. Billy didn't have to wash up or dress right or go home when his mother said he had to. He was free. He lived in the woods like a savage, something all of them aspired to become but knew, deep inside, that they never would.

Sometimes Billy's idea of what was "really neat" could be distressing, like the dead cat he insisted on cutting into fine pieces with a long, incredibly sharp knife while Oliver and the others looked on in disgust and fascination—both at the insides of the cat and at the spectacle of Billy flaying it with such obvious relish, muttering all the while as if carrying on some obscure argument with himself. One hand would seize the other and force the knife away, and the blade would weave back and forth in the air in front of all their wide-eyed faces. Then, suddenly it jerked down and Billy stabbed himself in his round stomach. Daniel screamed. Oliver forced Billy's arms aside and had a look, but it was just a scratch. Blood trickled through the grime.

But Billy remained oblivious to them all and completed

his operation, meticulously saving the cat's heart, lungs, liver, intestines, and even its penis in plastic jars.

Oliver watched with a terrible, breathless expectancy he couldn't even put into words.

Then Billy yanked the remaining hide off the carcass and held the bare skull up, his hands slimy with blood.

"Isn't that *neat?*" he said.

"No!" Oliver said. "It's *horrible . . .*"

"Maybe you're lying," Billy said softly. "Just maybe you *like* it."

"No!"

"Maybe it's not enough for you. I think you want more. Wouldn't it be neat to do this to *people?* Wouldn't that *really* be something?"

What frightened Oliver more than anything else was the realization that deep inside a part of him thought doing it to people *would* be neat. Somehow, the way Billy said it, or just the fact *that* Billy and not, say, Howard Gilmore had made such a suggestion overwhelmed all objections, enchanted him, and an inner voice said, *Yes, that would be neat,* and for just the barest instant he agreed with all his heart and soul—before his sanity returned and he recoiled from what he was thinking. But the thought remained, like a stain.

Nobody said anything more. Daniel went home crying that day. Oliver was silent for a long time.

Billy was the first one to figure out how to masturbate. He showed the others. He set up a bull's-eye target on the wall of the fort and he was the only one who could hit it. But he never got any further than that. He never developed any interest in girls.

The boys were older by then; but that was the odd thing: they were changing, and Billy was not. Oliver read more and more books. He wanted to talk about rocketships and explorers and outer space. Billy preferred dead animals he could take apart. By now the inside of his fort stank like a garbage bin, and skulls and skins and wings decorated the walls.

"Come and see something *neat*," he still said, but the others didn't always come. When they were with girls they pretended they didn't know him. The girls held their noses with exaggerated gestures and whined, "Eeew! Gross!" And Billy would scream at them and vanish back into his woods and everyone would laugh.

Nobody saw Billy pass from grade to grade like the rest. He went to some other school somewhere. Rumor had it it was a place for retarded kids. That brought more laughter.

Only Oliver knew that couldn't be true, that Billy had chosen some secret, magical path which kept him apart, which changed him and wouldn't let him change again. Oliver *didn't* laugh.

But certainly Billy was losing whatever charm he had. What was fascinating at nine is okay at eleven and a bit boring at thirteen, and when the human body stays that dirty and gets older, it starts to stink. After puberty you learn about B.O. Billy had it in epic proportions.

"Come on!" he pleaded. "I know something *neat!* What's the matter? Are you afraid?"

Not even Daniel visited the fort much anymore.

Oliver went one last time when he was fourteen. It was one of those growing-up things, like the last time you play with your electric trains. He somehow knew it would be the last.

He had been a freshman at Cardinal O'Hara for two months. It was October, but almost as warm as summer. In the evening, after he'd finished delivering his newspapers, Oliver stood among the fallen leaves behind the Drake house at the top of the embankment, waiting, remembering; and suddenly Billy was there, as he had always been, clad in dirt and a pair of cut-offs that were ripped up both sides almost to the waist so that he looked like a jungle cannibal in a loin-cloth. He wore a necklace like one, too, of dried snakeskins and animal bones.

"Hello, Billy."

The other said nothing and Oliver followed him down the embankment under the thorn-bushes and vines, trying very hard not to soil or tear the new jacket he'd gotten for his birthday a week before.

The golf course was being torn up to build a Sears but the construction area was deserted, and skulking among the huge piles of earth and among the idle machines was an acceptable substitute for the bushes that were no longer there.

He sat with Billy on the threshold of the fort for what must have been an hour. The woods grew dark. The first stars appeared and the rising full moon shone fleetingly among the tree trunks. Oliver zipped up his jacket, but Billy didn't seem cold.

Billy talked about bats, his latest fascination.

"I like bats too," Oliver said. "Did you see *The Kiss of the Vampire* where they killed the vampires at the end—?"

But, no, Billy meant real bats, soft, warm, sharp-clawed things like mice with wings. Sometimes he would lie in his fort at night listening to the distant howling of the Blood Goblin still angrily searching for its stolen body, and the bats came to cover him up like a chirping blanket. He *really* liked that. It was neat. The bats told him all their secrets. He had learned their language.

He made a chittering, whistling sound.

Oliver shivered, laughed nervously. "You're making this up . . ."

"No!" Billy leapt to his feet, towering over Oliver, his fists bunched up, his belly wriggling. "Don't be a asshole!"

That was how he said it, Oliver would always remember. Not *an asshole* but *a asshole*.

"Hey, I'm sorry, Billy. I mean it."

Billy spat and sat down, his chin on his grubby fists.

"If you're really sorry, you'll look at the neat thing I got to show you."

"Okay, Billy . . . " Oliver was more than uneasy then, definitely afraid. He could sense the magic in Billy, the power which wanted to anchor him here, to drag him back from fourteen to nine again and keep him that way forever.

"It's something the bats showed me," Billy said. "They can do it with their wings. I always wanted to see the insides of things. They showed me how."

"Huh?"

"Just watch. You promised."

"Yeah. I promised."

Oliver had no idea what was to follow. He sat there watching as Billy sat very still, his hands folded, eyes closed, head down. That was the strangest thing of all. Oliver had to control his impulse to laugh. It was impossible to imagine Billy *praying*.

Then Billy lowered his folded hands until the edges touched the dirt floor of the fort; and he parted them, brushing a little dirt aside. Suddenly there was an *opening*. Not a hole. No. He hadn't scooped out that much dirt. It was as if the earth were scum on the surface of a pond, and Billy's hands had broken it. The blackness suggested an infinite depth.

"Jesus!"

"Now look down there," Billy said. "You promised. Just look and see what the insides of the world are filled up with."

Oliver looked, and suddenly felt Billy's hands grab him by the shoulders of his jacket, yanking his head down; and then Billy was on top of him, heavy and fat and hot, breathing hard, his stench almost unbearable. He forced Oliver's head down into the hole and held it there.

"Look! Dead people! The world is full of dead people! Look! There's your grandmother! Isn't that *neat?"* He laughed, squealed, grunted like a pig, shaking Oliver, pressing him down, down—

Oliver opened his eyes in the darkness, flinching from the expected dirt, but there was none. He seemed to be hanging in a dark space . . . and then he saw the dead people, like pale bubbles suspended in the black fluid of the night, the array of them extending into infinite distance, their faces and naked skulls glowing like stars, like dim moons. They were all somehow aware of him, angry that he had intruded upon them. They froze him with their terrible gaze, those shrivelled corpses, those skeletons, those heaps of scraps and darkened bones. Nearby, an ancient lady in an old-fashioned dress, lying with her hands folded over rosary beads, glared up at him.

She opened her mouth as if to speak. He shouted, "No! Go away!" But she was *not* going away and there was no sound. Her voice, he knew, would be the most horrible thing of all, and he would never stop hearing it.

But she said nothing. There were only wriggling worms.

"Isn't that *neat?*" Billy whispered.

He let go and Oliver broke free, running through the darkened woods, tripping over vines, tearing his precious jacket among the thorns. Once he fell and landed face-down in a stream.

At last he came to the edge of the woods, where two holes remained of the old golf course. Alice, his girlfriend, lived nearby. He had planned to visit her tonight. He was late and a mess but he didn't think he would make it all the way back to his own house. He would be safe with her.

"What happened to *you?*" she said, giggling when she saw him.

"I fell," was all he could say.

Afterward, Oliver glimpsed Billy only at a distance once or twice, crouched under a bush, watching. He was almost able to deny him, to convince himself that he had never been fascinated with the things Billy considered neat. Almost.

Alice was succeeded by Marlene, who was succeeded by

Janice, then Jeanne, then Dora, and that took him to the end of high school. College was more a matter of books, then computers. All that talk about spaceships was rapidly turning him into an astro-physicist.

But he dreamed of Billy Porter at the oddest times. Once he seemed to doze off in a lecture hall, and someone nudged him on the shoulder; and there was Billy beside him, naked and dirty, garlanded with dead leaves. He followed Billy out of the hall while the professor droned on and no one seemed to notice he was going. Outside was not the corridor that should have been there, but the deep woods where the wind rattled branches and heaved vines, and the trees were alive with presences which welcomed Billy and rejected Oliver. They came to the fort and Billy squatted down before the fire, then lifted his head off until his spine and entrails dripped in the air. Oliver let out a cry and awoke back in his seat in the lecture hall. The students around him turned to look, and a couple snickered, but the professor didn't seem to have noticed.

At twenty-three, he began graduate work at the University of Pennsylvania, and, after that was done, moved to Princeton. There he met and married Eileen. For several years, that looked like the best idea he'd ever had, and for several more after that, the worst.

He couldn't begin to say precisely when the marriage went bad, but it did, with the glacial inevitability of a mansion built on an unsound foundation, tottering to a fall. The petty bickerings started, continued, became almost constant, over just anything—who was right in El Salvador, whether or not flying saucers exist—*anything*. It didn't matter. They weren't really fighting over the ostensible topics, Oliver wearily concluded, any more than the people of the Middle Ages *really* fought wars over which way you make the sign of the cross or whether the spirit flows from the Father and the Son, or from the Father alone. It was all ego, authority-turf, conquest and humiliation, territorial squabbles in that most personal of personal spaces, the mind.

At the end, he suspected Eileen had a lover. He didn't care. Fine and good-riddance, he told himself.

But she wouldn't let him off so easily. She was going to make it messy. At the very end they found themselves screaming at one another, and before he knew it he'd raised a silver candlestick like a club.

"Go on, you stupid fuck," she said, her voice even, contemptuous and not at all afraid. "Go on and kill me. That'll solve everything."

He walked out of the house, got in his car, just started driving. He had no idea where he was going. Just *going*. He joked to himself that he'd always thought that driving your emotions away with a car was a California trait, but no, they do it in New Jersey too. Driving, on and on like a record that's come to the end but the needle won't lift, so there's nothing left but an empty rasping noise.

An hour passed, more. His mind was on autopilot. Autopilot took him across the Ben Franklin Bridge into Pennsylvania. Autopilot turned west on the Schuykill Expressway and exited at Gulph Mills. His motions were as mindless as the orbits of asteroids—

"My God," he said aloud. "St. David's PA."

His mind cleared somewhat as he recognized the old neighborhood, or what was left of it. The Sears which had replaced the golf course was itself gone, turned into a corporate center. Across the street a B. Altman's had come and gone, the building empty. He didn't turn left to see if the parking lot had obliterated Cabbage Creek Woods. Instead, he continued on, turned right into Cambria Court, his old street, parked, and got out to walk.

He wanted to proceed slowly. He wanted to touch and feel and hear, not just to glance from a moving car. More than that, he wanted to put off the time before he'd have to inevitably go back and face Eileen. He wanted this moment to last forever.

It was dusk on a long summer evening like so many he'd known here. He walked past the house with the arched gateway over the path where he'd come that Halloween when he was fourteen, the very last time he'd ever gone trick-or-treating, and the man had said, "You're getting a little tall for this, aren't you?" Not old, tall.

He knew these places, every tree, every stone, for a child can trespass into any number of back yards without being noticed or driven away. Now he could only stand in the street and look.

The upper court was hardly recognizable. An apartment building had wiped out his own family's old house and the empty lot behind where, when he was very small, a Victorian pile had burned to the ground amid screaming sirens, flashing lights, and thick smoke. It was his most vivid memory from the beginning of his life: the firemen dragging hoses across the lawn, the snapping as the sparks and cinders flew into the air. He remembered standing in the driveway holding his mother's hand while his father hurried to pile valuables into the car in case the fire spread and they had to leave.

Now he could only look for traces of that former place, what was his whole world then. Yes, there was one twisted dogwood tree at the edge of the street which had been in their yard, but that was all.

As he stood there, as the evening shadows deepened, he was able to imagine what it had been like. But the scale was all off. Things were smaller: that dogwood tree, even though it should have grown, was no longer the labyrinthine tower of wood and leaves it had been. It was just a tree. And across the street, behind him, was a walnut atop the rising ground at the edge of the Drake property. He remembered crawling up that little hill on his hands and knees, resting beneath the tree. Now it was no more than a foot above the road surface. He could take the journey in a single step.

He leaned down and picked up a walnut, its green and black shell peeling to reveal the nut inside. Nobody ever ate them, but he remembered the strong, almost sweet smell which got on your hands and stayed for hours.

* * *

"Hello."

He turned, still holding the walnut. "I used to live here," he said quickly.

"I know."

He took the other for a handyman of some sort, a stocky fellow dressed in a dirty, dark uniform of the sort filling-station attendants sometimes wear. But there was something about the way the man moved, some unforgotten tone in his voice that made him hesitate. For just an instant, he felt a touch of the old fear again. *That* he recognized unquestionably.

Then he saw the face clearly. A face as it ages is like a waxen mask slowly melting, stretching. The basic pattern remains for a long time.

"Bil-ly?"

"Hey old pal, wanna see something *neat?*"

It was so easy, so utterly effortless to follow Billy through the hedge and into the Drakes' yard, even as some voice in the back of his mind said, *Wait a minute. We're grown men, we're trespassing on these people's property.* He crawled down the embankment, under the arching forsythias, through the thorns, and it was much easier than he thought it would be. He followed, even as he thought again, *How could you possibly know I would be here this particular night?* and Billy seemed to answer in his mind: *You thought of me and I waited. You were the very last one to come to my fort, and I waited.*

Billy took him by the arm, led him along the tracks. He cringed at that, because everyone knew that trainmen went by and took pictures of people who walked along the tracks.

He noticed that Billy was barefoot and his clothes were rags.

He climbed down the second embankment to the stream, clumsily, sliding amid a shower of sticks and gravel. Billy was ahead of him somewhere, in the trees perhaps, moving swiftly, easily; then waiting for him by the stream.

They walked out onto the deserted St. David's Golf Course in the deep twilight, and fireflies rose from the green earth; and a part of his mind said, *There's been no golf course here since JFK was president.* And a part of him thought it odd that he marked time that way, since JFK, *not* since he was in the sixth grade; and he reflected how each of us matters so little against the larger pattern of events. But the whole of his mind did not listen to those voices and they receded to a nonsensical whisper.

It was so easy. A downhill slide away from pain, where Eileen could not follow.

They came to the clump of trees behind the clubhouse, where some kid or other supposedly found a Spanish-American War sword once. Oliver wondered if Billy had that sword now, among his collection of neat things.

In Cabbage Creek Woods, among the skunk cabbages, the soft mud was almost frigid between their toes.

And, finally, the two of them crouched in Billy's fort before a smoldering fire, dirty, almost naked, clutching stone-tipped spears, hooting and howling into the night.

(Like the kids in *Lord of the Flies,* that other voice said. But he didn't understand. *No, this is all wrong. You're thirty-five. For Christ's sake what happened to your clothes?*)

"Isn't this *neat?*" Billy said.

Shaking, sobbing at some memory he could no longer quite define, Oliver said, "Yes. Neat."

"Here. Let me show you something."

Billy folded his hands, then brushed his own bare, mud-streaked chest, splashing away the skin like scum on pondwater, and Oliver could see Billy's ribs clearly, his lungs inflating like bags, his heart beating deep inside.

"My God—"

For an instant Oliver remembered. He struggled back into himself like a drowning man reaching for the surface. He remembered that he was a full professor at Princeton, that he'd parked his car over in Cambria Court. But he looked down at his slender, hairless legs, at his muddy knees and feet, and he wept and thought, *This can't be real. What is happening to me?*

"Neat, huh?" Billy laughed, like a kid who's just chewed up some food but not swallowed it, and opens his mouth in order to be deliberately disgusting.

It was so easy to stop weeping, to sit with Billy, to try to be just like him, to listen to his stories of the Blood Goblin and of the wild Indians who lived in these woods once, and what terrible tortures they performed on their enemies. If he listened very hard, if he stared intently out into the darkening woods, he could hear the tom-toms and the screams, far away.

Something moved furtively among the nettles by the stream, ruffling them.

"Billy," he said slowly. "I want to stay here. I want to learn to see everything you see. I want you to teach me."

(*No!* his adult self screamed within, like a prisoner in a cage being wheeled to execution. He tried to remember science, equations, the names of stars.)

Billy stood up. He opened his arms wide and the whole forest was transformed. It was utterly dark now. The bird-calls were exotic screeches. Something huge, like a giant on stilts, stalked among the trees, its bestial head glaring. Below the fort, by the stream, a huge serpent coiled, its scales gleaming with their own light. Its face was that of a bare human skull. Its tongue flickered between the rotting teeth like a thin knife.

"Just like me," Billy said, putting his hand on Oliver's shoulder in what had to be a gesture of acceptance at last, of genuine friendship. The master of the forest had accepted an apprentice.

(*No!* the buried, adult Oliver screamed from within his head. *I don't want to be like you. I'm not like you. I grew up! You never did!*)

"You're *exactly* like me," Billy said aloud.

And the two of them crouched inside the fort. Oliver, looking up for Billy's approval first, leaned down, placing his folded hands in the dust.

It was so easy. He didn't have to be forced. He looked down into the hole as if peering through a ceiling from the floor above, and he saw Eileen there, lying on the kitchen floor in their house back in Princeton, blood pooling around her throat. She gasped softly. Her fingers opened, closed, opened, were still.

He screamed, turned away. For an instant he crouched low beneath the cramped roof of the fort, his back pressing into dirt and roots, naked, a savage, yes, but in his adult body, and he saw the wild boy before him and was filled with horror and disgust. He shoved Billy aside, crawled to the doorway of the fort—

(What do you really want? Be honest. Really.)

(And all he could think of was that time when they were children, when Billy held up the bloody animal skull and said, *"Wouldn't you like to do this to people?"* and for an instant he'd known he *did*. Then the idea was like a horrible jack-in-the-box he had to shove back inside with enormous effort, but he had done it, and closed the lid. Now the lid had burst right off its hinges, useless, gone.)

The Blood Goblin rose out of the nettles by the stream, eyes glaring, its spine dangling below.

Billy spoke. His voice was deep and harsh. "You will slay her. You will resume your former guise long enough to execute the appointed task, then return and dwell here forever."

That wasn't Billy talking. Billy never used words like *former guise* and *execute the appointed task*. That was the Blood Goblin, grown eloquent in the long years of searching for rest.

Not Billy.

Billy was a dirty little boy. He didn't mean any harm.

"Something *neat*," Billy said solemnly. He put a stone

dagger into Oliver's hand, closing his reluctant fingers over it.

And Oliver began to chant, softly, hardly realizing he was doing it, "Slit her throat. Kill her dead. Drink her blood. Bash her head."

Billy smiled. He seemed to like that a lot.

'No," Oliver said aloud, his voice rising in tone, sinking into youth, into childishness, cracking, even as his body changed, as the room was comfortably-sized again, as his bare, hairless legs gleamed in the firelight. "I don't want to hurt her. I don't hate her. If only she'd leave me alone." He was pleading now. "If only we could talk it out like civilized human beings."

(Civilized? We're savages, remember?)

Billy was pounding on the dirt with hands and feet. "Slit her throat! Kill her dead! Drink her blood! Bash her head!"

Oliver-within-Oliver, drowning, struggled one last time for the surface, reached up but didn't make it. So easy to let go. To sink down. It made things so simple.

(I won't let you do this to me. I won't.)

Oliver crouched down by the fire, chanting along, "Slit her throat! Kill her dead!"

(You will. You'll do it yourself, to yourself.)

He looked at Billy as if he'd seen him truly for the first time. It was so easy, like letting go, sinking down.

(What makes you think I want to be like you?)

(You already are.)

And the Blood Goblin hovered before the fort's single opening, and the huge thing among the trees leaned down and whispered terrifying things; and the wild Indians crouched with them in the darkness, describing whom they had tortured and how. The great, bone-faced serpent entered the fort and circled around the two boys, again and again.

Oliver looked into Billy's eyes and understood fully, and he thought that Billy understood him, and for the first time it was Billy who was afraid.

(No. This isn't happening. You are a teacher, a scientist,

a grown, decent man. No. Billy was a dirty little boy you knew years and years ago. What was that voice? It was so easy to ignore it.)

Oliver looked into Billy's eyes, and he understood that there could be no two masters of the forest, that there could be no apprentice. It was not like that. The fort was built for one.

He knew what to do now. It was clear. Billy had shown him the way, had been showing him the way all these years, had ultimately seduced him, even as he allowed himself to be seduced.

"It'll be *neat,*" Oliver said. *'Really, really neat."*

Billy screamed and Oliver opened him up. He methodically peeled Billy apart, tearing out his ribs, his lungs, his heart, dropping them down the hole into the kitchen, on top of his wife's body (Whose wife?), while the forest birds screamed and the Blood Goblin chanted and the sound of the wind through the trees was a kind of song.

Very carefully, he placed Billy's skull among the trophies in the collection.

(*Try to remember.* Gone.)

He crawled out of the fort. The doorway was too small for him. His bare, broad shoulders brushed it on either side.

In the end he stood there above the stream, naked but for his loincloth, conversing with the Blood Goblin whose entrails dripped down over his shoulders and chest.

In the end, he smeared himself with blood like warpaint, and he held up his stone knife and Billy's stinking hide and shouted a great shout of triumph, of victory. The master of the fort and forest had come home.

(So easy to slide down. Into darkness. He'd always wanted to, ever since he was a child. Now he was just being honest with himself.)

He had to get back to Eileen. To explain. To resolve things once and for all.

He raised his knife and shouted a great shout.

The Collapse of Civilization

Ray Russell

The Collapse of Civilization has always been an out-of-sight group—those four topless teeners yelling their guts out and sweating real sweat, mean as life and all for you in your very own digs on your very own holographic video cassette—but they didn't make it really big-big until last year, that runaway hit of theirs.

The popularity had very little to do with the music, or even with the lyric, which was not what you might call brilliant—

> *Honey baby sweetie when you hold me tight*
> *When you grabba hold o' me and treat me right*
> > *When you give me all you got*
> > *Never mind the speed or pot*
> *It's like*
> > *RED! HOT! NEEDLES!*
> *In my fingers and my toes!*
> *Gloryosky, it's like*
> > *RED! HOT! NEEDLES!*
> *In my nipples and my nose!*
> *Leapin' lizards, it's like*

> *RED! HOT! NEEDLES!*
> *In my belly and my buns!*
> *Hallelujah, Lord, it's*
>   *RED! HOT! NEEDLES!*
> *Like a flamin' pair o' guns!*
> *Oh I'm tellin' you, it's*
>   *RED! HOT! NEEDLES!*
> *In my soul and in my brain!*
> Gotta have those crazy
>   *RED! HOT! NEEDLES!*
> *Though they're drivin' me insane!*

A long way from genius, but "Red Hot Needles" had been top-of-the-charts for a whole lot of weeks, and some of the smart freaks thought maybe the background sound effects had something to do with it.

The way the rumor had it, it was all Torquemada's idea.

She's the head-head of the group, Trish Torquemada, not her square name, of course. The brainblower was sort of a spin-off from their previous hit, a funky little number called "Ball," which had a background noise of a sister gasping and moaning and carrying on like she was making it. And it wasn't acting, they say. It was Trish herself, recorded later on a separate track, being balled by some dude she had around for a while. The record was a smash as a single. The guy, they say, had been Joanie's before Trish trashed him, but you know these show-biz rumors, there's probably nothing in it. Joanie is the junior member of the group.

Anyway, that's supposed to be how Trish flashed the idea for "Red Hot Needles." She wrote the song first, and they recorded it straight, without sound effects. Then, when they were rapping one day and smoking zilchsticks, she popped the wad to the other sisters in the group.

"It's *heavy*," said Joanie, "but how we gone find someone dumb enough to let us stick red hot needles into her?"

"Simple," said Trish. "There are four of us. We draw straws. Whoever loses . . ."

Joanie lost.

They made a deal with the recording boys, and late one night, they got it all together. Stripped Joanie down to the raw and spreadeagled her to the legs of an up-ended table right there in the studio. The other three—wearing motorman's gloves—heated big long darning needles in the flame of a blowtorch and started in on Joanie. She got those needles every place the song said and in a few places it didn't. They recorded for about half an hour, and later they picked out the best screams and laid them on the record, behind the song.

It was a real bummer for Joanie, but she's all right now, they say. Spent some time in a private hospital, being treated for burns and a bad case of nerves, but she rejoined the group. That's the story, anyhow.

"Simply Shocking" was their next big score—all those electronic effects and lots of *double entendre* with "hot seat" and "plugin-socket" and so on. Then they did "Rack and Ruin." You must remember it—

> *Goin' to rack*
> *And ruin*
> *Breakin' my back*
> *With screwin'*
> *Makin' me black*
> *Makin' me blue*
> *Makin' me crack*
> *Splittin' in two*
> *Makin' me shriek*
> *Makin' me weak*
> *Makin' me feeeeeeeeeeeeel*
> *Your love*
> *Crankin' the wheeeeeeeeel*
> *Of love*
> *Goin' to rip-rip-rack and ruin over you!*

There were all sorts of stories about that one. You don't have to believe them if you don't want to. I don't think I do.

Anymore than I believe the one about their next song, "Crash." You know that background noise of screeching brakes and some guy yelling and then that enormous crunch and explosion when the car hits the wall on the last note? They say Trish engineered that one, too, and the stud in the car was the same one she used on the "Ball" record. People love to heap the hype.

Nobody's seen Trish Torquemada for a while. The rest of the sisters get all vague when you ask about her. Vacation, they say, resting up, and like that. Maybe so. But I wonder.

Collapse's next release, coming out next week, is called "Witch." I heard a demo. The group expects to get a Grammy and a Gold Record and ten million balloons for this one. The sound effects are something else, and the lyric isn't bad. Joanie wrote it—

> Oh she stole my lovin' guy
> So that witch is gotta die
> And the way that witches die
> Is ablaze!
> She's a traitor and a liar,
> See the smoke a-climbin' higher,
> Hear her screamin' in the fire
> As she pays . . .

Animal Husbandry

Bruce Boston

When Stuart Evers came home with a vasectomy, his wife Marilyn threw what he could only describe as a tantrum. She stood in the center of their spacious living room with its high Victorian ceiling. Her fists were balled, her face red, her body wracked with sobs. Tears seeped from the corners of her eyes and ran down her cheeks.

"I don't understand!" she screeched in a voice bordering on hysteria. "Why didn't you ask me first?"

Stuart, sprawled in the leather easy lounger, was glancing through a copy of *Forbes* and sipping a glass of white zinfandel. He was astonished at his wife's reaction, but not about to show it. In twelve years of marriage he had hardly heard her raise her voice.

"But we agreed years ago," he stated without looking up, "that we didn't *want* any children."

"That's just the point, it *was* years ago," Marilyn shouted. He could see from the corner of his eye that she was shaking her fist at him. At the same time she was trembling. "How do you know I haven't changed my mind?"

Stuart didn't care for this behavior from his wife. He dropped the magazine and met her accusing stare head on. "Children are dangerous at your age," he informed her.

"I'm only thirty-five! My mother had William when she was forty-two."

"And look how he turned out," Stuart smirked. "An unemployed steeplejack who makes illegal drugs in his bathtub. He hasn't been coming around here again, has he?"

"Willie's a writer and a damn good one at that. It's not his fault if society is too crass to appreciate his talent."

"Sure, just like you're a *brilliant* artist."

There! He'd said it at last.

Marilyn screamed, she actually screamed. Bending to the coffee table she picked up the cut glass ashtray, the one they'd bought last year in Bimini, and hurled it across the room. Stuart was too surprised to even duck. The ashtray rebounded from the wall, taking a large chunk out of the plaster, and thudded solidly to the carpet. If Marilyn's aim had been better, the chunk, Stuart realized, would have been out of his skull.

Over the next few days an uncomfortable silence settled upon their lives. Marilyn still performed the domestic duties that Stuart expected of her. The house remained clean. There were fresh shirts in his drawer. When he came home each night he found his dinner in the refrigerator, waiting to be warmed up. Other than that, she treated him like an unwanted boarder. She only spoke to him when it was absolutely necessary, and she spent most of the time locked in her studio.

By the third night of his wife's retreat, Stuart had to admit that their king-sized bed was beginning to feel other than spacious. His doctor had claimed that he'd be functional within a week, and when the time came, he didn't want any delays. Stuart put on his robe, went back downstairs, and knocked on the door of the studio. He had already tried pounding, at great length and to no avail.

"Marilee . . . honey . . . why don't you come out so we can talk?"

Silence.

"You were right, dear, I should have asked you first. But I did it for the both of us. I thought it would improve our sex life."

A muffled laugh.

Stuart had never thought of his wife as a bitch, but he was beginning to get the idea.

"Marilee, you know what I've been thinking?"

A loud thump.

"Maybe we should get ourselves a pet. I've always liked animals."

Silence.

Stuart had exhausted both humility and patience, so he made his way back upstairs. If he'd known what was to follow his suggestion, he would have bitten his tongue on the way.

Stuart arrived home later than usual to find Marilyn's brother waiting for him in the kitchen. William had helped himself to Stuart's imported pilsner. He was drinking directly from the bottle, his third. His boots were up on the kitchen table and he was stretched out and balanced, rocking back and forth, so that only two legs of his chair were on the floor. Stuart felt an urge to kick the chair from beneath him.

"You should have never done it, Stu," William growled at him. "This time you've gone too far. A marriage is a sacred trust and you've betrayed it. Your body is a temple and you've desecrated it."

The hairiness of the man appalled him. William's beard disappeared into the collar of his shirt with no visible sign of a neck between. The hair on his head was even longer than the last time Stuart had seen him and now trailed down his back. In truth, everything about William appalled him. His slothfulness, his disregard for accepted fashion or mores, his theatrical pronouncements. Yet most of all, Stuart suddenly realized, it was the way William smelled. Even from across the room, he was positively gamy. Naturally, Stuart thought; his bathtub was always full of some mind-bending and no doubt gene-mangling brew. He knew that before their marriage, Marilyn had sampled more than a few of these concoctions. Reason enough for them not to have children. There was no telling what sort of monstrosity the woman might produce.

"It's none of your damn business what I do!" Stuart shouted. "Particularly this. And don't call me Stu."

"It's just no way to treat my sister, Stu. Even if you don't care about her anymore, *I do.*" William swung his legs off the table and his chair clumped to the floor. His brow furrowed as he rose to his full six-three, half a head taller than Stuart, who suddenly found himself backing away. "You know I warned you even before you married her." The man was *threatening him* in his own home.

"If you don't get out of here," Stuart stated, "I'm calling the police."

William snorted and took another step forward. Stuart moved back, never taking his eyes off William, and reached behind him for the wall phone. "I'm not kidding!" The receiver came loose from its cradle, slipped from his grasp, and banged loudly against the counter. A plaintive howl sounded from the back yard.

William took another swallow of his beer. "We got that pet you wanted."

He was in the habit, Stuart remembered, of referring to himself and Marilyn in the first person plural, as if *they* were the couple. There was no doubt about it, the man was disturbed.

"We put his food under the sink," William added as he strolled out of the kitchen, "and he needs to be fed."

"Go get a haircut," Stuart called after him.

In the backyard he found a dog, a St. Bernard of all things. At first the animal growled at him when he tried to approach, but once he filled its dish it settled into dinner and ignored him. As he watched the dog eating, he sighed deeply. He supposed he could learn to live with it.

Back in the house there was no sign of William except for his third beer bottle, empty, on the arm of the living room sofa. Stuart made sure the front door was locked so he couldn't return. Then he went to Marilyn's studio. A thin crack of light showed under the door.

"Marilee," he called, "I like the dog."

Silence.

"Do you have a name for it yet? I had a dog when I was a kid. We named it 'Buck.' He was a collie. Remember, I told you about him." This was ridiculous, Stuart thought. Having a conversation with oak paneling. And veneer at that! "Well, any name's okay with me, as long as it isn't 'William,'" he added spitefully.

He was turning back to the kitchen to get something to eat, when he heard voices from the studio. Not a voice, but voices. Damn, Stuart thought.

"Is he in there, Marilee? I told you I don't want that man in the house. He's unstable. For all we know, there's a warrant out for him right now. It wouldn't be the first time. And I don't want you taking any of his drugs!"

Stuart considered pounding again, but the heel of his palm was still sore from the last time.

On Friday morning Stuart left for a management conference in Houston that would run through the weekend. The conference was a washout: a series of boring exhibits and tedious presentations. He hadn't expected much else. His frequent out-of-town trips weren't taken with the expectation of any professional development, but rather for the extramarital opportunities they provided.

On Sunday night, three hours before his return flight was to leave, he met an ethereal and glitzy blonde in the hotel bar. She was the perfect counterpoint, Stuart thought, to Marilyn's increasingly stocky domesticity. When he steered the conversation in the right direction and told her of his recent surgery and its as yet untried results, the inevitable followed. Back in his room, which he had reserved through Monday in the hopes of such an encounter, he confirmed his doctor's claim more than once.

When he finally reached home at four in the morning, an endearing Texas drawl still echoing in his ears, he heard the St. Bernard howling in the yard. Stuart found its empty dish on the kitchen floor. He opened a can of dog food, the foul gravy spurting out and staining the sleeve of his suit coat. When Stuart deposited the dish on the back porch, the animal was so ravenous it nearly took his thumb off.

After he bandaged the cut, his mind rife with thoughts of blood poisoning and rabies, all Stuart wanted to do was get to bed. In the upstairs hall he was stopped in his tracks once again.

An aquarium, twenty-five gallons if it were an ounce, now dominated their French provincial sideboard. As he edged past the loudly bubbling tank, edged quite literally in the narrow hall, he couldn't help but take a look. The water seemed overcrowded . . . and with one of the oddest assortments of tropicals he'd ever seen. A transparent worm-like creature, resembling a centipede more than a fish, scurried up and down one side of the glass. On the floor of the tank, which was covered with multicolored gravel, what he had at first taken for a large red rock suddenly darted behind a ceramic treasure chest from which bubbles spewed. Near the top of the water, a black angelfish, a species he *could* identify, listed badly to one side and swam in circles. Its delicate fins were slack and ragged. A school of smaller fish tracked its death dance and nipped at it unmercifully.

Stuart grimaced and stumbled into the bedroom where once more there was no sign of Marilyn. He slammed the door to block out the bubbling of the tank.

* * *

In the next few weeks additional pets continued to appear at the house with frightening regularity. Stuart would arrive home from work, usually late, increasingly intoxicated, never knowing what new animal he would have to confront or what catastrophe he would have to assimilate into his evening.

Tuesday. A plump calico cat was perched atop his easy lounger, its claw marks already visible upon the leather. Stuart chased it into the yard where it immediately tangled with the dog.

Friday. A pair of guinea pigs in a wire cage in one corner of the kitchen, arduously mating while he ate his warmed-over dinner.

The following Monday. A large green parrot, so tame it was cageless, perched by the bay windows in the living room, its droppings staining the hardwood floor Stuart had refinished himself. He spread newspapers under the perch and sent a prayer on high that whatever pet store Marilyn was frequenting didn't stock orangutans or asps.

Stuart decided that the animals must be Marilyn's way of punishing him. Then it occurred to him that it could be William who was responsible. He swore his imported beer was disappearing faster than he was drinking it. At least once he thought he detected his brother-in-law's distinctive odor, though he couldn't be sure since the downstairs reeked from the cat box and the upstairs from the aquarium, which had quickly transformed itself from crystal clarity to a disgustingly cloudy morass.

Stuart had always thought of himself as someone who liked animals. On the other hand, he now realized that he didn't like taking care of them. He remembered that was how he had lost Buck. His father had taken the dog to the pound because he always forgot to feed it. And besides the time and trouble, there was the expense. Financial freedom was one of his reasons for not having children. Granted, the pets would never go to college or get married, but the food bills for this burgeoning menagerie were no pittance and the trips to the vet had already begun: the dog had developed an abscess in one eye where the cat had mauled it. Yet what annoyed Stuart most, beyond the time spent, beyond the money expended, was the parrot.

For the most part the bird remained as motionless on its perch as a piece of bric-a-brac. It was nothing the parrot did that upset him, but what it said. Only one phrase, repeated endlessly: "Tell them Willie-boy was here. Tell them Willie-boy was here." A coincidence, Stuart thought, or further evidence that William was involved?

Regardless of who was responsible for the pets, his wife, her brother, or the pair of them in conspiracy, the presence of the animals had done nothing to soften Marilyn's behavior toward him. If anything, she was even more remote than upon first hearing about his operation. Every time Stuart entered the house, she retreated to her studio and locked the door. No amount of pounding—the veneer was beginning to splinter—or pleading could elicit a response. Their sex life, which he had sincerely hoped the vasectomy would help, was nonexistent. And their once-active social life had followed suit.

At first he tried to go to the usual round of parties, to see their usual friends and maintain appearances. Stuart quickly grew tired of making excuses for his wife, excuses that were met increasingly with knowing nods. His so-called friends, most of them divorced or already on their second or third marriage, seemed to be taking a perverse pleasure in the fact that his marriage was on the ropes. Stuart had never dreamt that his life could disintegrate so rapidly, or that so many would take so much satisfaction in its collapse.

Returning home early from one of these parties, Stuart sank into a morose reverie. His worst fears took flight in a nightmare scenario of exaggerated proportions. He saw his house transformed by William into a zoo both animal and human, inhabited by a hippie cult, with black-light posters on the walls, cat shit on the floors, dog fights in the hall, heavy metal on his turntable, his demented and ursine brother-in-law

presiding over an unwashed assemblage of freaks and burn-
outs, dispensing unknown drugs in indiscriminate quantities
and preaching on the demise of civilization. It was just such
an environment he had rescued Marilyn from in the early days
of their relationship, and as his imagination continued to play,
he saw her returning to her old ways, glassy-eyed, heavily
adorned with costume jewelry, lighting incense and wearing
beaded shawls. But no, he assured himself, even William
couldn't pull that off. People just didn't live that way anymore.

He was very drunk. He was balanced on one foot on the
gas meter at the back of the house. The tips of his fingers,
in an uncertain purchase on the window ledge, were holding him in place. He was trying to peer into Marilyn's studio
while beneath him the St. Bernard crouched, growling softly
yet from deep within its throat. Unless he was actually feeding the animal, it remained hostile.

Through the thinly cracked slats of the wooden blinds he
saw only part of the room, and no sign of Marilyn. What he
could see were her paintings, a half dozen new canvases
mounted about the walls. At first he thought they were ab-
stracts, like the rest of her work, but as he looked more
closely he noticed that these pieces were representational.
And they were all depicting the same thing. Embryos.
Dozens of embryos in every shape, size and stage of development. Incipient embryos with their cargo still boneless
and gilled. Final trimester embryos with full-fledged infants
already sucking their thumbs. All of them a mottled and
sickly green.

At that moment the St. Bernard began tugging at his pant
leg and Stuart toppled from his perch into the damp hy-
drangeas.

His temples were pounding timpani. His mouth was
stuffed with spackle and rancid cotton. Stuart cracked one

eyelid . . . peered at the clock on the bedside table . . . and felt the rush of panic.

He was two hours late for work!

Struggling with his robe as the room performed several cartwheels, he tottered to the hall. Before he could reach the bathroom, Stuart pitched head first onto the carpet. He groaned mournfully as he rolled over into a sitting position and leaned back against the wall. Something had tripped him . . . and that something was . . . a turtle!

Stuart couldn't believe his eyes. It was in the middle of the hall, drawn back into its shell, and the damn thing must have been two feet long. As to when it had arrived at the house he had no idea and he suddenly didn't care. Despite his hangover, despite the fact that his toe was bleeding, despite the fact that he liked animals, yes, he really did, a blinding rage seized him. A wave of blood red washed across his vision as he grabbed the turtle and standing with difficulty beneath its weight, hurled it at the aquarium with all the force he could manage.

The glass exploded in an earsplitting crunch. Slimy water cascaded, flooding the floor with writhing fish and a shower of multicolored gravel. Stuart hopped back awkwardly to avoid the deluge and nearly fell again.

As he watched the turtle slowly poke its head from its shell and begin to lumber into the bedroom, he realized it was Saturday. He didn't have to go to work.

The day had been well spent, Stuart thought.

He savored the silence as he cracked his second bottle of cabernet. He suspected he should cut down on his drinking, but the now animal-less house seemed cause for celebration. Now only one problem remained.

It had been days since Stuart had seen anything of Marilyn except her back as she scurried into her studio. Their relationship had become more of a cold war than a marriage. He would give her one more chance, he decided, then it was over.

He marched down the hall and pounded on the studio door, being careful to avoid the splinters.

"In case you haven't noticed," he shouted, "I've gotten rid of your animals. Every damn one of them!"

Silence.

"This is your last chance, Marilyn, either come out of there right now and come to bed . . . or I'm leaving you!"

Silence.

"To hell with you, then!"

Upstairs, Stuart quickly packed a suitcase and zippered a few suits into carrying bags. First thing in the morning he would take a hotel room in the city, something close to work, while he looked for an apartment. Of course that would be temporary. He knew a good divorce lawyer, and one way or another he would make sure the house remained in his name. As for women, he'd never had trouble finding one in the past, and he didn't expect to have trouble finding another one now.

Stuart awoke in the middle of the night to hear footsteps on the stairs. For a moment he was startled, but then he saw his wife's familiar silhouette, framed by the hall light, as she paused in the bedroom doorway.

At last, his waking mind thought with satisfaction, she'd come to her senses.

Yet as Marilyn moved across the room, Stuart sensed that something was wrong . . . terribly wrong. For although it was his wife who lowered herself onto the bed beside him, she now seemed to smell exactly like William.

"Marilee . . . ?" he whispered hesitantly.

In the dark, Stuart reached out to touch his wife's arm . . . and suddenly realized how hairy it had become. He heard a fierce growl rising from deep within her throat. He felt the claws of her nails, impossibly long, as she ripped the pajama top from his chest.

Sounds

Kathryn Ptacek

Hammer, hammer, hammer.

Faye Goodwin pursed her lips, sighed and pulled the pillow over her head. Damned roofers.

Hammer, hammer.

Even through the thickness of feathers, she could still hear the whacking of the workmen's hammers on the slate roof next door.

She opened an eye. Read the clock. 7:07. In the morning, for God's sake, on her one day off this month—a Friday to make a long and very welcome weekend—and she had to be awakened by that damned whacking.

Someone started a buzzsaw. She winced. She glanced over at her husband, Tommy, lying serenely on his back, one arm flung over his face. He was soundly asleep, would remain soundly asleep no matter what noise followed.

She envied him. She sighed, punched up her pillow, closed her eyes. She would fall asleep again and sleep until nine, maybe even ten, and then—

A drill whined.

She sat up in bed.

"W-What?" her husband mumbled, only disturbed a little from her abrupt motion. Then he was asleep again, snoring mildly.

Snoring.

There'd be no more sleep for her today.

She shook her head, pushed the covers back and got out of bed. She went to the window in the hallway and stared out at the workmen. They went on their ways blithely, completely unaware of her baleful glare.

She knew the workmen had to get an early start or they'd be working too many hours in the 90-plus temperatures under a burning sun. But still. Couldn't they go about these improvements a little more silently? She grinned at the thought. She went into the bathroom, washed her face, and even over the running water she could hear the rapping.

Ignore it, she told herself, not for the first time. She tried to blot out the alien sound, tried to concentrate on the rushing water, a much more serene sound. A gentle, soothing frequency, hypnotic almost, peaceful and—

Tap, tap, tap.

No good.

She stepped into the shower, turned on the water full blast, and only then under the stinging stream did the other noise fade away.

She dressed, swallowed an aspirin. It was going to be one of those days.

Downstairs she retrieved the newspaper off the porch steps, sat down at the table to enjoy her first cup of hot tea for the day. The dining room windows faced onto the house under renovation, and she could see the crew crawling like immense ants over the grey roof.

Before she could get irritated, she got up and pulled the windows down. The noise dimmed a little, but didn't go away.

A few minutes later Tommy came downstairs. "Mornin'," he said, as he bent over to kiss her. He smelled of some lemony aftershave, and she smiled.

"Sleep well?" she asked.

"As always," he said, going into the kitchen. "You?"

She shrugged.

"Woke up again, huh?"

"Yeah."

"Maybe you need some sort of sleeping pill, something over the counter."

She sloshed her tea around in the mug. "I think I've tried just about every one out there. They work for the first night or two, you know, and then after that I keep waking up. In fact, I think they keep me awake."

"Well," Tommy said, sliding into the chair opposite her and dipping his spoon into his bowl of cereal, "maybe you should go to see a—"

"A therapist?" Faye asked, her voice a slightly sarcastic.

"Let me finish, okay? I was going to say a hypnotist."

"Oh. I hadn't thought of that."

"A guy at the office went to one—I could probably get the name, if you want—and he quit smoking. He used to smoke two-three packs a day."

She nodded thoughtfully. "Get the name, if it's no bother. I think that might be good. Sure is worth a try, I guess."

"Maybe you can take a nap today."

"Not with that going on," she pointed with her chin toward the windows.

"Isn't it kind of warm? Do you really want the windows closed, Faye?"

"It cuts down on the racket."

He gave her That Look—the expression she always hated, and always felt held more than a little condescension. "Hon, you've really got to do something about that. Face it, we live in a noisy world, and it's not going to get any quieter." He took his bowl out to the kitchen and ran water in it.

She made a face at his back, then looked down at her mug. She didn't know why she did that, except that she always suspected that he really didn't understand how horrible it was for her. How bad the level of noise could get.

"It would be much more quiet if we lived in the country," she said. "Hon, don't start on that again. I told you that with the cost of property, we just can't afford it. At least right now. If one of us gets a raise, maybe we can sock the extra dough away. Until then you'll just have to put up with a boisterous town. At least it's not the city."

She said nothing.

"See you." He kissed her again, picked up his jacket and a few minutes later she heard him chatting with the work-men. A few minutes later the car started up. It popped and sputtered; the engine needed tuning.

Faye gritted her teeth.

With mug in hand, she wandered into the living room and draped herself across the easy chair and turned on the tv. She didn't normally watch television in the daytime, but she was curious to see what was on at this hour. An earnest-looking host talking about incest, and some quiz show with lots of buzzers and flashing lights, a nature show about koalas, a couple of music stations, the weather channel, CNN, others. She flipped through the stations, then again as if expecting to find something else, then finally turned the tv off. Too much noise.

From one of the houses across the street she heard the faint beat of rock music. Something by some heavy metal group.

Swell.

A car went by, the windows rolled down, a Bach concerto blasting out.

Not even the classics were sacred, she thought with a faint smile.

Enough of this. Faye stood, looked around the room. So, what was she going to do? Well, she could go to the mall, but that meant a thirty-minute drive, crowds and that mad-dening piped-in music that followed her everywhere. Couldn't people survive without having to listen to some-thing every minute?

The mall was definitely out. The grocery store was not. Once there, she claimed a cart and started up and down the aisles.

The p.a. system played songs from the late '60s, all homogenized into bland music. The system crackled and a man's voice announced a special today on lean ground beef. He droned on about the different uses for ground beef. Finally, the ad ended, and the music—the Beatles' "I Want to Hold Your Hand," one of her favorites—came on in mid-tune.

That irritated her even more, but she wasn't sure which was more offensive—the lackluster renditions of the music or just the plain fact that there was music. She didn't know why she hated noise so much; from her early childhood on she had been particularly noise-sensitive, at least that's what her mother had called it. Faye had always disliked loud voices and sounds, and had always crawled into her parents' large walk-in closet when thunder boomed outside. She could hear the whine of air conditioning as she walked into department stores when no one else could. Once she had begun crying as a small airplane circled over their house. Her father had sworn it was simply a stage that she would outgrow; only she hadn't.

It hadn't gotten better with age; it had grown worse, much worse.

Most of the time she had an uneasy truce with her sensitivity. Then there were the other times . . . days like today.

Somewhere, maybe a few rows over, a young child began crying. Faye waited for the child to stop, but it didn't; it was building to an enthusiastic crescendo. It was a wonder those small lungs didn't give out. Her hands clenched on the cart handle. She braked before the paper products and tossed in paper towels.

The wailing grew louder. The high-pitched voice rose and fell in a pathetic undulation. The mother's voice was shrill and she was telling her child that the child really shouldn't cry.

Faye shook her head in disgust. The mother ought to just say no, and then bop the kid on the butt once or twice. That would stop the whining. God knows, it had happened enough to her. Of course, she hadn't been prone to pitching temper tantrums, either. That wasn't allowed in her family.

A gentle throbbing began in her temple; her headache was returning. Faye pushed her cart toward the end of the aisle, trying to get away from the noise. But it followed her wherever she went.

She hurried through the produce section, lobbed lettuce and radishes and spinach into the basket. She would surprise Tommy with a really big salad. Somewhere else in the store another child began crying, picking up the refrain of the first. Then a third started whimpering.

When she got to the check-out stand, Faye flung her items onto the belt as quickly as possible and watched the checker ring them up one by one.

"How can you stand to work with all this noise? These kids must drive you crazy."

The checker, a woman with a big black mole on her chin, shook her head. "Don't hear it after a while. It just sort of blends together pretty soon."

"You're lucky."

"Yeah, I guess so. That's twenty-three fifty. You should have been here when they were remodeling the store. All that hammering and drilling day in, day out—it was terrible."

Faye shuddered, drove home. The workers were still next door; she had entertained some vague hope that they might have called it quits. Right.

After she had taken several more aspirin, she wandered into the living room. She was going to read. She should do a little housework, but she knew she couldn't take the howling of the vacuum cleaner. She read for a while and only gradually became aware of another noise, a clanging and banging. She glanced out the window and saw the garbage men. Why, she wondered, when the garbage cans were plastic now, did these guys have to make all this noise? The truck moved slowly down the street, the noise finally receding.

It was noisy at the office, too, where she worked as staff writer. Her job was to translate computer talk into people talk, and the constant clatter of printers and phones and people talking, chairs squeaking, doors being slammed grated. Some days she wondered how anyone—how she—could take it. But no one complained about the noise, and she figured she was just being sensitive.

Too damned sensitive for her own good—wasn't that what Dad always said?

At lunch she fixed a simple cheese sandwich and had a soda, and while she was sitting at the dining room table still reading, she heard a high-pitched whining. Like a buzzsaw, only she knew that sound very well. Even over the sound of hammering and the shouts of the workmen, she could hear that grating noise, though.

She stepped out onto the front porch; the sound grew louder.

Something bright flashed along the street. The whining came from it.

It turned out to be one of those remote control cars, and she watched as a man with his young son played with the toy. Around it went, then up and down in front of her house. It was nice that he was with his son, she thought, but why couldn't they have found something silent, like a kite, to play with?

She found herself gritting her teeth, forced herself to relax, went back in and closed the front door and windows facing that direction.

Not good enough, but the best she could do.

She read until the kids came home from school, then, her finger marking her place in the book, she looked out the window and watched as the junior high kids cut across her lawn. They were yelling to one another, and one of them held a large silver radio that blasted out some loud song with a fast beat. They cursed at each other and pushed each other around, and shouted, even though they were standing only a few feet away from each other.

Didn't kids speak in civil tones any more? In *hushed* tones? she wondered.

It had always been hard to deal with, this noise sensitivity. She'd tried ear plugs years before, but they really hadn't helped. She tried ignoring the sounds, but couldn't concentrate fully.

Maybe the hypnotist Tommy had mentioned that morning would help, though; she hoped so. All these noises were driving her crazy.

It didn't help that Tommy snored so loudly sometimes at night that she woke up and was unable to go back to sleep until she came downstairs and camped out on the sofa. Even then, she'd be able to hear the snoring faintly, but at least it no longer kept her awake.

And he always kept the television volume much too high, just like her father had. Her father had been slightly deaf, though; Tommy was young yet. Maybe she would suggest that he have his hearing checked out.

She knew hers didn't need it.

At least, she thought, the boy and his father and the awful toy had gone off. Maybe the thing was broken; that would be good news.

Her mother had been the type to slam drawers and doors. If she was mad, slam went a dresser drawer. Or the door to the oven. Or the backdoor. With each jar, Faye had jumped. She was always glad that she came from a family of three rather than thirteen.

After a while she heard the ticking of the clock in the hallway. Tommy had bought that for their anniversary. With each swing of the brass pendulum there was a resonant echo, like the striking of a padded hammer on wood. Almost a muffled sound. Not muffled enough.

The refrigerator went on. The appliance needed work, and for years it had made cooing noises, like a dove. Sometimes at night as she lay in bed, trying to sleep, she could hear that persistent cooing.

Water dripped from the kitchen faucet. Drop by drop. She would have to remind Tommy again this weekend to get a new washer for the faucet. They were wasting too much water.

Her headache was back, and growing worse. It was centered over one eye and throbbed. She bet if she put her fingers on that spot she'd feel it pulsating. She got up and took some more aspirin, took a deep breath, and told herself to relax.

Somewhere, on the other side of the street, a phone rang and a loud voice answered it, and she listened to a conversation she didn't want to hear.

Kids squealed as they played in their front yards.

Bluejays squawked at each other in the mulberry tree outside her window. A lawn mower growled two houses down.

Tommy really was pretty good about all of this, she told herself. She tried not to complain about the noise, because he didn't understand. No one—not even her closest friends—did, because none of them could hear as well as she could. They all complained about varying hearing loss, and she always thought that they were the lucky ones, that she was the cursed one.

A jet shrieked overhead.

You're too sensitive, her father always grumbled, as if it were really something she could control.

The neighbor next door began working on the sports car he never drove. She heard the racing engine, a grinding of gears, the beeping of the horn.

Another phone shrilled.

It was just that she never could seem to get away from the noise. It was always badgering her, assaulting her. She hated it.

A television blared.

Too sensitive.

A piano—someone playing "Heart and Soul" over and over and over.

The pulsating pain returned.

An ambulance, or perhaps it was a police car, raced down

the next block out, the wailing siren rising and falling, rising and falling.

Another lawn mower roared into life, while the kid and his father returned with the remote control car.

Too damned sensitive . . .

The refrigerator hummed again, while the furnace rumbled on.

Her phone rang. And rang, and rang, and rang, and still she sat on the couch, and listened to all the noises of the house and her neighborhood.

Tommy parked the car in the driveway, waved to old Mr. Miller who was just finishing clipping his hedges two doors down. He went into the house.

"Faye, hi, I'm home." He heard nothing but the ticking of the grandfather clock in the hallway. He listened for running water, thinking she might be taking a bath, but he didn't hear it. Maybe she was out back.

"Faye?" This time louder.

Still no answer.

He heard something in the kitchen then, and he realized she was out there, probably making dinner.

He stopped on the threshold of the kitchen. "Hi, hon, how are you?" She stood at the counter with her back to him. She was cutting up vegetables for a salad.

"Hon?" Was this a game, he thought with a sly smile? Then: was she mad at him for some reason and ignoring him?

He stepped closer.

On the counter, not far from the salad bowl, he saw an icepick, and a smear of something red on the countertop.

"Honey, I got the name of the hypnotist; it's some guy who just—" he began, then stopped when Faye turned around and he saw the blood trickling from her ears.

Whispers of the Unrepentant

t. Winter-Damon

I.

I a mbored with this grey, untextured tapestry—
    These chafing shackles of restrained banality,
        Unleavened wafers,
           Tepid water,
              Saltless meat . . .
Your perfumes no longer seem so sweet,
    Fire without warmth,
        Frost without chill . . .
Your laughter is silent, the strains of your music still.
        I AM THE HELLRAKE . . .
           I am the footsteps in the
              darkness

I crave—
    To shed the fabric and stain it red;
        These moral chains to smash and rend;
           To glutton the blue and mouldy bread;
              To swill the Dark Gods' crimson wine;
                To gorge on savory, dripping
                    flesh.

My pulse throbs—
>To the coffin's wild, necrotic scent,
>>To the warm and fragrant musk of blood;
>>>Hell's fires fill me with their molten flame;
>>>>Arctic ecstasy the stolen corpse cold
>>>>kiss.
Demons' laughter echoes in the wind.
>The dirge rapture sets my head awhirl.
>>The choirs of The Damned: quicksilver bliss . . .
>>>I AM THE HELLRAKE . . .
>>>>*I am the footsteps in the
>>>>darkness*

II.
Sister Drusilla, dearest of the three—
>Shall we wash our hands in blood while you sit upon
>my knee?
>>>I AM THE HELLRAKE . . .

My name the epithet for lust-inflicted pain—
>That fixation of disgust soon waxes pleasurable as
>cherished vices wane . . .
>>>*I am the footsteps in the
>>>darkness*

Whitechapel five? or seven? harlots wedded to my
blade—
>>Lawyer? surgeon? jew? or prince? What a novel
>>masquerade!
>>>I AM THE HELLRAKE . . .

Death to pigs! Acid family, blind carnage yet to wreak—
>Apocalypse in black and white the vision that I seek . . .
>>*I am the footsteps in the
>>darkness*

* * *

This is my cold and sweating hand that holds the .44—
    You know it is the mongrel's voice that leads me to
       your door!
          I AM THE HELLRAKE . . .

My wife's head turns backwards in mock disbelief—
    I have a freezer full of secrets and some most
       suspicious beef . . .
               I am the footsteps in the
                     darkness

III.
Cloying Virtue's sugared promise, bile upon my lips,
    Dark Angel rising through The Well of Time.
Your cretin philosophies term each crimson masterpiece
    Yet another violent crime . . .
          I AM THE HELLRAKE . . .
               I am the footsteps in
                  the darkness.

Obscene Phone Calls

John Coyne

"You're a sonovabitch!" It was a woman's voice, strong and wide awake.

"Hello?" Steve yawned and glanced at his SONY Digimatic glowing in the dark. It was already past midnight.

"You're a bastard!" She spoke again with authority. "I've been up half the night and you're not going to sleep at my expense."

"Hey, what's this?" Steve whispered back. Beside him, the woman stirred.

"Why are you whispering? Got some woman with you?" Her voice was quick and sharp.

"Say, listen, sweetheart, you've got the wrong guy . . ."

"You really are something else!"

"It's the middle of the goddamn night, and you've got the wrong number, sister."

"Your name is Steve Mirachi and you live in an apartment on Hillyer Place above Dupont Circle and this evening at Discount Records you spent ten minutes eyeballing me and I just wanted you to know I think you're a goddamn sonovabitch!" She slammed the receiver in his ear.

"Bitch!" Steve swore and then, shaking his head, replaced the headpiece.

"What's that?" the woman mumbled.

"I have no idea. A wrong number, I guess." He slid down next to the sleeping woman.

He remembered watching several women in the record store, but he always watched girls, and now no face or body came to mind. Whoever it was must have followed him home, seen where he lived. Weird! The thought made him nervous.

He had gone out again later in the evening, around the corner to Childe Harold and there he had met Wendy. He glanced at the girl burrowed in bed beside him. Or was her name Tiby? He couldn't remember and he fell asleep trying to recall her first name.

The next morning he was up early and out of the apartment before the girl woke. He disliked awkward morning goodbyes and he only left her a note next to the Taster's Choice.

I'm off; Saturday shopping day!
Leave a phone number, okay?
We'll get together . . .
Love ya,
Steve

Steve had been transferred by his company to Washington only that spring and when he wasn't on the road selling his line of leather goods, he'd spend his Saturday mornings in Georgetown, wandering from shop to shop, watching the women. Then he'd go to Clyde's for a Bloody Mary and omelet and stand by the bar so he could see the door.

He had never seen so many women: tall and thin and braless. Breathtakingly beautiful women! They'd come through the door, toss their long hair into place with a flip of their heads while scanning the room with wide dark eyes. They never missed a thing, or a man. He could see their eyes register when they spotted him.

On Saturday mornings he always dressed well. The clothes alone attracted their attention this Saturday. He was wearing a bold flower design shirt and had left the four top buttons open to show his chest and, in his patch of thick black chest hair, an imitation Roman coin dangled on a gold chain.

Steve was built like an offensive lineman, with short legs, a thickly trunk and no neck whatsoever. His square head appeared as if it was driven down between his shoulders with a sledge.

It was a head with surprisingly small features. The nose, lips, and ears were tiny and delicate, almost feminine. His eyes were gray, the color of soot, and set too close together. He had lots of hair and that he let grow, but it was fine hair and wouldn't hold its shape, even with conditioner.

Steve spent at least two hours every Saturday at Clyde's, watching and meeting women. It was an odd Saturday when he didn't come home with a new name and telephone number. Steve was on a first name basis with all the bartenders at Clyde's. He was also known at Mr. Smith and up Wisconsin at the Third Edition, and at most of the bars on M Street. For a newcomer in town, he thought with some pride, he had gotten around, become known.

"You've been a pig with a friend of mine." She phoned again a week later, and again it was after midnight.

"Who are you?" Steve whispered. The girl beside him began to stir.

"Don't you respect women?"

He strained to recognize the voice.

"You only make a woman once or twice, is that the average?

"Go screw yourself!" Steve slammed down the phone, and it rang again immediately.

"Who's it?" the woman in the bed mumbled.

"Some goddamn nut case . . . " The phone kept ringing. Steve swore again and, climbing out of bed, took the receiver off the hook. He wrapped a towel around the headpiece, as if he were smothering a small animal, and put the telephone in a dresser drawer. The next morning, he told himself, he would have his number changed and left unlisted.

Nevertheless, for several weeks afterwards whenever he brought a woman home with him, he'd take the phone off the receiver and place it in a drawer, out of sight and sound. He also found himself searching for the caller. He listened carefully to all the women he met on the job and after work in the Washington bars. He made lists of the women he had slept with since moving to the District and eliminated those he knew wouldn't call.

Still, he wasn't certain. He became less sure of himself around stretched the cord and peered through the front window. She was there, he knew. Somewhere in the dark houses across the quiet street, she was watching him. It gave him the creeps.

"Quit staring out the window. I'm not outside. I don't live across the street."

"How do you know I'm looking?"

"You're the type. You don't have much imagination. Now, come on, Stevie, let me talk to the woman, or are you afraid?"

Steve muffled the receiver with his palm and explained to his date. "It's some crazy chick that keeps calling me. She wants to talk to you."

"Oh, no!" The teenager backed away.

"It's okay. I'm here." He smiled his little boy smile to show she had nothing to fear and coaxed her towards the phone.

She took the receiver cautiously and, keeping it at bay, whispered hello. She was a cute peaches 'n' cream high school graduate from Virginia that Steve had met that night at The Greenery. Steve wasn't sure, but he thought her name was Shirley.

Shirley listened attentively to his caller and Steve had a moment's panic. He had an urge to pull the telephone from her, but he didn't want to seem nervous. Instead, he went into the kitchen to mix drinks, and when he returned, the girl was replacing the phone as if she had just heard bad news.

"I'd like to leave," she whispered.

"For Chrissake . . . what did that dyke say?"

"She's not . . . that way."

"Like hell! That's the reason she's after me. I know about that stuff." He kept talking rapidly, afraid to let the girl talk.

"Would you please call a taxi?" she finally managed to say.

"You can't pull that crap on me! I have a right to know what she said."

"It doesn't concern you."

"It's my damn telephone!" He began to stride about the apartment, pacing to its walls, then spinning around and striking off for the other side of the room. "Goddamn dyke!" he mumbled and finished off his drink. To the girl, he said, "If you want to leave, leave, but find your own taxi!"

She left without a word and when Steve heard the door close behind him, he spun around and gave the finger to the empty room.

He now couldn't find a date in Washington. The word, he knew, had spread about him. That woman had done it to him. At night when he wandered up and down M Street, women looked away. It was done subtly. Their eyes swept across his face when he walked into a bar. The eyes registered him, then moved off. No one seemed to even see him. It was as if he wasn't there any longer.

He went home early after work, turned on the tube or worked with his weights. Then before ten o'clock, he took a cold shower and dropped into bed. He let the radio play all night to keep him company.

At work when he made his calls none of the saleswomen noticed him. And there were women in those stores that he had taken home, who had cried for him in the night, and whimpered against his chest. Now they let him pass. His swaggering attitude crumbled. He no longer winked at strangers, checked out women's legs. He began to hedge with work, phone for orders, and never left his desk. He took days off to sit by the window of his apartment and watch the street like an abandoned pet, left home alone.

"Are you sorry?" She telephoned again, early one evening.

"I haven't done anything. I'm no worse than the next guy. You're being unfair."

"Have you been fair to us? The women you've taken home?" Her voice had a curl to it.

"They came of their own free will. I'm the one being punished. No one in Washington will date me. You started this!"

"It's not my fault you can't date. Washington's a small town. Word gets around."

"You owe me at least one meeting, you know, after all of this." Steve began to pace. "I'm not giving you a line. How 'bout a drink some night? I'll meet you at Bixby's . . . you like that place."

She was silent and Steve let her take her time deciding. With women like this, he knew he had to be cool.

"I'm not sure."

"One drink. A half hour. I'd like to ask you a few questions. I have to hear your rap, okay? Maybe you've got a point."

"No drinks."

"Okay. Lunch?"

"No. I'll meet you at five o'clock in Dupont Circle."

"Fine! How will I know you?"

"Don't worry. I'll find you." And she hung up.

Steve would have rather met her at the Dupont Circle Hotel. A nice, cool and dark afternoon lounge where there were private booths, well-dressed people, the feeling of leather under his fingers. He appreciated quality and operated best in such places. But Dupont Circle! The park was full of young people and the homeless. They cluttered the grass like litter.

He sat away from the center fountain, picked a spot in the

shade away from the crowd. He had come ten minutes early to give himself time to be settled and positioned. Steve had taken time dressing. He wanted to look good for this woman.

He had dressed conservatively and wore a navy blazer, a striped tie, white shirt, and summer linen slacks. It would impress her, he knew. Also he had a couple days of early summer tan and his weight was down. Just thinking about the fine impression he'd make made him feel great.

He'd be boyish with her, he decided. He'd keep the conversation general, and not push her for a date. Only a name and a phone number. She was going to be someone special. Anyway, he thought, it was about time he dropped all those salesgirls and secretaries. A guy with his position, the whole District as his territory; he could do a lot better, he knew.

"Hi!" A woman spoke to him.

Steve glanced along the bench at the young girl that had been sitting there. He looked over at her defensively, expecting trouble. She smiled. She was wearing a short dress, sandals. Her blond hair was long and loose. She wasn't bad looking, with big brown eyes and a bright smile. She looked, however, about sixteen.

"Your questions?" She tossed her hair away from her face and stared regally at him. Her brown eyes tightened and her wide mouth sealed up like a long white envelope.

"You?" He began to perspire.

She nodded.

"Well . . . ah . . . I was . . . I guess I was expecting someone else." He shifted around, clapped his hands together as if gripping a football, and thought: she made the whole story up. She was some kind of sex freak. He had never in his life tried to pick up a kid. "Okay, sister, you're not what I had in mind. Forget I arranged this, okay? We don't have anything to say to each other."

"You poor bastard."

"Why don't you stay with your gang?" He waved toward the grass.

"What's the matter? You don't hustle young girls?"

"I wouldn't touch you with rubber gloves. No street traffic for me." He wiped his face with a handkerchief, looked away.

"I bet you're something in bed." She kept a smile on her face like an insult.

"Better than anything you've had, sister." He sat up straight.

"I'm not going to call you again," she said calmly. "I had this notion I might be able to reach you, but you're such a pathetic person. Oh, you'll get women to date you, Steve. Silly women who don't know better. But you have nothing to offer a real woman."

"Hey, bitch, you don't know me."

"Stevie, you boys are all alike." And with that she left him alone on the bench.

He retreated to the cool, dark bar of Dupont Circle where he bought the only other guy at the bar—a furniture salesman from North Carolina—a round of drinks. Steve told him about the girl, about his phone calls and meeting her in the park, but the salesman didn't see the joke. Well, Steve summed up, you had to have been there.

He stood back from the bar, shook his head and grinned, "Goddamn bitch!"

He'd get another apartment, he decided. He'd move out of the District. He'd live somewhere over in Virginia or Maryland, maybe Vienna. He'd live out where normal people lived, and get away from the crazies in the city.

Several months later, just before he did move out of the District, not to Vienna but instead to Gaithersburg, he saw her again. Steve's boss was in town and he had taken him to the Hay-Adams for lunch. It was the kind of restaurant Steve liked to be seen in. People in position and with money, he knew, ate there, and sitting among them made him feel special.

He saw her when she was leaving the restaurant. She was passing tables and causing a stir. All around the room businessmen looked up and smiled at her. She moved gracefully and quickly through the tables, her long blond hair styled and swept away from her face. She was wearing makeup, but not enough to draw attention away from her brilliant bright eyes, her perfect white skin.

She was wearing a pinstripe trouser skirt, long-sleeve shirt, weskit and blazer. In one hand she carried a thin leather attache case. Steve realized as he watched her that she was the most beautiful woman in the city.

She saw him. Her large brown eyes held him briefly in focus and then she looked away and continued past him. He didn't exist at all.

The Children Never Lie

Cameron Nolan

"I tellya, Addie, it's our chance. Almost as good as winning the Lottery. Hell, maybe better." He picked up his coffee mug, the one with his Valencia County Sheriffs shield on the side, a personalized (and cheap) gift from the Chamber of Commerce. Twenty-five years of service. He shook his head at the thought. Too long. As he took a swig from the cup he looked out the kitchen window at the flat brown fields which rolled toward the purple mountains in the distance.

Cotton and sugar beets, not what usually came to mind when people thought of California. Five thousand square miles of farms, just like back home in Libertyville, Nebraska, only there it had been corn and sorghum. He'd come 1,500 miles to trade corn and sorghum for cotton and sugar beets, and a county sheriffs pissy salary.

But things were due to change.

He thought about the beautiful Spanish colonial sign outside the La Palma Mobile Home Estates in San Diego. He already had the lot for a trailer picked out: Number 15-A. It overlooked the ocean, had palm trees front and back, a sweet little side yard, and a clear view of San Diego twenty miles to the south. Blue sky and blue ocean and white sea gulls . . . It was all going to be theirs, he really believed it now. For the first time, he really *believed* it.

He took a long drag on his Marlboro and fingered the collar of his uniform shirt where it rubbed against the wrinkled flesh of his neck. He knew he looked older than his sixty years. Too damn much sun, he thought. It was hard to avoid in farming country.

He looked over to where his wife was flouring the meat for chicken fried steak. "Dr. Martin says these kids were 'probably' molested. *'Probably,'* he says! Shit!"

He sighed and took another drag on his cigarette. "I called Ben in Sacramento—at the Attorney General's office—and he told me to phone the Sarazan Center in San Francisco and have their psychologists come down to examine all the children. So when I call them, they tell me they'd be *happy* to do it—for their regular fee. Gonna run over a thousand per kid before this thing is over, maybe a whole lot more than that. Last election the good voters of this county decide they can't raise my salary a lousy two thousand a year, and suddenly they're pleased as punch to pay maybe fifty thousand to some head doctors from Frisco. It isn't fair, Addie. It just isn't."

She looked up from the boiled potatoes she was mashing. "Millie at the grocery store told me people want to pay whatever's necessary. She says it's all anybody talks about these days. Clint, do *you* think it's true? You know more than anybody else right now. Do *you* believe it?"

He looked at her quickly, then shifted his eyes back out the window again, looking deep into the horizon. He shook his head. "I don't know, Addie. I just don't. It seems unbelievable that something like this could happen out here in the sticks. But it's my responsibility as an officer of the law to investigate this to the fullest extent. That's what I'm gonna do."

He drank from his mug. "Whatever happens, I give the big city papers two days—maybe three—before they pick up on it. And once it's in the headlines up and down the state, *everybody* is going to know who Clinton Lansdale, Sheriff of Valencia County, California, is.

"And then two things are gonna happen. First, we're going to get a lot of calls from movie and TV producers who want to buy the story. Just like that teacher up in Placerville a few months ago who got two dozen calls from producers after his story hit the big city papers. So that guy's set for life—all 'cause he got fired for doing too good a job! One way or another, I tellya, we're going to be seeing some real money real fast."

He looked at her, his eyes intense.

"The second thing that's gonna happen is the people of this county are going to see me in a whole new light. I'm going to be Big Time, Addie, a real celebrity. And when elections come up next year, they'll be *proud* to vote me a salary increase. So no matter what happens now, we're gonna be okay. Honest to God, honey, we're gonna be okay."

"The children *have* been molested, Sheriff Lansdale. Every one of them. We have proof." The smartly-dressed woman searched through her expensive leather briefcase for some papers.

"Here we have a preliminary summary of the results of our examinations. The completed examinations are all on videotape, of course, for use in court, and we still have several weeks of investigation ahead of us. More detailed information from each child is needed; obtaining that data is our next task. But the preliminary results are quite important. Just look at these."

Melissa Hamilton handed over several sheets of expensive paper with the Sarazan Center logo engraved at the top of each one.

Class, Clint thought. He didn't have much use for psychologists but Melissa Hamilton and this Sarazan Center were class all the way.

"As you'll see, we have documented a variety of criminal

charges for you to choose from when you and the District Attorney prepare your indictments. We at the Sarazan Center pride ourselves on the professionalism we bring to our legal services. We offer depth *and* breadth, in order that local law officials can create airtight cases that are virtually guaranteed to result in guilty verdicts."

He looked over the summary sheets, blinked. What he was reading was bizarre, beyond belief. "It says here that some of the children were taken to Nevada and used in child prostitution!" he exclaimed incredulously.

"Oh, yes, we found that quite interesting. We have established scenarios in both Reno and Las Vegas."

"What's all this devil worship stuff?" He looked at Melissa Hamilton skeptically. "We sure don't have any devil worshippers here in Valencia County."

She smiled with the syrupy condescension of the sophisticated city professional towards the country bumpkin.

"Of course, this is a shock to you, Sheriff Lansdale. We run into such disbelief all the time. What you must realize is that the sexual abuse of children is the most well-hidden of crimes. Usually, no one other than the abuser and the victim knows what is occurring. We're lucky in this case because we have more than two dozen children involved, and the abusers appear to number at least ten. We're not sure yet just how many people are involved or exactly who those particular people are, because our established investigation format focuses first on breaking down each child's personal privacy boundaries. *Then* we detail specific acts which have occurred. That's where we are now. After we get the children to trust us—tell us the things they thought they couldn't tell anyone—we then go into the specifics of exactly who did what to them, how many times, under what conditions, and so on. It's a multi-step procedure which has been developed in order to maximally utilize the memory potentials of the children we are examining."

He put the papers down on the desk. "How do you know the children are telling the truth?"

"We have scientifically-approved ways of establishing data," she said. "Initially, we use anatomically correct dolls in which the genitals are greatly enlarged. When a child manipulates two or more dolls in such a manner as to indicate oral sex, for example, we know that such an act has occurred in the life of that child."

"Couldn't they just be playing with the dolls and however they put them, it's still just a child playing?"

"Oh, no. When a child manipulates an anatomically correct doll, each action has specific meaning. That's been well established in scientific literature."

"And how do you know who supposedly did this to them? Do you ask the child for names?"

"We do, of course. But we seldom get a direct answer. Instead, the children answer *indirectly;* all children do. We give them crayons and paper and they draw pictures. Whenever they draw monsters, we ask them who the monsters are, what the monsters are named. *That* they tell us—*then* we know who the 'monsters' in their real lives are. Once a child identifies an abuser, we ask the other children about that particular person. They are relieved the secret is out and usually admit quite readily that that person also abused them."

"You mean, you take a child and give it naked dolls with big genitals—some crayons and paper—and whatever the child seems to indicate, you depend on that being the *truth?"*

"Oh, absolutely. It's well established medical procedure used by virtually all child abuse investigators throughout the United States."

Clint shook his head in disbelief. The county was paying thousands of dollars for just this information, and he couldn't accept any of it. Well, maybe sometimes it worked, some of it. But *all* the time? These people might be doctors and have initials after their names out the ass, but he'd developed a lot of common sense over the years and his gut told him this was, mostly, totally nuts. But he held a tiger by the tail now and he knew it. One way or another all this had to be seen through. Besides, these Sarazan Center people were *professionals*. Surely they knew what they were doing.

One way or another, his future and Addie's depended on him doing his job and doing it right.

If only it didn't seem so crazy.

"What do you do now?" he asked her.

"At the moment, we don't have any idea who did these things to the children. The next step is determining who is involved. We must quantify data: names, dates, times of day, locations."

"How long do you expect everything to take?"

"Another two weeks, perhaps three. I have five experienced interviewers working on the children now. We ought to begin getting specific data within the next day or so. My interviewers know what they're doing, Sheriff," she added. "We've obtained data on some of the most resistant cases imaginable. Compared to some, this is a piece of cake."

"And you're *certain* this is *real*? This is the *truth?*"

"Just remember the first rule of child sexual abuse, Sheriff: The children *never* lie."

There was a hoot owl outside and he always felt good when he heard a hoot owl greeting the moon. Comforted. You knew that wise bird (all owls *were* wise, he'd been convinced of it since he was a child) was somehow watching over you. Which made life a bit easier to take when everything seemed so all-fired crazy. Clint looked out into the lonely moonlit fields from the living room. He'd stubbed out three Marlboros since he sat down, unable to sleep, and now he sat in the dark without even the friendly red glow of a cigarette to keep him company.

The last of the arrests was over, he hoped. Twelve people—people he'd thought were among the good people of Valencia County—were now in the county jail. Which meant, of course, that the jail was three hundred percent over maximum legal capacity. Nobody'd ever figured on a series of crimes like this in Valencia County when the jail was built. God, he still couldn't believe it.

Duane MacAllister, who owned the feed and supply store, the principal sponsor of the Valencia County 4-H Club. Agnes Hobson, the music teacher for all the Valencia County public schools. Pete Dubrevick, who carried the mail for half the county. And Dr. Martin, the one who'd said the kids had "probably" been molested. He was one too. It was like the whole world had suddenly gone nuts. These people he'd known intimately all these years.

It was sick and awful, his soul hurt, and there wasn't a damn thing he could do to make sense out of it. If all these people were guilty, then Sheriff Clinton Lansdale didn't know a damn thing about human nature.

It was time, he realized suddenly, for him to retire.

The realization had been coming a long time. Hell, he probably would have done it five years ago if he'd had the money. But he didn't then, and now he did. Well, almost. The producers had been calling, just like he'd promised Addie. It was the biggest news story of the month and not just in California, either. It was all over national television—even around the world—and Clinton Lansdale was now an honest-to-God celebrity. A week ago he'd even gone to San Francisco to appear on "Nightline" with Ted Koppel. The network had sent their own plane, flown him to San Francisco, put him up in a suite at the St. Francis, and then flown him home again.

He'd never been so scared in his life, not even the time years ago when that murderer had escaped from San Quentin and was ready to kill him in Mike Cahill's barn. But he'd looked fine on TV—everybody said so—and it was a shoo-in for him to get a fat raise in the next election.

But he didn't have to depend on that now. No, he was going to sell his story to the TV movies for a quarter of a million dollars. That was the price and the contracts were being drawn up. Two hundred and fifty thousand dollars. Enough for the rest of their lives in San Diego.

Another six months, and Number 15-A at the La Palma Mobile Home Estates would be Home, Sweet Home.

Outside the living room window he saw the glint of shiny metal moving in the night. Someone was in the front yard. His cop's senses aroused, he suddenly realized there was more than one person. He could see dark motion by the eucalyptus tree, more over by the wooden fence. Quietly, Clint stood and went for his weapon.

He couldn't figure out why, but the house was under siege. Terrorists? Drug-crazed motorcycle freaks? He didn't know, but he *did* know that it would take at least ten minutes for backup to arrive from town. By that time, if he wasn't careful, he and Addie could both be dead.

Adrenalin pumping, his mind clearer than it had been in years, Clint walked softly towards the bedroom to wake her. Every second counted.

The door exploded open with light and sound. A spotlight, his mind registered—the type used by city SWAT teams. He was pinned in its beam, unable to move. He noticed that he could see the weave on his cotton pajamas, each hair on the back of his hands. Those lights were damn good, some part of his mind registered. I wish Valencia County could afford one.

"Freeze!" an authoritative voice ordered. "This is the FBI. Turn around and face the wall, hands in plain sight. Spread your legs apart."

Incredulously, automatically, he did what he had ordered so many others to do over the years. The hands that patted him down were professional. It didn't make any sense, but these were no terrorists or hippies. They *were* the law.

The man in charge, keeping him covered, came nearer. "You are under arrest. You have the right to remain silent. If you give up the right to remain silent, anything you say can and will . . . "

Addie was suddenly there. Nobody could have slept

through the last five minutes. When had she appeared in the doorway? Clint didn't know. She was looking at him oddly, which he found strange. Then the other FBI man, dressed in camouflage, was talking quietly to her. Her eyes were getting big and round like she couldn't understand what the man was saying, except she did.

He'd never seen that expression before on Addie's face, but he'd seen it on lots of others. First was years ago when he'd had to go over to Emma Dunham's place and tell her Frank had been killed in a tractor accident near the bridge. That was the first time he'd seen that expression—just a couple of months after he became a deputy sheriff—but he'd seen it plenty of times since. Total disbelief mixed with total belief, all at the same time.

It was the horrible look of a human being stretched to the limits of endurance, and now it was on his own wife's face.

The trial was a nightmare. At first, in the months before the trial began, Addie came to visit him every week. Then gradually, as his bail was denied and the press and television went to work, she came less and less. She was in court the day the verdict came in—he saw her sitting next to the back door—but she acted as if she'd never seen him before. Her face didn't have any expression on it. She was just going through the motions, living each day as it came until God called her home, just like she'd been taught at the First Baptist Church back in Nebraska when she was a little girl.

His last thought before the verdict was read was that he wasn't married anymore. His wife had died, though her body continued to function. It was a sobering thought: it hit him more deeply than the guilty verdict which he had already come to expect.

It didn't matter that he'd never done any of the things he was accused of. He was innocent, but he knew that his innocence was irrelevant in this age of scientific knowledge and expert witnesses. The children had identified him.

They'd told immensely detailed stories of how he had done ghastly perverted things to them, and to chickens and rabbits and geese and sheep and cows and horses and dogs and cats.

They told of things he'd never heard of in all his career as a law officer.

It had happened—was *supposed* to have happened—Wednesday nights. Those interminable Wednesdays when he had all night patrol duty. But the children said those were the nights he did things to them and to the animals. He had no alibi—why would a sheriff, doing his job as he was supposed to do, need an alibi?—and the children were so sincere, so detailed, so . . . *right*.

Except none of it ever happened.

After a while, as the trial dragged on (one of the longest trials in California history), he gave up. He didn't know how to answer the child abuse experts with their degrees and their graphs and their scientific studies and their videotapes of children identifying him as the ringleader of the "cult."

That's what the newspapers and the experts called it, a "cult."

It seemed so weak just to say that it never happened.

But the children never lie. "The children never lie." Over and over and over again the numerous official experts agreed: the children *never* lie.

The verdict was guilty on all counts.

The prison sentence didn't matter to him. He was past feeling. What *did* matter was that the producers of the TV movie about him and Valencia County didn't pay Addie a dime for the rights to the story. They didn't have to. He was a convicted child molester, and the facts were on record. So the dream was over. Addie was going to live the rest of her life in Valencia County. Eventually she would die there, a broken woman with a broken soul.

Somewhere inside, Clint knew that he was crying for her and for him and for their destroyed lives. But the tears were so deep that his eyes were never moistened. He doubted he would shed a tear again.

James Hutchings, twenty-seven-year-old accountant, was undergoing hypnosis in the office of therapist Jon Sherman, trying to determine the actual source of his post-traumatic stress syndrome disorder. Not that the source was ever in great question: as a child, Hutchings had been one of the many victims of the Valencia County child sexual abuse ring. Not only had his initial molestation experiences been traumatic, but the subsequent trial of the defendants, which lasted for more than two years—with him testifying before the world via television cameras and in open court—had further traumatized him greatly.

Afterward, he'd gone on to a seemingly "normal" high school and university life, become licensed as a top flight C.P.A., and earned, at a very early age, respect for his professional accomplishments.

But the post-traumatic syndrome had surfaced three years ago: nightmares, impotence, hallucinations, eating disorders, addictive behavior, suddenly stressed interpersonal relationships. His marriage failed, his two children were being raised three thousand miles away, and Hutchings couldn't seem to get it together in any phase of his life other than work.

Nine-to-five he was "normal"—brilliant, actually—and every other hour Hutchings was a walking disaster case. He'd tried psychotherapy; it hadn't helped. He'd tried all the different groups which had helped so many, but they had resulted in only cosmetic improvements.

He was strongly considering suicide and his turn to hypnotherapy was the very last try Hutchings would make to regain his mental health. If this failed, he had already decided to kill himself.

"And now that you are completely relaxed, more relaxed than you have ever been before, I want you to breathe slowly and deeply. Take a deep, deep, slow breath and then hold it, hold it . . . now exhale slowly . . . slowly . . . slowly. Exhale completely. Inhale deeply again.

"I want you to go back into your existence, Jim, back through your entire history. I want you find the source of your present troubles. Be there, but realize that you are actually here with me, right now. It is safe for you to be there mentally, at the source of your problems, and tell me what you are experiencing.

"Where are you, Jim?"

"In a . . . a barn, I think. There's hay, and there are cows and chickens . . . yes, it has to be a barn."

"Good. That's very good. Now tell me what's happening."

"It's night. It's dark outside, it's cold. I'm cold. I'm so cold."

"Why are you cold, Jim?"

"Because I don't have any clothes on. Oh, I'm scared! I'm *so* scared! It's the night of the ritual, and I'm supposed to be in it."

"What ritual, Jim?"

"The wedding of the devil. The devil is going to get married tonight, and I'm to be a gift for him on his wedding night. They're going to do . . . things! . . . to me. I'm so cold and I'm so scared."

"That's okay, Jim. You aren't really there. You're here, in Los Angeles, and you're safe. It's okay to relive what went on back then, but realize that you're safe *now* and no one is going to do anything to you. Do you know you're safe?"

"Yeah. Um . . . uh, nobody *looks* right. Everybody looks different. Sheriff Lansdale is here but he doesn't look like he does now. He's wearing a cape and his hair is different. And he's got a big scar on the side of his cheek. He never had a scar when I knew him, but he has a scar, a real big, ugly scar. Why didn't he have one when I was a kid? But he *had* to have a scar, because that's when I knew him . . ."

"That's okay, Jim. Don't worry about the scar. Let's go to

something else. I want to get you out of that barn. Let's go to your house. What do you see in your house?"

"Uh . . . it's my house, I know that. But it's just one room! It's made of stones, and there's straw on the floor where we sleep, and a fire in one corner, and the walls are all black where the smoke goes. I don't understand! I *know* this is my house, but it *isn't* the house I grew up in!"

"That's okay, Jim. Don't worry about the discrepancies. Let's just go with what you're getting. Is your mother in the house?"

"Yes, she's coming in the door. She's got roots in her hands—she's all dirty. She's been out digging roots for us to eat. She looks like she's never taken a bath in her life! And she's got scars all over her face—the pox, I think. And she's dressed funny. She's got on a long skirt and her hair is all wrapped up in a cloth and she smells bad—oh, my God, does that woman stink!"

"Jim, how old are you?"

"Fourteen. I know 'cause it's time for me to get married. My pa's arranged for me to marry the girl from the next estate. We're going to get married on Whitsun, and then I won't have to be in the rituals anymore."

There was a long moment of silence, which only the hypnotist noticed. When Jim Hutchings was fourteen, Sheriff Lansdale had already been in police custody for over five years. And the boy certainly had never been part of an arranged marriage at that age. A thought . . .

"Jim, can you tell me what year it is?"

"It's the tenth year of the reign of our king, Edward of Caernarvon. We had the celebration last month."

"Jim—what country are you in?"

"England, of course. What country do you *think* King Edward rules? Are you French? Are you an enemy of our king?" Hutchings was moving about on the couch, obviously disturbed, completely involved in his hypnotic experience.

"No, Jim, I'm definitely not an enemy. I'm your friend.

I'm going to check on something and, while I'm checking, you just see whatever it is you want to see. I'll be right back."

He went over to his bookcase to pull out a pocket encyclopedia. The list of English monarchs was, Sherman was grateful to see, complete. King Edward II (Edward of Caernarvon) had ruled from 1307 to 1327.

Over six hundred years ago.

The standing room only crowd in the packed hotel auditorium was silent, totally involved in the words Jon Sherman, Ph.D., was speaking. It was the best attended lecture in the history of the conventions of the American Association of Child Abuse Professionals. Reporters and news crews clustered in the aisles and in front of the dais and only the insistent clicking of Nikons punctuated the hypnotist's amplified voice.

"And so what I'm saying to you, fellow professionals, is that our knowledge of the human potential is so limited even today, that often we don't know what we *assume* we have already scientifically established.

"I have now regressed all twenty-six of the people who, as children, were involved with the Valencia County child sexual abuse ring. Every one of these adults relived a lifetime in the target year 1317, near Lancaster, England—where they were, indeed, victims of such a ring. According to historical documents which I have carefully researched, a severe famine existed in England during this period. Worship of the devil was considered by many to be a way to bring about the end of the famine. These victims all agree that the person you know as ex-Sheriff Clinton Lansdale—as well as the storekeeper, the music teacher, the mail carrier, the doctor and all the others—were also involved in this ancient ring of devil worshippers.

"It may well be true that 'the children never lie.' But I put the question to you: Are we, as a modern society, prepared to punish people for what they did hundreds or even thousands of years ago? Is that our responsibility? Because, while I have no doubt that these people did molest these children, I also have no doubt that this mass molestation took place across the Atlantic Ocean over six hundred years ago.

"And I strongly suggest that when we, as professionals, use advanced psychiatric techniques—some of which border dangerously close to the methods used to brainwash political prisoners—to access the memory banks of children or adults, we may be obtaining far more information than we are capable of dealing with. We may be dooming people who are innocent in the present, but whose guilty pasts have not been forgotten by their victims."

Clinton Lansdale, California penitentiary prisoner number 344187, read the cover stories in *Time* and *Newsweek* with great interest. Now, at last, he knew for sure he wasn't crazy. He wasn't angry at the system because he knew, as a lifelong law officer, that guilty people must pay for their crimes. After six hundred years, he was paying the price for his.

He got out a piece of prison stationery to begin a letter to Jon Sherman. He knew the prison authorities would allow him to be hypnotized by a qualified hypnotherapist, especially one as famous as Sherman was now. It might gain him a new trial, and a new verdict. Hollywood was sure to be interested. There would be a lot of money after all—and at last, Addie could buy the trailer in San Diego. *She* could live in it even if he couldn't.

His lips curved upward into a smile as he envisioned the ocean as it looked from the yard of Number 15-A. He could see the gulls swooping across the sky, hear their cries as they searched the beach for food.

It was going to be one hell of a story.

The Other Woman

Lois Tilton

I lie naked on the bed, wet hair covering my face. I can't see, and I panic for a second until I discover I can lift my hand to brush it away. It's time, again.

I can hear my mother's cold silence in the hallway: the disapproving footsteps that stop just outside my door, then move on. "Why do you keep doing this to yourself?" she always asks. "He's a married man, almost twice your age. Don't you have any shame?"

The warm glow from the shower is fading, my skin prickles with the chill, and I get up, wrap my robe around me and switch on the hair dryer, filling the silence with the rush of heated air. I can't argue about it with her. I know she's only thinking of me, but she just can't understand how it is, what we have to go through just to be together. Even this way.

I shake out my hair, halfway dry already. My face is a little flushed from the hair dryer's heat, and I turn it off for a second to look into the mirror, lightly brushing a finger across my cheek, the smoothness of the skin. With makeup, the faded scars are almost invisible.

"I'm pretty," I tell myself, still not quite believing in the miracle. His gift, the money to pay for the treatments. So much I owe him, I think, finishing my hair and shaking it out so it flows down my back the way he likes it. I dress slowly, for him, as if he were here watching me. The panties, real silk, so sheer they reveal more than they hide—I feel shameless and love how I feel. I won't wear a bra or slip tonight; the fabric of the dress caresses my bare skin, glides sensuously across the silk.

Earrings, the diamond pendant—I never asked for such things, but he likes to see me wearing them. I look at my watch. 6:45. Two more minutes until the car will pull up.

My mother sees me coming down the stairs. *You look like a whore,* says the set of her head, averted. Then her eyes, more merciful, turn back. *Don't you know he'll never marry you? Never be able to give up his wife?*

But I do, I do know. What I can't explain is that it doesn't matter, that nothing else matters except being with him. Our few hours together are worth all the pain.

I see the headlights of the car turning into the drive, and I open the door to leave without looking back.

He already has the car door open, and I slide down into the smooth leather of the seat. He's just shaved, I can catch the faint mint scent of his shaving cream, and I lean close against him, fingertips lightly tracing the lean smooth line of his jaw. Oh, how I want him!

Suddenly his whole body stiffens. My breath catches in my throat. I see it in the mirror, the car driving past in the darkness, its headlights off . . .

She's seen us!

But the car turns the corner without slowing and we both exhale in shaken relief. He turns to kiss me, cupping my chin in his palms, and I open my mouth to his desperate intensity, forgetting about the car, about everything. We only have time for each other now—so little time. Finally we break apart, and I can see his hands are trembling as he puts the car into reverse, backs down the driveway. It's harder for him, I know it is, having to live with her.

In less than half an hour we're outside the city limits, heading down the highway into the night. I don't ask where we're going. I know we can't risk being seen together. She's suspicious already.

I remember the first time I saw her, only a few weeks after I was hired—my very first job, right out of high school. She was coming out of his office, I was crossing the hallway on the way to the copier room. I remember how her look stopped me, and I pressed my lips together to try to hide my overbite while her eyes took in every detail of my face, my body, my clothes. I'd never felt so ugly, so ashamed.

Later, looking around the office, I realized that there wasn't a woman working in the place who could even be considered marginally attractive. Naturally, naturally, they had hired *me*.

"Who was that woman?" I asked Beverly at lunch. Beverly was his secretary then, swarthy, with a mustache on her upper lip. She weighed close to three hundred pounds. "This morning, with the full-length fur coat, the heavy perfume?"

Her thick eyebrows lifted. "You don't know? Listen, this whole company belongs to her, every share of stock. *He* just runs it, and you'd better believe she don't let him forget it, either." She shook her head emphatically, added, "She's in and out of here all the time. And let me tell you something else: you want to keep your job, you stay away from *him*."

So I learned to keep my face down whenever she came into the office, which was three or four times a week. Maybe it helped me keep my mind on my job, knowing that at any time I might look up to find her narrow, suspicious eyes watching, her lips pressed thin with distrust. When Beverly quit, when she couldn't stand it any more, she warned me not to take her job, but I needed the money; my mother had hospital bills and she couldn't even work part time any more. And the benefits were good. The company's dental plan paid for the braces I'd needed since I was twelve.

It wasn't long before I learned to be alert for the heavy

scent of musk perfume wafting across my desk. "Is he in?" she'd demand, then push through the door of his office before I could get out an answer—as if she could catch him that way, unprepared. It made me sick to have to listen to the screaming from behind the closed door, the insane accusations, the threats. I came into the room once with some papers, five minutes or so after she'd gone. I saw him there with his face buried in his hands, his shoulders shaking. I backed out, saying, "I'm sorry, sir, I thought you were alone." Pretending like he did that there was nothing wrong, as if I didn't know, as if the whole office didn't know.

Then one day he called me in. He had a folder on his desk and he looked slightly uncomfortable as he opened it and looked up at me. He cleared his throat.

"I hope this isn't something too personal, but I see here that the company's medical insurance has turned you down for a procedure—cosmetic surgery?"

My face went hot and I knew how I must look with the acne scars all flaring red. I shook my head, keeping my head as low as I could. "It was for dermabrasion treatments. But, no, they said the insurance wouldn't pay, not for—something like that."

His voice was so soft, careful not to embarrass me. "If a loan would help, I could arrange it. Not through the company, I mean. You could repay the money out of your salary, a little bit each month. I can understand . . . what it might mean to you."

Oh, I know, Mother said he was only doing it to take advantage of me. But she was wrong, they were all wrong. There was nothing else, we never even touched each other. Not until that day . . .

The scent of her perfume warned me to look up just as she brushed past my desk, ready to push open his door. Then, suddenly, she froze, staring at me. My face flushed. My braces had just come off a week before and the raw look from the dermabrasion was starting to fade. Now, the way she looked at me, the way her face went—all brittle with hate. Malicious, jealous hate. Her fingers curved into claws, and I flinched away involuntarily.

She stormed into his office. I had never heard such screaming: *bitch . . . whore . . .* I couldn't stand it. I ran into the ladies room and hid in one of the stalls, in case she might come in after me.

When I got back, he was waiting by my desk. His face was pale, as if he were in shock. "I'm sorry. I'm afraid I'll have to ask you—"

I spared him, saying quickly, "I understand. I don't want to cause you more trouble."

He nodded but then, suddenly, he caught my hand in his, so tightly it hurt. But I would never have pulled away, not if he'd held me for a thousand years. Our eyes met and the hurt I saw in his made me burst out. "I'm sorry, I'm so sorry."

"Will you meet me?" It was a whisper so low I almost doubted what I had heard. But I already knew my answer. "Yes."

Yes. It would always be yes, no matter what we had to go through to be together. It always will.

I sigh as his hand strokes up the length of my thigh. I move closer to him while he drives, fitting my body against his. He turns his head slightly to catch a glimpse of my breasts visible beneath the sheer fabric of my dress. I can hear the intake of his breath, his wanting me.

We stop at a bed-and-breakfast place in the country. A car behind us slows slightly, accelerates. I glance at him to see if he noticed, but his face shows nothing.

Our reservations are under an assumed name. The room is pleasant, decorated in Williamsburg style with landscape prints on the walls, but we ignore the amenities, we ignore everything else to press ourselves against each other. His hands slide up the backs of my thighs, across the silk panties. He pulls them down. His mouth is on mine, it moves to my throat, my breasts. I can feel his hardness against my belly.

We can't wait. My dress is on the floor, I'm lying on the bed, lifting my hips. He fills me with himself.

It's over too quickly. I bend over him. My tongue teases his nipples, moves lower. He reaches up to pull me down on top of him. I can hear the sound of a car outside in the driveway. So little time left. I close my eyes, closing out everything else but the sensation of him. With my body I worship. I cry out, shuddering with pleasure almost too much to endure. His hands clutch my hips. He gasps. We look into each other's eyes with awe.

I fall onto the bed next to him. We lie next to each other, my head on his shoulder. I breathe in the scent of him. I wonder for an instant that I have never found her scent on him, the musk she always wears; he feels my shudder. He pulls me closer to him and we cling to each other. Our eyes are closed. This is the moment when I always think: let it stop here. Let time stop here and leave us together like this forever.

I hear a noise—the creak of the door hinges—then a sound like wood splitting. His body jerks violently in my arms, and warmth hits my face, fragments of him splashing me.

"Bitch!" The voice spits venom. I turn away from the bloody ruin on the pillow next to me to see her standing in the doorway with the gun still in her hand. It has a silencer on the barrel. I want to scream but terror is choking my throat. The insane, hateful satisfaction on her face tells me everything. She's *glad*. I realize now that she had driven him to this all along, tormented him with her jealousy until he was desperate enough to risk both of us. But I—I'm the one she really hates. Younger than she is, prettier than she is.

The gun had been for him. Now she closes the door and takes the razor from her purse, the old-fashioned straight razor. *This* is what she means to use on me.

I panic, I try to rush past her to the door, but the razor is a bright flash slicing open my breast. I try to fend it off but the razor lays open my palms, my forearms. My blood is spattered on her face. It smears the polished surface of the razor like a crimson oil. I'm screaming now, but her laughter is more shrill. Her face is alive with insane hate, her eyes burn with it. She's been wanting this for a very long time.

I fall back onto the bed, and hot pain slashes across my belly. I scream again, but she pulls my arms away and the razor slices across my throat. Silenced, I still struggle, gasping for breath, inhaling my own blood through my gaping windpipe. It starts to fill my lungs.

She's still laughing as she starts to cut my face. My face, my breasts. Angry slashes between my legs. A great rip across my scalp, pulling it away, blinding me with my own hair. The scent of her perfume is suffocating. The pain is fading, sensation ebbs with my blood. It will be over soon.

More noise now, a banging on the door, shouts from outside. Too late, too late. Her laughter is breaking down into sobs. Through the bloody veil of my hair I see her put the gun to her own head. Suddenly she falls across the bed, across his legs.

We are all together now. Again.

I'm fading, the cold is spreading through me, but I still can't let go. Never to see him again. *It was worth it. I would go through it again. For him. To be with him one more time.*

I lie naked on the bed and brush the wet hair out of my face. I shiver a little and reach for my robe. The warmth from the shower is fading.

My mother's footsteps pause in the hallway outside my door. *Why do you keep doing this to yourself?*

I stand up, pulling on my robe. I don't want to argue with her. She can't understand.

But to myself, I whisper the answer. "Because I love him."

Love, Hate, and the Beautiful Junkyard Sea

Mort Castle

It wasn't until the third grade I learned I could love. It was in third grade I met Caralynn Pitts.

Before that, seems to me all I did was hate. I had reason. As everyone in Harlinville knew and let me know, I was trash. The Deweys were so low-down you couldn't get lower if you dug straight to China and kept on going. My daddy was skinny, slit-eyed, and silent except in his drunken, grunt-shouting, crazy fits that set him to beating on my mother or me. Maybe it was the dark and dust of the coal mine—he worked Old Ben Number Three—that got inside him, poisoned him to turn him mean like that.

My mother might have tried to be a good momma, I don't know, but by the time I was able to think anything about it, she must have just given up. In a day she never said more than ten words to me. Sometimes in a week, maybe she didn't say ten words to me. At night, she cried an awful lot. I think that's what I mostly remember about my momma, her crying that way.

So trash, no-account trash, bad as any and worse than most you find in southern Illinois, that's what I was; and if you're trash, you start out hating yourself and your folks and hating the God Who made you trash and plans to keep you that way, but soon you get so hate filled, you have to let it out or just bust, and so you get to hating other people. I hated kids who came to school in nice clothes, with a different shirt everyday, the kids who had Bugs Bunny lunchboxes with two sandwiches on bread so white it made me think of hospitals, the kids who lost teeth and got quarters from a tooth fairy, the kids whose daddies never got drunk and always took them on vacations to Starved Rock State Park or 'way faraway, like Disneyland or the Grand Canyon. I hated all the mommas up at the pay laundry every Monday morning, washing the clothes so clean for their families. I hated Mr. Mueller at the Texaco, who always told me, "Take a hike, Bradford Dewey," or "Boy, jump in a hole and pull it in after you," when I wanted to watch cars go up on the grease rack, and I hated Mr. Eikenberry, the postmaster. Mr. Eikenberry had that breeze-tingly smell of Old Spice on him. What my daddy smelled like was whiskey and wickedness.

If you hate somebody, you want to hurt them, and I thought of hateful, hurting things happening to all the people I hated. There wasn't a one in Harlinville I didn't set my mind on a wish picture for, a hate-hurt picture that left them busted up, bleeding and dead. I imagined a monster big as an Oldsmobile grabbing up Rodney Carlisle—his father owned the hardware store on the square—and ripping off his arms and legs, a snake as long as the Mississippi River swallowing Claire Bobbit, Patty Marsel, Edith Hebb, *all* the girls who used to tease me, and an invisible vampire ripping the throats out of all the teachers at McKinley School.

You might think maybe that I really did try to hurt people, I mean, use my hands, punch them in the nose or fling stones at them, or hit them on the head with a ball bat or something like that, but that is not so. Never in my whole life have I done that kind of hurt to anyone.

What I did was to find another way to get people. What I did was, I started lying. It's this way: You tell someone the truth, it means you trust them. It's like you got something you like them enough to *share* with them. Doesn't have to be an important piece of truth, either, it can be a little nothing: "I went to the show last night and that was one fine picture they had," or "It's really a pretty day," or "My cat had kittens," or anything at all. You tell someone the truth, it's just about the same as liking them.

So when you *lie* to a person, it's because you got no use for them, you hate their guts—and what makes it really so fine is you're doing it without ever having to flat-out say what you *feel*.

So I lied, lied my head off. I told little lies, like my Uncle Everett sent me five dollars because I was his favorite nephew and I did so have a wonderful birthday gift for Rodney Carlisle but I wasn't giving it to him because he didn't ask me to his party; and I told monster whopper lies, some of them super-crazy, like I was just adopted by the Deweys but my real parents were Hollywood movie stars, or once I saw a ghost who had this big red butt like a baboon, or I had to kill this three-hundred-pound wolf with just my bare hands when it attacked me out at the junkyard.

I didn't really fool anyone with my lies, you know. That wasn't what I was trying to do. All in all, I'd say Miss Krydell, the third grade teacher, was right when she used to say, "Bradford, you are a hateful little liar."

But all that changed when Caralynn Pitts came and showed me the beautiful junkyard sea.

You've probably had to do it yourself, I bet—stand in front of the whole class and tell who you are and all because you're the new kid—and you're supposed to be making friends right off. It was the first week in May, already too hot and too damp, an oily spring like you get in southern Illinois. The new girl up by Miss Krydell's desk was Caralynn. She had this peepy voice about one squeak lower than Minnie Mouse. Her eyes and hair were the same shade of black, and she was wearing this blue and dark green plaid dress.

Caralynn Pitts didn't say much except her name and that she lived on Elmscourt Lane, but in a town the size of Harlinville, everyone knew most everything about her a week before she'd even moved in. Her daddy was a doctor and he was going to work at the county hospital and her momma was dead.

Well, Caralynn Pitts wasn't anything to me, not yet. I went back to drilling a hole in my desktop with my yellow pencil. Some kids do that sort of a thing without even thinking about it, just something to do, but with me, well, I could feel hate running down my arm into the grinding pencil and all the time I was doing that, I was mashing my back teeth together, if you know what I mean.

It was a week later I talked to Caralynn Pitts for the first time.

It was ten o'clock, the big Regulator clock up near the flag ticking off the long, hot and miserable seconds, and that was "arithmetic period," so, like always, Miss Krydell asked who didn't do the homework, and then she started right in on me, first off, of course: "Bradford Dewey, do you have the fractions?"

"No, ma'am."

"Please stand, Bradford, and stop the mumbling. It would help, too, if you were to take the surly look off your face."

"Yes, ma'am."

"Didn't you *do* the homework?"

I actually had tried to do it but, when I was working at the kitchen table, my daddy came up and popped me alongside the head for no reason except he felt like it, so I lit out of the house.

Not that I was going to tell Miss Krydell any such thing. "Ma'am, I did *so* do the homework. I don't *have* it, is all."

"Why is that?" said Miss Krydell.

I felt this good one, a real twisty lie getting bigger, working its way out of me. "What it was, see, I was on the way to school and I had my fractions, and next thing I knew, the scurlets come up all around me. And that's how I lost my homework."

"The scurlets," said Miss Krydell. You just know the kind of face she was making when she said that. "Please tell us about 'the scurlets.'"

There was a laugh from the first row and someone echoing it a row over, but Miss Krydell gave the classroom her special poison radiation eyes and it got dead quiet real quick.

I said, "Well, the scurlets aren't all that big. No bigger than puppies. But they are plenty mean. There's a lot of them around every time it gets to be spring."

"Oh, is that so?" Miss Krydell said.

"Yes, ma'am. It was running away from the scurlets so they wouldn't get me that I dropped my homework, and I couldn't go on back for it, could I? See, the scurlets have pointy tails with a stinger on them, and if they sting you, you swell up and turn blue and you *die*. And when you're dead, the scurlets eat you up . . . " I was really running with it now. "They start on your face and they bite out your eyes, first thing . . ."

"That will be enough, Bradford."

". . . I guess for a scurlet, your eye is kind of like a real tasty grape. It goes 'pop' when they bite down on it—"

"Enough."

I stop right there. Miss Krydell says, "You are a liar, Bradford, and I am sick and tired of your lies. You'll stay after school and write 'I promise to tell the truth' five hundred times."

I sat down, thinking how much five hundred was, how much I hated Miss Krydell, and how bad my hand was going to feel when I finished writing all that rubbish.

The day went on, and, it was strange, but every time I happened to look around the room, there was Caralynn Pitts looking at me with those black eyes big as the wolfs in "Little Red Riding Hood." I didn't quite know what to make of that. I did not know if I liked it or not or what.

After school, I wrote and wrote and wrote, each "I promise to tell the truth" sloppier than the one before it. Miss Krydell didn't take her eyes off me, either, so I couldn't do it in columns, which is a lot easier way. With my hand feeling like someone had taken a sledgehammer to it, Miss Krydell finally let me go.

I cut back of the school through the playground to take the long way home. I heard this *shh-click* like someone running on the gravel, and then she was calling my name—somehow I knew it was her, right off—so I stopped and turned around.

She ran up to me and, before I could say anything, she said, "You can see things, can't you?"

Not knowing what to make of that, I said, "Huh?"

"*See* things," she says.

I figured Caralynn Pitts had hung around school just to tease me and pick at me the way Claire Bobbit, Patty Marsel, and Edith Hebb always did, and so I answered kind of nasty, "Sure can." I pointed over at the monkey bars. "You go hang by your knees over there and I can see your underpants. What do you think about that?"

Caralynn said, "You can see things other people don't, can't you, Bradford? Like the scurlets."

Then Caralynn started talking real quiet, like she was in church or something. "Bradford, *I* can see things, all kinds of things, too. I can see tiny people living under sunflowers and I can see giants jumping from cloud to cloud and bugs that fly in moonlight and spell out your name on their wings and once I saw a stone in the sunshine and it was trying to turn itself into apple jelly!"

I said, "What are you talking about?"

"Both of us, we can *see things*, so that means we ought to be friends."

I said, "No sense to what you're talking, Caralynn. I can't

see anything much, nothing like what you're saying, and if *you* can, then you sound crazy."

Caralynn said, "I can't tell my daddy about what I see because he says it's only pretend and I'm too old to pretend that way. I used to tell Momma, before she died. She said I had imagination and sometimes, when there was nothing worth seeing in the whole world, all you had was your imagination. When Momma was so sick, dying, I guess, it seems like it rained every day. I used to sit with her, and we'd look out the window; and every day, Bradford, *every day* I could see a rainbow. It had twelve colors, that rainbow, colors like you don't ever see in a plain old rainbow. I used to tell Momma how the sun made the colors change from second to second. Momma said that was our rainbow. That was the rainbow over the graveyard the day we buried her. It wasn't even raining, but I looked up and there it was, and where it bent and disappeared on the other side of the world, I saw Momma, and she was waving to me."

"I don't know," I said. "I don't know anything about that or rainbows."

"Bradford," Caralynn said, "there's something I want to show you. Something beautiful. Can I?"

"I guess," I said.

I'm not a bit sorry about saying that, and I haven't been since the words slid off my lips. But in all these years gone by, I sure have asked myself why I didn't tell Caralynn to just go on and get lost. Maybe the reason is, I was small and dirty, my whole life was small and dirty, but packed inside me was this big hate—and hate is such an ugly thing—so I guess I was tired of all that ugly and there was something inside me, too, that was ready to be shown something . . . *beautiful*.

Oh, not that I believed Caralynn had a thing to show me. To tell the truth, I thought she was off some—and we're talking more than a little. But I did go with her, all the way past the edge of town, through Neidmeyer's Meadow, and then along the railroad tracks until we came to the curve;

and there, by this rusted steel building that I guess the railroad must have once had a use for but didn't anymore, there was the old junkyard.

It wasn't the kind of business junkyard where you go to sell your falling apart car. It was an acre or so where everybody dumped the trash that wouldn't burn and was too big for the garbage men to haul off. It was all useless, twisted garbage, a three-legged wringer washer with the wires sticking out the bottom, and a refrigerator with the basket coil on top, and an old trunk without a lid like maybe a sailor once had, and a steam radiator, and a bathtub, and hundreds of pipes, and a couple of shells of cars, and thousands of tin cans. Everywhere you looked were hills and mountains of steel and glass and plastic, all kinds of trash that came from you didn't know *what* stuff. Flies swarmed in bunches like black cyclones, and over it all, hanging so stink-heavy you could see it, was the terrible smell.

And that was what Caralynn Pitts had to show me.

Not more than a spit away, a rat peeked from under a torn square of pink linoleum, its nasty whiskers quivering. I chucked a stone at it. I told Caralynn Pitts maybe she thought she was funny but I didn't think she was funny— and I started to run off.

I didn't get a step before she had my elbow. "Bradford— can't you see it?"

"It's the junkyard. That's all."

"It's the *sea,* Bradford, it's the beautiful junkyard sea. You have to look at it the right way. You have to want to see it to see how beautiful it is. *Please* look, Bradford."

Then Caralynn Pitts started talking to me in this whispery voice that seemed to crawl from my ear right into my brain. "Look at the water. Can't you see how blue and green it is? See the waves . . ."

. . . the water goes on forever and sends the waves to us from beyond nowhere, the waves gentle as night breeze, the rippling tiny hills rolling in to wash against the diamond dotted golden sands where we stand . . .

". . . and a sea gull . . ."

. . . its wings are white fire cutting through layered-blue sky, its eyes magic black . . .

". . . and way out there . . ."

. . . there, at the horizon line where water and sky are one . . .

". . . a whale . . ."

. . . whales, placid giants, their strange squeaking pips and rumbles unearthly and eternal . . .

"Bradford," Caralynn said. "Can you see it, the beautiful junkyard sea?"

"No," I said, and that was the truth. But in the moment before I said it, I think I *almost* saw it. It was like someone had painted a picture of the junkyard on an old bedsheet and the wind catching that sheet as it hung on a line was making everything ripple and change before my eyes.

It was because I almost saw it—and because, I know now, there was a fierce *want* in me to see it—I came back to the junkyard day after day with Caralynn Pitts.

And on a Wednesday, in the afternoon—a week after school let out—it happened.

I saw the beautiful junkyard sea.

The forever waters, sun light slanting, cutting through foam and fathom upon fathom, then diminishing, vanishing into the ever night depths. The sea gulls, winged arrows cutting random arcs over the rippling waves. A dolphin bursts from the sea, bejeweled droplets and glory, another dolphin, another and another, an explosion of dolphins . . . explosions of joy . . .

Far off a beckoning atoll, a palm-treed island. Far off a coral reef living land. Far off the promise of magic, the assurance that a lie is only a dream and that dreams are true.

Good thing you do not have to learn or practice love, that it just happens.

In the fine sea spray
in the clean mist of air and salt water
in the best moment of my life

I kissed Caralynn Pitts on the lips.

I told her I loved her.

And I loved the beautiful junkyard sea.

Every day that summer, Caralynn and I visited the beautiful junkyard sea. It was always there for us.

Then late in August, she told me she was moving. Her daddy was joining the staff of a hospital in Seattle. She told me she cried when her daddy told her about it.

I said I would always love her. She said she would always love me.

"But what about the beautiful junkyard sea?" I asked her.

"It will always be ours," she said. "It will always be here for us." She promised to write to give me her address once they were settled in Seattle. We would keep on loving each other and, when we grew up, we'd get married and be together forever.

The next week, she moved. Months and then years went by and there was no letter.

But I had the beautiful junkyard sea.

And this is the truth: I never stopped loving Caralynn Pitts or believing she would return.

She did.

I was 22 years old. When I was 12, my daddy got drunk and drove the car into a tree and killed himself. My momma did not cry when he was buried. She said she had already used up all the tears my daddy was entitled to.

What with my father's miner's benefits and insurance, and no money going out on whiskey, Momma and I got by. I scraped through high school, pretty bad grades, but I learned in shop class that I did have a way with engines. Pop the hood and hand me a wrench, chances were good to better yet that I could fix any problem there was, and so I was working at Mueller's Texaco.

On a sunny day in late April, Caralynn Pitts drove her white LTD up to the regular pump and asked me to fill it up, check the oil, battery, and transmission fluid.

Stooped over, I just kind of stood there by the open car window, jaw hanging like a moron. There was a question in Caralynn Pitt's big eyes for a second—and then she knew.

"It is Bradford, right?"

"Yes," I said.

"You've changed so much."

"I guess you have too," I said. That was probably the right thing to say but to tell the truth, she hadn't done that much changing. It was like she was still the kid she had been, only bigger.

"Growing up's a strange thing," Caralynn said.

"You came back, Caralynn," I said.

She gave me another funny look, then she laughed. "I guess I have. I work out of Chicago—I'm in advertising—and I was on my way to St. Louis and, well, I needed gas, so I didn't even think about it . . . just pulled off I-57 and here I am."

"You came back for the beautiful junkyard sea," I said.

"Huh?" Caralynn Pitts said. "Huh?" is something most women just can't say right and it bothered me to hear her say it.

She laughed again. "Oh, I get it. I remember. 'The beautiful junkyard sea,' that was some game we had. I guess both of us had pretty wild imaginations."

"It was no game, Caralynn," I said. "It isn't."

"Well, I don't know . . ." She tapped her fingers on the steering wheel, looked through the windshield. "Could you fill it up, please? And do you have a restroom?"

I told her, "Inside." I filled the tank. Everything checked out under the hood. When she came back a minute or two later, I said, "Maybe we could talk just a little, Caralynn? It's been a long time and all and we used to be good friends. We used to be special friends."

She took a quick look at her wristwatch. Then in her eyes

I saw something like what used to be there so many years ago. "We were, weren't we?" she said. "Maybe a quick cup of coffee or something. Is there someplace we could go?"

"Sure," I said, "I know the place. Just let me tell Mueller I'll be gone awhile."

I drove her LTD. She told me she had gone to college, Washington State, majored in business. She told me she and a guy—I forget his name—were getting serious about one another, thinking about getting engaged. She told me she hoped to be moving up in advertising, to become an account executive in another year or so.

When we got out past the town limits, she said. "Bradford, where are you taking us?"

"You know," I said.

"Bradford . . . I don't know what's going on. What are you doing? You're acting, well, you're acting strange." I heard it in her voice. She was frightened. She didn't have to be frightened, is what I thought then. She'd understand as soon as she saw it.

"There's something I want to show you," I told her, and I drove to the junkyard.

She didn't want to get out of the car. She was scared. She said, "Bradford, don't . . . don't hurt me."

"I could never hurt you, Caralynn," I said.

I took her arm. I could feel how stiff she was holding herself, like her spine was steel.

"Here it is," I said. "Here we are."

We stood on the sun-washed shore of the beautiful junkyard sea.

She jerked like she wanted to pull away from me but I held her arm even tighter. "I don't know what you want, Bradford. What am I supposed to say? What am I supposed to do?"

"What do you see, Caralynn?" I asked.

"I . . . I don't see . . . anything, Bradford."

"Don't say that, Caralynn. I love you." What I was thinking then was, *Don't make me hate you. Please, please don't . . .*

"Bradford, I . . . I can't see what isn't there. This is a junk-yard. That's all it is. It's ugly. And it stinks. It's a junkyard! *Please* . . ."

They never found Caralynn Pitts. I left her car there, walked back to town. The police did have questions, of course, since I was the last person to see her, but like I said, I know how to lie, and so I made up a few little lies and one or two big ones and that took care of the police.

All these years, I haven't gone back to the beautiful junk-yard sea. Maybe I never will.

But I cannot forget, won't ever forget, and I think I don't want to forget how Caralynn looked

when the waters turned black and churning and the light-ning shattered the sky and the sea gulls shrieked and the fins of sharks circled and circled and the first tentacle whipped out of the foam and hooked her leg, and another shot out, circled her waist, and then one more, across her face, choking off her screams, as she was dragged toward that thing rising in the angry water, that great, gray-green, puffy bag that was its head, yellow eyes shining hungrily, the corn-colored, curved beak clattering, as it dragged her deeper, deeper, and then she disappeared and there was blood on the water and that was all until, at last

the sun shone
and all was quiet in
            the beautiful junkyard sea

The Sources of the Nile

Rick Hautala

"Why are you tormenting me like this?" Marianne Wilcox said. I looked at her, cringing beside me in the soft darkness of my car, her blue eyes illuminated by the faint glow of a distant streetlight. I couldn't have denied the over-powering swell of emotion I felt for her at that moment. I wanted to take her right then—that instant! I knew that, but I couldn't—not yet . . . no, not quite yet . . .

"Look, I don't *like* having to be the one to break it to you this way," I replied. "Honest! I mean—Christ, I just met you for the first time . . . when? Last week, at the Hendersons' party. You hardly even know me, and I'd understand if you didn't trust me; but you would have learned the truth sooner or later."

"Maybe I . . . maybe I didn't *want* to learn the truth. Not really," she said. Her chest hitched; her eyes glistened as tears formed, threatening to spill. "Maybe I just *wanted* a . . . wanted a . . . Oh, *Christ!* I don't know what I wanted!"

She beat her small fists on the padded dashboard once, then heaved a deep sigh. Blinking her eyes rapidly, she turned away and looked out the side window. We were parked at the far end of the parking lot at the Holiday Inn in Portland, back where it was dark so we wouldn't be noticed. Minutes ago, we had watched Ronald Wilcox, her husband, walk into the motel arm in arm with another woman. This wasn't the first time—nor was it the first "other" woman.

"Look, I'm just telling you this because—well, I've known your husband for quite some time—through mutual friends, you know. And frankly, I like you," I said, struggling hard to keep my voice as soft and sympathetic as possible. Women fall apart when you talk to them like that. "Something like this hurts me too, you know? But after meeting you, I felt a—I don't know, an obligation, I guess, to let you know that your husband was having an affair." I nodded toward the motel entrance. "Now you've seen that for yourself. As painful as it might be, you asked me to bring you here. I . . . I didn't want to do this to you."

"I know that," she said, glancing back at me for a moment. My heart started beating faster when I saw the tears filling her eyes. They would spill any second now. A cold, tight tingling filled my belly and I can't deny that my erection hardened as I shifted closer to her and placed one hand gently on her shoulder.

"I don't *like* seeing you upset like this," I said. "I'm not *enjoying* this, but you have to remember that *I'm* not the one who has hurt you. It's *him*." I jerked my thumb toward the motel. After a moment of silence, I leaned forward and withdrew a manila envelope from underneath the car seat. "If you'd like, I could show you these photographs I—"

"No!"

Her lower lip trembled as she looked at me. Her eyes were two luminous, watery globes. Just seeing the wash of tears building up there twisted my heart. I tried to push aside, to resist the powerful urge to take her in my arms and caress her, but I couldn't deny that there was an element of spite in what I was doing. I wanted her to see *everything*. I wanted her to *imagine* it all; and if she couldn't imagine it, I was ready to *show* it to her—every instance, every second of her husband's infidelity. I wanted—I *needed*—to push her until she broke because after she broke—ahh, sweetness!—*after* she broke, she would be mine!

"No, I don't . . . don't need to see your—your photographs." Her voice was tight, constricted. "I don't *want*
them!"

"Of course not," I whispered, tossing the envelope onto
the dashboard and inching closer to her. "I understand."

My heart throbbed in my throat when I saw a single,
crystal tear spill from the corner of her eye and run down
her cheek. It slid in a slow, sinuous, glimmering line that
paused a moment on the edge of her chin and then, pushed
by the gathering flood of more tears, ran down her neck and
inside her coat collar. Gone . . . lost . . . !

"Please—don't cry," I whispered, knowing it was a lie. I
brought my face close to hers, feeling the heat of my breath
rebound from her smooth, white skin. My gaze was fastened
on the flow of tears as they coursed from her eyes, streak-
ing in silvery lines down both sides of her face. Her
shoulders hunched inward as if she wanted to disappear inside herself.

"But I—I—"

She couldn't say anything more as she stared at me, her
glazed eyes wide—two lustrous, blue orbs swimming in the
pristine, salty wash of tears. My hand trembled as I traced
the tracks of her tears from her chin to her cheek. Heated
rushes of emotion filled me when I raised my moist finger
up to the light and studied the teardrop suspended from the
tip. It shimmered like a diamond in the darkness. Slowly, savoring every delicious instant, I brought it to my lips. The
taste was sweet, salty. The instant I swallowed it, I knew I
loved her as deeply as I have ever loved any woman.

"I—I wish I could have spared you all of this pain," I
whispered as I lowered my face and kissed her lightly on the
cheek. The briny taste of her tears exploded in my mouth.
The effect was overpowering; I could no longer hold myself
back. Like a snake, my tongue darted between my lips and,
flickering, trembling, caressed her skin. I grew dizzy, intoxicated by the hot, sweet taste of her.

She moaned softly, barely at the edge of hearing. My arm

went around her, pulling her closer—comforting, reassuring, like a good friend.

"Go on," I whispered. "If you have to cry, let it out. Let it *all* out." I could barely hear my own voice above the roaring rush in my ears as my face brushed against hers. Ever so lightly, my tongue worked its way up from her chin, over the soft contours of her cheek until—at last—I reached her eyes. My hand grasped the back of her head, turned her gently to face me, and pulled her tightly against my greedy, eager mouth. Moving my head from side to side, I kissed and lapped her lower eyelids, savoring the salty explosion of taste on my tongue. With slow, sensuous flicks, I licked the bulging circles of her closed eyes.

"No—please!" she whispered, squirming on the seat. "Not now . . . not here!" But I knew she didn't mean it. Her body was molded against me like a tight-fitting glove. The passion consuming me filled her, too. I could feel it thrumming through her body like an electric current. Her hands worked around behind my back, clutching, clinging desperately to my coat. She shook with repressed sobs as I moved back and forth, kissing the corners of each eye. While I was busy drinking the flood of tears from one eye, my hand wiped the other until it was slick with moisture. Then I slipped my fingers into my mouth and sucked them clean, not wanting to miss a single delicious drop.

"Please . . ." she moaned, and I knew what she was asking for. This wasn't denial; it was passion, raw and desperate. Puckering my lips, I feverishly kissed first one eye, then the other. She gasped for breath, the tears streamed down her face, but my lips were there—eager to savor every pearly drop. Oceans of passions raged in my head, my heart pounded heavily in my chest as I pressed myself against her, crushing her back against the seat of my car. The world outside disappeared in swirling passion. For a flashing instant, I knew she sensed danger, but it was already too late. I possessed the source of her tears, the twin rivers that fed the raging of my desire.

"White Nile"—I said before kissing her left eye, "—and Blue Nile," before I kissed the other. Then I clamped my mouth over her right eye and, pressing my tongue hard against her eyelid, began to suck—at first gently, then more insistently. I'm sure she thought I was lost in sexual desire but I knew she would never truly understand. None of them ever did. I applied more pressure, suctioning hard until her eyeball bulged against her closed lid.

She began to struggle, making soft, whimpering sounds; but here in the shadowed corner of the parking lot, I knew no one was going to notice us. As my sucking grew stronger, more insistent, she screamed, sharp and shrill. I covered her mouth with one hand, pulled back, and stared at her eyes, glistening and round with fear.

"Please—*don't*," she said, her voice a wet rasp. Her throat was raw with tortured emotions and the tears she had already shed. Her fists beat helplessly against my back as I leaned forward and sucked all the harder. Her resistance was futile. She was mine now. I *had* her!

Her low, bubbling scream continued to rise, stifled by my hand. I was afraid I'd have to kill her before I could finish. It usually happens that way no matter how hard I try to keep them quiet. Marianne thrashed with frantic resistance, but I wouldn't stop, I *couldn't* stop. I had to have her—I had to lay claim to the source of my passion! I was only dimly aware of her long, agonized screech as my cheeks, working like strong bellows, sucked harder and harder until—*at last*—something warm, round, and jellied popped into my mouth. I nibbled on it until I felt the resilient tube of her optic nerve between my teeth, then bit down hard, severing it. A warm, salty gush of tears and blood—an exquisite combination—flooded my throat. I was dizzy with ecstasy as I reached down to the car floor, found the jar I kept under the seat for nights such as this, spun open the top—and spat her eyeball into it.

Then I went back to draining the empty socket dry of tears and blood. Precious drops dribbled from the corners of my mouth, but I eagerly wiped them up with my finger-tips.

"I . . . love . . . you," I gasped. With one hand still covering her mouth, I sat back to wipe my chin with the back of my wrist. Then, moaning softly, I shifted over to her left eye and clamped the suction of my mouth over it. She struggled again, harder now, writhing and screaming in pain and terror; but my weight held her fast while I dragged the tip of my tongue hard against her eye, lapping up more tears. Then, unable to hold back any longer, I sucked her other eyeball out of its socket and spat it, too, into the jar.

For long, dizzying minutes, I pressed her down against the seat while my tongue tenderly probed both empty holes for the last traces of tears. After a while, her body shivered; then she lay still as her heart quietly slowed and stopped. My rapid-fire pulse eventually lessened as well—but all of this happened nearly four weeks ago, and I feel it coming on me again. I have to go out tonight. That urge, that demanding, thirsty need is strong inside me . . . like the irresistible pull of the ocean's salty tide.

Collaborationists

J. N. Williamson

As if it had been ordained by Someone on High, Mel always came to the convention with Valerie, his wife. I'm certain he knew we would expect to see that old horror writer's most supportive fan but there was no decent opportunity to ask Mel why she *wasn't* present this year until the final day of the convention, Sunday, and he hadn't uttered a word about her absence. I was, frankly, mildly hurt.

Until this convention, Valerie and Mel, Carol and I had made it a matter of course to attend the awards banquet and for the four of us to sit together. But Carol and I had suffered a bad year financially, hadn't bought banquet tickets, and our plane for home would leave in a couple of hours. Carol left the hotel to look around town and, I supposed, to avoid any risk of embarrassment. I waited in the lobby and was startled when Mel dropped heavily into the leather chair beside me.

I said, "Aren't you going to the banquet either?"

"No," he said. "It won't really be any fun without Valerie." He crossed his long legs, busied himself lighting a cigarette. That surprised me too because Mel had quit smoking two years back. "Go ahead and ask," he told me. "I won't like it, but you might as well get the question off your chest."

I took that for one of his customary sardonic replies. "All right." Casually, I sipped at a coke—this was Sunday, remember—I'd brought out to the lobby with me. "Why isn't Valerie with you at this convention?"

Mel swiveled his oblong head around to peer directly at me and I was reminded of some aging horse that had learned even his stud services were no longer required. He took a moment. "On Thursday, a week ago," he said, "Valerie woke up and found that she was an entirely happy woman."

"Why," I breathed, "that's wonderful." Now came Mel's famous punch line.

"No. It is not." He took his time about getting a long drag into his lungs and tried not to cough when it came back out. "I'm afraid you aren't understanding me."

"I'm sorry."

"My fault. I'm not getting it right."

"Why don't you try again?"

"All right," Mel said. His eyes burned into mine. "Val said she was in a condition of absolute ecstasy."

"Good Lord."

"Had been, she said, for at least twenty-four hours."

"My God," I said. "How? Not to be overly inquisitive, but why?"

"That's what I asked her. I mean . . . I'm a *writer.*"

I said, "My point exactly." I shifted nervously in my leather chair. "How could a thing like that happen to a writer's wife?" I found the concept wholly confounding. "Was she drinking?"

"Not a drop. Remember; she never cared for the stuff." Mel gazed thoughtfully at the burning end of his Winston but it had no answers for him. "Well, I tried not to make too much of it; played it down. Not time yet for hysterics, I thought. Then I poked around in her things." A deepening frown. "I was looking for it, you know. Dope."

"Why, certainly." I tried to be as reassuring as humanly possible. Drugs was as good a guess at explaining Valerie's condition as anything, I thought. I added to Mel, manfully, "You had no other choice."

"But there was nothing narcotic anywhere I looked," he said. "Except for a fantasy novel—leprechauns and unicorns, you know—and one of those exquisitely subtle horror anthologies." His shoulders moved. "Nothing, however, she could possibly put into her nose or arm or could conceivably swallow."

Wonderingly, I slowly shook my head. I yearned to help, but I could not bear imagining what I might do if Carol was ever—

"My Val has been a genuinely decent woman, a devoted wife, always," Mel choked. I tried not to see his eyes at that instant. "Truly devoted. Understand, I don't want to make Valerie out to be some kind of angel—"

"But she was," I said. I changed it hastily. *"Is.* Listened to every word you got down on paper, I know. Typed your manuscripts. Put off having more children, even held down the basest, most menial jobs just so you could—"

"It was *together,"* Mel interposed a trifle sharply. "For *both* of us. The long climb up, grubbing for a dollar, an agent; prostituting oneself. You know how it goes."

"How true," I said and chuckled. Mel and I had often laughed together about the deceit, the lies, the royalty departments, computer downtime, though I didn't know why. "Mel, I know. I remember when—"

"You *can't* know," my friend argued. "You *can not know* what passes through one's mind when your wife, out of the blue, announces that she is one hundred percent content."

"You're right," I nodded, "I can't."

"Well, *try,"* he urged me.

"I cannot. I wouldn't know where to start," I admitted. "Mel, surely she didn't mean what she said. Not literally."

"One hundred percent," he answered with a stricken, stately nod. "I sought immediate clarification, suggested eighty-nine, proposed ninety-four. She swore that she meant every percentage point. Just sat there, grinning. Smirking like a devil."

"No one has ever heard of such a thing." Then the idea hit me. "A possibility comes to mind, one only—a single, nebulous, wholly absurd, exceedingly remote possibility."

"Thought of it in the wee hours." He had stopped with his cigarette an inch or two from his lips. "You're wondering if she's having an affair. Has taken a lover."

"No!" I shouted. One of the people moving around behind the check-in desk almost lifted his head to look at me. "Well, *yes*." I felt my cheeks color. "But only because it can happen to the best of us. Remember Allen? And Wally?"

Mel looked me in the eye. "I demanded the truth of Valerie and she swore that there has never been a man in her life since we married."

I used the occasion of my friend's growing ash drawing within inches of my nose to raise a hand and conceal my errant smile. Mel, meanwhile, tapped hell out of the cigarette in a tray.

And then—to my astonishment—he was beaming the broadest of smiles at me. "Put two and two together and you can imagine what I did next." He made his face go blank, glanced carefully around and then back at me. "I took advantage of the situation."

"You mean, you and Valerie . . . ?"

Light reflected off his high forehead as his head bobbed. "Took Val straight to bed. We had at it. We had at it." He went on nodding.

"And?"

"It was as good for me as ever." His expression remained blank.

"But?" I prodded.

His chin lowered. "She said it was fine."

"Lord," I sighed, "that bad?"

He spoke into the collarless neck of his sweater but I heard him. "It was as good as it had ever been for her, too—and she was *still* perfectly happy. 'Ecstatic' remained her exact term." The mumbling got worse. "She said she had no complaints about either that particular sex or our sex life in general. Absolutely none."

"Sweet Jesus," I remarked. "She's in even worse shape than I'd thought."

He didn't hear me. "She strongly implied that that aspect of our marriage should in no way be held responsible either for how awful she used to feel *or* how ecstatic she felt after we'd just had 'our little romp.' It was . . . *fiiiiine.*"

This was intolerable! "My poor, old friend. What happened next?"

"What else could I do but accept it? I was neither responsible for making my wife miserable nor for making her content." Mel's face was a mask of horror. "A husband can occasionally strike out; we all know that. But I was no longer even a member of our marital team! It wasn't as if I couldn't get the bat on the ball, it was as if—"

"I understand," I told him, and edged slightly away.

"Well, the kids came over. Not because I phoned them; they'd already been invited to dinner."

In mind's eye I saw my friend's grown children and their mates. Mel, Junior, had a wife I'd had to use—on paper, that is. The daughter was as lacking in talent as Junior. "How awful was it?"

"Awful enough." His shudder started out life as a sigh. Perhaps everything did, I thought, and tried to remember the insight till I got to make note of it. "Before they were through the door, I had to tell them about Valerie. 'Your mother is happy,' I said. 'She has just informed me that she's never before felt so fulfilled.'"

"That was her choice of words, 'fulfilled?'" I stammered. *"That?"* Nothing had prepared me for such a disclosure. I doubt anything could.

"Do you know what Junior asked me?" His baseball mitt of a hand squeezed my knee. "Do you *know?*" His face was red so I winked back tears of pain and he continued. "He asked if his mother—*my* wife—had asked for a divorce!"

"He wasn't expecting such news, Mel," I reasoned. "He's a man, too."

Mel's fingertips dug in. "That little son of a bitch!"

"Easy, buddy." Prying his fingers out of my knee was like extracting steel pins. Mel has written several million words. "It's a dreadful thing to ask his father, but he's your own flesh and blood. You must try to forgive him." We were sitting side by side and I began to wonder what was detaining Carol, my wife. Into my friend's sudden, growing silence, I whispered: *"Did* Valerie go to an attorney?"

Mel snatched the can of coke from my hand. For a moment, I swear, I think he wanted to dash it into my face. Then, emitting a moan unlike any I'd heard from an unfettered man, he crushed the can between his typewriter-trained fingers and paid no heed to the drops raining on our knees. "She did not. *I* thought about it, but the only one I know is a man who was always out of town when I wanted him to read a multi-book contract. Besides, if I *did* seek a divorce, I'm reasonably sure . . ."

I was staring at him when his words began to trail away. "Go on," I said.

Mel turned to peer at the check-in desk. The people behind it were obviously trying not to look at us. "I'm sure that if I got a divorce, it would mean no more to Valerie than if I *didn't*. It's—all the *same* to her, now. She's *happy!"*

I let seconds tick away, to think. What I needed to say to Mel then was hard, very hard, and Mel's face looked as if a powerful storm was building, broodingly, behind it. "Mel . . . old friend . . . there's a possibility"—I broke off in order to furnish suspense—"that Val has . . . gone."

"Gone?" he repeated. "How do you mean, 'gone'?" One eyebrow lifted. "Do you mean her soul may have been replaced by that of some demonic entity—that sort of 'gone'?"

I considered the idea for an instant, then shook my head. Valerie wasn't Catholic. "No, I meant that writers' wives are often under great pressure. Since they lack the creative outlets we possess, at least when the child-bearing years have passed, a few of them have been known to—become neurotic. Flip out, as it were."

"Not Valerie." Rather wearisomely, Mel again shook his head. "Carrie, our daughter, ruled that out. She had a little heart-to-heart with Val and said she's perfectly sound mentally. Or did I tell you Carrie graduated from that psych course she took? 'Everything You Needed to Know about Your Woman's Mind but He Wouldn't Let You." My girl is *Doctor* Carrie now."

"Then I'm at a complete loss to understand Val's problem," I confessed. A surreptitious glance at my watch told me the plane home would leave in an hour and Carol was still window-shopping in town. Several ideas played torturously at the fringes of my mind, one of them worth writing down, but I remembered my friend still had not said why his wife had not come to the convention. I approached the matter with delicacy.

"Did you ever sit Valerie down and demand to know what was making her imagine she is contented; fulfilled? Did you confront her?"

"In a way," he replied vaguely. "I asked if I was the last to know of her damnable ecstasy. It seems Val admitted it to two friends. One of them got quite angry, I understand. The second believed Valerie was just making it up."

"That's not like Val," I mused. "I doubt she's ever imagined a thing."

"Well, I counted on that, of course." Something in Mel's tone informed me that he hadn't said it all, that he was getting to it at last. "Before telling me, she went to a doctor. I gather he gave her a complete examination, asked many of the questions we've asked, but he confessed it was beyond his expertise and sent her home. I spoke to him on the phone. Good health is over his head, that's the size of it."

"He's a doctor," I murmured, relieved to hear Valerie's condition did not appear to be contagious. "Of course it is."

Laughter from the ballroom where the convention awards

were being presented trickled to my ears when the door opened briefly and one of the losers fled to the rest room. When I next looked at Mel, he summoned his courage and finally started to explain the reason for his wife Valerie's singular condition of happiness.

"I did not say," he began, "that Val did not accompany me to this city. You just assumed it. She's here."

"Where?" I turned my gaze in every direction. "In the hotel?"

"No, in this metropolis of commercial sin," he said. "In its suburbs, to be more precise. At another, newer, more sumptuous hotel."

A gleam of insight became an icicle at the back of my head. Dimly, I recalled hearing that another writers convention was going on here at the same time.

Seized by panic, I leapt to my feet. "Where in heaven's name is Carol?" I checked my watch once more. "Mel, I'm sorry. But if we don't get to the airport by 3:40—"

"I know," said my fellow writer with a meaningful nod. "Yet if you catch that plane, you will be flying home . . . alone."

"What do you mean?" I asked it while my heart thundered in my chest.

"You've been deep in your next novel or you might have seen it for yourself." Mel spoke with infinite gentleness, and clear regret. "Your wife, too, is supremely happy." He blinked his eyes shut, snapped them open. "She is with Valerie this minute. In a way, she has been with Valerie for weeks now."

I could no longer stand. I toppled back into my lobby chair, gaping at him.

"Carol and Valerie are collaborators," Mel continued remorselessly, getting it all said. "No; don't think of *Casablanca* or other theaters of war. Think of the frilly, very feminine dress Carol was wearing when you arose this morning."

I nodded, but my mind was a blank. It contained no memory of my wife's apparel. For the fraction of an instant, it contained no recollection of Carol's face. "Collaborators?" I said feebly.

"Both of us should have seen the signs," Mel admitted. "The sudden preference for large quantities of time alone. Few complaints when we were late for meals. Happiness predicated upon absolutely nothing real. Their eyes raised, fixed upon sights and scenes only they could see."

"They are *writers?*" I cried, and I suppose my mouth fell open. *"Our wives?"*

"Unreasoning tolerance of one's surroundings, that's the first clue. Smirking. Joy which surpasseth understanding when nothing whatever has improved." Mel was relentless. He gripped my biceps as if to prevent me from hurting myself. "No poorly-concealed anxiety when the mortgage goes unpaid. No threat to leave unless *we* abandon our plans to attend the convention—instead, *real interest* in being here . . . where each woman keeps her little secret and mysteriously melts, seemingly alone, into the big city."

"They've *sold* their *book?*"

"Far worse," Mel hissed, bracing my arms to keep me from falling from the chair—"they were nominated for a major award!"

"Oh, dear God," I gasped, weeping briefly against my friend's shoulder. Then I stared up at Mel. "But, *how?* They cannot have put much time into it. My meals, my clean clothes, have been done on time. Carol hasn't been a moment late typing my pages." An idea occurred to me. "Now I think of it, she has had a faraway look of late. She did have her hair done before we flew here. Rather girlishly, as I recall, but there were only going to be other writers of horror here, and I—"

Mel gave me a solemn nod and assisted me so that I could rest my head back against the chair. Quickly, he lit two cigarettes, and I took the second one between shaking fingers. He went on sadly nodding.

Valerie's condition of absolute ecstasy; the novel finished

fast, and already nominated for an award. Carol's frilly costume, her girlish hair style. Valerie, untouched and unmoved by sex with her husband. Carol, leaving me alone in the lobby . . . keeping to herself . . . wandering off to another hotel with her collaborator to be feted in the most romantic of ways.

"It's a romance novel the two of them wrote," I gasped into my friend's persistent nodding. "They're—*romance writers!*"

Only Mel's already-tested, steady gaze kept me from going over the deep end.

"I've had time to get used to it," he said softly after gesturing at me to stop using such words at an audible level. "Not that I have; not that I ever can. I knew no other way to break the news to you than face to face. But I have thought of two ameliorative facts that might hearten you and ease the blow."

I mumbled, "Go ahead. But they'll do no good."

"My Valerie," Mel said in a whisper, "doesn't *mind* having intercourse now. She—doesn't notice it, as I remarked."

I looked hopefully at him from between half-hooded lids. "She did tell you it was 'fine'?"

"She did," he said. "Off in her own little world, it seems. And the other fact . . ."

"Yes?" I prodded him.

"The demand for those so-called romantic novels turns out to be virtually insatiable." Mel's eyes seemed to be in bold face. "Carol and Valerie can knock one out in less time that it takes a publisher to accept one of our contracted novels!" His lifted hand made certain no lip-readers detected what he was whispering. *"Our wives can sell one of those babies every couple of months for up to ten grand each. Ten grand."*

"Several books a year," I asked, "and they're splitting the take?"

"Val told me," Mel said, "fifty-fifty."

"Upfront, right?" I said, doublechecking. "On acceptance?"

Mel was nodding again. "They're something like dot-to-dot books, or fill-in-the-missing-word. It's Follow the Magic Formula time, said Valerie." Mel had a look to him then that was the first living demonstration of the clichéd "dancing eyes" that I had ever seen. "Fill in the words just so, and the check follows like day the night. The girls will have a feeling of accomplishment over this, of course."

"Of course," I said, and found I was smiling. Laughing, really. In waves that kept coming up to the moment I saw Carol and Valerie hurrying into the lobby.

"Why are you laughing?" Mel demanded under his breath. I noticed our wives were also trying to subdue a mood of hilarity.

"Because it just dawned on me that they've done a collaboration," I explained, holding it down.

"Go on," he said—"but hurry!" Carol and Val were drawing nearer. "Well, the author's byline on romance novels is always sweetly feminine or borrows a man's name such as 'Alex' or something, and is so pretentious that no one in the real world could possibly believe that it was anything but a pseudonym."

The smile was restored to Mel's face. "So there's no chance in the world they they would take either of *our* names and ruin them!"

"Right," I hissed back at my friend, slapping his knee. "Kuntzedale and McWilton are safely preserved in horror!"

We were on our feet to make it a foursome again, our wives' wearing the most apologetic of expressions, and I saw clearly that my term "girlish" for Carol's new hair style might well have been far too hasty.

My Private Memoirs of the Hoffer Stigmata Pandemic

Dan Simmons

My Dearest Son—

The fact that you will never read this does not matter. Peter, my son, I think it is time I explained the events of thirty years ago to you. I feel a great urge to do this, even though there is much I do not understand—much that no one understands—and the time before the Change has long since become vague and dream-like for most of us. Still, I think your mother and I owe you an explanation, and I shall do my best to provide one.

I was watching television when the Change came. I would guess that a majority of Americans were in front of their TVs that evening. As luck would have it, I was tuned to the *CBS Evening News with Dan Rather,* and because we lived in the Eastern time zone then, the news was live.

Now some think that because the Change began first in our hemisphere, that it was the result of the Earth passing through some belt of cosmic radiation. Other "experts" suggest that it was a micro-virus that came filtering down through the atmosphere that day and just spread like algae in a stagnant pond. The religionists—back then when there were religionists—used to talk about God's judgment beginning with America because it was the Sodom and Gomorrah of its day. But the truth is, no one knew then where the hell the Change came from, or what caused it, or why it began in the Western Hemisphere first, and the truth is that no one knows now.

And we don't really give a damn, to tell you the truth, Peter.

It came, and I was watching the *CBS Evening News with Dan Rather* when it came. Your mother was cooking dinner. You were in the crib that we kept in the dining room. Dan Rather was on the screen talking about Palestinians when suddenly he got a startled expression on his face sort of like that time a few years earlier when protesters got in the studio and started screwing around while he was on the air, only this time he was alone.

What was happening was that Dan's face was melting. Well, not melting exactly, but *flowing,* shifting, sort of running downhill like it had been turned into wax and held over a hot stove.

For a minute I thought it was the TV or the damn cable company again and I was halfway to the phone to give the cable people a piece of my mind when I saw that Dan Rather had stopped talking and was grabbing his face as it flowed and shifted and reformed like silly putty, so I put the phone down and sat back in my chair and yelled "Myra, come in here!"

I had to shout again but finally your mother came in, wiping her hands on a dish towel and complaining that dinner would never be done if I kept yelling at her and . . . she stopped in mid-sentence. "What's happening to Dan?" she said then.

"I dunno," I said. "Some sort of joke, maybe."

It didn't look like a joke. It looked awful. Dan's aging-but-still-handsome face had quit running like melted wax but was twitching and reforming into something else. The muscles and bones under the skin of his face were moving around like rats under a tarp. His left eye seemed to be . . . well, *migrating* . . . moving across his face like a chunk of white chicken floating in a bowl of flesh-colored soup.

There were shouts from off-camera, the picture blurred and bounced, then cut away to the *CBS Evening News with Dan Rather* logo, but a few seconds later we were back live to the shot of Dan and the news desk, as if someone in the control room or whatever you call that place where the director works had decided that *this* is news and to hell with it.

Dan had gotten up and was stumbling around then, his hands still holding his face, obviously peering in monitors as if they were mirrors. Whatever had happened, I could see that the silly-putty part was over. Nothing was moving under those splayed fingers any more. Dan was making sort of choking sounds, although he'd ripped his microphone thingee out so the sounds were distant and echoey. Then Dan dropped his hands.

"Jesus Christ," said your mother. She never cursed, never took the Lord's name in vain. "Jesus H. Christ," she said a second time.

Dan Rather's face had turned into something out of one of those *Tales from the Crypt* shows we used to avoid on HBO. But not really like that, because no matter how good make-up is, you can always tell that it's make-up. Just like you could tell that this was *real*.

Dan Rather's face had Changed. His forehead had sort of collapsed so his combed mop of graying hair—we'd noticed he'd just gotten a haircut that week—was down about where the bridge of his nose had been two minutes before. He didn't have a nose any more, just an open-holed scoop of a snout— a sort of tapering, anteater-like proboscis that sloped down below his jaw and ended in a pulsing pink membrane that looked like you imagine your eardrum might look. If it was infected. And every time it pulsed, you could see right into Dan's face—I don't mean into his eyes or anything, I mean *in-*

side his face—all the green, mucusy things in there, and bones and flesh from the inside and other things, glistening things.

Dan's left eye had stopped migrating about where his left cheekbone used to be. That eye seemed much larger now and was bright yellow. His other eye was fine and looked familiar, but above it and below it, the red wattles began growing. These wattles hung down from what used to be his cheek and what had once been his brow and they seemed to congregate along that scaly, bony ridge that had grown out of his right cheek like the whatchamacallits on the back of a stegosaurus.

And Dan's teeth. Well, we soon knew what everything meant—the hypocrisy proboscis, the power-abuser scales on the cheek, the Ambition teeth curling in and out of the skin around the flesh-sutured mouth like that—but you have to realize that this was the first time that we'd seen the Change and we didn't have any idea that the stigmata had something to do with a person's IQ or temperament or character.

Dan Rather tried to scream then, the Ambition teeth cut through cheek muscle, and your mother and I screamed for him. Then the director *did* cut away—to a Preparation H commercial—and your mother said, "How about the other channels?"

"No," I managed to say, "I'm sure it's just Dan." But I clicked over to ABC and there was Peter Jennings pulling at what looked like a pink, half-eviscerated squid that had attached itself to his face. It took us almost a minute of slack-jawed staring to realize that this *was* his face.

Tom Brokaw had been the least affected, but he'd clapped his hands over the power-abuser scales erupting from his cheek, jaw, and neck and run from the set. We saw it later on tape. But right then, all we saw was the empty NBC set and all we heard was a sound like a coyote gargling rocks. We found out later that this was John Chancellor screaming when the mucus began erupting from his pores.

Finally I clicked off the TV, too shocked to keep watching. Besides, it was all commercials by then. So I turned to your mother to say something, but the Change had started on her by then.

I pointed and tried to say something, but my mouth was too dry and it felt like it was full of jagged potato chips or something. Your mother pointed at me and screamed, the sound seeming filtered coming as it did through the rows of baleen that had replaced her teeth and made her face look something like the grill of a '48 Buick. The rest of her face was still flowing and dripping and clumping.

I felt my own face twitch. My hands went up to my cheeks, but the cheeks were no longer there. Something else was: something that felt like a cluster of fleshy, pulsing grapes. Something had grown out of my forehead enough to block the vision in my left eye.

Your mother and I looked at each other again, pointed again, screamed in unison, and ran for the bathroom mirror.

I should say right up front, Peter, that you were fine. When we finally could think again, we went into the dining room and peered down into the crib with some trepidation, but you were the same healthy, handsome ten-month-old who had been there half an hour before.

When you looked up at us, you started crying.

I won't pull any punches, my dearest son. I had the fleshy blood-horns that only adulterers grew. We didn't know what it meant for a few weeks. It took a while—sorting everything out, I mean. But we had time. The Change was permanent. Not necessarily complete, we soon learned, but permanent. There was no going back.

The pulpy-looking masses of flesh-grapes on my cheek and neck were later called Barabbas papillomata by whoever the hell named all this stuff. The Surgeon General maybe. Anyway, the Barabbas papillomata only showed up if you'd played a little fast and loose with other people's money. With me it was just a few thousand bucks overlooked on some pissant IRS forms. But Christ, you should've seen the photos of Donald Trump in *The National Enquirer* that next month after the Change. He had papilloma so thick that he looked like an ambulatory grape arbor, only not as pretty since you could see through the skin and see the veins and yellow ichor and all that.

Your mother's baleen mouth, we found out later, was connected with malicious gossip. If she looked like a '48 Buick, you should have seen Barbara Walters, Liz Smith, and that bunch. When their pictures first leaked out, we thought we were looking at a *fleet* of Buicks.

Your mother's Quasimodo eye and mantis maxilla were the results of small cruelties, hidden racial prejudices, and self-imposed stupidities. I had the same symptoms. Almost everyone did. Within a month, I considered myself lucky to have only the adulterer's bloodhorns, a moderate cluster of Barabbas papillomata, mantis maxilla, a trace of Rather-snout, some apathy osseus turning my brow into Neanderthal ledges, and the usual case of Liar's leprosy that took my left ear and most of my remaining left nostril before I learned how to control it.

I need to say again that you were untouched, Peter. Most children under twelve were, and all infants. Your face looked up at us from its crib or cradle and you were perfect.

Perfect.

Those first few hours and days were wild. Some people committed suicide, some went nuts, but most of us stayed indoors and watched television.

It was more like radio, actually, since no one at the networks wanted to go in front of the camera. For a while they tried showing a preChange photograph of the reporter or anchorman or whatever while you heard his or her voice in the background—sort of like when we were getting telephone reports from Baghdad during the war a few years ago—but that made people angry, and after a few thousand phone calls they dumped the pictures and just showed the network logo while someone read the news.

They announced that the President would address the nation at 10 P.M. E.ST. that night, but that was soon cancelled. They didn't explain why, but we all knew. He gave a radio address the next evening.

None of us were very surprised when pictures of the President finally leaked out, although the bloodhorns and treachery-tumors were a bit of a shock. It was his wife that took everyone by surprise. She'd had such good press that we half expected her to be unChanged. For several months we heard and saw nothing of her, but when she finally appeared in public we could see through her Elephant Man veil that she had not only multiple horns but the face-turned-inside-out look of the Ultimate Arrogance Syndrome.

Still and all, she fared better than Nancy Reagan. Word was that the former First Lady wasn't even recognizably human during the first minutes of the Change and was gunned down in disgust by her own Secret Service guards. Official word was that Mrs. Reagan died of shock at the sight of her husband after the Change. It's true that Ron's case of Liar's leprosy, apathy osseus, and stupidity sarcoma was impressive, but the old gentleman took it good-naturedly and probably would not even have curtailed his schedule of paid public appearances if Nancy's demise had not intervened.

As for the then-current Vice President . . . well, word is that one had to be there to believe it. The press and media had been unkind over the previous years, but we discovered that their unkind remarks about the VP's limited IQ had been dramatic understatement. The young man who had been only a heartbeat away from the presidency is said to have deliquesced like so much wet cardboard left out in the rain. Word was that the stupidity sarcoma was so widespread that there wasn't much left but a suit, shirt, and red-and-blue striped tie lying amidst a heap of twitching snot.

The Vice President's wife became a textbook case of Ambition dentitus. It's not true that there was nothing left of her but the four-foot-long teeth, but that's the impression we had at the time.

Before you get the wrong idea, Peter, you have to understand that I'm not picking on the Republicans. Neither did the stigmata. Both sides of the aisle suffered equally. Our elected officials were so hard hit by the Change that the verb "senatored" soon came into use to describe anyone who had lost almost all humanity to their stigmata. They were a resilient bunch though, and some—like Ted Kennedy, they say—were out hunting new sexual conquests before the papilloma, sarcoma, fibroid masses, supraorbital distortions, and longitudinal sulci had quit pulsing and oozing.

For a while the TV kept showing reruns and old commercials—obviously none of the actors or pitchmen were spared in the Change—but eventually they started filming new stuff. It was about a year before we could go out to the movies and see post-Change actors, and by then we were ready for them. By then I wasn't bothered by the sight of Dustin Hoffman's UA-syndrome inside-out visage, or Eddie Murphy's racist albino-pox mottling, or the absolute ego-dripping, sex-obsessed-tentacled mess for a face that Warren Beatty's personality had given him, but I could no longer stand to look at pre-Change images of people. They seemed as strange as aliens to me. Most people felt exactly the same by then.

But I'm getting ahead of myself. Sorry, Peter.

Those first few weeks were nuts, to put it mildly. Almost nobody went to work. Mirrors were smashed. Suicides and homicides and unprovoked attacks reached such a high rate that the whole country began to have casualty figures as high as New York City's. I'm not exaggerating.

Today, of course, New York's violence has all but disappeared now that racial differences go almost unnoticed and the gangs have disappeared after it was shown that lip and eyebrow pus-lesions were the inevitable result of belonging to a gang. (Although some still wear the lesions with pride . . . but these idiots are easy to avoid.) Also, the Barabbas papillomata discourage a lot of the theft and . . .

Sorry, I'm way ahead of myself again.

Those first few days and weeks were crazy. We stayed in our homes, listened to TV, waited for the twice-daily news conferences from the Centers for Disease Control, smashed our mirrors, avoided our spouses, and then spent a lot of time seeking out reflections in any shiny surface we hadn't destroyed: toasters, silver platters, butter knives . . . . It was crazy, Peter.

A lot of couples split up then, Peter, but your mother and I never considered it. The bloodhorns took some explaining, but there was so much else going on that it didn't seem all that important at the time.

Eventually people started going back to work. Some never really quit working—reporters (newspaper reporters stuck by their jobs more often than TV people), firefighters, a lot of lower level medical personnel (the rich doctors were busy dealing with their Usury gluteal malformations), pickpockets (who quickly donned hoods to hide their peculiar strain of Barabbas papillomata), and cops.

Cops were perhaps the least affected of all professions. As individuals, they'd known for years the scum and pus and malformed souls that hid behind the pre-Change blandness of skin and bone. Now they tended to look at their own distortions, shrug, and carry on with their jobs which—if anything—had been made much easier by people wearing their insides on their faces. It was the rest of us—the multitudes who had pretended that human nature was essentially benign—who had trouble adapting.

But eventually we adapted. First we ventured out on the streets under hoods and balaclavas and old hats dug out of the closet, found the others in the supermarkets and liquor stores hooded and hidden the same way, and found that the shame is not so bad when *everyone* is in the same condition.

I went back to work after a week. I wore my baseball cap with the mosquito-netting veil during the first few days in the office, but I had trouble seeing the VDT and soon began taking it off once I was in the office. MacGregor from accounting still wears his Banana Republic mask to this day, but we know the Barabbas paps are there—you can smell them. Our boss didn't show for almost a month, but when he did he had nothing on his head. That took courage with his stupidity sarcoma so rampant that new fibroid pustules would appear between lunch and quitting time.

Everyone was oozing and dripping and squeezing and popping and lancing their paps and pusts in the restrooms, and pretty soon there was a company policy that we had to do it in the privacy of the stalls, where mirrors and handy-wipes were installed. The only guy I know who got rich during those first post-Change months was Tommy Pechota from Mergers and Acquisitions who invested heavily in Kleenex stock.

But back to those first few days.

The Russians had about ten hours to laugh their asses off at us and talk about the Western Decadence Disease before the Change hit them. It hit them hard. There was even a stigmata peculiar to current and ex-KGB guys that turned their faces into the equivalent of roadkill that you can't quite identify but definitely don't want to get too near. Gorbachev and Yeltsin got their share of what one Moscow analyst called the Commie Zits, but Gorbie had more problems than a few cosmetic difficulties. The Change got the March Revolution going in earnest and before summer started, the new leaders were in power. They weren't much to look at either—several had Ambition teeth—but at least none were oozing from Commiepox.

The Japanese took it pretty much in stride and began to see how the Change would affect the international market.

The Europeans went a little berserk: the French launched a nuclear missile at the moon for no particular reason—but it seemed to settle them down a bit—the British Parliament passed a law making it a criminal offense to comment on another's appearance and then adjourned forever, and the Germans remained calm for three months and then, almost as a reflex action since the world's attention was distracted, invaded Poland.

No one had anticipated the Aggressor-simplex malformation. You see, we'd thought the Change was more or less complete. We didn't know at the time that even passive participation in an evil *national* act could add new and dramatic wrinkles to the physiognomy.

We know now. We know that the human face can twist, bend, and fold itself so dramatically during the throes of Aggressor-simplex dynamic that a living, breathing human being can walk around with a face that is almost indistinguishable from an anus with eyes. It's very easy these days to pick out a German who supported the Polish incursion, or an Israeli or Palestinian since most of them suffered Agg-simplex during the Change itself, or anyone—and we're talking several million people here—too active in the American military-industrial complex.

Speaking personally, Peter, it made me glad to be carrying the stigmata I had.

Churches were filled during those first few weeks and months, although one glance at most ministers, pastors, and priests did quite a bit to empty the pews. In all fairness, a high percentage of the men and women of the cloth did no better or worse than the rest of us during the change. It's just that it's hard to concentrate on a sermon when Liar's leprosy is eating away someone's eyelids while you watch. It didn't prove that religion was a lie, only that the majority of those peddling religion *thought* that they were lying.

The TV ministers were the worst, of course. Worse than

senators, worse than insurance salesmen (and we all re-member *that* stigmata), and even worse than the tentacles-in-place-of-tongue, polyps-in-lieu-of-lips stig-mata of car salesmen.

Your mother and I watched on cable that first night, Peter, when the TV ministers self-destructed on camera, one after the other. The Barabbas papillomata came first, of course, but these paps were infinitely worse than the mere blood-and-ichor tumors on my cheek and neck. Most of the TV evangelists became nothing *but* papilloma, tentacles, and polyps. Even their eyes grew bumps and bloodwarts. Then the Liar's leprosy began eating at them, their paps suppurated and exploded, the centers of their faces began to grow inward in a style similar to the Aggressor-simplex mode only to pustulate again into something very much resembling an inflamed he-morrhoid . . . and then the process started over. We watched Jimmy Swaggart go through this cycle three times before we were able to change channels and get into the bathroom to throw up.

Not a whole lot of these TV evangelists are still on the air.

I guess I've been off the subject, Peter. I promised you an explanation . . . or as close to one as I could get.

Well, it's not an explanation, but I'll get to the facts and they may suffice.

Children were the hardest to watch. They generally began their own Change around the age of eleven or twelve, some-times at puberty but not always, although some kids Changed much younger and a few lasted until their late teens.

They all Changed.

And we could see the reason. It was us. The parents. The adults. The culture-givers and wisdom-sharers.

Only the culture-giving brought on the racism albino pox

in the children, and the wisdom-sharing tended to increase their chance for stupidity sarcoma and a dozen other stigmata.

It was heart-wrenching to watch, not only for what it did to the young people but for what it said about ourselves. Then the first post-Change babies were born and the stigmata were smaller, unearned, but already in place and growing. Our genes now carried the stigmata information and our personalities had been impressed even upon fetuses during the Change.

But you were perfect, Peter. By that June, you were one year old, healthy, happy, and perfect.

I remember it was a pleasant evening in the city when your mother and I dressed you in your finest blue baby clothes, tied on a little cap because the nights were still cold, and carried you down to the city park. Actually, your mother carried you while I lugged along a big box with all of our pre-Change snapshots, photo albums, home movies, and videotapes. There had been no official announcement about that first Catharsis Gathering in the park, but word of mouth must have been rampant for days before, if not weeks.

I remember that there were no official speakers and no one from the crowd spoke either. We simply gathered around the huge heap of kerosene-impregnated wood and broken furniture there on the parking lot near the municipal pool. There was silence except for the nervous barking of a few dogs that had tagged along: silence except for the barking and the cries and quickly hushed shouts of a few of the hundreds of children who had been brought along.

Then someone—I have no idea who—stepped forward and lighted the bonfire. An elderly woman with a lifetime's share of stigmata stepped forward then and began emptying her box of photographs. For a moment she was a lone silhouette against the flames and then some of the others began shuffling forward, usually the men while their wives held the children, and with no dialogue and no sense of ceremony, we began ridding ourselves of our boxes of photographs. I remember how the videotape cassettes melted and wrinkled and popped—so much like our faces during the Change.

Then we'd all emptied our boxes and backpacks and we stepped back, one hand raised to shield our faces from the terrible heat of the oversized bonfire. We could see nothing of the city behind us now, only the flames and the sparks rising into the starless night above us and the stigmatatized and heat-reddened faces of our neighbors and friends and fellow citizens.

I remember how excited your blue eyes were, Peter. Your cheeks were red in the reflected firelight and your eyes were luminous and you tried to smile, but some scent of madness in the air made your one-year-old's smile somewhat tremulous.

I remember how calm I was.

Your mother and I had not discussed it and we did not discuss it now. I looked at her with my good eye and she looked back and already our new faces seemed normal and necessary.

Then she handed you to me.

Most of those approaching the bonfire now were the fathers, although there were some women—single mothers possibly—and even a smattering of grandparents. Some of the children began to cry as we moved closer to the circle of heat.

You did not cry, Peter. You turned your face into my shoulder, closed your eyes, and curled your fists as if you could make a bad dream go away by not looking.

There was no hesitation. The man next to me threw at the same second, with the same motion, as I did. His little boy screamed as he flew deep into the bonfire. I heard nothing from you as you rose over the outer periphery of flame, seemed to hover a second as if considering flying upward with the sparks, and then dropped into the heart of the roaring bonfire.

The whole thing took less than ten minutes.

Your mother and I walked back toward the house and when I glanced back once, everyone had left except for members of the fire department who were standing by with a pumper truck to make sure that the bonfire burned itself out safely. I remember that your mother and I did not talk during the walk home. I remember how fresh and wonderful the newly mowed lawns and recently watered gardens smelled that night.

It wasn't that night but perhaps a week later that I first saw the graffiti spray-painted on a wall near the train station:

What monstrosities would walk the streets were some people's faces as unfinished as their minds.
                                                    —*Eric Hoffer*

I didn't know then who Eric Hoffer was and I admit that I haven't taken the time to find out. I don't know if he's still alive, but I hope that he is. I hope that he was around for the Change.

I saw that slogan scribbled several places after that, although it's been years since I've noticed it and I may have gotten the words wrong. I know that some of the CDC people refer to the change as the Hoffer Stigmata Pandemic, but I think they're referring to that German neurologist who was the first to come up with that active-RNA enhanced plasticity or whatever-you-call-it retrovirus theory.

Big deal. It doesn't matter anymore because even the experts admit that the Change is final and there's no going back.

We don't want to go back. The Change was painful; a Changeback would be too much to endure. Besides, it would be almost impossible to live in a world where one had to guess what paps and sulci and lesions lurked hidden under the smiling, pink-skinned surfaces of our mates and friends and co-workers.

* * *

That's about all, Peter. It's about time for the *CBS Evening News* so I have to close.

I feel better having written to you. I'll put the letter away here in the box in the attic with the baby clothes that your mother carefully folded away so many years ago.

I just wanted to explain.

To explain and to say that I remain . . .

Your Loving Father

The Secret

Steve Allen

I didn't know I was dead until I walked into the bathroom and looked in the mirror.

In fact I didn't even know it at that exact moment. The only thing I knew for sure then was that I couldn't see anything in the mirror except the wallpaper behind me and the small table with the hair-brushes on it low against the wall.

I think I just stood there for perhaps ten seconds. Then I reached out and tried to touch the mirror, because I thought I was still asleep on the couch in the den and I figured that if I moved around a bit, so to speak, in my dream I could sort of jar myself awake. I know it isn't a very logical way to think, but in moments of stress we all do unusual things.

The first moment I really knew I was dead was when I couldn't feel the mirror. I couldn't even see the hand I had stretched out to touch it. That's when I knew there was nothing physical about me. I had identity, I was conscious, but I was invisible. I knew then I had to be either dead or a raving maniac.

Just to be sure, I stepped back into the den. I felt better when I saw my body lying on the couch. I guess that sounds like a peculiar thing to say too, but what I mean is, I'd rather be dead than insane. Maybe *you* wouldn't but that's what makes horse races.

My next sensation (that's the only word I can think of to convey my meaning to you) was that there was something pressing on my mind, some nagging matter I had almost forgotten. It was very much like the feeling you sometimes have when you walk over to a bookshelf or a clothes closet, let's say, and then suddenly just stand there and say to yourself, "Now why did I come over here?" I felt a bit as if I had an imminent appointment.

I went over to the couch and looked down at myself. The magazine was open on the floor where it had slipped from my hand, and my right foot had fallen down as if I might have been making an effort to get up when I died.

It must have been the round of golf that did it. Larkin had warned me about exertion as long as three years ago, but after a fearful six months I had gotten steadily more over-confident. I was physically big, robust, muscular. I had played football at college. Inactivity annoyed the hell out of me. I remembered the headache that had plagued me over the last three holes, the feeling of utter weariness in the locker room after the game. But the cold shower had re-freshed me a bit and a drink had relaxed me. I felt pretty good when I got home, except for an inner weariness and a lingering trace of the headache.

It had come while I was asleep, that's why I didn't recog-nize it. I mean if it comes in the form of a death-bed scene, with people standing around you shaking their heads, or if it comes in the form of a bullet from an angry gun, or in the form of drowning, well, it certainly comes as no surprise. But it came to me while I was lying there asleep in the den after reading a magazine. What with the sun and the exer-cise and the drink, I was a little groggy anyway and my dreams were sort of wild and confused. Naturally when I found myself standing in front of the mirror I thought it was all just another part of a dream.

It wasn't, of course. You know that. You do if you read the papers, anyway, because they played it up pretty big on page one. "Westchester Man 'Dead' for 16 Minutes." That was the headline in the *Herald Tribune*. In the Chicago *Daily News* the headline on the story was "New Yorker 'Dead,' Revived by Doctors." Notice those quotation marks around the word *dead*. That's always the way the papers handle it. I say always because it happens all the time. Last year alone there were nine of us around the country. Ask any of us about it and we'll just laugh good-naturedly and tell you that papers were right, we weren't dead. Of course we'll tell you that. What else could we tell you?

So there I was, beside the couch, staring down at myself. I remember looking around the room, but I was alone. They hadn't come yet. I felt a flicker of some kind that would be hard to describe—an urgency, an anxiety, a realization that I had left a few things undone. Then I tried a ridiculous thing. I tried to get back into myself. But it wouldn't work. I couldn't do it alone.

Jo would have to help, although we had just had a bitter argument. She had been in the kitchen when I had gone in to take a nap. I hurried to the kitchen. She was still there. Shelling peas, I think, and talking to the cook. "Jo," I said, but of course she couldn't hear me. I moved close to her and tried to tell her. I felt like a dog trying to interest a distracted master.

"Agnes," she said, "would you please close the window."

That's all she said. Then she stood up, wiped her hands, and walked out of the kitchen and down the hall to the den. I don't know how I did it, but in a vague way she had gotten the message.

She let out a tiny scream when she saw the color of my face. Then she shook me twice and then she said, "Oh, my God," and started to cry, quietly. She did not go to pieces. Thank God she didn't go to pieces or I wouldn't be able to tell the tale today.

Still crying, she ran to the hall phone and called Larkin. He ordered an ambulance and met it at the house inside of ten minutes. In all, only twelve minutes had elapsed since I had tried to look at myself in the mirror.

I remember Larkin came in on the run without talking. He ran past me as I stood at the door of the den and knelt down beside my body on the couch.

"When did you find him?" he said.

"Ten minutes ago," Jo said.

He took something out of his bag and injected the body with adrenalin, and then they bundled "me" off to the hospital. I followed. It was five minutes away.

I never would have believed a crew could work so fast. Oxygen. More adrenalin. And then one of the doctors pushed a button and the table my body was on began to lift slowly, first at one end and then at the other, like a slow teeter-totter.

"Watch for blood pressure," Larkin whispered to an assistant, who squeezed a rubber bulb.

I was so fascinated watching them I did not at first realize I had visitors.

"Interesting," a voice said.

"Yes," I answered, without consciously directing my attention away from the body on the tilting table. Then I felt at one and the same time a pang of fear and the release of the nagging anxiety that had troubled me earlier.

I must have been expecting them. There was one on each side of me.

The second one looked at the body, then at Larkin and the others. "Do you think they'll succeed?" he said.

"I don't know," I said. "I hope so."

The answer seemed significant. The two looked at each other.

"We must be very certain," he said. "Would it matter so much to you either way?"

"Why, yes," I said. "I suppose it would. I mean, there's work I've left unfinished."

"Work isn't important *now*, is it?" asked the first one.

"No," I agreed. "It isn't. But there are other things. Things I have to do for Jo. For the children."

Again the two seemed to confer, silently.

"What sort of things?"

"Oh," I said, "there are some business details I've left up in the air. There'll be legal trouble, I'm sure, about the distribution of the assets of my firm."

"Is that all?" the first one said, coming closer to me. Larkin began to shake his head slowly. He looked as if he were losing hope.

Then I thought of something else. "You'll laugh," I said, "but something silly just came into my mind."

"What is it?" asked the second one.

"I would like to apologize to Jo," I said, "because we had an argument this afternoon. I'd forgotten I'd promised to take her and the children out to dinner and a movie. We had an argument about it. I suppose it sounds ridiculous at a time like this to talk about something that may seem so trivial, but that's what I'd like to do. I'd like to apologize to her for the things I said, and I'd like to keep that date. I'd like to take the children to see that movie, even if it is some cowboys-and-Indians thing that'll bore the hell out of me."

That's when it all began to happen. I can't say that suddenly the two were gone. To say I was gone would be more to the point. They didn't leave me. I left them. I was still unconscious, but now I was on the table. I was back inside my head. I was dreaming and I was dizzy. I didn't know what was happening in the room then, of course. I didn't know anything till later that night when I woke up. I felt weak and shaky and for a few minutes I wasn't aware that Larkin and some other doctors and Jo were standing around my bed. There was some kind of an oxygen tent over my chest and head, and my mouth felt dry and stiff. My tongue was like a piece of wood but I was alive. And I could see Jo. She looked tired and wan but she looked mighty beautiful to me.

The next day the men from the papers came around and interviewed me. They wrote that I was in good spirits and was sitting up in bed swapping jokes with the nurses, which was something of an exaggeration.

It was almost a month before I could keep that date with Jo and the kids, and by that time the picture wasn't even playing in our neighborhood. We had to drive all the way over to Claremont to see it, but we stopped at a nice tearoom on the way and had a wonderful dinner.

People still ask me what I felt while I was "dead." They always say it just that way, getting quotation marks into their voices, treating it as something a little bit amusing, the way the newspapers did. And I go along with it, of course. You can't say to them, "Why, yes, I was dead." They'd lock you up.

Funny thing about it all was that I'd always been more or less afraid of the idea of death. But after dying, I wasn't. I always knew I'd eventually go again, but it never worried me. I did my best to make a go of my relationships with other people and that was about the size of it. One other thing I did was write this little story and give it to a friend of mine, to be published only after my death.

If you're reading it, that means I've gone again. But this time I won't be back.

Feel the Seduction of
Pinnacle Horror

Scare Up One of These Pinnacle Horrors